THE RED HUNTER

Center Point
Large Print

Also by Lisa Unger and available from
Center Point Large Print:

In the Blood
Crazy Love You
Ink and Bone

**This Large Print Book carries the
Seal of Approval of N.A.V.H.**

THE RED HUNTER

Lisa Unger

CENTER POINT LARGE PRINT
THORNDIKE, MAINE

This Center Point Large Print edition
is published in the year 2017 by arrangement with
Touchstone, a division of Simon & Schuster, Inc.

The text of this Large Print edition is unabridged.
In other aspects, this book may vary
from the original edition.
Printed in the United States of America
on permanent paper.
Set in 16-point Times New Roman type.

ISBN: 978-1-68324-501-8

Library of Congress Cataloging-in-Publication Data

Names: Unger, Lisa, 1970– author.
Title: The red hunter / Lisa Unger.
Description: Center Point Large Print edition. | Thorndike, Maine :
    Center Point Large Print, 2017.
Identifiers: LCCN 2017024633 | ISBN 9781683245018
    (hardcover : alk. paper)
Subjects: LCSH: Revenge—Fiction. | Psychological fiction. |
    Large type books. | BISAC: FICTION / Suspense. | FICTION /
    Mystery & Detective / General. | FICTION / Thrillers. | GSAFD:
    Suspense fiction.
Classification: LCC PS3621.N486 R43 2017b | DDC 813/.6—dc23
LC record available at https://lccn.loc.gov/2017024633

To Joe and Jen Pamlanye

Thank you for the blessing of your friendship
and for the precious gift you gave me
—space and time.

THE RED HUNTER

today

There's nothing about me that you would ever notice. I am neither especially thin, nor overweight. My face will not be one you remember. With dark eyes and pale skin, hair the color of straw, cheeks round and just rosy enough that you won't wonder if I'm ill, I will blend into the sea of other plain faces you saw before and after as you went about your day. Nothing about my clothes will capture your notice. No brands that incite jealousy, or anything revealing, no stains, maybe just wrinkled or worn enough that you'll dismiss me as someone without much money, though not poor enough to be in need. If I'm wearing a uniform, I don't even exist. I am the checkout clerk at the grocery store, or the maid that cleans your hotel room, the girl who answered the phone, or the young lady at the information desk. No, you would say later, you can't recall her name or what she looked like, not really. The truth is you don't see me; your eyes glance over me, never coming to rest. But I see you.

Today I am trying not to emit the energy of excitement. I use my breath to control the pulse of adrenaline, just as I have been taught. I keep my head bent and my pace easy as I trail behind him. He moves slowly, haltingly, relying heavily on his cane, pauses long at the curbs, edging down cautiously. Occasionally, I have to slow my stride or stop altogether, glance at clothing I wouldn't buy in windows that cast back my reflection, someone narrow and still amid the bustle of city dwellers shuttling through their frenetic lives.

My hands are small and soft but stronger than you would imagine. Where I train we smack our palms and knuckles against cinderblocks. This action creates tiny fissures in the bones. When those fissures heal, the bone is stronger. I can put the blade of my palm through a two-by-four. But my hands are not calloused in the way of the fighter; they are smooth and hard as beach stones. Because I am not big, I must be fast. Because I am not big, I must come in close and hard, use elbows, knees, deliver unflinching blows to kidneys and groin, the soft notch at the base of the throat, the jugular. Eyes are good, too. Eyes can be a fight ender if you get it right.

A fight, when you must fight, is a dance. You can prepare but not strategize. You are married to your opponent, his movements dictating your own; his weaknesses are your strengths, his mistakes, your opportunities. You must be present, focused, and—most of all—you must breathe. No panic. No anger. Just the breath.

His right hand grips the cane. In his left, he

clutches a green reusable sack. It's Wednesday, his day to go to the farmers' market where he buys berries, bread, honey, kale, carrots, and a tub of hummus. The vendors know him, but he is rarely greeted with smiles. He is cantankerous, unfriendly, and something more. Maybe others can smell what I know to be true about him. They catch the scent but can't place it. They recoil ever so slightly, want to draw their hands back quickly when they give over his purchase or change. Only the old woman at the hummus stand openly scowls at him. You only know it if you've seen it before. It's death. There's a rot inside that sweats from his pores, stares back at you from the abyss of his eyes. Whether you can name it or not, if you're sensitive to such things, it repels you.

He crosses the street. Once he reaches the far curb, I follow quickly just as the light is about to change. He wears a frayed tweed jacket and a mud-colored fedora, khakis, and brown walking shoes. Though he is decently turned out, no one looks at him. No one sees the old, the frail, the infirm; they are invisible like me. No one looks as he turns off Broadway onto Twenty-Sixth Street. He stands in front of the metal door, loops his hand through the handles of the bag, and fishes his key from his pocket. With the key in the lock, leaning on the cane, he struggles to push open the door. This is his moment of vulnerability.

"Can I help you with that, sir?" I ask coming up

11

behind him, pushing the door open easily from over his shoulder.

"I don't need any help," he says, not even glancing at me. I dance around him and step inside the small vestibule. There's another door. I need him to give me the key.

"It's no trouble," I say brightly. "I'm Eve? From the third floor?"

I am not Eve. I do not live on the third floor. I take the sack from his hand.

"Give that back," he says. A little spittle travels from his lip to my cheek. I wipe it away. "Leave me alone."

"Give me the key," I say. "I'll let you in."

He doesn't hand it over, so I reach and take the key from him. His grip is weak and shaky, and his face is getting red from anger, from a kind of twitching powerlessness. I remember him as a powerful man, with a steely grip and cruel smile, blank eyes—which is all I ever saw of his face. And this moment in the vestibule gives me the briefest pause, a stuttering disconnect between the past and the present. *He's just an old man. Helpless. Weak.* Then, I remember the vise of his stony fingers on the soft flesh of my arm. I remember my mother shrieking my name, a wobbling pitch and tenor I'd never heard before and would never, all my life after, forget. I remember him. But he does not remember me. Once, I was afraid of him. He was, in fact, my worst nightmare. Today, it's almost too easy.

I put the key in the lock and push open the interior door. It's here that I experience another moment of doubt, a hollow that opens through my middle. *This is wrong. Part of you knows that.*

"Number 103, right?" I say.

He's staring at me now. There's a slight tremor to his head, almost like he's shaking it no. His eyes are a watery brown, still blank, but weak, not strong and cold like I remembered. His body has failed him. Years in prison, hard living, and illness have aged him terribly. I've seen men his age look fit, robust. Not him.

He doesn't have much longer, and his life is grim and lonely. I could just leave him be. The possibility hovers, a flicker of light teasing in the periphery of my consciousness. I could take another path.

But. He doesn't deserve to eat fresh berries and spend the morning watching television, does he? He doesn't get to go to the park later and feed his stale bread to the pigeons. He's doesn't deserve those simple human pleasures at the end of life.

You don't get to decide who deserves what.

Oh, but I do.

I unlock the door to his apartment and walk inside. It's dark and bare, just an old recliner and a television on a stand. A bed in the corner, neatly made. A picture of a woman in a frame, a paperback novel, and a glass of water sitting on a wobbly end table. And, of all things, a Bible open on the kitchen counter by the phone.

"Have you found Jesus?" I ask him. "Are you saved?"

"Get out of here," he says, snatching the groceries from my hand, pushing past me. "Go on now. Get out."

I close the door. He turns and takes me in with those eyes.

There he is.

The monster I remember.

"Who are you?" he asks.

"Don't you know me?" I ask with a smile. It has been many years, and a lot has happened between then and now. A whole lifetime really.

But he does know me. He does. I can see it as he starts to back away.

"You."

"That's right," I say. "Me."

He stumbles back a little more, as I lock and chain the door. He falls heavily into his old recliner. His breathing is labored, filling the room with its wheeze. It's lung cancer, I have learned.

"Where is it?" I say.

"What?" he asks. But his glance over toward the bed gives him away. I reach under the mattress and retrieve the gun I was sure he had. I put it on the counter, well out of his reach.

I have something of my own. I take it out of my

pocket and hold it up so that he can see. I wonder if he recognizes it. He used it on me once. I still bear its marks. Outside and in. A single tear trails down his cheek. His lips are moving in a whisper. It takes me a second to realize he's praying.

Is this who you want to be?

It's my uncle's voice, the uncle who is not an uncle and somehow more like a father because he took me in, loved me, taught me everything I know.

I take a step toward the man. A faint skein of music leaks in from the apartment next door. There are things I need to say. Questions I want to ask, but they are lost in the red fog that crowds my thoughts.

Yes, it is, I answer to the voice in my head. *It is precisely who I want to be.*

part one

TWO GRAVES

Raven looked repentant, but Claudia knew that she wasn't. The girl had her head bent, and the sheets of her blue-black hair, thick and impossibly glossy, fell to hide her face. It was October. A week from Halloween, and this was Claudia's *second* time in the principal's office since school began. The first one was about grades. Raven was already struggling. *We can see from her test scores that she's capable of more,* the desperate math teacher said. *But it's like she's just not here. Not paying attention. Leaving answers blank on her test. Mrs. Bishop, she's not even trying.*

Claudia could already see it on Principal Blake's face: The Look. It was the expression that careful people, kind people got when they started to wonder if there was something wrong with Raven.

"It's difficult to start a new school," said Principal Blake. "But here at Lost Valley Central we have a zero-tolerance policy for physical violence."

Physical violence? That was new. Claudia still wasn't sure what Raven had done. She'd raced in as soon as Principal Blake had called. A bland man with a soft voice and graying head of hair, he had greeted her in the office with an understanding smile. *We've had a problem in the cafeteria. A girl has gone home.*

"Oh, really?" said Raven. "So, it's okay for *her* to be verbally abusive to me, and I just have to sit there and take it?"

"That's enough, Raven," said Claudia. She wondered if she sounded as exhausted by her daughter as she felt. The kid's capacity for outrage was endless.

"There are other ways to solve your problems that don't involve flipping a lunch tray onto someone," said the principal easily. "What did she say to you exactly? What made you so angry?"

Raven shook her head. "It doesn't matter."

The principal answered her with a quick nod, like he got it, like he knew how cruel kids could be and how words could hurt as badly as any blow.

"I understand that bullying can be verbal and emotional as well as physical. And Clara Parker has had her moments; she's sat here with me more than once. Still, when we step over that line into the physical, that can't be tolerated."

Oh, god, thought Claudia. *She's going to be suspended—expelled.* She could just hear her sister Martha crowing, *I told you that changing schools wasn't the solution. You can't just keep running away.*

"I need a clearer picture of what happened," said Claudia. She looked at Raven. who had turned her head away.

"Apparently, Clara and a friend had some unkind words for Raven. I am not sure what was said since neither Raven, Clara, or her friend Beth will say. But, in response, Raven flipped a tray that was in front of them, covering both the girls with food."

Claudia felt the tug of a smile but bit it back.

"It was an accident," said Raven unconvincingly. "I was picking it up to walk away and finish my lunch elsewhere."

"It was meatball and spaghetti day at school today, so it made quite a mess."

"So it's not that she *hit* anyone," said Claudia. She didn't want to be one of those parents, the kind that rushed to the defense of her obnoxious, misbehaved child. But it was important that she be clear on exactly what happened.

"I didn't hit anyone," Raven said. "It was an accident. Clara went home because I ruined her *outfit,* not because I hurt her."

Principal Blake nodded carefully, cocking his head and wrinkling his eyes a little. "People around the girls said that it *seemed like* Raven purposely dumped the tray onto Clara."

"Yeah," said Raven, sitting up a little. "All her *friends,* who were *laughing* while she was verbally abusing me."

21

Claudia struggled against a flush of anger, a surge of protectiveness for Raven. "So, basically," she said, trying to keep her voice mild. "A group of girls surrounded Raven, saying unkind words—to use your phrase—and when Raven got up to leave, she tipped her tray either by accident or on purpose and ruined another girl's outfit. Is that right?"

Raven gave a light nod. "It *was* an accident."

Claudia was reasonably sure that it wasn't an accident. She knew Raven's temper was a flash flood, surging against everything in its path and then quickly receding, leaving regret in its wake.

"That's what I gather," said the principal reasonably. He seemed like a nice man, trying to do his job.

"Were the other girls reprimanded?" asked Claudia.

"It's unclear what was said," said the principal. "So it's difficult to address."

"Okay," said Claudia. She took and released a breath. "So where are we with this? Is Raven going to be punished?"

"Look . . . it's Thursday," said Principle Blake. He had nice hands, long thin fingers, and a white-gold wedding band, clean, pink nails. You could tell a lot about a person by his hands. He was careful, responsible, tried to follow the rules. He laced his fingers in front of him on the green desk blotter.

"I'm not going to suspend Raven; it's not going on her record," he went on. "Let's just have her take the day off tomorrow and we can all start fresh on Monday, let her think about what happened and reflect on how she could have handled things better. Maybe on Monday we can have a conference with each girl and her parents to discuss how we can better handle conflict. How does that sound?"

It sounded like shit actually. A "day off" was a suspension, even if it didn't go on her permanent record. She would have to attend the conference alone while Raven sulked unapologetic, and Principal Blake played benevolent mediator. This *Clara* and her parents *The Parkers* would play the injured party, and Claudia and Raven would be the outsiders. But she found herself nodding.

Claudia wanted to say something. She wanted to say thank you, and assure him that she was going to make sure that Raven understood the seriousness of her actions, but also ask that this Clara be made to understand the power of words.

Instead, there was a big sob stuck in her throat, a bulb of anger and frustration and sadness. She was afraid that if she opened her mouth, she wouldn't be able to contain it. So, instead, she just kept nodding and rose. She felt Raven's dark eyes on her. Only her daughter, and maybe her sister, knew that silence from Claudia was more

23

serious than yelling—which she didn't do very often either.

"Ms. Bishop?" said Principal Blake. He was staring at her with concern. "Are you all right?"

"I'm fine," she managed. "Thank you for your patience with Raven. She and I will talk over the weekend, and of course, there will be consequences at home."

There. She didn't burst into tears. Was there any more vulnerable position than being the single parent of a badly behaved child, sitting in the principal's office? Weren't you the one being reprimanded, really? Because wasn't it, after all, your fault that your child couldn't control herself?

"Raven," she said. "Do you have something you want to say to Principal Blake?"

"I'm sorry," she said dutifully. "I lost my temper and I shouldn't have."

The principal smiled warmly. "It takes a big person to admit when she's wrong. I think that's a good start. Write me an email over the weekend, okay? With your reflections?"

Raven nodded. "I will."

Claudia draped an arm around her daughter's slender shoulders as the girl stood, gave her a little squeeze, then nudged her out the door.

Claudia stood beside Raven's locker while the girl stuffed her belongings—iPad, binder, dirty

24

gym clothes—into her knapsack. Claudia had hated school—the ugly lights, the cafeteria smells, gym class, the pathetic social hierarchy where looks and athleticism trumped brains and character (not that *that* ever changed). The scent of the hallway—what *was* that smell?—brought it back vividly.

"It's not my fault," said Raven, slamming shut the locker door.

"It never is, is it?" said Claudia.

That glare, those dark eyes in that ivory skin. That full, pink mouth and ridiculously long eyelashes. Raven's beauty was shocking, frightening in its intensity, in her utter obliviousness to it. *We need to get a burka on that kid,* Martha had joked. *A body like that? On a fifteen-year-old? It should be illegal.*

Luckily, Raven's gorgeousness was tempered by the boyish way she carried herself. She *loped*. If Claudia didn't insist on showers and hair brushing, the girl would look most of the time as if she'd been dragged through a bush. And still, the way they *stared*. Men, boys, the same stunned goofy expression, eyes wide, smile wolfish on male faces young and old. Raven didn't even *see*. Claudia took to carrying pepper spray in her bag. *She's a baby,* Claudia had to keep herself from screaming. *Don't you look at her like that!*

Claudia knew that she was a fairly attractive woman still, and she'd been pretty hot when she

25

was younger—blonde and bubbly, with glittery blue eyes. Never *thin,* never one of those waifish, patrician women she'd always admired. She was full-bodied and curvy, never smaller than a size 12, sometimes bigger than that when she wasn't watching *every single goddamn bite* of food she put into her mouth. Still, she'd turned her share of heads.

But she'd never looked anything like Raven—a princess, a fairy, a siren, men climbing towers, and slaying dragons, and crashing themselves upon jagged rocks, dying happy. More disturbing though was the way *women* looked at Raven— with a kind of naked hatred, unmasked envy. They knew what a commodity had been bestowed upon Raven, through no fault of her own. The kid had won some kind of genetic lotto. Did anyone really know how isolating it was? How dangerous? No doubt it was part of the reason Raven was drawing fire from her classmates.

"Mom!" Was it only Raven who could imbue the single syllable with so much annoyance? "You're doing it again."

"Sorry." Getting lost, drifting off into her own thoughts, being somewhere else. According to her daughter, Claudia did that *all the time*. God forbid a mother should have her own inner life.

"What did she say?" Claudia asked as they exited the building and headed to the car. She dropped an arm around her daughter's shoulder again, pulling her in. And the girl shifted closer, matching her gait.

Raven shook her head. "It doesn't matter."

And maybe Raven was right. It didn't matter what Clara had said. What was important—what had been important back in the city—was that Raven couldn't control herself, her mouth, her temper. Impulse control was the problem.

They climbed into the rattling old Ford pickup, almost an antique, still a workhorse, which she needed in her business, something she wasn't worried about scratching or dinging, something that could haul loads.

"I hate this truck," said Raven. It was a far cry from Raven's father's Range Rover, certainly.

"I know," said Claudia, pulling out of the school driveway and onto the road home.

Claudia always found it funny—not *funny* but rather interesting or notable—that one moment or really a series of moments might derail your entire life. There you are, moving along on one track, full speed. You have your destination clearly in mind, and the journey itself is not half bad either. In fact, you're quite happy with the whole package.

And then one thing, or a series of things . . .

Maybe a woman, suffering from depression, drives her car onto the tracks a moment too late for the conductor to stop the train on which you're commuting. Your path (and the conductor's and other commuters') and hers collide. What happened to her in her life and what happened to you in yours—everything, where you were born, how you were raised, if your parents were nice, if you were bullied in school, if the gene for depression was turned on in her or not, or in you, all of these infinitesimal elements of her existence and yours lead you to be in the exact same place at the exact same moment and—KABOOM.

Or a gust of wind takes your scarf, and who should catch it but your husband-to-be, who happens to be walking past you on the same street, in the direction the wind is blowing at the exact moment on the right trajectory so that it trails beside him a flash of red and he reaches for it and turns around and your eyes meet and—SHAZAM. Love at first sight. These moments—less dramatic but equally meaningful—happened *every* day, Claudia often thought, and almost no one seems to notice how many things have to go wrong or right for them to occur.

It's never one thing that leads to a tragic accident, she was sure she'd read once—though she couldn't say where. It's usually seven things—seven mistakes, or errors in judgment, or acts of negligence. If you reverse engineer any major disaster—oil spill or train derailment or airplane crash—there are usually seven things that had to go wrong in order for them to occur.

Claudia had spent a lot of time thinking about that theory, even though what happened to her wasn't an accident by any measure. Especially in the darker moments—like this one—when she questioned the wisdom of almost every decision she'd made since that night. It was comforting in an odd way to look back and think that if she had changed any one of those seven things, she'd still be on that figurative train heading in the right direction.

The first thing was that her (now ex-) husband Ayers wanted to live in Midtown, since it was where they both worked. But she was in love with the East Village and had been since college. That was the real New York City—Yaffa Café and Trash and Vaudeville and St. Marks Books. There was still grit, even though it was very stylized now, and most of those wonderful places were gone or going. And very expensive even then. But she'd found a place she just loved on Fifth Street. Out back there was a garden, and it butted up against a church and an old graveyard, and the windows opened. It was utterly unlike the place Ayers wanted in Midtown, a tower with a doorman and central air, a pristine gym, and Friday socials on the sun deck.

Ayers was not a fan of grit. But he gave Claudia her way, because that's the kind of man he was. The kind of man who subordinated his wants and needs for Claudia's. A good man, a darling husband who she knew right away would be a lovely father.

There were gates on the back windows, of course there were. It was the East Village and as much as New York City was gentrified, junkies still busted in and took your stuff if you didn't have bars on the windows. So they got bars, even though it bummed Ayers out. He loved unmarred city vistas. They were *nice* gates, painted white, with wrought-iron ivy and twisting branches, and they opened like French doors. Claudia was terrible about closing them and locking them. She forgot sometimes. That was two.

They had been married a year and they were trying to have a baby. Not in that sad, desperate way that people often seemed to. More in a joyful, let's fuck all the time with no protection because we're—wink wink—*trying for a baby*. They'd been trying for about eight months, and no baby. *But hey,* said Ayers, *it's about the journey, not the destination! Now take off your panties, you little tart.*

Because they'd had a glass of Prosecco, Ayers got frisky. Then they messed around, having a quickie with her underpants around her ankles and her skirt hiked up, while he took her from behind over the couch. They were late to meet his parents at Café des Artistes. She never went back upstairs in their charming duplex, but mopped up carelessly in the little bath off the kitchen, putting on lipstick and sweeping up her hair, feeling dirty and naughty and loving it because Ayers's mother was so proper. Neither Claudia nor Ayers went back to the bedroom to close the gates. That was three.

Claudia and her mother-in-law were almost exact opposites—which was probably why they got along. Claudia admired Sophie's buttoned-up, ever stylish, cool (not cold, but unflappable) demeanor. And Claudia often caught Sophie smiling at her when she rambled on, or got exuberant, or passionate. If Sophie was pressed linen, Claudia was crinoline. If Sophie was crepe, Claudia was sequins. It worked. And her father-in-law Chuck was a bear of a man, always sweet and looking sleep-tousled, with a big appetite and sudden, explosive laugh.

After dinner, Claudia tried to convince everyone to have one last drink. But Ayers said he was tired, that he had an early meeting and wanted to work out first thing in the morning. That was four.

She was drunk. No, not *drunk*. Tipsy. Not puking, falling down, ugly drunk, of course— never that. But she was bouncy, giggly, silly. OTM was the code Claudia and her girlfriends used: One. Too. Many. OTM and you might get teary, telling your friends how much you love them, or laugh too loud, or dance with abandon—

even though you were a terrible dancer. Which was *fine* under most circumstances. Perhaps not with your in-laws. But any more and you were going to regret it. Any more and tomorrow was going to be a bad day. Maybe that was the real reason Ayers wanted to go home. Because for his mother, there were limits. Pressed linen, it creased terribly. You could never tell if crinoline had been hugged too long or too tight. *I love my mother,* Ayers often said, as if such a thing needed saying. *But I remember as a kid that she only had so much patience for affection.* Claudia had no idea what that meant. Why would you need patience for affection? Claudia had maybe drifted too close to the line; there had been lots of hugging and declarations of affection (from Claudia to Sophie), and maybe Sophie *was* getting a little stiff. Anyway, if Claudia hadn't been OTM, she might have noticed as soon as she came home what they only noticed later: That the lights in the kitchen were on, when they hadn't been before. That a coat had been knocked from one of the hooks on the wall beneath the stairs. If she hadn't been OTM, she might have seen those things and deduced the truth before it was too late. There was someone in the apartment. That was five.

Ayers was still outside, and Claudia came into the apartment alone. Claudia had *taken on* Mrs. Swanson, their impossibly elderly landlord.

Which meant that she often loaned Ayers out to her. *Oh, Ayers will help you with that. Won't you, honey?* They helped her with small things—like changing lightbulbs and getting dead mice away from Mittens, her ginger tabby. When Claudia was at the store, she often picked up eggs, bread, and 2 percent milk, dropping them off on her way upstairs. Usually Ashley, Mrs. Swanson's daughter, came to take the trash out. But Ashley was sick with the flu that night, so Ayers had promised to do it. That's what he was doing. That was why Claudia went alone into their apartment. That was six.

Stumbling up the narrow duplex stairs, she'd noticed a strange smell. Something musky. She dismissed it. That was one of the reasons she'd wanted to live in the East Village, in an apartment where the windows opened. The city had a smell, especially in summer. And it wasn't just garbage and bums and dog piss. There were aromas from trees and flowers, from bakeries and fine restaurants, from baristas and something else, hot asphalt and rubber, something indefinably New York. And you couldn't smell it in Midtown. She thought absently on entering—see, she did it even then—had she forgotten to close the window? Was she too exuberant with Sophie? Was Ayers embarrassed by her? Maybe she shouldn't have told that story about her friend Misha who had recently dyed her unapologetically long underarm hair neon green and delighted in showing it off everywhere possible. Her absentmindedness often kept her from seeing things that were right in front of her. That was seven.

A lot of women don't remember the event, her doctor told her. And that must be a wonderful mercy. Because Claudia *remembered*. Every crushing, bruising, airless second from the moment he stepped out of the bedroom in front of her and grabbed her by her hair, pulling her inside and closing and locking the door. Every detail of his face from his dark eyes, to the stubble on his jaw, to the scar on his chin, to the rank of his breath, the black stains on his teeth. He punched her with a closed fist right in the face—so jarring, so brutal, blinding white stars and pain that traveled from her jaw and the bridge of her nose, up over the crown of her head, her neck snapping back.

She struggled for orientation. No, no, this wasn't happening. Couldn't be. He pressed his arm over her throat, cutting off air. She couldn't breathe so she couldn't scream. Funny how that went. She wouldn't have thought about that. No air, no sound. She was silent, writhing. Utterly powerless against his far, far superior physical strength. She took kickboxing! She had thick powerful legs, athletic calves that *never* fit into those sleek high boots she so adored. She was bigger than Ayers—there was no carrying

Claudia over the threshold, nothing that would have been pretty. They play wrestled all the time. He was strong, Ayers, but not like this. She couldn't *move*. She was as helpless as a child. His eyes. They were blank, totally blank. He didn't see *her;* she wasn't even *there*. He thrust himself into her, a heinous ripping impact. The violation. It was unspeakable, beyond comprehension, and the pain. A horrible, tearing, burning. One, two, three. He shuddered, eyes closing—release, not pleasure—and it was done. He hit her again.

Stop looking at me! A hard crack against her cheekbone.

She fell back, and he kicked her brutally in the ribs. She threw up on the floor and managed to be humiliated about it even though he was already gone, out that window that offered such a pretty view of Mrs. Swanson's garden and the graveyard. She lost herself then. Went somewhere else. The next thing she remembered was the door crashing in. Not Ayers but a uniformed cop. Why *not* Ayers? Why wasn't he the first person through that door?

"Oh Jesus," the young cop said. Claudia wanted to apologize about the vomit. Crazy, wasn't that? Then she was out again.

It was two weeks later that she knew she was pregnant. No AIDS, no other sexually transmitted diseases. It *was* possible to determine paternity in vitro, but the test was invasive and caused risk to the fetus. They both decided. She *thought* that they *both* decided (though Ayers would later claim that it was all about Claudia, that he was just doing what he thought she needed) that they didn't want to know. A baby was a gift, no matter how it was delivered. Wasn't it? They would love the child. They would *never* seek to discover the true paternity. No matter what, they'd raise the baby as their own.

Don't do this, Martha had begged. *You don't know how you're going to feel. It's not fair to the child.*

So it's fair to—terminate the pregnancy?

Claudia was shocked at how unanimous was the sentiment that she should have an abortion. What a horrible word: the brutal end of something before it began. Even her doctor seemed to assume. *Do you want to schedule the D&C? No,* said Claudia. *I don't know.*

Life at any cost, then? Martha asked.

This baby is proof that even out of the most horrific possible moment, in your darkest hour, something wonderful is possible, Claudia had countered.

Martha, who was fifteen years older than Claudia, just shook her head, looked off into the middle distance as if she were the long-suffering knower of all things, just waiting for her little sister to catch up.

Ayers and I were together that night. It is equally possible that it is his child.

And if it isn't?

It won't matter. We're enough—strong enough, in love enough. It's possible. I've done the research.

Claudia remembered gazing out at the vista from their *new* apartment in a luxury Chelsea high-rise with windows that couldn't be opened and a doorman who looked like a professional wrestler (they'd moved within two weeks of the attack) hoping—*praying* that she was right. She wasn't right, not by a long shot. Not about that. Not about anything, it seemed, since that.

Claudia pulled up the long drive to their farmhouse. Twenty acres, most of them wooded, in a dot on the map called Lost Valley, New Jersey. *Lost Valley?* Raven had raged. *Are you kidding? You're moving us from Manhattan to a place with a name like that? It's like something out of a horror movie.* This land had been in her family for decades, bought with cash on one of her father's real estate whims—one of many. He got it for a song—$15,000 for twenty acres in the seventies, the barn and old house falling to pieces. He'd never set foot on it in all the years he owned it, then left it to Claudia when he died.

Claudia never set foot on the farmhouse property either, until one day she got it in her head that she'd renovate the buildings and start a blog about it. Single city mom moves to the country and renovates two historic properties. She'd take pictures. Eventually it would become a book—poignant, moving, inspiring. It wasn't just about the property. It was about rebuilding in the spiritual sense. Never mind that she wasn't really a writer or a photographer, or that she didn't have *any* experience with home renovation. And she liked the name of the town. It was romantic, wasn't it? A secret place, a hidden gem, a place where magic was still possible.

Weirdly, it was all kind of working. Claudia was in fact a quite decent writer, according to Martha. And her photographs had a "certain special energy," according to Ayers. She had blog "subscribers," was "building a platform," had a query yesterday from an advertiser. And she was—dare she say it?—happy-ish. Something she never would have believed possible once. Now, if she could just get Raven on track.

"You're doing it again."

Claudia had pulled the old pickup to a stop. How long had they been sitting there, with her just staring at the barn door—which, by the way, looked like it was going to fall off its hinges any minute?

"Jesus, Mom," said Raven, climbing out of the truck and slamming the door as hard as she could. "*Wake* up!"

Claudia watched as Raven stormed up to the house and slammed through the front door. You were never so acutely aware of your own flaws as you were in the presence of your child. Why was that?

The sky overhead was a menacing gunmetal. She was staring up at it when a blue car, a Toyota Camry, pulled into the drive. It came to a stop and a man, a stranger, climbed out. It had been more than fifteen years since her rape in the East Village. Her heart didn't thump with alarm every time a strange man approached anymore. She didn't think every unknown person was a potential assailant. What *was* different about the woman she was now versus the girl she was then, was that she was prepared if he was. She'd taken a self-defense class and spent nearly a year training every Tuesday and Thursday, when Raven was still a toddler, with a former Navy SEAL named Jet. *Defense starts on approach,* he used to say. *Watch the body language, the eyes. Trust your instincts. If it feels like something's not right, it probably isn't.*

What she noticed about the man who got out of the blue Camry first was a careful aura, a gentleness. He hung back a bit, lifted a hand, and offered a smile. That's what good men did, they kept their distance. Selfish men, arrogant men, dangerous men, the first thing they usually did was violate the space bubble, or the respect bubble—moving in too close, or maybe making some inappropriate comment, calling you sweetie or babe. Maybe he squeezed your hand too hard when you shook for the first time, signaling his strength.

"Hey, there," he said. "Mrs. Bishop?"

She wasn't technically Mrs. Bishop. She never took Ayer's last name. Bishop was her maiden name. If she'd at any point been a "Mrs.," she would have been "Mrs. Martin," which she didn't like as much as Bishop. Raven had both their last names Bishop-Martin, which Claudia thought sounded very big and important, and had a nice rhythm: Raven Bishop-Martin. A girl could do anything, *be* anything, with a name like that.

"That's right," she said, not smiling, just standing her ground. It was so hard for her not to smile, not to be exuberantly friendly. It was a discipline, something she'd worked on. *You don't have to throw yourself into everybody's arms, Claudia,* Martha was fond of saying.

He fished for something in his pocket, withdrew a sheet of paper. "You had a flier in the coffee shop for a handyman."

Oh, right. "Yes," she said.

"I'm Josh Beckham." He ran a big hand through sandy blond hair. "Did Madge tell you about me?"

"Oh," she said. Madge, the lady who owned the bakery. Claudia, a talker all her life, had been

40

mentioning that she needed some help with the house. And Madge suggested that she put up a flier. *We have a lot of boomerang kids around here, looking for work. One or two of them can manage to hammer a nail into something.* She *had* mentioned someone named Josh, living with his elderly mother, taking care of her. She hadn't mentioned the sky-blue eyes or the muscles that pressed against the sleeves of his blue tee-shirt.

"Not a good time?" he said. She could see that he was eyeing the barn door.

Oh, no, she wanted to enthuse. *Thank you so much for coming. It's a perfect time. I have so much that needs doing!*

"It's fine," she said. Why did it feel rude to be calm and measured, to hold herself back? "Madge mentioned you."

He squinted at her, gave a nod.

"I've been doing handyman work around here for a few years." He pulled another piece of folded paper out of his pocket. "I brought you a list of references. Folks you can call who'll tell you I show up, on time, and charge a fair price."

The sun had managed to peek out from the clouds, casting an orange-yellow glow against which he lifted a shading palm now.

"Thanks," she said. "Can I give you a call tomorrow?"

"Sure thing."

She always jumped into things too quickly and

41

often regretted it. She had always thought that she was just following her instincts; that's how she rationalized it. But her instincts sometimes failed her because—as Martha was quick to remind her—Claudia was just too nice, too trusting. *You think everyone you meet is as pure of heart as you are. They're not, kid. We both know that.* She wanted to hire him on the spot. Instead, she was going to do as Martha would. She would call the references and then, if he still seemed okay, she'd ask him to come out and *do one thing* and see where it went from there. That was the opposite of what her instincts told her—which was to hand him her list and tell him he was hired.

He handed her a card, his list of references, and gave her a friendly nod. "Hope to hear from you."

He moved toward his Toyota, then turned back. "That door—just saying? It doesn't look safe. Doesn't have to be me. There's a company in town, Just Old Doors. They specialize in fixing them or replacing them up to the historic code. Not cheap, but they do good work. You might get it looked at before you open it again. Okay?"

She smiled at him. "I will. Thanks."

She watched him drive away. His energy. It wasn't just careful or gentle. It was sad, too. And was there something just a little bit off? When his car was gone, she released the tension she didn't know she'd been holding in her shoulders.

What was that noise? Something faint and discordant on the air. She looked toward the house in time to see Raven open her window. Music poured out. The angry tones of Nine Inch Nails slicing through the darkening afternoon.

two

I carried the groceries up the stairs—four bags, five flights. At the landing, I put the bags down and fished the key from my pocket. Inside, the television droned. I jiggled the lock and then forced the door open with a push of my hip. East Village postwar construction, not to be confused with prewar. These were the buildings that were put up slapdash after World War II to house the burgeoning immigrant population. These days, a lot of them are sagging—doorframes crooked, floors dipping, façades crumbling. Uncle Paul has lived in this apartment for thirty years, since he was a New York City beat cop in Midtown North. I lived here, too, for a while. It's as much a home as I have.

He was waiting for me—sitting at the small kitchen table with a cup of coffee, his cane resting against the back of his chair, a newspaper folded open in front of him.

I didn't say anything as I carried the groceries to the counter and started unpacking. Neither of us is big on talking. Coffee and hummus from Sahadi's out in Brooklyn Heights, handmade mozzarella from Russo's on Eleventh Street, fresh fruit and vegetables from the farmers' market on Union Square. Shopping for my uncle was an adventure, a trek through the city to purveyors of fresh foods. He has always been a foodie, but after twenty-five years of eating pizza and donuts and hot dogs and gyros on the beat, he had chosen to go fresh and organic in his retirement.

"When did you find him?" he asked by way of greeting. "How?"

I just kept putting the groceries away. I didn't want to talk about it; there wasn't anything to say. I shelved three cans of San Marzano tomatoes, closed the cabinet door.

"I can't condone this," he said. There was a wheeze to his breathing that I didn't like.

Silence—other than the low chatter of the television, which was really just white noise for him, I think, a reminder that the world continued on even though most of his days passed in this small apartment. He drew in and released a jagged, labored breath.

"They wouldn't want this for you."

I was not so sure about that.

"And now what?" Another rasping breath. "Have you thought about that?"

He had smoked a pack a day for almost forty years. Now, he suffered with emphysema, had a hard time with those stairs. He could still make it, but it took ages, and he has to rest on every floor. Lately, though, he was short of breath even when he was just sitting. I was trying not to think about it. He was all I had.

45

"I have no idea what you're talking about," I said.

I ground some beans, put the grinds in the French press, and put on the water for coffee. I sat across from him, and he rested his ghostly blue eyes on me, ran a hand over the white cap of his shorn hair. His face was a filigree of tiny lines around his eyes and mouth. It was hard, with mountain ridges for cheekbones and a boulder for a chin.

"I think about it," he said. "They'd hate me for how I've failed you."

"Stop it."

I looked down at the article in front of him. MAN MURDERED IN HOME INVASION. He caught me looking.

"Says here he was sixty-five years old. He had cancer, a bad leg, couldn't walk without a cane."

"Yeah, I know," I said. "Quiet. Kept to himself. Just a nice old guy who fed the pigeons in the park. Who would do such a thing?"

I'd seen the article, too. But that's what they always say, isn't it? About victims and perpetrators alike? What would people say about me? I wondered. My McJob du Jour was as a waitress at a place called the Sidewalk Café on Avenue A. I showed up on time, didn't make mistakes, and left when my shift was over. I smiled blandly at anyone who caught my eye, was polite-almost-friendly to my coworkers (not one of whom I could name). If someone needed to change a shift, I always said yes. It was a busy place and the tips were good, especially on the weekend late nights when people were out partying. I never tried to hold on to the cash that came my way (these days most people tipped with credit cards), always put any money in the jar to share with the busboys and dishwashers. I'd seen a couple of the other girls pocket the random cash tips they received. Of course, I never said a word.

What would *they,* my coworkers, say if they knew what I was? All the same things they said about him. That I was quiet. Kept to myself. They would have a hard time reconciling the pale, silent, nondescript girl who worked beside them.

I usually call him Paul, not Uncle Paul. Technically, he's not my uncle. He is my father's stepbrother. They were raised together and were lifelong best friends. I don't know much about their childhood in New Jersey; neither of them talked about it much. My grandfather was a city bus driver. My grandmother was a teacher who died of pancreatic cancer when my dad was small. My grandfather married Paul's mother, Sherry, who was a 911 dispatcher. Their life was simple and uneventful, according to Paul. Both Paul and my father, Chad, wound up as police officers. Paul moved to New York City and stayed a beat cop by choice. My dad was a homicide detective in New Jersey. My mom was "justamom," as she jokingly referred to herself, the rare stay-at-home mom in a world of two-career families. She made cookies and did laundry, paid the bills, cooked the dinner.

"We're not going to talk about this," I said.

"We are," he said, tapping his finger, one hard knock, on the page. "This is wrong."

"Is it?" A lash of anger caused me to rise. Then I sat again, leaned into him. "How? How is it *wrong?* In what just universe is it wrong?"

"When we hurt other people, we hurt ourselves, Zoey. You must know that by now."

He bowed his head and struggled to breathe. I put my hand on his. I slowed my breathing, hoping it would signal him to slow his. It did.

"What do you want me to make for your dinner?" I asked. "I'm working tonight, so I'll make it now and Betsy can heat it up when you're hungry."

He didn't answer me. So I moved over to the cabinets and removed those cans of tomatoes. "I was thinking I'd make a marinara with meatballs and sausage. I'll make a lot so we can freeze it."

"Zoey."

Out his kitchen window, I could see right into the dining room of the loft apartment across the alley. It's one of those newer buildings, everything espresso and white, clean lines and glittering backsplash. Cold and modern the way

48

people seem to like things these days. My uncle's kitchen by contrast is all Formica and peeling wallpaper, things so old and stained from use that they'll never really be cleaned no matter how hard I scrub.

The rest of the apartment is similarly old-school New York. No central air in this building. There's an air-conditioning unit in the window of his bedroom. I sleep on the pullout couch when I stay here, now—which I sometimes do when I don't like his breathing. When I moved in here with him at fourteen years old, he let me have the bedroom, and he slept on the couch until I left for the dorms at NYU. Four years he slept on a pullout couch.

"I'll put it in a Tupperware, and Betsy can just heat it up and make some pasta tonight. And a salad."

Betsy was the nurse who came in every day to check on his meds, help him with things he wouldn't let me do, make sure he ate when I couldn't come by.

"Please," he rasped.

"It's done."

"It'll never be done, kid," he said. "Not like this."

Even though I already suspected that he might be right about that, was already aware of a kind of hollow opening inside me that might never be filled, there was really nothing I could do. There are certain dark doorways in this life, and when you open one and step inside, you can't come back out. The door locks behind you and you have to stay. No one ever tells you that. Or if they do, you don't listen. You never *really* understand until it's too late.

I poured the olive oil in the bottom of the heavy-bottomed pot that belonged to my mother. I minced the garlic by hand and slid it from the cutting board into the oil, then put the heat on low. I opened the cans of tomatoes and sniffed the air. Only the nose can tell when the garlic is ready, right before it turns brown and has to be thrown out.

When it was time, I dumped the crushed tomatoes (my mother would have picked them from our garden, but I'm less ambitious about things like that—and I don't have a garden) into the oil and listened to the sizzle. I tore up leaves of fresh basil and watched them flutter into the red. Salt. Pepper. A tiny bit of sugar to cut the bitterness. And let it simmer. Like all good recipes, there's almost nothing to it, just quality ingredients, a little attention, and time.

When I turned back to my uncle, he had his head in his hand, the rasping growing worse.

"It's okay," I said. "I'm okay."

He shook his head, didn't seem able to talk. So I helped him into the bedroom. The air conditioning was on in there, the shades drawn, so it was cool and dark. I tried not to notice that he looked thinner, that his arm felt smaller in my grip. I could hear the kids playing in the schoolyard across the street, faintly over the hum of the window unit.

"Do you want the oxygen?" There was a green and silver tank by the bed. He nodded and sat heavily on the mattress. I lifted his legs onto the bed and helped him get the oxygen on. He used to lift me up over his head and spin me around in my parents' backyard. I used to ride on his back, or make him drag me in stocking feet across the hardwood floors in our great room in a game we called Airplane.

You're too big for that, Zoey! My mother would chide. *Uncle Paul has a bad back.* But he would just smile and shake his head, and I knew it was okay.

I didn't know anything about emphysema until my uncle got it. It had seemed to my ignorant mind innocuous, a little trouble breathing. I didn't know that it slowly destroyed your lung function, that it wasted you. The lungs eventually lose so much function that they can no longer support the metabolic processes of the body and supply oxygen. I think it's one of those ugly things that no one ever talks about. It's such a quiet, nasty way to slowly die.

I covered him with the blanket resting over the chair in the corner. He pointed over to the

51

television, and I switched it on, handing him the remote. I checked the inhalers on his bedside table—Advair, Combivent, Flovent. He took Accolate twice a day and has prednisone for flare-ups. He was at less than 50 percent lung function, and it was only going to get worse.

There was a picture in a cheap plastic frame by the bed of my parents and me, next to his retired shield and his department ring. Other than that, there was just the bed, his reading chair, two bedside tables, and shelves and shelves of books, kiltered every which way, in checkered, colored stacks—history, biographies, detective fiction, science. My uncle never stopped reading. He had a stack of three by his bed: the new Lee Child, a book about birds, and a biography of Alexander Hamilton.

"Police have no leads in the home invasion death of an elderly man," said the pert blonde NY 1 News reporter from outside an apartment building.

I pretended not to be listening, fixed his blanket, went to refill his water jug.

"John Martin Didion lived alone. According to the building super Anthony Ruiz, he was quiet and polite, had lived in the building for several years, a rent-controlled unit grandfathered to him by his elderly mother, who he cared for until she died."

"He kept to himself, you know. Never any

52

trouble," said the middle-aged Latino man, wringing his hands self-consciously and staring off camera. "I don't get this city. Who would do such a thing?"

The newscast cut to grainy footage. It took me a second to realize it was the front door of Didion's building. He limps up to the doorway as a slender hooded figure approaches from behind, then the two disappear through the door.

"Footage captured from a convenience store security camera across the street shows Mr. Didion being accosted at the doorway. Inside his apartment, he was stabbed once through the heart. His body was discovered by a neighbor, concerned that the door was ajar."

The camera cut back to the young reporter. Her hair blew prettily in the breeze; her makeup was perfect. She looked like a doll, something you would dress up and put in a sports car. She'd have a perfect plastic boyfriend, a dream house with a pool.

"Sloppy," said Paul. He drew in deeply through the nasal cannula. "You know there are eyes everywhere in this city."

"I don't know what you're talking about," I said. I tucked the blanket around him and gave him a kiss on the head. "You're an old man. Stop making up stories."

My pulse was racing, though. To see myself like that; it was odd. An out-of-body experience.

And, yes, very, very careless. I'd done my recon. How could I have missed that camera?

"Police continue their investigation and ask that anyone with information about the hooded figure in the doorway come forward," the plastic newscaster continued.

Shit.

He closed his eyes, shook his head. He leaned his head back, arms slack at his side, his chest rising and falling, that rasping like he was sipping air through a tiny straw. Sometimes he just fell asleep like that and slept for hours exhausted from the effort of just being alive. I moved toward the door looking back at him. Before I closed it completely, he caught my eyes, and I heard him whisper:

"Be more careful."

I finished the cooking, then cleaned up, left a note for Betsy about what to do for his dinner. When I checked on him again, he was sleeping. I hoped he'd stay asleep until Betsy came. I'd feel better if he'd have twenty-four-hour care, but he wouldn't hear of it. *I'm not an invalid. I can take care of myself.* This was increasingly untrue. But it's hard to argue with the people who used to give you piggyback rides.

In addition to my illustrious waitressing career, I was also a serial cat sitter, plant waterer, house watcher. For the last month and for possibly the next six, I had stayed in a loft on Greenwich and Vestry. The kind of place where about 1 percent of the population, less, might ever be able to consider living. I headed there after leaving Paul's East Village walk-up.

The doorman in the cool museum of a lobby acknowledged me with the slight nod reserved for the help—nannies, housekeepers, cooks, personal trainers, massage therapists, cat sitters. His dark, lidded eyes slid past me, not lingering, as I drifted over marble and past snow-white walls adorned with towering modern art oils in shining white frames. I knew his name, Bruno— tight black curls and a nasty scar on his neck. He had bulk, standing nearly six feet, and edge. In a fight, he'd get dirty. I bet he carried a knife, which is a highly effective weapon if you have nerve, aren't afraid to get in close.

On a console table in the elevator lobby, a towering vase of white calla lilies offered a funereal odor, filling the space, tickling my sinuses. The elevator opened, and a willowy blonde dressed in a draping, expensive white fabric brushed past me without seeing, staring at the enormous smartphone in her hand.

"Have a good day, Miss Dykstra," I heard the doorman say, his voice bright and obsequious. I bet his eyes lingered on *her*—the spun gold of her hair, the elegant sway of her body.

He rushed to open the door for her. From where

I stood, I didn't even see her acknowledge him with an upward glance from her phone. He was invisible to most people, as well. He just didn't realize it. Maybe somewhere, to someone, he mattered. But not here.

Inside the elevator, it was quiet and mercifully dim, no mirrors. I hated elevator mirrors, standing in a box, staring at myself. I avoided mirrors as a general rule, turned away from my reflection. I stepped into the private hallway that the owner had kept spare and undecorated and walked down to the door at the end.

Tiger greeted me as I stepped inside. He was more like a dog-cat, curious, always getting into trouble by tipping plants and tearing up throw pillows, sloppily affectionate, a big eater. At night, he slept on the pillow beside me in the gigantic king bed in the gigantic white room—white walls, white dresser, white down comforter, white sheets, white Eames chair in the corner—with views of downtown.

As usual, Tiger had scattered food all over the floor in the kitchen.

"Bad kitty," I said mildly, petting him as he wound himself in furry figure eights around my ankles.

I swept up the mess from the gray slate floor and refilled the bowl with the stupidly expensive cat food I had to pick up from the organic pet supply store in the West Village. Tiger purred madly, then set to eating as though he hadn't eaten in days though I'd filled his bowl that morning and had only been gone a few hours. He was lonely. I felt bad for him.

I had never met the artist that owned the apartment. He contacted me via the website where I list my services, checked my references, and then hired me without ever meeting me. He paid me via PayPal. It was possible we'd never meet, as had been the case with many of my previous employers. I preferred that. No connections. No personal contact.

But something about Tiger's loneliness niggled at me. After sitting with him awhile on the couch, petting him, thinking about Paul, about John Didion, I got up, grabbed my laptop, and wrote Nate Shelby an email:

> Tiger's lonely. Maybe you should consider another cat.

He wrote back promptly.

> Nate@NateShelby.com.
> I'll think about it. Thanks.

Okay, great. The encounter led me to look up his website. It was spare and beautiful like his apartment, all neutrals, the only bright colors in the large-format oils, some of which I recognized from around the apartment. Big bold strokes of color, spheres, spirals, angry splashes, thick black jags that looked like tears in the canvas. His bio had no picture: *Nate Shelby, a graduate of The Cooper Union, is a renowned artist who works primarily in oil on canvas. His work has appeared in galleries and museums around the world. He divides his time between New York and Paris.*

In a world where people were promoting themselves from every possible platform, Nate Shelby didn't seem to feel the need. I searched around online for some pictures of him and only found a couple. One when he was still at The Cooper Union. He stood in a room of other artists surrounding a nude woman who reclined on a chaise. He was thin and pale with a thick mop of black hair, his face a mask of concentration. There was another one of him, grainy, black and white, walking on the Brooklyn Bridge, hands in his pockets, head down. There were no shots of him at glamorous art parties in SoHo or Paris, no publicity images, no profiles in art magazines.

It wasn't my habit to search out my clients. Usually, I could tell almost everything about someone by his home—what photos were displayed, and weren't, objects collected, cluttered or tidy, what was in their medicine cabinet (that was a big one), the pantry, the state of the master closet, the home office. I got a sense after living in someone's space for a while, an energy that settled on me. I knew the person even if we never met. I remembered the apartment and how it felt and smelled, like a relationship that ended amicably but forever.

The maid had been here. I could tell because the whole space smelled of astringent lemon, a tingling clean smell that was still unpleasant. Tiger settled on the windowsill, finding a lovely patch of light close to me. And I abandoned my laptop and sat in front of Nate Shelby's gigantic Mac and opened the browser and entered the name that had been hovering on the edge of my consciousness all day, a tickle, a tune I couldn't get out of my head.

three

I t was the one thing he could always do, the thing that always made sense. He could build; he could fix. He could understand how a broken thing worked and make it work again. In school, he'd struggled. Words swam on the board, a muddle. He needed glasses, but no one figured it out until fourth grade, so he had trouble learning to read. Math? The only things less understandable than letters were numbers. But in the shop with his father, with the hum of the saw, and the sound of the hammer, and sandpaper on wood, the smell of varnish and sawdust—that's where it all worked, where the pieces fit together. There was never any question, no abstraction. In the shop, if you had the right tools, you could fix anything. Not so in the world outside.

He wiped down the surface of the work area. His dad was long gone, but Joshua Beckham still followed the rules of the shop. A place for everything and everything in its place. Keep the work area uncluttered. Clean up at night before you go home.

He'd fixed Mr. Smyth's vacuum. He wasn't going to charge the old man because it was just that the roller was full of hair; that's why it had stopped moving. It had only taken him a few

60

minutes to clean it and there was nothing to it. His dad wouldn't have charged for a thing like that, and neither would Josh. Mr. Smyth, he knew, didn't have much money—otherwise he'd have just replaced the old vacuum like anyone else would have.

After that, Josh had just finished sanding down and refinishing an old table for Jennifer Warbler; she'd found it at a garage sale and asked if he could "work some magic." He could.

The table came to him gouged and wobbly, scratches and dull places on the surface, a chip out of the leg. He loved stripping a thing down, sanding away the old, patching up the wounds, watching it come back to life with a brand-new coat of stain.

He wasn't sure what he'd charge Jennifer. She had three boys who ran her ragged, and she was a good customer, had Joshua out at her place six or seven times a year at least, most recently to fix a hole the oldest boy Brendan put in the drywall—with his brother's head. (Jennifer: *Thank goodness he was wearing his skateboarding helmet!*) The loose dowel in the banister, a closet door off its hinges, clogged plumbing, some electrical (though he mainly needed to call in Todd for that—you didn't mess with wires if you didn't know what you were doing). Jennifer was married to Wayne Warbler, who commuted into the city to work. *You know Wayne is a smart man, but he is* not *handy. I love my hubby, but I'm not sure he would even know what to do if I handed him a hammer.*

Josh wanted to take the table over to the Warblers after he'd finished work, but the varnish wasn't dry. It was better to do it anyway during the day when Wayne and the boys weren't there. Jennifer was different when she was alone, when her husband was at work and the boys were at school. She was more exuberant, less distracted. Joshua wanted her to enjoy the table, to see how beautiful he'd made it, not be pulled in a million different directions. *Fabulous, Josh! What do I owe you?* Like it was just another thing she had to cross off her list. He knew if she had a minute, that she'd see and appreciate how an old thing, one she'd found and recognized as beautiful, had been made new again. She was a person who recognized good work and beauty. Few others did.

He pulled the door to the workshop shut behind him and locked it. He had a lot of expensive power tools inside, and there had been a rash of thefts and burglaries in the area. The property he shared with his elderly mother was isolated, a total of ten acres now though it had been bigger once. He'd sold off a parcel of twenty acres after his father passed to pay off the old man's debts and help to take care of his mother. But the house was still far from the road and surrounded by trees; it was just him and his mom now. Nurses came in during the day and some evenings to help with her meals, bath, and medicine. Her best friend from childhood helped out sometimes, too.

The night was cool as he moved up the path between the shop and the house, a path his father had walked every day just before supper. Josh hadn't imagined that it would have been his path as well. When he was young, he'd dreamed of being all kinds of things—a firefighter, a cop, an acrobat, an astronaut, an ice cream man. No little boy dreams of being a handyman, the guy you call to clean out your gutters because your very successful hedge fund manager husband just doesn't have the time for that kind of work. But, all things considered, it wasn't that bad. When his father had passed, and his clients just started calling Josh instead, he fell into it easily. It was right, familiar. And he didn't have anything else going on after a string of failures: he didn't pass the psych evaluation on the police exam (which he *still* didn't understand). He'd abandoned the real estate course he was taking online. The lead singer for the band in which he played bass guitar got a DUI and was in rehab. They hadn't been getting many gigs anyway—mainly because they weren't that good.

As he approached the house, Josh saw that Mom's light was still on upstairs but that the nurse's car was gone. The nurse had probably left around nine, and his mother was most likely propped up in bed, watching reruns of *Criminal Minds*, her favorite show, when she really should be sleeping.

Inside, he went to the kitchen (it was *exactly* the same as it had always been except that some of the appliances had been upgraded ten years ago and needed upgrading again), grabbed a beer from the fridge, and headed upstairs.

"Ma," he said, pushing the door open a little. "You should be asleep."

She was, as predicted, propped up in bed, her white hair a little wild, her flannel nightgown too big.

"Hmm," she said, squinting at the screen. "That's what *I* used to say to *you*. Did you listen?"

He sat in the chair by her bed, took a swig of his beer. On the dresser by the television were his parents' framed wedding picture and another one of his ma holding him in front of the hospital, a yellow tinge to both photos, she looking impossibly young and pretty like a girl he wouldn't mind meeting. Even now she still had that sparkle in her hazel eyes—mischief.

"Guess not," he said, kicking off his boots and propping his feet up next to her on the bed.

"Always with that Game Boy under the sheets," she said. "Your brother with his books."

"Yeah," he said, smiling.

"No one who is told to go to bed ever wants to,

young or old," she said. "The end of another day."

He watched the rest of the show with her, not really paying attention, just being with her. When the credits rolled, she turned it off, and he told her about his day—about the table and the woman he went to see about her renovation. Fact was, he hadn't stopped thinking about Claudia Bishop since he'd been out to her place.

"That would be a good thing," she said. "To have the regular big job and fit the other small jobs in."

"Instead of *just* the small jobs," he said. There was always a need for a handyman; he always had work. But the bigger jobs usually went to a crew. Sometimes he worked for a contractor in town and that was good; he might get a regular thing that went on for a couple of months— doing floors or painting in a larger renovation. But when the market was slow and people had stopped building, there was less work to go around. He'd had a couple of lean years, though things were picking up again.

"Someone's been calling," she said, after he thought she'd drifted off.

"The home phone?" he said. "Just telemarketers probably."

He lifted his cell phone from his pocket, noticing that he had varnish underneath his nails. No messages—no texts or voicemails—except one from his buddy earlier today asking if he was going up to Lucky's where they usually played pool on Thursday nights. If he brought his bass, he might get to play with the band for a few songs.

"More than usual," she said. She reached out a small, papery soft hand to him, and he took it in his. He touched his thumb to her wedding ring, which he'd had adjusted earlier that year to fit better.

"I'll check the voicemail," he said.

He tried to press it back, a tickle of unease that had been hovering. It was always there, a kind of odd buzz, a tune you couldn't get out of your head. As long as he was working, busy, he could ignore it, a joker shuffled among the other cards of his thoughts. But once the day was done and there was nothing left to do but watch television and go to bed, it found its way to the top of the deck. So many years had passed. And still.

"You look tired," she said.

"I'm okay."

"Sleeping?"

"Well enough."

"Your father was a bad sleeper, always wandering around in the night."

"I remember."

That's because he was drowning in debt, Ma. We almost lost everything when he died. But she didn't know. They had an old-school marriage. Dad worked, paid the bills, handled the finances.

Mom cooked and cleaned and raised the kids. She had no idea the mess he was in. Not before he died and not after. *Take care of her, Josh. Your brother is useless. You're the one who has to stay on.*

Josh turned out the light and kissed his mom on the head, pulling the covers up around her shoulders, a mirror of how she used to tuck him and Rhett in at night. It wasn't cold in the house, but she got cold. Sometimes he got up in the night to make sure she was still covered.

He walked down the creaking staircase and back to the kitchen where he picked up the cordless phone and dialed the voicemail. Auditory junk mail—a campaign ad, a survey call, the bank offering another credit card. And then, there it was, the voice he wished to never hear again.

"Hey, buddy." Josh listened to the whispering sound in the background—wind through the trees, tires on asphalt? The long, slow sound of a distant horn. A deep drag and a sharp release of air. Smoking still. "Long time, no see, right? So, look. We have a problem. Let's—uh—get together. You still in the same place?"

Josh listened to five more messages, all of them hang ups. He put the phone down and rested his head against the cabinet, one that his father had made. It was solid, the smell of wood and stain a comfort. His heart thumped and his throat had gone dry.

We never outrun our sins, his dad had warned him. *Someday they come back on you, one way or another.*

Josh still thought he knew a few things back then—was it ten years ago now? Did time really pass that fast? Did you blink your eyes and find yourself on the cusp of middle age having accomplished next to nothing? Living in the house where you grew up? Taking care of your mother? Josh had loved his dad, but he'd thought the old man was terribly naïve. The old man was hardworking but not worldly, had never been anywhere, done anything. Not like Josh, who knew and had seen it all back then, or so he thought, who had the whole world before him and a catalog of grand plans.

Dad's simple ideas: Measure twice, cut once. Don't use the table saw when you're tired. Slow and steady wins the race. But philosophies like that were for another time, Josh had thought back then, another universe where things moved more slowly and people still played by the rules.

Things don't change as much as you think they do.

Josh turned off the lights in the kitchen and made sure the doors were locked. In the cupboard beneath the stairs, he checked the revolver he'd stowed on the high shelf toward the back. It was clean and oiled, fully loaded just as his father had always kept it, and now Josh did the same.

Josh pushed the gun back far and locked the cupboard door. He was the only one with the key. He was about to climb the stairs when the light in the dark hallway changed. He walked to the window where in the black outside he saw the twin yellow eyes of an approaching car. He went back for the gun.

four

Claudia often dreamed of Ayers. And these dreams—they were so real, so pleasant. They were just lying on the white couch they'd had in that East Village apartment. She had her feet in his lap, and he was massaging them the way he used to, while she drank a cup of tea. Outside, it was windy and the room was filled with that Indian flute music he loved. She felt light, free, the way she used to on Saturday afternoons when they were first married—before.

"Will it always be just like this?" she asked.

"I hope so, darling," he said, with that peaceful smile he wore so often. "Or even better."

A crash and the world went dark. Ayers was gone, and the pleasant day outside had turned black, wind howling. And then Claudia was awake, the echo of that bang still hovering on the edge of her consciousness. What was it? Was it real?

"Mom! Mom?" Distant, down the hall. Was she still dreaming?

It was pouring, rain sheeting against her window.

"MOM!"

Claudia was running then, her heart a hammer against the cage of her chest. She and Raven met in the hallway reaching for each other.

"Mom!" said Raven, looking so, so much like the little girl she recently was. "*What* was that?"

"I don't know," said Claudia, her throat constricted with fear, hands shaking.

She went back to her room and grabbed the baseball bat she kept by her door, all of Ayers's warnings about living alone on an isolated property in a strange town ringing in her head.

"Go into my bedroom and lock the door," she told Raven, who'd looked at her wide-eyed.

"Really?"

"Call the police if—"

"If *what?*" Raven's voice went up a worried octave.

"If—anything." She tried to keep her voice low, calming.

Claudia had no intention of waiting in the bedroom, hiding. No. She'd come too far for that. She wasn't even sure what she'd heard. Inside or out? In the basement or the attic? She closed the door on Raven, waiting until she heard it lock. Then she stared down the dark stairway. She paused, listening. Just the wind outside, moaning, strong enough that the windows rattled.

She'd read an article once about how a predator had lay in wait in a woman's attic for days, biding his time until she was alone in the house, listening to her through the ceiling. He'd snuck down from the opening in the closet, raped and killed her in her own bed. This story had haunted Claudia for days, the idea that he'd been up there, listening to all the private moments of her life before he ended it. It came back to her now, but she pushed it away.

Claudia headed down the stairs, slowly, still shaking, flipping on lights. The doors to the outside and the basement were locked; she saw that right away. No windows broken. Pretty quickly, she was reasonably sure that there was no one inside. Her heart rate slowed. Whatever she heard must have been outside, she thought.

The truth was—and she was surprised by this and a little ashamed—that she was already narrating it, thinking about how she'd write it for her blog. Things that go bump in the night! Something like that. Once upon a time, she'd have been paralyzed with fear, barricaded in a room with Raven, waiting for the police. Time, enough of it, fades everything like hot sun on cloth, even the worst trauma—if you let it. She thought her therapist would applaud her bravery, if not her judgment. In the years after the attack, Claudia had wanted *so badly* for the world to be okay again, and eventually it sort of was.

"Mom!" called Raven.

Raven came halfway down the stairs, her black hair up and wild, her sleep shirt, a giant purple tee she'd gotten when they saw *Wicked* on Broadway last month, shifting down to expose her shoulder.

Her eyes were red, glistening on the lashes. "I called the police."

"You did?" Claudia was surprised. Raven was not so tough after all.

"I was scared."

"Okay," said Claudia, reaching for her. "Better safe than sorry."

Raven came to her and wrapped her arms around tight, holding on, sinking in like she used to do when she was small, as if she wanted to close off all space between their bodies. Claudia grieved the physical intimacy she used to have with her daughter, the heat of that little body, the silk of her peaches and cream skin, the smell of her hair. When they're small, they're part of you, on you in bed, showering with you, climbing onto your lap, holding on to your leg. Slowly, slowly, they start to move away, and if you love them, if you want them to feel safe and free to explore the world, you have to let them go. Mostly.

"We're okay," said Claudia, relishing the feel of Raven in her arms. "We'll wait for them to come. I'm not going into that basement alone."

"No," said Raven, shaking her head. Claudia looked at the door, still bolted from the outside. "No way."

It was a horror movie basement—huge, more dark corners and shadows than spaces where the light reached, bulbs hanging from wires that dimmed and brightened mysteriously, cold spots and boxes full of she didn't even know what. The electric in the house was old, needed a total overhaul—which Claudia could *not* afford— so that explained why the lights in the house were always browning out. But it seemed like there was an energy to it. Things went dark at odd moments—like when Raven was having a tantrum, or Claudia was alone in the house, wondering what the hell she'd gotten herself into. It would be just like the lights to go off when she was down in the basement, alone and terrified. The thought made her shudder.

There was so much work to be done there. There had been some flooding last year, so there was water damage. And two of the beams had come down, which apparently didn't compromise the house, according to the engineer that had been out. *Still,* he'd said, *I wouldn't spend a whole lot of time down here until you shore up those areas. You never know what else is going to come down.* He'd pointed out some cracking in the other beams. Maybe that was what had made the noise. Perhaps another beam had come down.

And there were so many boxes down there, old furniture from a past tenant, just junk. There was a workbench, rusted tools, an old exercise bike, clothes, papers, books, a box of old toys. Claudia had no idea who any of it belonged to, why it had just been abandoned down there. There had been multiple tenants on the property since her father bought it. But no one had lived there in more than ten years. Who just left a house with all their stuff and never came back? Claudia could spin out a hundred dark scenarios, but now was probably not the time. Sorting, donating, selling, junking all that stuff—it was all on her ridiculously long "to do" list.

But there was something about the basement that repelled her. She couldn't be down there alone, and Raven hated it, too. So they'd been avoiding it.

Claudia and Raven huddled on the stairs together, baseball bat beside them, afghan from the couch wrapped around them.

"I'm sorry about today, Mom," said Raven. "It's just hard sometimes. To just ignore people and the things they say."

"I know, baby," she said. "I get it. But when you lash out at people, you just give them energy, make things worse. When you stay silent, hold your head up, and walk away, you take everything away from them."

"But isn't that just like saying it's okay?" said Raven. "When do you get to stand up to people?"

Claudia sighed. She didn't have all the answers. Not by a long shot. "Sometimes that *is* standing up."

"I want the test, Mom," her daughter whispered. "I want to *know*."

Claudia blinked at Raven, who held her stare like a prizefighter.

"What does that have to do with anything?" asked Claudia. "Was today—was it about *that?*"

Raven shook her head, sighing, as if Claudia were terribly slow.

"Somehow *everything* is about that. How do you not understand that?"

The headlights of the approaching police cruiser traveled across the walls, saving Claudia from getting into it with Raven. She knew this day was going to come; she thought she was prepared for it. She wasn't. There was no script for a situation like theirs. People barely even wanted to talk about it.

Claudia stepped out onto the porch and down the steps to greet the officer, who looked like he wasn't much older than Raven. Really. His unlined face and wide green eyes, his beefy arms made him look like a high school football player. He even had a smattering of acne on his chin. How old *did you* have to be to be a police officer, actually?

"Ma'am," he said. "I'm Officer Dilbert. You called about a suspicious noise."

Yeah, that was right. She was a *ma'am*. She was nearly forty, young looking, in shape (not skinny, but *fit*). Still the days of "miss" and "honey," of the goofy smitten stares at her prettiness? They were fading fast. Not that she cared. Hey, everyone was young for the same amount of time; every girl gets her turn for a blushing youth. And at the end of the day, pretty didn't seem to be worth very much at all. But Claudia was noticing it lately, how she had almost receded from the stage, from any hope of hotness. After a certain age, women who were trying to look "hot" were really just succeeding at looking sad. Lately, she was going for well-turned-out, elegant, attractive. Which in sweatpants and oversized tee, hair crazed from sleep—nowhere close.

"That's right," she said, taking her hair down from the knot at her crown. "Thanks for coming out."

"I think I saw your problem on the way up the drive," he said, glancing back at the barn. "That barn door looks like it fell off?"

The millennial way of ending a statement like a question. It annoyed some people she knew, like Martha, for example, who was annoyed by most things. But Claudia didn't mind it. There was something modest, something gentle about it. It acknowledged the many possibilities of a situation. As if, it *looked* like the barn door fell off and that's what made the noise, but, you know, hey, maybe that wasn't it at all.

Yes, of course, the barn door. Claudia was certain that's what it was. What else could have made such a bang? Somewhere in her subconscious, she must have registered it otherwise she might have been more afraid.

Claudia walked over to the barn with young Officer Dilbert, him towering, as big as a refrigerator, which was a rather nice quality in a cop. The rain had stopped, but the ground was saturated, the trees around them bending and whispering in the high wind.

There it was, the huge barn door laying flat on the ground. Officer Dilbert removed a big black flashlight from his belt and shined it, moving in close. Claudia could see where the hinges had ripped from the wood, leaving rusted, exposed nails. The latch at the door had ripped completely off, lay on the ground practically dissolving into a pile of rust. The barn was another thing she hadn't had time for. They'd been there only a month. Which was weird. In a way, it felt as if she had always been there.

"It looks like—and it's hard to tell because the wood is so old?" he said, moving in closer. "Could someone have pried this off?"

She came up behind him and saw the scratches he was examining. She remembered how it looked that afternoon; even the handyman had noticed it. The one she *hadn't* hired on the spot the way she wanted to. She put a finger to the gouges in the wood. There it was, the dark creep of suspicion, the edge of paranoia. But, no. No. He wouldn't have come back here and done that, just to get the work. No, that was crazy. Or was it? The world was a dangerous place, and she knew that better than most. People did all kinds of unthinkable things, all the time. But he was a nice guy; she could see that. Couldn't she? And he came highly recommended by Madge.

"Oh, no," said Claudia. "I don't think so. It was really needing repair. I put a call in to Just Old Doors this afternoon. They're coming out early next week."

He gave a quick nod. "I'll take a look around just the same if you don't mind?"

"Of course," she said. "Thank you."

He looked very serious as he made his way around the back of the barn, his hand resting on the gun in the holster at his waist. She fought back the urge to tell him what a good job he was doing, very thorough and brave. *Why do you always treat people like they're in kindergarten and you're the teacher?* Ayers had recently asked her, not unkindly really. Actually kind of amused. He'd been down at the school for orientation day. She'd been talking to the principal, complimenting him on something or other. Did she do that? She really didn't think so. Martha was like that, but surely not Claudia, who really didn't consider herself an authority on anything.

Raven had put on some clothes and a long sweater and was standing on the porch, arms folded, watching as Claudia returned.

"Just that barn door," Claudia said. "It finally fell apart."

"Like everything else around here."

The sullen, oh-so-disdainful Raven had returned. The sweet clingy one, the one who loved Claudia and had always thought she was so wonderful, was gone again; she came and went. Every time she disappeared, Claudia prayed she wasn't gone for good. That little person was the truest friend she'd ever had, the kindest, the most honest, funniest, sweetest little dear. In the dim orange light of the lamp beside the door, her daughter looked more like an unfriendly stranger.

"Well," said Claudia, forcing brightness. "That's why we're fixing the place up."

Raven glanced away, wrinkling her nose. Disgust. With the place? With her mother? Claudia didn't dare ask.

"I want to stay with Dad this weekend," she said, looking down at her toes—which she'd painted black. Once upon a time it had been all pink and sparkles, princesses and unicorns. Now Raven's fashion palette was black, slate gray, and light gray, and black again. "He said I could."

Claudia nodded, wrapping her arms around her center. "That's fine. Sure."

It crushed Claudia when she did that. It shouldn't. It was normal for a teenager to pull away from her mother, to try to pit her divorced parents against each other, to want to hurt Claudia a little. But the twist, the anguish Claudia felt—as if someone were mercilessly squeezing her vital organs (it wasn't an exaggeration; she literally felt physical pain sometimes)—almost always brought tears to her eyes.

She turned back toward the barn so Raven couldn't see her face. Claudia had never been good at hiding her feelings. Anyway, Raven wasn't looking, didn't care; her perpetually angry teen went back inside, slamming the screen door behind her.

five

Maybe it's my imagination, but I wouldn't say you seem overly happy to see me, brother."

"Of course, I am," said Josh, staring at the eggs in the pan. The words sounded fake on the air, probably because he was definitely not happy to see his older brother Rhett. Not at all. In fact, he'd hoped never to see him again. The fact that Rhett was back was a little like thinking you had beaten cancer only to discover during a routine visit to the doctor that it had returned, more virulent than before.

Their mother, on the other hand, was as giddy as a schoolgirl. He'd never seen her face light up the way it did when Rhett walked in through the door of her bedroom last night, as if Jesus Christ himself had come down from heaven.

"My baby," she'd said. "My Rhett. Am I dreaming?"

He'd sat beside her, and she'd petted his head, tears welling up in her eyes.

"Hello, Mama," Rhett said, leaning his forehead against hers. "I've missed you. I'm sorry I've been away so long."

"Never mind that now," she said. "We're just glad you're here. Aren't we, Josh?"

She didn't remember. There were so many

big dark spots in her memory now; sometimes Josh could tell it took her a second to recognize him. The dementia seemed to come and go. She remembered things from his childhood that he had long forgotten: his red bicycle, the striped shirt he insisted on wearing every day when he was five, screaming bloody murder when she wanted to wash it, his stuffed bear Buttons. He noticed that it was the unpleasant things mostly she claimed that she couldn't recall—like the reason Rhett had been away for as long as he had. And Rhett knew that Josh wouldn't be the one to remind her. *Mama's boy*. The taunt still echoed around in his head, like so many of the things Rhett had said over the years.

"Sure are," Josh had said a beat too late, earning a dark sideways glance from his brother. Even now that look could make him shudder.

"You don't look a day older," she'd told him.

"Neither do you," he'd said. "You're as pretty as you were when we were boys, Mama."

"Oh, silly," she said, clearly pleased and placing a palm to each of his cheeks. "You always were a charmer."

Rhett did look older, his face a landscape of deep lines, his black hair thinning and going gray. But his body was lean, muscles sinewy and rock hard, hands thick with calluses. If anything, he looked stronger than he had when he was younger. He was still broad through the shoulders and a good four inches taller than Josh. Any softness there might have been to him once—and there hadn't been much—was gone. He was hard hewn, as jagged and stealthy as a shiv.

"What are you doing here?" Josh said now. He'd served his mother her breakfast, bringing it upstairs on a tray like he did every morning before work. Now he put a plate in front of his brother. Eggs, bacon, buttered toast. He poured coffee in the red mug with the chipped handle, put it down on the table.

"A man can't visit his family?" Rhett said.

Josh poured coffee for himself and pulled up a chair. His father had made the long wood table. He'd used wood from an oak that had been struck by lightning in the backyard. One of the larger branches smashed through the roof of his father's workshop. How old had Josh been—maybe ten? The sound had been so loud that he had jumped to his feet before he even fully woke up, hearing his father and brother already thundering down the stairs.

"My goodness," said his mother. She clutched at her nightgown and reached for him as he walked out into the hallway. "What in the world was that?"

He'd stayed behind with her, the storm raging outside. From the window, they could see how the branch had fallen, hanging by splinters still, the bottom of it piercing the gabled roof of the workshop. Josh marveled. Such solid things . . . the old oak, the barn turned workshop, things that seemed so fixed in the world, immutable— fallen, smashed. His father was swearing downstairs; his mother had Josh wrapped up tight. He would always rather be with her than with them.

He ran his hand along the surface of the table. In the grains of the wood he always thought he could see the old man's face, pulled long in disappointment the way it often was in life. The table, like everything his father made, was as solid as it was the day they carried it into the kitchen. Josh ran his hand along the perfectly straight edge. Measure twice, cut once.

Josh was aware of that notch in his throat that he always seemed to get when Rhett was around. His brother was a loaded gun waved in the air, a storm gathering in the distance. You just didn't know what was going to happen. Maybe nothing. Maybe something awful.

"The truth is," his brother said, pushing at his eggs. "I need work."

Josh felt a dump of dread and resentment in his middle, rubbed at his eyes with a calloused thumb and forefinger so that Rhett wouldn't see it on his face. He heard the television come on upstairs, the dripping of water from the leaky kitchen sink faucet. He'd redone the counters and resurfaced the cabinets last year, but the kitchen with its old four-paned window and fading floral wallpaper needed an overhaul.

"I don't have any place else to go," his brother went on when Josh didn't say anything.

"More trouble?"

"Some," said Rhett with a shrug. He shoved the eggs into his mouth like he hadn't eaten in a week.

"Is it going to follow you here?"

Rhett offered a vigorous shake of his head. "No," he said. "Course not. I wouldn't do that to Ma."

Josh nodded.

"Who's going to hire me?" asked Rhett, locking Josh's gaze.

Right. Who was going to hire an ex-con who went to prison for being part of an armed robbery, which wasn't nearly as bad as other things for which he'd never been caught? Who was lazy and shifty and looked like a thug, to boot?

It took Josh a long time to understand what his brother was, and what he himself became when his brother was around. Josh took a sip of his coffee. The back door stood open, and the October air was still warm, smelling like the last stand of Indian summer, the last moment of green before brown, the last lingering of long days before short.

"There's not a lot of work right now," said Josh.

Rhett polished off the rest of his meal, rubbing

crumbs out of his thick, dark goatee. He leaned back, ran big hands through the mass of his black hair. Sideburns made twin *L*s along his jawline. It was a look.

"Ma said you might have a regular gig," said Rhett. "Handyman on some rich lady's restoration project."

Josh had left them to talk last night. He shouldn't have.

"I haven't been hired."

Rhett dropped his gaze on Josh, and Josh tried not to shrink from it.

"You're still so *pretty,* little brother." Funny how an innocent word like that could be a razor blade, could slice painful and small, going so deep, so fast as to draw blood. "I bet if you tried hard enough, you could get that girl to hire you."

"She's not looking for a *date,*" said Josh. "She's looking for a handyman."

Rhett cocked his head to the side, cracking his neck, squinting. "Dad always wanted us to work together. That was his dream, that we'd take over his business."

Josh let out a little snort. "Dad had a lot of dreams that didn't work out."

"Thanks to me?" said Rhett. His voice as cool and flat as a blade. "Is that what you were going to say?"

"Don't start."

He hadn't seen his brother in five years, and

yet it might have been yesterday that they were boys fighting over everything from friends, to video games, to comic books, to girls. Their life together had been one long wrestling match. And yet. And yet. Beneath that antipathy ran a current of laughter, of affection. Even now. Even after everything and so much time passed. There were things they understood about each other, things no one else could see.

Josh cleared the plates, loaded them into the dishwasher feeling his brother's eyes boring hot and mean into the back of his neck.

"You were there, too," said Rhett. His voice was just a whisper. "Let's not forget that. I protected you, took care of you."

Josh shook his head but kept silent. That was really not how it went down. Not even close.

"I've changed," Rhett said as Josh washed his hands, dried them on the worn dish towel. In the window over the metal sink, Josh could see his brother's faint, ghostly reflection; he looked slouched and old, beaten. But if that's what Josh was seeing in him, that's what Rhett wanted him to see. All psychopaths were skilled manipulators. Words were the least of their tricks.

"I know you don't believe it," Rhett went on. "But I have."

Josh turned to face his brother, who had lifted his empty orange juice glass and was peering into it.

"I can help you around here," said Rhett. Josh looked around and saw what Rhett saw—water stain on the ceiling, rusted hinges on the door, floor that needed replacing. Dad wouldn't be happy with the way the place looked. *Never walk by something that needs repairing without repairing it.* But between working and caring for Ma, the days seemed short. And there wasn't a whole lot of money.

"Alright then," Josh said.

He wasn't surprised to hear the words come out of his mouth, even though he never intended to say them. He always gave in to Rhett, always did what his brother wanted, whether Josh wanted to or not. It was a compulsion, almost a biological imperative. "I've got some work in the shop—some shelves I have to put together, a chair that needs fixing."

Rhett looked up with a smile. "Yeah?"

"If you want to get started on those, I'll follow up with that other job."

"The Bishop place," said Rhett. He pinned Josh in a dark stare. "That's what Ma said."

"Look. We've been all through this," said Josh, lifting his palms. "There's nothing there."

Rhett's eyes had the hard glint of bad ideas. Josh understood then—why Rhett was back. The Bishop place under renovation, the phone call, the other news. That tight knot in Josh's throat expanded. Rhett hadn't changed, not one bit.

But then Rhett leapt up and took Josh into a hard hug. "You won't be sorry, man. You'll see. Let me get another cup of coffee and I'll get right to it."

Josh *would* be sorry; he knew that. He was already sorry. He had spent a *lifetime* being sorry for doing things his brother had asked him to do. Josh had the strong urge to call his sponsor, Lee. One of Lee's big things was staying away from the people and places that reminded you of what it felt like to be high, to do wrong, to lose yourself. *Some relationships are like pythons: they wrap around you, slowly squeezing until you can't breathe.* Josh wondered what Lee would say when Josh told him Rhett was back; he could already feel the air being pressed out of his lungs.

six

I n the damp, sunny morning that followed, the drama of the night before seemed far away.

"Just—" Claudia said, trying not to lose her patience before nine in the morning. "Can you push the hair out of your eyes?"

A sullen eye roll, a toss of her head, then a careless brush of bangs. Big fake smile. Claudia had never touched Raven in anger, not a spank on the bottom, not that angry arm grab she'd seen too many times on the playground. But lately she *thought* about it sometimes. She really did. Wasn't that *horrible?* Sometimes Claudia just ached to smack that teenage, know-it-all look right off her face. But not really. It *was* extremely annoying, though.

She snapped a picture instead. Could you say "snap" when you took a picture with your smartphone? It wasn't a snap exactly anymore, was it, even though the device issued a facsimile of that noise? The photo was a good one with that morning light coming through the trees, catching Raven's hair and making it shine purple. Her smile didn't look fake at all. It was radiant, like the natural flush on her daughter's cheeks, the shine in her eyes. Raven leaned cheekily against the barn door, which was leaning against the structure now that Claudia and Raven had pushed it upright. Teamwork.

"Do you ever feel bad about exploiting me in your blog?" Raven asked.

"Uh," Claudia said, putting a finger to her cheek and glancing up as if considering. "No."

She filtered the image. "Chrome" was her favorite. And it was perfect—bright and moody at the same time, heightening colors, lightening lights.

"You're the one always going on about internet predators," said Raven. "What if there's someone out there, trolling for pictures of nubile young girls in any context?"

It struck a chord, as it was no doubt intended to do, opened a cold place in her belly.

"Uh . . ." said Claudia brilliantly.

She'd done some thinking about this subject, some discussing with her new agent and with Martha. But ultimately they'd decided that since Claudia's blog was about home renovation, rebuilding, single parenting, and life in general, the occasional photo of Raven (just called "R" online) was not a violation of her personhood. Claudia had never revealed the address of the house, the town they were in. Since she used a different name for her blog—Claudia Davidson, her mother's maiden name—their identities were protected. Of course, if Raven didn't want to be a part of it, that was another matter.

"I don't have to use it," said Claudia, lowering her phone and looking seriously at her daughter. "I mean, if you don't want to be a part of this, it's *totally* fine. We've talked about this. You know that."

Raven glanced over at the door, then back at Claudia.

"No," Raven said. "It's okay. I like doing this with you. It's fun."

They locked eyes for a moment and then both started to laugh.

Now, in the bright morning sun, the night before seemed funny. Wasn't that always the way? Nothing ever seemed as bad when the sun came up. She and Raven huddled on the stairs, the earnest young cop, Claudia catching sight of herself in the mirror, seeing what a crazed middle-aged wreck she looked. Then lying awake all night worrying. The French call them *les pensées qui viennent dans le nuit*, "the thoughts that come in the night." Most nights, Claudia fell asleep hard and fast, almost as soon as Raven was asleep. But often she would wake around three, usually with a start, thinking that she heard something. She'd shuttle over to Raven's room, where the girl was always sprawled across her bed, arms thrown wide, mouth agape, sound asleep.

Claudia would return to bed and entertain the parade of fears, dark imaginings, wonderings about death. That's what happened last night after the door fell and the police officer had left. She just lay there for hours. Sometimes, even now, she still thought about "it," the event that divided her life into before and after. Sometimes, she still remembered that night in vivid detail, moments flashing back on her—his flat, empty eyes, the hard, mean grip of his hand on her arm, the smell of him, his *odor*. He was dead now. She never thought "before" that she'd ever wish anyone dead. But she had wished it, and he was dead and she was glad. But that moment, it was alive and well. Her shrink said that it was normal. *Some things don't leave us,* he said. *We just learn to live with them better. And those memories, they do fade some. They will—some.*

"So are you going to call that guy?" asked Raven. Claudia posted the photo on Instagram. It was pretty and bright, Raven a dark-eyed angel in the golden morning sun. *That door finally fell off. Time to get started on the barn. #needahandyman*

She was gratified to get three likes almost instantly. Validation in the palm of your hand.

"Who?" asked Claudia absently, moving toward the car.

"The hot one," said Raven. "From yesterday. I think he liked you."

"The handyman?" said Claudia. "Don't be silly. He didn't *like* me. He wants a job."

God, but yes, he was hot. Again that dark

94

thought presented itself. Would he have come over and pried off that door, just so she'd call? No. Who would do that?

"Are you going to give him one? A *job*."

Claudia glanced over at her daughter, who was smiling slyly. Was her fifteen-year-old being filthy? No. No. At fifteen Claudia had had *no idea* about anything like that, of course, she didn't. Certainly, Claudia had never discussed it with Raven. They'd talked about sex, about how it worked, about boundaries, about treating her body with respect, protecting herself on all levels. They'd had talks about biology and all its implications; they'd talked about disease, about pregnancy. But they hadn't talked about pleasure, giving and receiving. No, that wasn't part of the dialogue. Certainly not. Claudia was positive that Raven was still a virgin. Positive. No way Claudia wouldn't be looped in on that.

"I don't know whether I'm going to give him—work," said Claudia impatiently. "I have to check his references. Did you do all your homework?"

"You should know," said Raven. "You checked it last night."

"Right," said Claudia. She put the truck in reverse and swung around to head up the long drive. "And moving forward, are you going to try to keep it together?"

"I'll try," said Raven, sullen again.

95

"What people think of you," she said. "It doesn't matter."

Raven blew out breath. "Trust me, Mom. It matters. What if you had to go somewhere all day where you knew no one? Where everyone else has known each other *forever,* and look at you like you're some kind of freak? If you had no one to sit with at lunch."

"I'd hold my head up high, focus on my work, and bring a book so that I always had something to do. You'll make friends. You've only been at this school for a few weeks. You'll find the cool people. Or they'll find you."

"There aren't any cool people," said Raven. "We live in a town called *Lost Valley*. Cool people *do not* live in a place with a name like that."

Guilt, worry, anxiety—the three furies of motherhood. They swirled around the car, shrieking and laughing. *You never should have brought her here. What if she never does meet anyone cool? Maybe she's marked by what happened to you. Maybe . . .*

"I want the test," said Raven. "I've been talking to Dad about it. Ella thinks it's time."

"*Ella* thinks it's time?" said Claudia, slamming her foot on the brake and bringing the vehicle to such a sharp halt that it jerked them both forward. The name was like acid in her throat. "*She* is not part of this conversation."

Raven lifted her palms, widening her eyes.

96

"Okay," she said, as though she were placating a crazy person. "Oh. *Kay*."

Ella, Ayers's girlfriend. Ella, who was everything Claudia might have been if not for the night that shattered her life with Ayers. In the years since their divorce, there had been other women in Ayers's life, one or two men in Claudia's (no one serious enough to introduce to Raven). But never anyone who was around for very long. Ella, tall, gorgeous, publishing executive, childless by choice, faultlessly kind yogi, who *loved Raven like her own,* had been dating Ayers for two years now. She was more or less living at his apartment, though she still maintained her own. Claudia would have to be a small, mean person to hate the lovely, sweet Ella—who truly had only ever been kind to Claudia and Raven. But she *did*. Why was it only Claudia who could see beneath that perfect façade to the vain, vacuous, self-serving bitch beneath? Claudia rested her head on the steering wheel, listening to the birds sing outside the window. They were going to be late for school.

"Have you thought about it?" asked Claudia into the space between her arms. Then she looked back at her daughter, who stared sulkily down at her nails. "You want the test and I get why you do. But have you really thought about how the results would affect you?"

"I *have* thought about it," said Raven, sounding

97

far older than her years. "I want to know. Either way, I want to own who I am."

Raven turned to look out the window, the sun and the green of the grass, and the autumn golds and reds casting her in silhouette. She had Claudia's button nose. Though her eyes were deep black, Claudia always thought that they were Ayers's eyes, almost but not quite almond shaped, heavily lashed. Raven was lean with delicate features—long fingers, high cheekbones—like Ayers's mom Sophie. She had Martha's rock-solid faith in her own abilities. And yet, she was just Raven, someone unique in all the universe, part of them all and yet all herself.

"But you can do that without the test," said Claudia. "You are who you are right now. Nothing will change that."

"Then let me do it," she said.

Claudia put the truck in gear and started driving. She pulled out of the drive and onto the road. She didn't have the right answer for this. But she could feel her resolve on this topic weakening for the first time. It was all well and good to make decisions for your children before they had opinions of their own.

"In less than three years, I'll be eighteen," said Raven. She tilted her chin up. "You won't be able to stop me then."

Was she counting the years until she owned

herself? The thought made Claudia unspeakably sad.

"Where are we going, anyway?" Raven asked.

"Hel-lo?" said Claudia. "We're going to school."

"I'm not going today. Remember?" she said. "Principal Blake wants me to *regroup, start fresh* on Monday."

Again, Claudia brought the truck to a stop. Of course. Claudia was the queen at blocking out the things she didn't want to remember. Raven was right. She was absentminded, distracted. A flake, Claudia's own mother would have said. Her mother was also gone, just two years after her father. Claudia was an orphan. A divorced orphan. She almost tripped into the abyss of self-pity and added single mother.

"What's in your backpack, then?" she asked.

"My clothes," said Raven. "I told you I wanted to go to Dad's this weekend. You said I could."

The prospect of the weekend alone in the house was bleak. On the other hand, there was a lot she could get done without Raven lurking around, complaining. She wouldn't have to make proper meals, or monitor her daughter's screen time, or suggest that they go to the gym or make a picnic to keep the kid from vegetating in front of the computer all day, texting with her friends in the city.

"What time is he expecting you?" she said, trying to stay light.

"He's taking a half day," Raven said. "Ella's going to be away. She has a yoga retreat."

Of course, she does. How nice for her. *Don't be catty, Claudia. It doesn't become you,* Martha would surely say. Then Martha would say something even cattier. Not catty. Biting, scathing, so close to the bone that even Claudia would cringe. If Claudia was a kitten, bearing her little claws now and then, Martha was a lioness. With a single effortless swipe, she could cut your throat.

"So run some errands with me, and we'll do breakfast," said Claudia. "Then I'll take you to the train."

"Okay," said Raven. She was looking at her phone, tapping with her thumbs.

Claudia should probably be punishing Raven. Shopping, breakfast out, and then an unscheduled trip to the city to see Ayers (the preferred parent) was not exactly a hard consequence for bad behavior. The guilt was making her soft. Claudia had moved Raven out here against her will, taking her away from her friends and her life in the city, so that Claudia could pursue this idea she had. Not just because of that. The city—it was such a crush, such a drain of energy and finances. Claudia had been struggling. And those friends of Raven's? Some of them were real trouble. Claudia had found a dime bag of marijuana in Raven's backpack, a slim package of rolling papers. It sealed her decision. Now Raven had to adjust to a new life while she was struggling with this big question of her identity.

And, really, who was Claudia to keep her daughter from this knowledge?

Claudia was all about the truth, speaking her pain, putting it out there, not just for herself but to help others who needed a voice. Soon after her attack and before Raven was born, Claudia joined an online support group; she shared her story and read the stories of others. Monsters thrive in the dark, she believed; if you dared to shine a light on the ugly things, they often shrank to nothing. Rape victims so often hid from what happened to them, blaming themselves, drowning in shame, suffering depression, PTSD. She didn't want to hide what happened to her. Admittedly, Claudia never even thought about what it meant to be the *child* of a rape victim, one who wasn't certain whether she was the product of that rape or not. Claudia never once, *never once,* allowed herself to think that Raven didn't belong to Ayers. It wasn't even an option. The universe just wasn't that cruel; that's what she told herself.

You told these people everything that happened to you? About Raven? Ayers had stammered when he first found out that she had joined an online discussion group. (That was right when things started to go bad between them, when he first got that she wasn't just going to *forget,* just *get over it.*) And that was even before the internet was what it is today, a huge barfing mouth of everybody's over-sharing. Now there was no more secret shame; it was all out there. But back then, those internet discussion groups still had the illusion of privacy. Typing in the dark, nothing lighting the room but the glow of the screen, sharing with anonymous other victims, baring it all. There she was just LostGirl—she could rage, she could whine, she could worry that she'd never be whole again. It was cathartic. It was the only thing that had helped her step back into the world of the living, knowing that she wasn't alone. She would look at other women she saw on the street and wonder, *What is your secret shame?*

Eventually, she started her own blog, more of an online diary about how she was moving forward. She posted weekly essays about motherhood after rape, everything from learning to be alone in the apartment again, to walking home at night without Ayers—really everything. It was a stream of consciousness. She had nothing to hide. That blog, Aftermath.com, grew to have lots of followers. The daily mail she received from people it was helping—well—it helped to heal her.

The new blog Makeoversandmeltdowns.com was about all about shedding skin, moving into the next phase of her life, single mom, victimhood behind her. She was even working on a book proposal with an agent. She was helping herself; she was helping others. She was all out there.

"You have three new sign-ups today on your newsletter," said Raven. "Your post with the video of mounting those photo shelves got a hundred likes and was shared thirteen times. That's pretty good."

Raven helped Claudia with social media, took pictures, helped with some of the work in the house (when she wasn't complaining about it or sulking in her room blasting angry music) and technical aspects of the blog—like laying it out, linking in pictures, linking to older, relevant blogs; Claudia paid her ten dollars an hour. Raven didn't resent it, even seemed to enjoy it—especially the social media stuff.

Even though Claudia had regrets about all the sharing she'd done, she was also proud that she had taught her daughter not to be ashamed of what had happened to Claudia, of who Raven was or where she may (or may not) have come from. There was nothing more corrosive than secrets. If Raven had discovered later that Claudia had hid Raven's origins, it would have broken trust, introduced shame. She'd raised Raven as openly and as honestly as she'd done everything else. Except for that one thing, the one thing that wasn't supposed to matter, but did.

"Okay," said Claudia. She knew when she was

beaten, when she was wrong. She didn't believe she'd started out wrong, but somehow her decision was wrong now. That was such a trick of parenthood, knowing the line between protecting and smothering, the line between loving and clinging.

"Okay?" asked Raven, glancing over sideways. She sat up a little in her seat, a kind of brightness coming onto her face.

"Okay," said Claudia. "You can have the test."

After dropping Raven at the train, Claudia stopped at the hardware store for a few basics, then drove back to the house. Exhaustion suddenly pulled at her eyelids, pushed down her shoulders. She sat in the truck for a minute, stared at the gaping hole where the barn door used to be, at the big gray beast of a house. They stared back at her like members of a rival gang, ready for a rumble.

"You will not beat me," she said, pulling herself out of the defeated slouch into which she'd fallen. "You will not."

The sun dipped behind a swath of gray clouds.

Ayers had come out here with her the first time, when she'd just had the initial idea for the project. They'd left Raven with her grandparents and driven out together.

"Okay," said Ayers, as he pulled the Range Rover to a stop. "Wow."

"Amazing, right?" she'd said.

"That's one word for it."

"What?"

"Claudia." He had this way of saying her name that made the first syllable sound like "cloud." "Do you know how much work this is going to be? How much money?"

He pointed up at the roof that sagged, where so many shingles were missing it looked like a design choice. "The roof alone."

He shook his head, blew out an amused breath.

She thought she knew—how much work, how much money. She was up to it. She always believed that; that she was up to any task, no matter how daunting, that lay before her. "But it's beautiful, isn't it?"

He watched her with his blue-gray eyes, with that sad, sweet expression he still had when he looked at her.

"Yes," he said, putting his hand on hers. "It is."

The tug back to him was still strong, so many years passed and still.

"How's Ella?" she asked. It was mean; but it worked. He drew away from her. Why? Why did she keep pushing him away?

"Oh," he said, looking back at the house. "You know."

"Sophie must love her," said Claudia. "She's so upright, so—proper."

"Sophie hates her, and you know it."

"I'm surprised," said Claudia. "They're so alike."

"Stop it." She saw the smile turn up the corners of his mouth just slightly. She felt that energy of laughter that never died between them. The universe was a joke, and just the two of them were in on it.

They went inside that day; she used the new video camera Martha had sent her. It was her first blog post about the house: *A New Start in an Old Place.*

Why did it seem so long ago?

Inside, she climbed the creaking stairs to the second level, then up the slim back staircase that led to the room where she'd set up her office. A tiny square of a space, with a quirky round window that looked out on to the woods. She called it level two and a half, since the room was suspended between the second floor and the attic. The engineer thought it was an addition, not original to the house, something created from a storage space that dropped down from the attic. It was a perfect office.

At her computer she went through the posts to find that first one, to remind her what she felt that day. The video was shaky and amateurish. And too dark; the lighting was bad.

"Uh," said Ayers on the video. He leaned in and inspected the banister, pulling lightly at one of the dowels, which broke off in his hand. He regarded it with dismay, held it up to her and they both started laughing.

"There is literally not one thing in this house that doesn't need repair. I mean—Claud, it's a gut job."

"Are you kidding?" she said from off-camera. "Look at this wainscoting."

It had been original to the house; it restored beautifully. "And this chandelier."

She panned to it. It had been grimy with dust, some of its glittering crystal teardrops missing. It too had come back to life with the help of her friend Blaire, who restored antiques. They were even able to find some crystal pieces online that matched almost perfectly. Today it shimmered over the dining room table.

She'd pointed the camera back at Ayers. He ran a hand through his thick, dark hair, then rubbed at the stubble on his jaw. She loved his hands, which were big and strong but still soft, gentle. "Well," he said. "If anyone can do it. You can. You're the strongest person I know."

She remembered feeling embarrassed; it was so far from true. She wasn't strong at all. She was a shivering wreck most of the time.

"I'm in," he said. "Whatever you guys need. I think it will be good for Raven. A project, the country, distance from the city."

The video ended when she tripped, the camera flying and landing in position to catch Ayers helping Claudia up.

"You okay?"

"Yeah," she said. They both cracked up again. She cut it there.

The post had been up there for a while, got a lot of views and comments.

> So, that's your EX husband? If my ex
>   looked like that, I'd have held on tight.
> You get that he still loves you, right?
> Your ex is a hottie. He can restore my
>   wainscoting any day. Wink, wink.
> Can I get the name of the friend who
>   refabbed your chandelier?

She watched the video a couple more times, thought of calling Ayers but didn't. Sometimes talking to him just reminded her how much she wanted him here, helping her. How things were so much easier when she didn't have to do them on her own. But she'd chosen this path. And she had no right to ask him for more than he already gave.

She checked the post about the fallen barn door, then wrote a few sentences about her plans to call Just Old Doors and have someone come out. She was rewarded with a swath of encouraging comments.

Then she girded herself and headed downstairs, ready to rumble.

seven

Raven waved to her mother from the train window. She imagined that her mother was a stranger, someone she'd never seen before—a pretty lady, not old, not young, stylish in rolled-up jeans and oversized white shirt, red ballet flats, and big, glittery bag over her shoulder. Her blonde hair was up in a let's-get-to-work messy bun; she had her sunglasses up on her head. She'd spend a minute when she got into the car looking for them before she remembered where they were. Ditzy, but smart ditzy. *Take it easy on your mom,* was her dad's constant refrain. *She's been through a lot.* Even Ella, whom Raven's mom *despised,* was always ready to jump to her defense. *We never understand our mothers until we are mothers ourselves. Until then, we should try not to judge. But, of course, we all judge them terribly.*

Her mom was smiling bright and happy, but Raven could always tell when her smile was fake. Her eyes were sad, and Raven felt it, that horrible twist of wanting to stay and wanting to be away all at once. She pressed her palm against the glass, and her mom blew a kiss, gave another big wave before walking back to the truck. She thought about getting off at the next stop and going back. Maybe she would.

What's up, buttercup?

Weird that her dad was texting her at exactly this moment. Like a poke in the ribs from the universe.

Not much. How's St. Lucia?
Better than biology class. Lol. You're on
   your way to class now, right?

He prided himself on knowing her exact schedule.

Yep. On my way there right now.

This was one of the little loopholes—and there were quite a few. One: Dad and Ella were having a long weekend in the Caribbean; they left after work last night. Mom didn't know because it wasn't supposed to be Dad's weekend with Raven, and Dad would never tell Mom about it (unless Mom said, "Hey, what are you and Ella doing this weekend?" and she never would). Two: Raven showed her mom an old text, so Claudia never questioned that Raven was going where she said she was going. Three: Her mom and dad only communicated directly about scheduling when there was (a) something wrong or (b) coordination was required beyond texts and email. So there were all kinds of ways Raven

110

could game the system to find a little freedom now and then.

Her parents didn't hate each other—far from it, they actually seemed to like each other. It was more like it *hurt* too much for some reason to be near each other. Her mother had a very particular soft, apologetic tone that she used only with Ayers, and, likewise, Ayers treated Claudia like a bird he was trying to get not to fly away. Neither one of them had *ever* said a negative word about the other. And four: Raven had begged her mom not to tell her dad about the quasi-suspension. Usually, there would be no chance that Claudia would keep something like that from Ayers but this time, for some reason unknown to Raven, Claudia had agreed. Maybe because Claudia was trying so hard to make a fresh start, she didn't want to admit that it wasn't going as well as she'd hoped.

Study hard.
Mom said I could get the test.

There was a long pause where Raven looked out the window, watching the blur of buildings give way to a blur of fields and trees, to a blur of concrete walls, then buildings again.

THE test?
Yeah. She'll probably change her mind.
But she said okay.

111

Why? What happened?
Nothing. It's just—time.

The station where Raven had considered turning around came and went. There were other points ahead, though, where she could change her mind. The sky outside grew darker, thick gray clouds floating together.

When I get back we need to all sit and talk. This is a big decision.

What? she thought. That was so like a grown-up. Why were they both so flip-floppy?

You said you were okay with it.
It's still something I want to talk through as a family.

As a family, she thought. What a crock.

Ella said she thought it was time.
Ella, whatever her opinion, is not part of this.

Oh, snap! There had been a bit more of that from her dad, sort of a hard shutout of Ella on bigger-picture things. Maybe there was trouble in paradise—maybe Dad didn't love being a vegan yogi as much as he said he did. Maybe Ella found out that he and Raven still scarfed down cheeseburgers and ice cream sundaes when they were alone together, lay around on the couch binging on television shows Claudia would never let her watch like *Game of Thrones* and *The Walking Dead*. It was hard not to like Ella (in theory) because she was so nice, so always, always kind. But, really, Raven wished that she'd just go away. *Just float away, skinny yogini, on your magical mat made of recycled materials.*

> Fine. We'll talk. But my mind is made
>   up. You can't stop me forever.
> Don't do anything without me.
> Duh. How could we?
> Uh, yeah. Right. When did you get so
>   smart?

She was far from smart. Ayers and Claudia were both smart in different ways—maybe not math or science geniuses but creative and sharp. Raven struggled—always, with everything—with reading, with math, with people. She was always behind, even had to repeat kindergarten. Her parents changed schools, hoping that she wouldn't notice that she had to do kindergarten again, but she noticed. Even now, even working hard, she was just a solid-C student, with the occasional B. She got A's in art and theater sometimes. But the rest of it was a constant challenge of attention and effort.

I had trouble in school, too, her mom said. *Creative people don't always do well in a traditional school environment.*

But Raven knew it wasn't true. She'd seen her mother's yearbook—she'd been beautiful and bright, editor of the school paper, most likely to succeed, homecoming queen. *Your mother couldn't pay attention,* her aunt Martha said, *because she was always thinking about boys, parties, and fashion. That's why she had a hard time.*

Another text from her dad:

Remember that you are my daughter in every real and significant way. Nothing can take that from us. No matter what. I love you, Kitten.

But it wasn't true. It just wasn't. She was either his biological daughter, or she was the daughter of a sociopathic criminal who raped her mother and left her for dead. There was no way to pretend that it didn't matter which. And lately, she felt it. She felt apart from them, different. Ayers and Claudia were one kind of person, and she was another. There was a darkness in her, an anger that was foreign and alive. Like yesterday, the girl that dumped that tray—yeah, on purpose— was not the girl who had been sitting quietly reading with her lunch just moments earlier. She was dark and mean and lived inside Raven, just

114

waiting to be invited out. And when she was out? There was always trouble.

> I know, Dad. I love you, too.
> I'll call your mom next week and we'll all
> get together.

If Raven were smart, she probably wouldn't have told him about the test until he got back. What if he called her mom to talk right away? But he wouldn't. Because then he'd have to tell her that he was in St. Lucia with Ella, since *not telling* her while he was calling her from the beach with a cocktail in his hand was the same as lying. Which her dad would never do. He was chronically honest. So, he'd mention where he was, try to make light of it. And, though her mom wouldn't say anything, it would hurt. (And no one wanted Claudia to be hurt any more than she already had been.) But the reminder that Ayers had happily moved on with his life wouldn't hurt as much as realizing that Raven had lied and was on her way into the city on her own to do who knew what. A shit storm for all involved would ensue.

Another station where she might have gotten off came and went. She even shouldered her bag and slid forward in her seat. But then she sat back down. She stuffed her phone in the pocket of her hoodie and leaned her head against the window.

It's not like she was running away or anything. She'd stay in touch and be home when she was supposed to go home. It was just that she had an errand to run, one neither of her parents would understand.

It was Ella who had given her the idea. The man who raped Claudia was dead. But he had a family—a family that might bc hcrs, as wcll. *What if you reached out to them,* Ella suggested. *Just, you know, to see if you have anything in common, if there's a connection.* It never occurred to Raven that Ella was anything but well meaning.

His name was easy enough to find, since Raven's own mother, in an effort to understand and forgive her rapist—had written extensively about him in an earlier blog. Melvin Cutter: abandoned by his mother to the system at age four, raised in foster care, arrested for the first time at fourteen, then three more times after that for various offenses from drug possession to assault. He held a job, a night watchman at a supermarket on Second Avenue. On the night he raped Claudia, he was twenty years old, illiterate, and high on meth. Police speculated that he'd likely broken into the apartment looking for something to steal and sell and ran into Raven's mother instead.

Cutter shouldn't have been free that night; he'd been in custody just hours earlier, brought in on suspicion of another rape. But lack of evidence caused the police to let him go. Cutter had a son, the child of a teenage girlfriend, that was being raised by his maternal grandmother. Eventually, he was murdered in prison by another inmate over some slight. *A wasted life, characterized by pain and misery, ending in tragedy,* Claudia had written. *He was a victim, too. Still, I find I can't forgive him. My body won't forgive him.*

Why would she *want* to forgive him? Raven marveled. What was the big deal about forgiveness? If it were Raven? She'd just want to kill him. In fact, she *did* want to kill him—even though he was already dead. She wished she could get in a time machine, *Terminator* style, and go back and kill him before he ever hurt her mother. But then, possibly, she would be killing herself, as well. That's why she needed to know who she was. That was part of it. It was complicated, a red tangle of anger and fear inside of her.

A little searching on Google and Raven found Andrew Cutter, who was twenty and a college student at CUNY. He was smart, a graduate of Bronx High School of Science. He had dark eyes like his father, and a mass of silky curls, but his features were fine where Melvin's were thick. He didn't have the vacant, disaffected look of his father. *A thinker. A wonderer who wants to make a difference in this place we share.* That

117

was his Twitter bio, his tag: @angryyoungman.

She followed him, and he followed her back. She wasn't supposed to have a Twitter account, but she did: @butterflydreams. She had a selfie up on her profile, overexposed and filtered, so that her skin looked paper white and her eyes dark as space. She knew it was too sexy and that it made her look much older than she was. Her mom wouldn't like it.

> I think we may have something in
> common @angryyoungman.
> Oh, yeah, @butterflydreams? I'd like to
> know what that is.

She DM'd him then: Melvin Cutter.
> I'm sorry, came the curt reply. But I don't
> have anything in common with him.
> Except that he's your father and might
> be mine, too.

He'd unfollowed her, then. It was kind of a slap in the face, one that smarted. But she could still see his posts in her newsfeed since she'd followed him. He was in a band called Trash and Angels, and they were playing this weekend at some dive bar on the Lower East Side. Raven and her forever best friend since kindergarten Troy were going. She wanted to see the boy who might be her half brother. She'd know right

118

away, wouldn't she? She'd feel the energy, that something, no matter how dark, connected them.

I'm on my way, she texted to Troy.

Are we totally sure about this?
Yeah. Totally.

She and Troy had been best friends since the first minute of the first day of kindergarten. They sat next to each other during circle time, and he reached for her hand because it was the first time he'd been away from his mom. Even though he was crying a little, he was still smiling. She took his hand because it was the first time *she'd* ever been away from her mom, and she knew just how he felt. He'd had a wild head of white-blond curls, in stark contrast to his dark skin, glasses, and a big toothless smile. Though his front teeth had since grown in, he didn't look that different now. He was taller than she was, even though he'd always been the littlest kid in class. Somewhere during the summer between seventh and eighth grade, he shot up. He still giggled like a little kid. He called her Birdie. And she was pretty sure she didn't have to tell him that she was not, in fact, totally sure about this or anything even when she pretended otherwise.

Okay, he wrote. Let's do it.

The train came to a stop at another little station. She grabbed her bag and almost got off. But then, she didn't. She sank back down and put her headphones on, David Bowie was singing about how there was a starman waiting in the sky. She watched the trees turn into a green-black blur, the train taking her toward what? She had no idea.

eight

Where is she?
            There's no one else here.
I saw her. Bring her to me.

I can still hear those voices. Some memories never go away. They stay. They get buried, tamped down, but then resurface in dreams, when you're tired, hungry, lonely. Or angry like I was today, practically vibrating with it. I was having a hard time keeping my composure, pulling that energetic curtain, my invisibility cloak, around me. I didn't have time to breathe through my feelings. So I started my shift jittery and unsettled.

It was the call from Seth that unstitched me. *Someone's moved into the house,* he said.

It wasn't big news. Or it shouldn't have been. But the words landed like a gut punch, knocking the air out of my lungs. It was so much easier to think of that place rotting and empty, falling to pieces. I'd been there so many times, walking those echoing halls, looking. It didn't seem as if lives could be lived there anymore.

"Who?" I managed.

"The old man's daughter, I think. She's renovating the place," he said. He paused a moment. I could feel him measuring his words. "There's a blog."

"A blog," I repeated. "About the house?"

"About the renovation," he said. "About her, you know, journey—or whatever."

I couldn't think of what to say.

"I know," said Seth. "It's weird."

We were still back there, Seth and I, in our very different ways. I guess I didn't think the house would be the first to move on.

"There's something else," he continued. He was used to long, protracted silences from me.

"What?"

"Beckham's back," Seth said. Something roared in my ears. "He was released a few months back. He's been drifting around. Finally found his way home."

A few months. He was supposed to be keeping tabs. This was important.

"Why didn't you tell me?"

"I'm telling you now," he said. "Just—"

"Just?"

"Are you sure that this is what you want?"

It was too late for questions like that. I'd started something, flipped some kind of karmic switch. I had no choice but to keep going.

"Zoey."

"I'm here."

If he knew about Didion, he hadn't said anything. Of course, he wouldn't.

"I have to think," I said. "I'll talk to you later."

He was saying something when I hung up. I didn't hear.

122

. . .

"You okay?" The voice snapped me back into the moment.

I wiped up the coffee that I'd spilled on the service counter. I never make mistakes. Never. Almost never. So when I do, it's like there's a big neon arrow pointing right at me. Mistakes call attention—sympathy, judgment, annoyance. Preoccupation had made me careless, and I'd overfilled a mug. Sloppy, I heard Paul's voice. Careless. Just like not noticing that camera. I thought I had a grip on the thing, the rage. Maybe not.

"I'm fine," I said. "Thanks."

"I'm Erik." I didn't want to look at him, but I did and found myself gazing into a pair of sea-glass green eyes. My pulse jumped a little; I don't like eyes on me.

"Zoey," I said, light, brisk, not rude but not inviting more talk.

I gave him a quick nod, then moved away swiftly with my tray of coffee cups, cursing myself. That's what happens when you let yourself feel something; you send off sparks of energy that attract the attentions of others. I took my break in the bathroom and did a quick meditation where I focus on my breathing, imagining myself as small and invisible, a wraith, someone who is there but isn't there. And the rest of my shift passed without incident—until I was getting ready to go home.

"Hey—Zoey?"

I turned to see Erik from earlier. He had a look, something going on beneath the surface smile. I stared at him longer than I should have, trying to figure out what it was. He looked down at his toes after holding my gaze a moment.

"So a bunch of us are going out for a drink." He did a little rocking thing, up on his toes then back on his heels. "Would you like to join us maybe?"

I shouldered my hoodie, put my backpack on. I tried for a regretful smile.

"I can't," I said. "I have to be somewhere."

He had his hands in his pockets, his shoulders hunched in a little. His blond hair was a careful mess as he gave an understanding nod. "Maybe another time."

"Yeah," I said. "Definitely."

Definitely not.

I got out of there as fast as possible, didn't stick around to see what kind of reaction he had to rejection. In my experience, men don't do well with it. You'll either see a flash of anger, maybe sadness, or maybe a mask will come down, something hard and protective. Few take it in stride.

With the ding of the little bell on the door, the light and noise of the restaurant was gone in the dark and cold of the street. Avenue A is always hopping, especially at night. I pulled my hood up and moved fast through the walkers, stumblers, shriekers, laughers. They didn't see me. I was invisible again. I wasn't lying to Erik of the green eyes. I did have someplace I needed to be.

Mike was already waiting for me when I walked through the door, my breath slightly labored from the six-floor walkup, which I took two stairs at a time. I was a little late, and I could see that he'd used the time to warm up. A hundred sit-ups, a hundred push-ups, a hundred jumping jacks. His forehead glowed, and he looked loose, ready.

"There's an elevator, you know," he said, as I bowed at the altar.

"What's the point of working out if you're just going to take the elevator?"

"To save your strength for the fight ahead."

The wood floors bounced a little beneath my feet, and I avoided my reflection in the floor-to-ceiling mirrors as I headed into the locker room. I stowed my stuff and stripped down to tank and sports bra. I pulled on my black pants and wrapped the fabric black belt around my waist. Then I exited to find him waiting in the middle of the floor, legs spread apart, arms folded.

"Your energy is not right," he said. "It's wobbly."

"I'm fine."

"Are you here?" he asked. "Are you all here?

We bow at the door and leave our burdens at the altar. Have you done that?"

"Yes," I lied. "I have."

"We'll see."

We faced each other, put our hands in prayer to our chests and bowed. He was right; I was wobbly. I was going to get my ass kicked.

Mike Lopez was the man who taught me how to fight. I came to him a kitten, scared and skittish, hiding behind my uncle. He turned me into a dragon.

"Learn to fight and you'll never be afraid again," he told me that first night while my uncle watched. "Learn to fight and you'll know yourself and understand your own power."

I was skinny and fourteen, newly orphaned, and in the throes of trauma. Maybe without my uncle and *sifu* (teacher), as I have come to think of Mike, I would have turned to drugs, or become a lifelong victim, broadcasting a signal of fear and weakness, drawing predators to me like an injured bird. Instead, he turned me into a warrior. I have never left fear behind me, nor should we, but I have conquered it.

We started small back then with stances (make it strong or always be off balance), basic punches (fast, loose, as if your fist is a rock on a chain), and blocks (twist your arm to deflect with the flesh not the bone), and we built from there into sequences of moves called Tao Lu. My uncle took me three days a week to the studio on Twenty-Seventh Street from six-thirty until eight-thirty in the morning, after which I went on to school. I hated it until I realized that when I left the temple after two hours of intense exercise and learning, I had no energy for misery. As my body grew stronger, so did I. More than therapy, of which there was plenty, kung fu healed me. Sort of.

Mike Lopez was a big man, so he always came in hard like a freight train. That's his advantage: size, strength, and a surprising speed for someone the approximate girth of a semi. But I am a cat, slipping away and behind, or coming in close, delivering blows to the kidneys or the abdomen. The trick, when you're a small fighter with a big opponent, is to get away fast, to dance, to never let it be a match of strength, never let the big hand close around your wrist, never take the full brunt of the blow.

We wrangled around for a while; he threw me, and I landed (that wood floor bounced for a reason) in a roll, hopping quickly back to my feet. I caught his slow but devastatingly heavy roundhouse kick and forced him to the ground. Side kick, forearm block, duck below his leg again, pull my upper cut to his chin, just touch him there. He tapped my temple, to indicate that he could have struck me there—a fight ender, possibly worse.

I am not better than he is; I won't ever be. But

127

I can hold my own. He has admitted as much. At that point, we trained together mostly; sparring was play. But I will always consider him my teacher. That is the condition of even the most advanced martial artist—student. There is always something to learn, even though now I was a teacher myself. I taught the Sunday morning girls' class, the ten- to twelve-year-olds. Most of them are just coming to terms with their own bodies, finding their confidence and power. How I have loved watching them turn from kittens into dragons. I think that's what I'll miss the most.

When we were done, we sat on the floor, leaning against the mirrors, and drank from big jugs of water, scarfed down protein bars.

"What's eating you?" he asked.

He had put on his glasses, gold-rimmed circular specs that made him look like a scholar, even with his bald head, tattoos, and giant muscles. He was as old as Paul, maybe older, but he seemed much younger. His body pulsed with health, and his energy was strong. There is an intimacy with people you fight regularly; they know your body better than lovers do.

"Nothing," I lie.

"Paul," he said. "He called. He's worried about you."

"There's nothing to worry about."

"Let me ask you a question."

"Is it a real question?" I ask. "Or is it a question

128

to which you already think you have the answer? Because that's annoying."

Mike has a belly laugh, a kind of funny shake he does, covering his mouth like a girl as he issues a sound that's more like a cough. When it passed, he grew serious again. The laughing Buddha.

"What is the difference between justice and revenge?" he asked.

It was a good question, one I've asked myself a number of times. Probably most victims of violent crime have reason to ask themselves this question. As a society, we have reason to ask when we try to convict criminals, send them away for life without parole, or, in the extreme, sentence them to death. Who has the right to judge? Who says what is the appropriate punishment for wrong? Juries and judges make the call most often. But what if the people who do wrong are not caught? What if there is no arrest, no trial, no sentence, no judgment day? What if the men who murdered your parents while you watched went free?

"Must there be a difference?" I asked.

He took a swig of water, ran a big hand over his crown. It sounded like sandpaper.

"There should be," he said. "What's the first rule of kung fu, as I have taught it to you."

"Walk away unless they won't let you. Then, stand your ground to defend yourself, no more."

He gave an assenting nod. "Better said: never do more harm than is necessary to walk away."

I stood up, stretched my hands high, catching sight of myself in the mirror, then quickly turned away. It's an uncomfortable position, to have parted company with your mentors. Mike always tells this story about the Buddhist monks who prayed for their killers while they were being slaughtered. It might be a myth, because I looked it up on the internet and couldn't find any articles about it. He speaks of them with awe and admiration; but the story always angered me. How could you pray for someone who hated you and wanted to kill you? I don't know if I have Mike's pacifist heart. What is the difference between pacifism and weakness?

"And if those people, the ones you walk away from, go on to hurt others," I said. "What then? Are you not at least somewhat responsible?"

He put a hand on my arm, and his skin was bark against the sand of mine. His mother was Jamaican, his father Puerto Rican. She was a singer; he was an electrical engineer. He was a harsh disciplinarian; she used to take Mike out of school so they could play hooky at Rockaway Beach. Mike's fighting style is a curious mix of precision and fluidity, almost predictable until it isn't. It's funny how two people meet and come together, and through their differences

130

form someone unique with a whole new set of gifts and quirks.

Mike forced me to meet his eyes, leaning in front of me so I had to look at him. "What happened was not your fault. And you're not responsible for anything that's happened since. You were just a kid."

"Well," I said, gently unwinding from his grasp. "I'm not a kid anymore."

I moved toward the locker room door.

"Revenge seeks chaos," he said. "Justice seeks balance. That's the difference."

His deep, resonant voice bounced off the walls, and the sound of it caused me to pause at the door, my palm on the wood.

"That seems pretty vague to me," I said. "Open to interpretation."

"Okay, how about this: when you plan revenge, you should dig two graves—one of them for yourself."

I decided not to mention that that's been the plan all along.

The first time it happened, it was an accident. Well, not an accident exactly, but unplanned. I was a freshman at NYU, eighteen years old, and I'd been fighting for four years, not to mention some informal earlier training from Paul—how to make a fist, how to draw power from your stance, in a street fight or to defend yourself, always go for the eyes and the groin.

I'd been studying at the temple for four years. There are no belts in kung fu, not at my school anyway. We earn degrees. The first degree came after two years if you passed a written and physical test. The second came a couple years after that. I'd just earned my second degree.

But I'd never been in a real street fight.

Don't look for it, Mike always warned us, worried that young people overconfident in their own abilities would go out into the city looking for trouble. Some did.

Even *I* wondered if outside the temple I could defend myself. Sparring is not the real deal. We didn't wear guards—except the men wore cups and the women wore breast shields inside their sports bras. But we took blows to the center body and limbs to learn what it feels like to get hit. And in sparring, we pulled our strikes to the head, vital organs, lower abdomen, tapping or slapping when a fist might do real damage, actions that taught control and discipline. But we still got hurt—a lot, marking each other with ugly black bruises, massaging each other when it was done. So I knew what it was like to take a blow. But when fear and adrenaline were part of the equation, what would that change? If someone had a real gun or a knife, was crazy, a gutter fighter, not following the rules of the kung fu temple, how would I fare?

The goal is never to find out, Mike answered when I asked.

It was late, that first time. I had spent my evening at Bobst Library, off Washington Square Park, studying and decided to walk home rather than cab it as my uncle would have preferred. It was early autumn, Halloween approaching, the air crisp but not cold. I wore my eternal hoodie, black jeans, and sneakers. It was the perfect invisibility cloak; tons of people in the city wearing exactly the same thing.

My parents had been dead for more than four years. I was constructed mainly of eggshells, emotionally speaking. I still couldn't bring myself to talk to anyone but Paul, some of my teachers, people at the temple. So I'm sure I came off as a bit of a freak, hollow-eyed and shrinking (or trying to) into a slate-gray hood. The world, to me, seemed like a field of shadows, everything suspect, everyone untrustworthy. I felt safe only at the temple, among stacks of books, or with Paul. Otherwise, I was a field mouse staying out of sight, always watching for the wings of death.

"I don't know what you're talking about." A shrill voice, young and frightened, startled me as I walked, heading east on Eighth Street. "Get away from me."

"What the fuck? Do you think I'm stupid?" Brooklyn, big round vowels, hard-edged consonants. "Save yourself, kid. I'm warning you. Give it back."

"You're making a mistake," the kid wailed. "Help!"

I came up behind them, the two men pushing a ratty-looking teenager up against a brick wall. The street wasn't deserted, but people were crossing to the other side to avoid the conflict.

The boy, a stick-skinny Latino with a row of piercings in his ear and a kind of dirty, neglected aura, had the wild-eyed look of a cornered animal. I'd lived in the city long enough to know a street kid when I saw one. His thick-necked assailants were grown-up frat boys, twin-like with close-shorn hair, red faces, well dressed in auras of entitlement.

"I don't want to hurt you," said one of the men, a blond, as he moved in closer.

"Then don't," I said.

The two men both swung to look at me. I hated having three sets of eyes on me, took a step back.

"Let him go," I said. I couldn't believe the way my voice sounded, deep, calm. My pulse wasn't even slightly elevated.

Taking advantage of the distraction, the kid tried to run. But the man with darker hair and one of those giant diver's watches that are supposed to let people know you make a lot of money, grabbed him, wrenching his arm. The boy—he *was* a boy, maybe not even as old as I was—let out a cry of pain.

There wasn't even a thought in my head. I moved in quick and brought my heel down hard on the darker man's expensive loafer, feeling a small bone snap beneath the strike. I was pushed back by the sound of his scream. The kid looked at me with something like awe, then scrambled down the street.

"What the fuck?" the blond, scared, angry, turned on me. "He took my wallet."

He reached in with both hands for me. I threaded my hands up through his arms and vise gripped his wrists, using his arms and weight to stabilize myself and bring my heel hard into his groin. He crumpled soundless into a pile of himself on the concrete, his neck gone bright red against the lavender checks of his Brooks Brothers Oxford. I knew it would take him a second to find sound. By the time he did, a great helpless wail of pain, I was gone, running up the street, heading east, pausing only when I got to Avenue C, ducking into a doorway to catch my breath. I tried to disappear into the dark.

"What the hell did I just do?" I asked no one.

There was a homeless man sleeping in the next doorway, buried beneath a pile of papers, emitting an impossibly strong stench, snoring peacefully.

That street kid probably *did* have that guy's

wallet. But I didn't care. It wasn't any excuse for brutality.

"Oh, and that wasn't brutal?" my dad asked. Did I mention that I sometimes see my dad? That he lingers in the edges of my life, offering commentary and unsolicited advice. Well, I do.

"It was defense," I said. "I defended the kid. And then I defended myself."

"Oh, really," said my dad. He issued a little laugh. "That blow to the jewels was strictly necessary, was it? You couldn't have gotten away without it, once the kid was clear?"

He lit a cigarette and leaned against the wall beside me. He was wearing that denim shirt over a navy blue tee, the one my mom loved because it made his eyes look like sapphires. He had that sleepy look, like he used to after he'd worked overtime and then slept in. He used to smoke out behind the barn, hiding from my mom.

"Meanwhile," my dad said. "The kid was a thief."

"A street kid," I said. "He probably needed the money for food."

"A junkie," he said with a sharp exhale. "He needed the money for drugs."

"You'd let those two goons pound him into the wall? They were looking for it. They wanted to hurt him, wallet or not."

"You don't know that."

My breath came back, my head cleared. There

was no wash of regret, no shaky, post-adrenaline nausea. I was calm and solid as I slipped out of the doorway, confident that I was one with the night. I wasn't concerned that the police would be looking for me. I didn't feel bad for hurting those men. In fact, I rarely felt anything at all.

"Sometimes right is right even when it's wrong," I said, walking by my father.

"You keep telling yourself that, kid."

As I moved up the street, heading back to Paul's—he was bound to be worried by now; might even come out and try to meet me on the path he knew I'd take home—another shadow slipped out of another doorway. He must have seen me run by, waited.

"Did you?" I asked as he came into view. "Take his wallet."

He held it out, and I took it from him.

"Did you take the cash?" I asked.

"No cash," he said. "Just credit cards. No one has cash anymore."

"Do you need money?" I asked.

He nodded. I had a twenty in my wallet, not more. I'd have to ask Paul for money for lunch tomorrow. I handed it to him. I didn't know if he was hungry or if he needed a fix, that was *his* karma.

"Why?" he asked.

"Why not?" I answered. He just shook his head at me like I was an apparition, something

137

he couldn't quite believe in, stuffed the bill in his pocket. Then he ran off without a word of thanks. Weirdly, I didn't need one.

I walked a little way with the wallet and then ducked into a dive bar where cops from the Fifth Precinct hung out, around the corner from Paul's, told the bartender that I'd found it in his doorway. He said he'd take care of it, and I knew that he would.

Paul was waiting for me when I got back, his brow knitted with worry.

"You're late," he said. He came in close, put a motherly hand on my forehead. "You look a little flushed. You okay?"

"Never better," I told him. And it was true.

Leaving the temple, almost six years since that night defending the street kid, I made sure my brick-red hood was up, my light backpack strapped on tight. That night long ago was the beginning of something. A wrong turn home led me in the right direction. Since then, I've had only one thing on my mind. In our touchy-feely culture, there's a lot of talk about forgiveness, a commonly held belief that the nurturing of hatred and anger is a toxin. No one ever tells you that it can be an engine, that it can keep you alive. I started jogging toward the TriBeCa loft, thinking about my next move.

nine

His references checked out . . . and then some.

"Oh, *Josh,*" effused Jennifer Warbler. "He's not a handyman, he's a *magician.* In fact, I should give you a bad reference because I don't want to share him!"

In the background, Claudia could hear a baby cooing. Oh, that sound! Those little noises and babbles! The tired cry, the checking-out-my-voice yell, all the funny one-syllable stabs at language—Claudia had loved every minute of Raven's babyhood. She'd never allowed the darkness to touch that; she fought it back with therapy and yoga and meditation. She'd worked so hard not to be like the women she read about who had a baby after rape. She'd read every horror story. The woman who saw her rapist's face every time she looked at her son. The girl who couldn't touch her daughter because she was so riven by trauma. More, worse. Claudia didn't even like to think about some of the things she'd read, worried that those thoughts could wiggle into her, a virus, a contagion.

Raven was *Ayers's* child, not *his* (she didn't even like to think his name), and *her* child. Claudia did not look into her child's face and see the face of her attacker. She had found joy, because she wouldn't accept anything less for herself or her daughter. It was a jaw-clenched, white-knuckled kind of happiness, but it had worked well enough.

Jennifer Warbler's baby cooed again loudly into the phone.

"Sorry. He can fix anything!" Jennifer went on. "I'm not kidding. My husband—such a good guy—*totally useless* when it comes to stuff like that. Can't even hang a picture straight. I found this table? At a garage sale? It was a mess. But Josh made it amazing! You're the one fixing up that old farmhouse, right?"

"Yes," said Claudia. "That's me."

"I've always wanted to do that," said Jennifer wistfully. "I have design fantasies. But, you know, with three kids, fantasies are about all I have time for!"

"I hear you," said Claudia. "I only have one, and she keeps me running ragged. I can *only imagine* three."

Mothers of multiple children needed a lot of commenting about how hard they worked, Claudia noticed. They wanted acknowledgment, especially from mothers of single children, of what a challenge it must be to juggle it all. Claudia never minded giving credit where it was due. Claudia would have had more children, always thought there was a big brood in her future; but it just didn't happen. Life was such a twisting helix of choice and circumstance, especially hers; she found it didn't make any sense to have regrets.

Ayers had wanted them to have another one. Not even a year after Raven was born, and when they were already pulling apart, they started talking about it. She got pregnant pretty quickly, but then she miscarried within a month. *You're under too much stress,* Martha had said. *You might be ready, but maybe your body isn't. Give it some time.*

But there hadn't been time. How much sadness could two people endure before it started to take them apart? She could always look at Raven with love and joy. But slowly it became harder to look at Ayers, his face a mirror of her own heart, trying so hard to soldier through it, wanting so badly to be okay again.

"Josh is *into* his work, you know?" Jennifer went on. "He likes helping and fixing things, and it shows. You can just tell, can't you? When people are passionate about what they do. You'll love him. Just make sure he still has time for me!"

Mr. Crawley, the second person on Josh's list, had similar things to say. "He's a good boy. A hard worker. He just brought back my vacuum cleaner, all fixed, didn't even charge me. Said it didn't take long enough to charge. Imagine that? There aren't too many honest people around these days, but he's one of them."

She called another woman, Wanda Crabb, but the woman didn't answer, so Claudia left a message. But she'd heard enough when the landline rang and it was Josh.

"Hey, Mrs. Bishop. It's Josh. The handyman? I don't want to be pushy, but I was just following up on my visit yesterday."

It was good to want something bad enough to call and follow up, right? It meant that he was eager, that he needed the work.

"Your ears must be ringing," she said. "Your clients have been singing your praises."

There was a bit of a pause where she wondered if the call had failed.

"That's nice to hear," he said finally.

Claudia glanced at her cell phone, watching the little blue dot that represented Raven. She'd spent the afternoon tracking Raven, between bouts of trying to peel off the wallpaper in the kitchen. Her daughter had departed the train and was now wandering around Ayers's neighborhood. Was Ayers with her? she wondered. Raven and Ayers had a good relationship, the kind Claudia had always wanted with her father. It was easy, loving, they liked the same things, could hang out. Claudia loved it, for both of them. They were kindred; more proof as Claudia saw it of their biological bond. And more reason not to care if there was one.

The wallpaper featured a hideous pattern of cornucopias, rows and rows of them, and it clung onto the wall as if someone had affixed it there with cement. She tried to imagine who might choose that kind of wallpaper. What about the beige background and shades of brown, orange, and gold appealed? She knew almost nothing about the last family to rent the house; it had sat empty for more than ten years. She kept meaning to look into it but just hadn't gotten around to it.

"I'm struggling with the wallpaper in the kitchen," she said to Josh. She stared in dismay at the mess around her, her ruined hands that were raw and red, glue embedded under her nails. The rumble was over. She'd lost.

"I can help you with that," he said easily. She liked the sound of his voice, sweet but masculine, not deep but resonant somehow.

The steamer she'd rented from the big box hardware store was not cutting it. It looked so easy on the YouTube video she'd watched. Except the paper wasn't peeling off in big sheets but in frustratingly small pieces.

She glanced at the clock. It was after two already.

"Can you come by today?" she asked. "We can talk and I'll show you what I need done?"

"I can come now, if you like." Was there something suspicious about someone who could "come now"? Everyone she knew in the city was so busy-addicted. Schedules were tight, not a minute to spare, dinner dates and lunches and coffees planned weeks in advance. No one she knew ever said, "I'm free right now."

"That's perfect," she said. "You can see what a mess I've made of the kitchen."

He laughed a little. "I'll look forward to it. Hey—remember, everything looks like a mess when you're in the middle of it. See you in a while."

After she'd hung up, she stood staring at the useless steamer humming in the corner and decided she was beaten. She'd attacked the job (like so many things), with so much vigor but all that initial energy had drained. She'd decided to make an espresso to give herself a little jolt. She picked up her phone and watched the little blue dot that was her daughter arrive at Ayers's Upper West Side building. She received a text from Raven just minutes later.

> You can stop tracking me! I'm here.
>   Love you.
> Okay. Love you. Have fun.

"What's the point of tracking her if she knows you're doing it?" That's what Ayers wanted to know.

"I don't want to spy on her. I just want her to

144

know I'm watching," she'd said. "With her—even when I'm not."

After some of the trouble Raven got into in the city—sneaking into clubs, some drinking, lying about where she was and who she was with—Ayers wanted to install spyware. It monitored everything that passed through her phone—calls, texts, emails, social media activity. It created a map of her activities. It could even turn the audio and camera on to see what she was doing in real time.

Claudia had balked, though it *was* tempting. What parent didn't want to know exactly what was going on in her teenager's brain? And monitoring Raven's cell phone was a pretty good clue. But Raven was still close to both of them, still talked to them about things. Sure, she was pushing the edges, but wasn't that normal? Wasn't secretly installing spyware crossing some kind of line, the line between caring and smothering, between being there and hovering? Didn't it say: I don't trust you or the world we live in and I expect bad things to happen? Didn't it put them and their daughter on opposing teams?

While she sipped her espresso and stared out the kitchen window at the hole in the barn where the door used to hang, she thought about calling Ayers. She was surprised that he hadn't called about the test: Raven had surely texted him as soon as she got on the train. He'd want a Big Talk. He was a communicator.

Ayers would probably want to come to the house for the weekend, which would be fine. He could help with the basement. And after Raven was asleep, maybe they'd find their way to each other. It had happened a number of times since they'd split; the attraction between them had never waned. The last time had been a couple of years ago. *Come back to me,* he'd whispered as they lay in the dark. She'd thought about it that time. But she'd thought too long. And now there was Ella.

She rested her hand on the phone, the landline, and was about to call her ex-husband when it started to ring. She saw the name on the caller ID and for some reason almost didn't answer. It was Wanda Crabb, the woman she'd called for a reference earlier.

Mrs. Crabb sounded like her name, older and a little crotchety.

"He does decent work, as much as anybody does these days," she said. "He refaced my cabinets. Work was fair at a fair price. I didn't have to call and call to see when he was going to show up like some of them. Seems to have grown into decent fellow. Not like his brother."

"Oh," said Claudia. "Do they work together?"

"No, no one's seen Rhett for years. Good riddance. He's probably in jail; that's the rumor anyway. I was the English teacher here at the local high school for twenty years; seen all kinds. Anyway, you must know all this. Rhett Beckham was a bad seed, if ever there was one."

There was something a little unsettling about a teacher referring to a child as a bad seed, wasn't there? It touched a nerve, a concept that Claudia could not allow herself to entertain. And—know all *what?* She found that happened a lot here; locals assumed a lot of knowledge on her part just because the property had been in her family for a long time. Anyway—stay focused, Claudia!

"But Josh?"

Wanda Crabb issued a cough, then another. It was an unsettling sound, deep and growling. Claudia noticed that she'd involuntarily put her hand to her own chest.

"Josh was an okay kid—as long as his brother wasn't around," she said finally, sounding raspy still. "Rhett was *that* kind of kid, the kind that could get otherwise good boys to do bad things. He knew how to exploit weakness."

"Oh," said Claudia.

She could hear the old woman breathing on the other line while she tried to think of what to say. Then: "Anyway, you said you were looking for a reference. That's my reference."

"Well," said Claudia. "Thank you so much."

She was about to go out on a limb and ask Wanda what it was that Claudia must know all

147

about it. But the other woman had already hung up. A hit and run; Claudia was exhausted. She'd always had an inability to protect herself against other people's negativity. She was fighting back the creep of anxiety and self-doubt when she saw him emerge from the trees, silent as a wraith as if he'd melted out from the color around him.

He was large, with a tawny coat, and long bushy tail, a regal, thoughtful face. She moved to the window, and he stood, watchful, looking at the house. She wasn't sure if he could see her, but she felt as if he could, as if he was looking right at her, wondering at her as she was at him. The first time she saw him, she'd thought he was a coyote. But a quick bit of research on the internet and she'd determined that he was a *coywolf,* a coyote-wolf hybrid. They were bigger than coyotes, less skittish of humans, with bigger heads, and longer, fuller tails. She'd given him a name, Scout, and she liked the sight of him, always felt a flush of excitement at his arrival, even though she didn't go out when he was around. There'd only been one human fatality involving a coywolf, a young girl killed in Canada by a coyote-wolf pack. Mainly, they were unseen by humans in their environments, which were increasingly urban. They were smart, adaptable, and good at hiding in plain sight.

Scout took a seat and lifted his nose toward the air. As Claudia watched him, a kind of calm came over her. She took and released a breath. She heard on the local news that a male coywolf had been killed a couple of towns over. Police claimed that his behavior was aggressive. Only afterward was it discovered that the coywolf was protecting the den where his pups and his mate were hiding. Coywolves mated for life; Claudia had spent an unreasonable amount of time worrying about the female and her pups. Would they be all right on their own? How did animals process loss? Would the mate just pull herself together and do what needed doing, leaving her cubs behind in the den as she went out to find food, returning later with her kill? Would she bay at the moon, mourning her lost love? Sometimes at night, you could hear them—yipping, talking, howling. It was a sad sound, lonely and distant.

Scout stood up abruptly, his reverie interrupted by something, then quickly turned and disappeared into the trees. Claudia always had a moment of disappointment when he went on his way. She turned to see that blue Toyota pulling up the drive, and she watched as Josh Beckham climbed out. For a second, she thought there was someone in the car with him, but he got out of the car alone. He stood a moment, looking at the barn door, shaking his head, running a hand through his unruly head of blond hair.

Wanda Crabb's words were still echoing, even though they had nothing to do with Josh really.

149

It was his brother that was the problem. So why couldn't Claudia shake it? That worried feeling. Trauma and its aftermath were tricky, even so many years later. Even though, emotionally, she had healed more or less, meaning she could function, love, trust, meet people, make friends, connect. Sometimes it was as if her body still remembered; she still jumped at shadows, was attuned to strange noises and even scents.

When he knocked, she hesitated a moment, then opened the door.

"So it came down after all," Josh said, stepping into the foyer. "I had a feeling."

He filled the room with the scent of sawdust and soap, something else—paint. It took her a second to remember what he was talking about.

"Oh, the door," she said. She glanced down at her watch. "They should be here soon, too. The guys from Just Old Doors."

She was happy they would all be here at the same time.

He nodded. "They're good guys," he said. "I'll talk to them and make sure they take care of you on the price."

"Thanks," she said. "Hopefully, some promotion on the blog will help, too."

"I liked your picture shelves," he said. "You did a good job—using the laser level and that digital stud finder and everything."

She laughed a little, pleased at his praise even

150

though she didn't want to be. She'd filmed her mistakes, as well as the final success, just so people could see that home repair and renovation wasn't as easy as they made it look on television. When you did it yourself, there was a learning curve. You made mistakes and tried again, hopefully finally getting it or maybe admitting defeat and calling a professional. She put it all up there. Luckily, when it came to home repair, there was almost always a fix—even if you had to bring in the drywall guy.

"I messed it up a couple of times before I got it right," she said.

"I like how you show your mistakes," he said. "That's how we learn."

Something about the way he said it had more weight than she thought he intended. He dug his hands deep into his pockets and glanced down at the floor, then around the foyer—up at the ceiling (water stain from leaky plumbing in the bathroom), at the wainscoting along the stairs (still big sections in need of refinishing), the banister (still loose).

"Want to walk through the house with me and talk about my punch list?" she said. "I thought we'd start with one project and see how it goes. Does that work?"

He gave her a nod. He had a nice smile, warm and open, that caused his eyes to squint a little. In his jeans and work boots, another long-sleeve

151

tee, this one fresh white, he had a disarming boyishness about him. As they walked through the house, talking about the endless number of projects, she forgot all about Wanda Crabb's negative energy and the unpleasant things she had to say about Josh's brother, who was—lucky for them all, she guessed—long gone.

ten

There's no one in there. It was just the dog.

I logged miles that night after sparring with Mike, walking from the dim desertion of residential Twenty-Seventh, up the constant melee of Broadway to Ninety-Sixth Street. Then I cut west and moved though the shadows of Riverside Park, heading north slowly, a watcher, gliding through the quiet streets. Often I roam, no destination in mind, until I am tired enough to think I might sleep.

After a while, fatigue finally tugging at me, I headed back downtown. As I moved from neighborhood to neighborhood—the eternal crush of Midtown, the sleepy West Village—my brain churned. I thought about what I knew, what I'd done, what I had yet to do. I thought about Paul and how angry he'd been with me. I thought about Seth's question and Mike's warning. I'd imagined I'd feel better after the plan was in play. But I didn't. No, there was something else now. A buzz, a white noise of anxiety.

What now? Paul had asked. *Have you thought about that?*

I actually hadn't thought about that, if I was honest. I didn't think there would be an "after."

The city is always alive with people, all

153

kinds—a circus of good and bad, wild and tame, freakish and square. Even at that hour, I wasn't alone. Paul always says that it's safer than it used to be. But it's still not safe. Nothing is. Not even the quiet, rural place where I grew up.

I loved that isolated farmhouse that my father rented for cheap from an old man who bought properties for investment. With its creaky floors, and fireplace, the big barn out back and acres of woods where I could get lost without ever being lost, it was a child's dream.

My dad loved it, too. We'd wander with our dog, Catcher, out in the woods, down to the river. It was a big luxury—all that land, all that space and sky—for a city boy like my dad, who had lived in an apartment most of his life. He hated the city, didn't even like to visit. Unlike Paul, who couldn't sleep without city noise, who could never imagine himself anywhere but the East Village. They were very different.

My parents and I felt like the place was ours, not a rental, because the old man who owned it never paid it any mind. If something went wrong—the toilet clogged, or the roof needed repairing—my dad would call Mr. Bishop, and the old man would either tell my dad to take care of it and deduct it from the rent, or if the repair required more money, time, or skill than my father possessed, Mr. Bishop would send someone to take care of it quickly. It was the rare relationship that worked without conflict. We probably would have stayed there forever.

By three in the morning, years and miles, eons away from the farmhouse, I was back at Nate Shelby's loft, loping into the opulent lobby under the suspicious eye of the night doorman, a thick guy with the scarred face of someone who once had terrible acne. There's something flat about his gaze, menacing about his gold-ringed hands. He would never pass muster for the day doorman, who needed at least a modicum of refinement.

"Where you staying again?" he asked as I tried to slink past him.

"I am house sitting for Mr. Shelby," I said. I didn't slow my pace toward the elevator.

"There's a package."

I paused, keeping my back to him.

"Where?"

"In the apartment," he said. "It came late. Mr. Shelby called, said to bring it inside."

"Okay," I said.

The conversation was going on too long. The elevator was slow, and he walked around the desk to keep talking. Which was weird.

"What's with the getup?" he asked. Finally, I had to turn to face him. It was too weird not to. "The hoodie, the backpack, the Chuck Taylors."

I looked down at myself. "It's not a getup. It's just what I wear."

"Just saying," he said. "You're a pretty girl. What are you hiding from?"

It wasn't wolfish or threatening. In fact, now that he was talking, there was a softness to him, an easy curiosity. A kind of twinkle. I didn't answer him, though. I am not much of a conversationalist.

"Good night," he said as I walked away, ducked into the waiting elevator. The doors closed. That made three times I'd been seen when I didn't want to be seen: caught on camera, green-eyed Erik asking me out for a drink, inappropriately curious doorman.

What was wrong with me? Why was I not invisible?

I knew the answer, though. It was getting to me. I was vibrating, giving off the energy of the thing I tried to hide and harness. I had given it a name. A thing that lived inside of me. The Red Hunter. Rage.

In the apartment's inner foyer there was a box, which I might have left where it was except there was a noise coming from it and Tiger was sniffing around it mewing loudly. There were wide holes in the side and on top; beside it was another box, filled with supplies. I flipped the lid with my toe, and sitting on a bed of newspaper was a white kitten with one blue eye and one green eye.

"Meow," he said, opening his tiny mouth wide. "Meow."

There was no hissing from either Tiger or this new addition, just some rubbing and a little purring. The white kitten climbed clumsily out of the box as I stood watching, trying to process this turn of events. There was a note on top of the supplies—toys, kitten food, litter, a tiny litter box, a bed, all from the expensive organic shop where I got Tiger's stuff.

Let's call him Milo.

Best,
Nate Shelby

Milo was cute, but the whole thing was an annoying distraction, one that I had created. This is what happened when you let yourself show; you attract things into your life. I had violated a personal policy and reached into Nate Shelby's world, causing a reaction in him. He had reached back into mine. The best thing to do would be to quit. To write him a note and say I got called away; he would need to find someone else.

But I didn't do that. Instead, I unpacked the supplies, filled Milo's litterbox, and put it next to Tiger's in the tiny laundry room. I put out Milo's food and some water across the kitchen from Tiger so there wouldn't be any issue about whose food was whose. Of course, there would be, but they would need to figure that out. Then

I watched the two of them tangle on the floor a little, finally settling on the windowsill together. I felt something I hadn't felt in a while. Was it pleasure?

If you open the door, life wanders in. It's harder to ask it to leave than never to invite it in the first place.

I almost went to bed. Fatigue weighted my limbs. I almost sank into the white bliss of Nate Shelby's bed. But the computer screen beckoned. I couldn't *unsee* what I had seen earlier. I needed to go back to it. I needed the information so that I could formulate the final stages of my plan. That's what I told myself.

It was surreal, dreamlike to see the house online, to see the hallway where our pictures used to hang, the room where I used to sleep. The corner where we used to put our Christmas tree. And the basement where every nightmare I ever had came true. As I scrolled through the photos, the videos she'd posted, I couldn't see anything as it was. I could only see it as it had been. Memory is like that; it colors the present like a patina.

Outside the tall windows of Nate Shelby's loft, the cats watching me from the sill, the city hummed—its ceaseless song of sirens and horns and voices and tires on asphalt. Inside, all I could hear was the thrumming of the engine in my chest, my deep breaths.

・・・

The night it happened, I snuck out to meet a boy. Seth Murphy and I had been dancing around each other for a couple of months, stealing glances in algebra, smiling at each other in gym class. Jenna asked his best friend if Seth liked me and the answer came back yes. Then, finally, he'd asked me to the movies. And my parents said yes— much to my surprise and delight. But then they went with us, smiling but watchful chaperones, sitting far behind us in the back row during the seven o'clock show of *Minority Report*.

Seth and I held hands in the dark as Tom Cruise tried to stop crimes before they occurred, and I could feel the heat of Seth's skin. When Seth leaned in to kiss me, his breath smelling of root beer and popcorn, my father cleared his throat loudly—unbelievably! humiliatingly!— from the back of the theater. Seth looked briefly embarrassed in the blue light from the screen, and then we both started laughing, earning annoyed shushing from the people around us.

The next Monday, Seth left a note taped on my locker.

Meet me at Old Bridge around 11? If you can. I'll wait. Just try.

My father was a cop, so sneaking out was no small feat. I knew that when he was home they

159

usually checked on me around ten, then went to sleep. So I waited, pretended to be sleeping until I heard my father come in. He placed a hand on my forehead, then left, turning out the light in the hall. I waited until it felt like the house was asleep. Then I crept downstairs. Catcher, our huge yellow Lab, was lying by the back door. He stared at me with sad eyes, his tail wagging hopefully.

I didn't have any choice. I had to take the big lug with me, otherwise I knew he'd start barking at the door after I left. So I did. I didn't lock the door behind me. It was cold, my breath coming out in clouds, my jacket too thin. The sky was clear and riven with stars, a bright high moon lighting the road in front of me. I remember feeling proud of myself, excited—I don't know if it was about Seth Murphy as much as it was just having a moment of freedom. My parents were strict, my dad especially. He wasn't so hard; I knew he loved me. He just thought the world was a bad place, filled with bad people, and he wanted to keep me safe as long as possible. Turned out that he was right.

But I didn't believe that then with my feet crunching on the gravel. I thought my dad was paranoid and my mother was too passive, always following his rules. Paul always said that the world was my oyster, that it wasn't small but big and full of possibilities. I was flushed with the excitement of meeting Seth Murphy alone in the night. With my dog.

I think they were already there waiting; they must have been. When I reconstruct that night, I try to remember. Could I have missed their vehicle, parked in the shadows waiting for hours of quiet before they went inside? I don't know. Did they see me leave? Did they wait for me to come back?

Seth Murphy didn't show. I waited an hour, then headed home, let down, disappointed—but weirdly relieved, too. What would come of meeting a boy at the bridge in the middle of the night? Catcher was his usual docile self, not perturbed in the least that we'd gone out together in the middle of the night.

When I moved out through the trees into the clearing where the farmhouse stood, I saw the light on in the kitchen and the bottom of my stomach dropped out. *Please let it be Mom,* I thought. Mom was easy, slow to anger. There was something between us, a shared desire to laugh things off that I didn't have with my father. I could tell my mother anything. I could tell her that I liked Seth and that I wanted to meet him but that he didn't show and I wouldn't have done anything with him anyway. I just wanted to know what it would be like to sneak out in the middle of the night and maybe, maybe kiss a boy. She would get it. We'd talk it through. She wouldn't hide it from my father, but she'd make it more palatable. If it was him, sitting there in the kitchen, waiting? There'd be yelling and tears, grounding. And that look, the stern frown of disapproval. That was the worst of all. I stood in the trees, trying to see inside from a distance. The gray of my father's tee-shirt or the pink of my mom's PJs. Someone walked quickly past the window. That's when Catcher started to growl, low and deep.

"What is it, boy?" I said. "Quiet."

I had to think of a lie. Catcher was sick? I took him for a walk? No one would ever believe that. I had to do a project about owls for school; I went out looking for some. Nope. My mother knew every single thing about my schoolwork. That wasn't going to fly. If there had been an owl project, she'd be out there with me.

We moved closer, Catcher growling, me holding on to the frayed red collar he'd worn as long as I could remember. The brush of his fur rubbed against my fingers, his dog smell strong and weirdly comforting as I crouched down low.

"Catch," I said. "I'm so dead. Stop growling."

How did he know there was something wrong all the way back there? How did he know? I stood up slowly and peered around the window frame. The scene was so odd, so strange that I almost couldn't understand what I was seeing at first.

Two men. One was smallish but muscled and

162

wiry, standing by the door, a gun nearly the size of his forearm gripped in his hand. One tall, broad through the shoulders, dressed in black. Both of them wearing black ski masks. Another man was sitting on a chair, arms tied, slumped, a bag pulled over his head. My father. He wore his Lost Valley Police Department tee-shirt. My mother was on the ground, her pink pajama top open to reveal her belly button—lying quiet and peaceful on her side, as if she were just sleeping. There was a third stranger, someone thin and small, a boyish body, also wearing a mask, at the kitchen table with his head in his hand. The taller man was standing in the doorway with a shotgun.

I drew in a ragged breath and swallowed a scream. Sinking onto my haunches, my mind raced. The next farmhouse was a little over a mile up the road. If I ran as fast as I could, I could make it in twelve minutes. My father kept a gun locker in the old barn. I wasn't supposed to know the code, but I did. The same code he used for everything, my mother's birthday. I knew how to fire every one—from the service revolver, to the Glock 9mm, to the Sig, to the shotgun. *Never pick up a gun unless you're prepared to kill someone with it. Hopefully, it won't come to that. But be ready if it does.* Our hunting trips hadn't gone well. I had bad aim and lacked the hunter's heart to take the life of a creature who never did anything but munch on leaves. But I knew the shotgun made up for bad aim and the men in my house were not deer or bunnies.

Catcher had gone quiet, issuing a low whine, feeling my fear, knowing instinctively to stay quiet. I put my arms around his neck.

Run for help or stay and fight? I asked him silently.

But when a shot rang out from inside, Catcher pulled away and ran to the door, his explosive barking filling the night. The pounding of footsteps, the screen door slammed open. I was already running toward the barn, fast as I could. A hole opened in the world that minute, a dark doorway though which I passed into a place where nothing would ever be what it was before.

There was a screaming child in my head, one in terror, afraid for herself and shattered by what she'd seen in the window. But there was also someone else, someone I've since come to know as "the watcher." The one who calmly observes the chaos around her, the one who can see exactly how far is the barn, can hear how close is the stranger behind her, the one who knows that there is no running for help now, only getting to the gun locker and arming herself before the man behind her catches her.

Catcher's barks were vicious and undercut by a feral growling behind me until there was a hard thud and primal yelp of pain, then silence. Then heavy footfalls again. I stopped at the

barn door—don't look, don't look, don't look—
and had to use all my strength to open it. Then
I pulled it closed hard and latched it, just as
someone thumped against it.

"Open the door," said the voice on the other
side. "I'm not going to hurt you."

I ran to the locker and to my great dismay found
both the doors standing open. The shotgun was
gone; yes, it was the one I'd seen in the stranger's
hand. The revolver. The semiautomatic. The
rifle. All gone. The only thing left was a serrated
hunting knife. The black oxide grip was molded
to my father's hand, a gift from Uncle Paul on my
father's fortieth birthday. I took and shoved it into
the inside pocket of my jacket. It was too big.

"There are no guns in there."

He was at the window, his voice muffled
through the glass. I dove to the side so that he
couldn't see me. Every nerve ending in my body
sizzled with terror.

"You're trapped in there now," he said. It was a
young voice. "If you know what's good for you,
you'll stay there."

"Who's out there?" Another voice, older, harder.

"No one," said the boy. He was just a boy.
"There's no one there, just the dog."

"Bullshit," said the other. "It's the kid, right?"

"No," he said. "Just the dog. He ran off into the
woods. I kicked him hard; he won't come back."

The window shattered then, an exploding

shower of slicing rain around me as I bowed my head into my arms. An impossibly hard grip on my hair yanked me from above, shards of glass digging into the back of my neck, my face. The razor edges sliced through my jacket as he dragged me with superhuman strength over that sill. I'm sure I was screaming, but I don't remember really. I clawed at his arms, but he didn't release me until I was lying on the ground at his feet. I turned on my side away from the mask that was his face and the terrified eyes of the boy, only to see Catcher lying before the trees where we'd just emerged. And the stars. And the clear, clear night white with moonlight.

He pulled me to my feet.

"She's cut," said the boy. "She's bleeding."

"Shut up," said the older man. And he started dragging me toward the house. That's when I heard my mother screaming my name; it hurt worse than the glass embedded in my skin, the pitch of her terror connecting to every nerve ending in my body.

I didn't want to think about it anymore. I slammed my fist down on the desk, startling the cats, who shot away silent, dark shadows. I went out of the apartment and took the stairway up to the roof—using my center and my breath, the pumping of my arms to carry me up.

I was breathing hard but not breathless as

I emerged onto the roof deck, downtown Manhattan splayed around me. I wanted to let out a scream into the sky; one scream among millions in this city. Instead, I swallowed the energy. Never grunt, blow breath, make a noise of effort—it's a shameful waste of power. Keep it all inside, a red-hot ball of flame in your center, your chi, your life force. Let it burn hot, let it fill you. The Red Hunter.

I climbed up to the ledge and stood looking at the vertiginous drop below me. Then I sat, cross-legged, on the thin edge—the concrete cutting at my ankles, digging into my bottom. There was nothing beneath me to keep me from falling all the way to the street below, a fall that would likely break every bone in my body, leaving me to bleed out on the sidewalk.

With my breath, I moved into the discomfort and then through it. With my breath, the sound beneath all other sounds, the cool at my nostrils, the rise and fall of my chest, my belly. The Red Hunter bowed and retreated. Pain, anger, fear, sadness, they receded clinging only for a few moments. They have no home in the present moment. Here there is only room for the breath. *I am breathing in. I am breathing out.* I took the seat of the watcher, the one who is quiet in the chaos.

eleven

Careless gold curls and wire-rimmed specs sat on the long bridge of his nose, in relief against sienna skin and blue eyes. Grace and Sophia were always going on and on about how *hot* Troy was, but Raven didn't see it. Not that she didn't *see* it. It's just that it didn't matter. Troy was Troy.

That's what had first drawn Raven to him, she thought, even though they were just little kids, even though he was crying a little because he missed his mom. He always seemed to know who he was. He was small, but no one picked on him. He was kooky, but everyone thought he was funny. Once he punched a bigger, older kid named Max right in the face because—why?—Raven couldn't even remember. Troy had been suspended. And when he came back he was a hero, and no one ever messed with him again.

"Do you want to marry me?" he asked her in kindergarten.

"Okay," she said, even though she was pretty sure you couldn't get married in kindergarten, and her father had told her to stay far away from boys as a general rule.

Troy took her hand then, and they'd been holding hands ever since. They *were* married in a totally nonsexual, pure-love kind of way, the way you can only love your childhood friends. Troy was Troy.

He lounged on the couch in her father's living room. The doorman, Carey, had known Raven all her life. He probably knew she shouldn't be there when Dad was away, but he was too cool to ask her any questions when she walked in earlier. He gave her a kind of look, though, a knowing sideways glance. He sent Troy up an hour later without even calling to say he was coming. Would he call her dad? Mom? Raven didn't think so.

"I guess what I'm thinking," said Troy, simultaneously tapping on his phone. "Is that this is a bad idea. I mean—I'm in. I'm with you. You know that. I just think you might be making a mistake."

His red sneakers dangled over the arm of the couch. Was he *that* tall?

"How can it be a mistake to try to find out who you are?" Raven asked.

He regarded her with that cool gaze he'd perfected. She sat on the chair opposite him, *her* legs over the arm of the chair and a half.

"Where you came from doesn't define you," he said. "You are who you are right now. And, he *unfollowed* you. To me that means he's not going to be happy to see you."

Troy was a good kid, a mama's boy, a straight-A student. He looked alternative, but he was a button-down geek at heart.

"*So what* if he's your half brother," Troy went on. "He's a stranger. You share biology and nothing more. I'm more your brother than he is."

He looked different somehow, his face fuller; maybe it was just that they didn't see each other every day like they used to—in person anyway. They FaceTimed almost daily, did their homework together. He had a little bit of stubble at his jaw. And his voice kept doing this weird thing, like he had a cold. It would get deeper, then higher. He kept coughing when it happened, looking at her weirdly.

She turned out her phone to show him a picture of Andrew Cutter, he was on stage—black jeans, red tee-shirt, combat boots. He stared down at the electric guitar in his arms.

He reached out and took the phone, stared, then looked back at her. "He does look like you—a little."

"A lot," she said.

He shook his head. "It's hard to tell from a picture. Lots of people have black hair and dark eyes."

"Lots of people have brown hair," she said, lifting a strand of her own. "Not black, not like this."

"If he doesn't want anything to do with his father, what makes you think he's going to want anything to do with you—even if you are, by some distant chance, his sister? *Half* sister."

"It's not a distant chance," she said. "It's like a fifty-fifty chance."

Troy sighed, tossed back her phone.

"Like I said." He sat up and leaned forward, arms on his knees. "I'm with you. I'm just—worried about you, Birdie. I don't want anyone to hurt you."

She moved over to the couch and sat next to him. He dropped an arm around her, and she let her head sink to his shoulder. They sat like that awhile, the afternoon sun washing in through the big west-facing windows.

"I'm already hurting," she said. "This is about trying to stop."

She wondered if that was true. If that's what this was really about—lying to her parents, Twitter stalking @angryyoungman, going to the club where his band was playing to try to talk to him.

Troy shifted to take out his wallet—a beat-up old pleather thing with the stamp of a shamrock. He slid two cards from one of the slots and held them up before her. She drew in a breath.

"You did it," she said. She was shocked. Maybe he wasn't such a goody two-shoes after all. She really didn't think he'd pull it off, even after they stopped in that copy shop and had their pictures taken, supposedly for passports.

"My cousin did it."

Oh, right, his mysterious cousin with supposed

ties to the Latin Kings, the Hispanic gang that ruled Riverside and East Harlem. She took the fake non-driver's ID from Troy, held it out. It looked real—like really real. It even had a glittery rainbow seal underneath the laminate. Raven Bishop-Martin, twenty-two years old. She could pass for twenty-two, couldn't she? She stood up and looked in the mirror over the couch. Hmm . . . maybe not. Her breasts were barely there. Without a padded bra, she was almost completely flat. With enough makeup, though? The right outfit? Maybe.

He took it back from her and shoved it in his wallet along with his.

"You promised only with me," he said. "And only this once. So I can keep it, right?"

"Yeah," she said. "You can keep it."

He got like that sometimes, all big brother, protector. Sometimes it was nice. Sometimes it was annoying. He was only older than her by eighteen days.

He flopped back down on the couch and started tapping with his thumbs again, texting, tweeting, Instagramming pictures of himself, whatever. Whenever she logged on to anything, it was a wall of Troy, pictures of himself, what he was eating, thinking, feeling, where he was, what he was doing.

How can you miss your friends? her mother asked. *Their entire consciousness is on display online*. Like Claudia should talk. If anyone was oversharing, it was Raven's mother. She was the poster child for TMI.

But there was more to people than that, though, wasn't there? What they posted about? The online Troy was not the guy on her couch, the one who held her hand in kindergarten. Her mom was not just a rape victim, a home repair blogger.

She walked over to the window, and the sun was already dipping low. She hated this time of day before the afternoon had fully ended and night was yet to begin. There was something about the transition between light and dark that made her sad. She wanted to call her mother and confess—where she was, what she was planning. Troy certainly wouldn't stop her.

But she didn't. There was a tug, something pulling her down the path she was on. It was too strong to resist. She went into her room to get changed.

twelve

Afternoon seemed to leak into early evening as Josh walked through the house following Claudia. He watched her, the way she threw her arms around when she talked, listened to the bright bell chime of her laugh. He examined the house. The way the stairs had creaked beneath his weight, how the old wood dipped. He observed the water stains on the ceiling. The banister was dangerously loose, and the wainscoting looked at is if termites might be getting at it. There were lots of problems he knew, many of them worse than she thought.

The basement was the worst of it, with those beams that had fallen. They'd need to be shored up before it was even safe. The last time he'd been down there, he'd heard a suspicious creaking. And it had been impossible to clear away the debris on his own.

But the bones were there. A good old house, solid in its foundation. Not like the crap that went up now, houses that felt like Styrofoam boxes, cheap and flimsy.

It's in there. I know it is.

It's not. I've been through every room, every closet, the attic, the cellar. It's not there. It never was.

174

It's in there.

Josh knew that house. Over the years, he'd come to know it intimately, his hands had been all over her, probing into all her private places. She had never given him what he was looking for. Rhett was convinced now that he'd have reason to really tear the place up, they'd find what was hidden. He was wrong. This house wasn't keeping any secrets.

From the kitchen window, Josh had watched Rhett slip from the backseat of the car and duck into the barn. Was he still in there? Or was he back in the car? Claudia had said the boys from Just Old Doors were coming out. Rhett better get his ass out of that barn before they did.

"What do you think?" asked Claudia, her back to the outside. "Do you think it's too much work for you? Do you think it's too much work, period?"

"No," he said. "It'll take time. I'll have to bring in some folks to help with plumbing and electricity. The basement is going to be a big project. But I think I can manage most things."

She turned to look at him, her smile cautious. She had a way of glancing at him with her face turned, peering over her glasses. She was pretty, like his mom had been. Lovely with creamy, soft skin. Even the tiny wrinkles at the edges of her eyes were pretty. She smelled like peppermint.

"So what's your rate?"

Rhett was already giving him a hard time about the business. Josh still charged close to what his father used to charge. Rhett wanted Josh to gouge her: "She's a rich city girl. In Manhattan she'd pay four times what you're charging. More."

"I charge $350 a day, for all work," he said. That's what he'd always charged folks. It was fair. "Plus materials. Other service professionals I bring in will have their own fee in addition to mine."

She nodded, bit the bottom of her lip. "That sounds fair. Are you insured?"

"Yes," he lied. "Bonded and insured."

Insurance cost a fortune, and he couldn't afford it. *Maybe if you charged more than Dad was charging in the eighties you'd be able to afford to do things right.* It was just like Rhett to be gone for five years, in prison no less, and then show up like he owned the place and knew everything.

He watched Rhett come out of the barn empty-handed and get back into the car, lying down in the backseat. Claudia caught Josh looking outside and turned to see what he was looking at—a split second after the car door closed. She turned back to look at him.

"The cop who came out said it looked as if it had been pried off," she said.

She thought he had been looking at the fallen door. She'd wrapped her arms around her middle

176

and was toeing a peeling corner of linoleum tile. Her dainty foot was bare.

He laughed a little. "I doubt it," he said. "That thing was ready to fall. And there's nothing in there, is there?"

"Just some rusted old tools."

The dark creep of suspicion distracted him from the prettiness of her manicured toes. Had he told Rhett about the barn door? Had his brother come out here last night? There was nothing Rhett wasn't willing to do to get what he wanted.

She ran a hand through her cloud of blonde curls. "Can I get you some coffee? I just made it."

"Sure," he said. "That would be great. Thanks."

She had light, quick movements. He tried not to stare at her full bottom, or how he could just see the lace of her bra peeking out from the tank top she wore under a blue-and-white checked shirt. She moved off to get the coffee, and he stared at the barn.

That night, so long ago, the car had been over-warm and Josh knew, he *knew* he shouldn't be there. He had been sound asleep in his own bed when his brother snuck into his room and shook him awake. There was no way not to go with him. You just didn't say *no* to Rhett.

You kind of didn't *want* to say no; that was the first thing. There was something about his older brother that made Josh want to please, want

177

to feel the glow of his approval. And you were afraid of what he'd do to you if he didn't get what he wanted. Nipple twists and friction burns, choke holds and arm bending, small but painful acts of coercion. Then taunts. *Aw, you little pussy, stop crying.*

"Where are we going?" Josh asked.

"Are we babysitters?" said a man Josh had never met. In addition to Rhett and Josh, there were two more men in the car, one driving, the other to Josh's left. The man beside him never said a word. Both men wore ski masks; Rhett, riding shotgun, held one in his hand, and had handed one to Josh. It was scratchy beneath his fingers. "Why'd you bring the kid?"

"We need a third man inside," said Rhett. "Anyway, he's not a kid. He's just skinny. He's nearly twenty."

That was a lie.

Maybe I'm dreaming, Josh kept thinking.

The smell of cigarette smoke radiated off the man beside Josh, acrid and foul. He was big, taking up a lot of space, and spreading his legs wide. Their thighs were close together; Josh thought that his looked likc a baseball bat next to a fallen log. The stranger stared out the window, chewing vigorously on the corner of his thumbnail. Rhett, up front, pumped his leg the way he did when he was nervous or angry.

"What are we doing?" Josh said again.

"Shut up," Rhett hissed.

The waxing gibbous moon had dipped behind the clouds, no streetlamps lit the rural road. So outside it was just black. They turned off onto an unpaved drive, a wall of trees on either side. The driver turned off the headlights, and they drifted in what seemed to Josh to be total darkness. Finally a house, lit only by a light at the porch, came into view. They stopped a good distance, killing the engine, and sat silent.

"Where are we?"

Rhett reached back to knock him on the head, and Josh decided not to ask any more questions, rubbing at the spot. How long were they going to sit there? No one said anything.

Josh was pretty sure that he was the only one who saw her, a thin girl and her dog cutting across the side yard and disappearing into the trees.

What was she doing? Where was she going? He looked up at Rhett, but his brother was just staring off at nothing, his face twisted in a scowl.

He didn't say a word, the pain on the side of his head still smarting. After a time—how long?—the man in the driver's seat said, "Let's go."

"So," Claudia said now, handing him a cup. "When can you start?"

"How's Monday?"

She offered a slow bob of her head, her

expression uncertain. He looked around at the mess she'd made of the wallpaper.

"Leave that," he said, pointing. "I'll take care of it."

She released a breath, relief or defeat, he couldn't say. Maybe both.

"Okay," she said. "Monday."

On his way back to the car, Josh leaned in close to inspect the hinges of the barn door. It *did* look as though someone had used a crowbar. He ran his fingers over the ridges and looked inside the large dim space. The gun locker he remembered was gone. The window had been covered with thick plastic and sealed with duct tape. There was a rusting old lawn mower, some boxes, a rickety bike. He stepped inside. That night was still with him. He still dreamed about it sometimes.

When Josh climbed back in the car, Rhett was on his back, arms folded across his chest as though he were lying in a coffin. He often slept in that position, too. Josh sat a second, staring at the barn door.

"Find anything?" asked Josh. He already knew the answer.

"Not shit."

"I told you," said Josh, backing up the drive and swinging the vehicle around. "I've been through this place a hundred times. Other people sneak out here, too, you know. Someone would have found something."

180

"It's in there," said Rhett. He had the stubbornness of the unintelligent. If he thought the world was flat, he'd kill you before he'd let you convince him otherwise.

"It was *never* there," said Josh. "He set you up. Someone wanted that cop dead. They *used* us."

He'd had a lot of time to think about it, turn over and over what they'd done, why, how it had turned out. Josh watched in the rearview mirror as Rhett shook his head, thinking.

"In fact, maybe it never existed in the first place," said Josh. "Ever think of that?"

"Shut up," said Rhett. "You have no idea what you're talking about."

Rhett never gave up on the idea of that money. It was his holy grail, the thing that was going to make every wrong thing right. Even from lockup, he'd call collect with ideas.

Maybe it was inside the walls; look for a seam in the drywall.

What about the attic?

For a long time, the Bishop house was empty. So Josh could just go over there and look around. Over the years, he'd inspected every square inch, never once thinking he'd find it. He knew *that night* that the money wasn't there. He could hear it in the cop's voice. The cop would have given it up to save his family. *You're making a mistake,* he'd said, desperation making his voice quaver. *What you're looking for? It's not here. Let my family go.*

"I've been all through that house, all over the property, in that barn."

"Yeah," said Rhett. "But you're a fucking moron. And you're lazy. You give up. Remember when we were kids, we'd play hide and seek? You'd just wind up crying or telling Mom that you couldn't find me. You could *never* find me."

God, thought Josh. *He is such an idiot.* It was true, though; he never could find Rhett when they played hide and seek. But maybe it was really because he didn't *want* to find Rhett. He'd usually just wind up using the time to get to the Nintendo and play by himself for a while.

"I'll believe it's not there when *I've* gone through that house," said Rhett.

Josh didn't say anything.

"While you're in there working," Rhett went on. "I'll be in there looking. This is a perfect opportunity. It's like the universe wants us to find that money."

Josh felt that familiar tingle of unease he always had around his brother. He was a bully; he'd get what he wanted, no matter what he had to do to you to get it.

"She thinks I work alone." Josh didn't want Rhett around Claudia, or her daughter. Josh didn't know them, but he knew what his brother would see when he looked at them.

"Tell her there's too much work," said Rhett.

"You need another man. And jack up the price. Three-fifty a day? That's bullshit."

"With a lunch break, that's fifty dollars an hour. That's fair."

Rhett blew out a breath of disdain. "Tell her five hundred a day with a second man and the work will get done faster. Tell her she'll actually be saving money. You got to learn how to work people, little brother."

Josh wasn't going to do any such thing. But he nodded. How was he going to get out of this? He could already feel the poison of Rhett leaking into the air of his life.

"Didion is dead," said Josh. "Do you know that?"

Josh pulled onto the main road, hung a right toward town. The weight of his words was heavy in the air, expanding. "Someone broke into his apartment and killed him."

"How do *you* know that?" Rhett asked. He sat up and climbed awkwardly into the front seat, knocking Josh in the head, causing him to swerve a little. Christ.

"The old man called," said Josh.

"Called *you?*"

Josh didn't say anything.

"When were you going to tell me this?" Rhett asked.

"I'm telling you now."

"When did he call?"

"The night you came home," Josh said. He didn't want to turn and look at Rhett, those staring eyes turned Josh into a puddle, made him feel like he was a little kid. "He called you, too, right? That's why you're here. It's not a coincidence."

"No one knows it was us that night," said Rhett, apropos of nothing, like he was having a whole different conversation in his head. There was a ragged edge to his voice. "We got away with it."

"Did we?" asked Josh. "We killed a cop and his wife. Left the girl for dead, except she wasn't dead. All for a pile of cash that wasn't there. You went to prison for something else. I'm still here working in Dad's shop. You're still looking for money that never existed. What did we get away with, exactly?"

"The money's there," said Rhett, not listening. "We just have to find it. We have to get into that house and tear it apart. When we find it, everything we've been through will be worth it."

A flutter of fear laced with anger moved up Josh's throat from his belly.

"Didion was killed with a hunting knife," said Josh.

"So?" asked Rhett, his expression blank.

Did he not remember that night? What they did to the woman and the girl? Did it mean so little to him, did he not hear their screams at night, like Josh sometimes did?

184

"So—I think we have a bigger problem than money that may never have existed."

Still nothing. "What's that?"

Josh pulled the car over onto the shoulder and turned to look at his brother. Rhett had a raggedness to him, now that Josh was really looking at him—time behind bars, booze and drugs and cigarettes and bad food taking their toll in his pasty complexion, the deep wrinkles around his eyes. There was a strange glistening to his stare, something like desperation residing in the corners.

"We didn't get away with *anything*," said Josh. He'd have to spell it out. "Someone *knows*."

Josh expected to see the dawning of fear, a realization that if in fact the universe wanted something for them, it wasn't a big payday. Josh's father was right. You don't get away with a thing like that. It hunts you down, one way or another.

Instead, a kind of steely resolve hardened his brother's face.

"Well, then, we don't have any time to lose, do we?" he said.

thirteen

Lately, I have been thinking about how I want to die. I don't want to slip away, a ghostlike figure disappearing into the mist between trees. I don't want normal, the things that other people seem to want. I don't want to fall in love with someone, get married, have children. I don't want to watch them grow, go away to college, get married, too. I don't want to then watch my grandchildren grow, then maybe watch my husband die, until something starts to gnaw at my insides, slowly taking me away bit by bit. I don't want to die like Paul will die, fighting for every last breath, every day an agony of the disconnect between his agile mind and his failing body.

I want to fall from a great height after leaping from buildings, watching, breathing all the way down until the concrete rises up to greet me, smashing my bones. Or having rushed into a burning building to save a crying baby, I want to go up in flames. Or gct torn apart by bullets in a gunfight. I want it to be big, loud. I want to leave a mess when I depart this world, leave a stain that can't be washed away.

That's what I was thinking about when my phone buzzed on the bedside table, announcing

186

a text. I grabbed it quickly, worried that it was Paul, needing me—not that he was one to text. Instead, it was Nate Shelby.

How's the new kitten?
You're a man of action.
Always.
Tiger and Milo are fast friends.
Good call.

I waited, watching the gray buttons pulse, sensing there was more to come.
Then:

So what's your story?

What's my story? How should I respond to that? I wondered. I shouldn't. I should just let the text slip into the oblivion of the unanswered. Maybe he'd get the hint that I didn't exist. Instead, I found my thumbs moving.

No story. I'm just the cat sitter.
Somehow, I'm not buying it.

I didn't write anything back, and neither did he. I stared at the canvas that hung on the wall across his bed, an angry swirl of red and black, bold strokes thick on the canvas. What's *your* story, Nate Shelby?

• • •

After a couple hours of my particular brand of unsleep, I rose and dressed, headed to Paul's. The morning air was cool, the sun a yellow ball, as I made my way up Broadway toward the East Village. It was just after seven, and the streets and coffee shops were already packed, traffic already heavy on Broadway. But once I turned at Eighth and crossed Third, it grew quieter. The East Village sleeps in, always, like Truman Capote said, has the aura of desertion.

Inside the foyer with the eternal black-and-white tile floor of all old New York buildings, I retrieved Paul's mail. Then I hoofed it up the stairs, hearing blow dryers and television shows, someone laughing—sounds wisping through doors like smoke. At the doorstep, I paused and looked down at his copy of the *Daily News*. He should have retrieved it by now. My heart gave a little pump as I pushed inside. I expected to find him in the kitchen. He's an early riser and always gets up and gets dressed, retrieves the paper, and makes himself a cup of coffee. Always. But the kitchen is empty, the apartment quiet.

"Paul," I say, walking down the hallway toward his room.

The nurse, Betsy, would have left last night at ten. They would have called if something were wrong then, if he'd seemed off or needed a treatment.

"Paul."

I paused with my hand on the doorknob and knocked. When there was no answer, I pushed inside. He was on the floor, halfway between the door and the bed, still in the sweatpants and tee-shirt that pass for pajamas. I dropped to my knees and leaned in close to hear the rasping of his breath. He reached for mc and gripped my wrist.

"Zoey," he said.

"Don't talk," I said, grabbing the phone in my pocket and dialing 911. When the dispatcher picked up, I asked for an ambulance, gave Paul's address.

"Please," he said. "Be careful."

His eyes stared into the middle distance, and his breath was coming in painful rasps.

"It's okay," I said. "They're coming."

I called the super, Mr. Rodriquez, and told him to wait for the EMTs to arrive and let them in downstairs. I knew I'd left the apartment door ajar. I grabbed a blanket from Paul's bed and covered him. I lifted his head onto my thigh and held his hand, listening to his breathing, rocking, tears streaming down my face.

"Don't leave me," I whispered. "Don't leave me here."

The milky light washed in from the window beside his bed, the minutes pulling and yawning, his breathing, his hand in mine, time standing still until I heard the clamor of feet on the stairs in the hallway.

The past mingles with the present, another day, another moment watching people I love suffer.

Where is it?

I don't know what you're talking about.

The money you took. A million. We know you took it.

No. You've got bad information, man. Look at where I live. You think I have a million dollars?

When they lifted the bag from his face, and my father saw me, all the color drained from his cheeks. He struggled against the bindings that kept him lashed to the chair, knocking the chair against the floor. My mother was motionless on the ground, but she was staring, her eyes blinking furiously.

You've got this wrong. I swear to God. I swear there's nothing. You think I would let you hurt my family for money. The last word was a roar.

That's when the stranger cut me the first time, drawing the blade along the side of my face, just under my jawline. It left a scar you can't see but from a certain angle. My fingers find it often. I'm sure I screamed, but I don't remember anything except the warm sluicing of blood down my neck.

How much is your daughter worth to you?

• • •

Crashing, banging outside Paul's door right now.

"Where are his meds?" The EMT. He had dark skin and a bald head, earnest, alert eyes, looking at me. His crisp white shirt strained against the big muscles in his arms and across his chest. The name on his tag read: Carter. "Miss, did you hear? His meds?"

"Yes."

I listed them off.

"Emphysema?"

"That's right."

"Where's his tank?"

I looked around. Where was it? Why didn't I look for it right away and put his mask on? But it wasn't there. Not by or under the bed.

"I don't know," I said. "It's always right here."

They lifted him off of me and onto the stretcher. "I'll get the medications," I said moving over to the bedside table.

"Bring everything with you. Are you coming in the bus?"

"The bus."

"The ambulance?"

"Yes."

Paul was grabbing for me, panicked. He was trying to say something. But they had already put an oxygen mask on him.

"It's better not to talk right now, sir," said the other EMT. "Just try to relax." Carter. Bedroom eyes and a full, pouty mouth, a nice lilt to his voice, an accent I couldn't place.

Paul reached for the oxygen mask and pulled it off.

"Zoey," he said. "They're coming for it."

"Who?" I asked. He was staring at me, lucid, aware. He wasn't just rambling. "For what?"

But then Carter was pushing the mask back on and wheeling him away. I chased after, clutching all his pills to my chest. On the way out, I saw the oxygen tank in the kitchen, the cannula hanging over the chair in which he usually sat. Why had he walked away from it?

By late afternoon, Dr. Burns had come and they'd run a bunch of tests. Paul was settled in a semiprivate room at NYU Medical Center, the hospital with which his doctor is affiliated. The room was dim, and he was a cyborg, hooked to a web of tubes and monitors, an oxygen mask over his face. I sat in a vinyl chair and watched the rise and fall of his chest. I'd had to call in sick for my shift, and my boss didn't sound happy. More attention drawn. I'd have to quit.

"Paul," I whispered, leaning in close. "What did you mean?"

I can't stop thinking about what he said. But he's out.

My father stood in the corner of the room, looking rakish and thin.

"We both started smoking in the sixth grade," he said. "Stupid."

I didn't answer him.

"I could say we didn't know," he went on. "But we *did* know. Everyone knows that smoking will kill you. We just didn't care, or really believe it. Your mom used to get so mad when she caught me smoking behind the barn."

He was not really there, and I knew this. My shrink and I have discussed it at length. He thinks it's a way I have of parenting myself, something related to the trauma of losing them so violently. Part of my mind can't accept their passing, so it confabulates for me. Crazy, sure. But harmless, according to my doctor, as long as I don't start believing he's really there.

"What do the doctors say?" my not-dad asked.

"His lung function has dropped below fifty percent," I whispered, looking around to see if anyone could hear me. I wanted him to be there. I wanted not to be alone.

"How much time?"

"They don't know." My throat is tight, and I feel like there is a weight on my chest. But I won't cry again.

"What happened?" My dad moved over to the bed, looked down at Paul.

"It looks like he walked away from his oxygen tank and couldn't make it back."

"Why would he do that?"

193

I'd been giving this some thought. He must have walked to the kitchen with the tank to make coffee, but then something caused him to walk back to the bedroom without it.

"Maybe the phone rang," said my dad.

There's only one extension in the apartment and it's by his bed where he is most of the time. I can't imagine him rushing for a phone call, though, since it's usually just telemarketers. But the more I think about it, the more sense it makes.

"Whatever that phone call was—it must have upset him," said my father.

I looked up toward him, but he'd gone.

Later, when the doctor assured me that Paul would rest comfortably for the rest of the night, I left and went back to Paul's apartment.

The building was quiet, my footfalls loud on the stairs. At the landing, I saw right away that the door was ajar. I probably left it open, but I would have thought Mr. Rodriquez would have come up to close it behind us. He's like that, careful, always looking out for his tenants.

I stood and listened—maybe Mr. Rodriquez was inside or maybe the nurse came. But I didn't hear anything, and finally I pushed the door. It drifted inward with a low squeak. The long hallway was clear, so I stepped in, closing the door behind me.

The kitchen was as we left it, the oxygen tank still near the chair where Paul might normally sit and have his coffee and toast. The coffee beans were out, the grinder lid open. Yes, that was it. He came to make the coffee, then went back to the room to answer the phone. I took a paring knife from the block by the window and slipped it into my pocket, then moved out of the kitchen and down the hall.

It took a second to register that the living room had been tossed—cushions thrown off the couch, books knocked from the shelves in piles on the floor. The area rug has been pulled up; the television knocked over. Adrenaline started to pulse, my heart thumping. I took three deep breaths to push back the throb of fear, of anger.

Who was here? What were they looking for? Some junkie taking the opportunity of an open door to look for money? Kids from the building disrespecting a sick old man who never did anything but help people all his life? They wouldn't find anything. Paul had saved some money, enough to be comfortable, but he owned next to nothing. An antimaterialist in a hyper-materialistic world. Even the television was ancient. He still used a VCR, rewatching old tapes from twenty years ago.

They're coming for it, Zoey. Be careful.

Or something more? Something else? Was there someone still here?

The bedroom door was open and the air-conditioning unit, left on from this morning, hummed. I stood to the side and waited, listening. Nothing. Finally, I moved inside. The space was empty but trashed like the living room—covers torn from the bed, drawers spilled open, closet ransacked. Boxes pulled from the shelves and contents spilled on the floor—reams of papers, folders, videotapes, old case files.

"They were looking for something."

My dad sat in the chair over by the window.

"What?" I asked. "What could they be looking for? He doesn't have anything."

My dad lifted his eyebrows and cocked his head.

I picked my way through the mess and reached for the phone beside Paul's bed. I dialed his voicemail and listened, deleting as I scrolled through the slew of spam from telemarketers, campaign ads, messages from banks, credit cards, his insurance company. Finally, I get to a message left last night.

It took me a long time to figure it out, old man. But I finally did. Time for you to give it up.

Cold moved through my body. I was having trouble connecting the dots, my mind reeling. I hung up and clicked through the caller ID until I found an unfamiliar number with an exchange I knew. I struggled for breath, all my training, all my calm leaving me. I called it back, but it went

196

straight to a generic voicemail, a robot voice repeating the number back. I hung up. Suddenly I was fourteen again. Helpless. Afraid.

That's when I heard it, the sound of movement toward the front of the apartment.

I took the knife from my pocket and moved soundlessly into the hall.

A creak of weight on the wood floor, the sound of someone moving slowly, quietly. I pressed myself against the wall. Other than the front door, there was no other exit from the apartment except the windows that led to the fire escape. The window in Paul's room was blocked by the air conditioner—an acknowledged hazard that we never got around to dealing with.

I would have no choice but to fight my way out. I could wait for whoever it is to turn the corner, but instead I decided to rush forward and use surprise to my advantage. I took a deep breath and sprinted.

I saw him in flashes—dark hair, tall, and broad shouldered—as I tackled him and took him to the ground hard. A surprised shout, a whoosh of air as the wind left him when my shoulder connected hard with his abdomen. And then I was on him, straddling his center, the paring knife to his throat. It happened quickly, fluidly.

"No, please." Panic. Fear. "Miss Zoey."

That's when I saw, with alarm, that it was Mr. Rodriquez, the super.

He was looking at me with pure terror in his eyes, gasping hard for air as I sat heavy on his lungs. I slumped with relief, blowing out a breath, removing the knife from his throat.

"I'm sorry," I said, struggling for air myself.

"Dios," he gasped. I climbed off of him, offering my hand. I helped him get to his feet. "Miss Zoey."

He doubled over, coughing. I hurried to the kitchen to get him some water.

"Someone broke into the apartment," I said, handing him the glass. He leaned heavily against the wall. "I thought you were an intruder."

"I saw you come up," he said. He takes a few sips but keeps coughing. "The door—was—open."

He was looking at me as if he'd never seen me before, which I get. I am half his size and I just knocked him to the ground and held a knife to his throat. Formerly, he saw me as a little girl, someone he watched grow. I guess he won't be seeing me that way again. I am all grown up.

"I came to give you this," he said.

He held out an envelope, my name written across in Paul's scrawling handwriting. "He brought it to me a couple of weeks ago."

I took it and stared, hefting it in my hand. It is small but heavyish, something, not paper, inside. I opened it and found an oddly shaped key, nothing else. No note or any indication to what the key might open. I held it in the palm of my hand.

"Did he say anything else?" I asked.

"Just that it was important," he said, looking at the tarnished key. "You don't know what it is?"

"No idea," I said. I looked in the envelope again, but there was nothing else. I put the key back inside and stuffed it in my pocket. It's not like Paul to be cryptic. I thought of his panicked eyes, his warning, this trashed apartment. I bit back a pulse of fear.

"Is he okay?" Mr. Rodriquez asked, still staring at me wide-eyed. He edged toward the door, away from me, maybe wondering if I'm going to attack him again.

"He's alive," I said. "But he's— not doing well."

He ran a hand through his graying hair, He nodded solemnly. His wife, Elmira, used to cook for us sometimes when Paul was working late and she knew I would be home alone. She'd bring pork, or chicken, with yellow rice and black beans, plantains. She would bring a ton, and we'd eat for days. Paul helped get her nephew out of a vandalism charge, gave him a scared-straight talking-to. They were good neighbors to each other, friends.

"He said if anything happened, I should give this to you," he said.

"Thank you," I said. "I'm sorry. About attacking you."

He lifted a hand, tried for a smile. "You're stronger than you look."

"I'm really sorry, Mr. Rodriquez."

"Who did this?" he asked looking into the living room. "Should we call the police?"

"No," I said, too quickly. He has his eyes on me, dark, wondering. "No police."

He nodded as if he understood, even though he didn't. I didn't even understand. But if the police came, it's another thing to deal with, and I couldn't handle more. And meanwhile, I was the last person who needed to be talking to the police.

"Did they take anything?" Mr. Rodriquez walked around the room, started picking up books and putting them back on the shelves. He righted the couch, the chair, the table, and I moved over to help him. The furniture was cheap, insubstantial. It didn't take much to put things back the way they were. The pillows were ruined, though, slashed and oozing stuffing.

"He didn't have anything," I said. "What were they looking for?"

"Cash, jewelry," he said with a shrug, a lifelong New Yorker resigned to crimes like these. "Anything they could sell. But how did they get in?"

He looked back at the door.

"The door was open," I said. "I must have forgotten it when we left."

He shook his head. "I came up," he said. "I'm sure I locked it."

He must have been mistaken. There were only three keys to this place. I had one, Paul did, and Mr. Rodriquez. I was sure of that.

"Let me help you finish cleaning up," he said.

"It's okay. I'll handle the rest."

I wanted him to leave, and he must have sensed that because he started moving toward the door. I had to think, figure this out.

"Call me?" He kept his eyes on me, wary, concerned. "Keep in touch about Paul, and let me know what you need, okay? I'll go see him tonight. We been friends a long time, Miss Zoey."

It's a term of endearment, not a way of indicating status. All I could do was nod, not trusting my voice. And then he was gone. I turned back to the apartment and moved into the mess. I had to figure out what they were looking for. Whoever they were.

fourteen

Chad Drake pulled his car into the lot, tires crunching on the gravel, and came to a stop under the oak tree in the north corner, far from the other vehicles. Most people parked as close as possible to their destination, but not him. He killed the engine and sat in the dark, letting the quiet wash over him. The days—how did they get so hectic, a rush, a mash of work and family and this demand and that worry? He was so tired all the time. Was it normal to be so tired?

The door to Burgers and Brew opened, and an arc of amber light and laughter and the sound of footfalls spilled out.

Please don't be drunk, he thought. *Please don't make me get out and ask if you've been drinking.*

He squinted into the dark and saw that it was Dr. Sherman and his wife, Lainey—walking steady, holding hands. He watched them make their way to their older but well-maintained Volvo. He got the door for her—nice. And then he climbed in the driver's side. The Shermans were good people, two boys in school with Zoey—one a year ahead of her and one a year behind. There were a couple of other pediatricians in town, but everyone said he was the best—careful, honest, slow to prescribe.

Zoey had been his patient since she was a few hours old.

The Volvo's engine came to life after a couple of minutes, then the headlights. Then they pulled slowly from the lot and onto the main road.

Thank you, he said silently.

If only decent people—the ones that didn't have to be taught how to live without hurting others—knew how much cops appreciated them.

He rubbed his eyes, waiting. Paul was late, which was not like him. Chad got out of the car and stretched long. Too much sitting—slouching in the prowler or hunched over the desk doing paperwork. There were two hard knots of pain between his spine and each shoulder blade. Only his wife, Heather, could work them out. She'd straddle his lower back and use the hard knobs of her elbows and get in deep, deeper while he howled.

"Big baby," she'd say. "Try to breathe into it. Release it."

"Stop, Heather," Chad would beg. "Please."

"What are you so worried about?" she'd ask. "What are you carrying around?"

Some of it she knew. Some of it she didn't. Some of it she'd never know, not if he had anything to do with it.

The twin beams of Paul's headlights caused him to raise a hand, shielding his eyes from the brightness. The beat-up old Suburban pulled to a stop beside him, and the man he thought of as a brother climbed out. They *were* brothers, closer than brothers because there was none of the sibling baggage.

"I stopped by to see Heather and Zoey," Paul said.

It was a cool night, but not cold. Halloween a few days away. Jack-o'-lanterns sat on every porch of their picture postcard of a town, leaves turning orange, red, gold. At the precinct, Mr. Bones, the old plastic skeleton had been pulled out of the supply closet and taken his place in the chair outside the evidence locker. There was a bucket beside him where folks dropped in their spare change and more to help fund the holiday party they'd throw for area "at-risk" kids at the Y.

"You didn't tell them I was coming," said Paul. "They were surprised to see me."

"It might have slipped my mind to mention it," he said.

"Nothing slips your mind, brother," Paul said. The older man pulled him into a powerful hug, slapped him on the back.

"Zoey is getting too grown up, man," Paul said with a shake of his head.

"Don't I know it."

"Good thing her uncle Paul taught her how to fight," he said. "I feel bad for the mope who messes with your girl."

His girl. Few things worried him more than Zoey. How do I provide for you? Protect you from the ugliness in this world? Make sure you know how to protect yourself after I'm gone?

"What is it?" asked Paul, squinting with concern. "What's on your mind?"

"You hungry?"

Paul's frown deepened. "Sure," he said. "I never met a burger or a beer that I didn't like."

It was nearly nine, so Burgers and Brew was quiet, just an hour from closing. It was Wednesday, a big game that night at the high school. It would be over now, folks heading back to their houses to finish up homework, get ready for the looming workday. Every good, law-abiding, family-centered person would be where he belonged—in front of the television or helping with homework, cleaning up after dinner. Heather, he knew, would be lying on Zoey's bed reading while Zoey studied for her algebra exam tomorrow. Or they'd be watching something together on the television in the master bedroom. After a certain hour, only the singles, the cops, and other night-shift workers, and the thugs were still out.

He and Paul took a booth toward the back.

"You've been on the job a long time," he said. "Like me."

"Sure," Paul said. "Yeah."

"Does it ever bother you?"

Peg, the waitress came and took their order—pale ale and a couple of towering, gooey cheeseburgers, fries. He'd have to lie to Heather; his cholesterol was through the roof. Paul didn't answer to anyone, never married, no kids, a New York City beat cop now for fifteen years. Neither of them ever wanted to be anything else, just like the old man. Well, not *just* like him.

"Does what bother me?"

"The unfairness of it all," Chad said. "The inequity."

"How so?"

He leaned in. "How some people have so much and other people so little. How the good guys struggle to make ends meet, but the thugs are driving Hummers?"

Paul flattened his big palm against the wood of the table, looked down at his hand.

"You sound like your dad."

"He was right."

"Okay," said Paul. "What if he was? Is it news that the world is an unfair place?"

Peg brought their beer. "There you go, boys. Enjoy."

They clinked glasses, each drank a swallow. It was cold and light, hops tingling and flavorful. The wash of it was a relief; he felt some of the day's tension washing away.

"I'm just saying," he said. "What if you had a chance to even the score just a little?"

Paul pinned him in an icy blue stare, took another swallow of his beer. "I don't know what that means."

"Well," he said. "I'm about to tell you."

No one ever really talked about debt, the weight of it, what it did to you. They never told you how it started small. For them, it was the engagement ring. It was too much, he knew that. She was a teacher and he was a cop. They were never going to be rich. Never. And it was never what they wanted. But the lady in the jewelry shop, she kept showing him ever bigger rings. *It's the purchase of a lifetime. Every time she looks at it, she'll know how much you love her. One day it will go to the daughter you have together, or maybe your future grandson's fiancée years from now. What seems like a lot right now won't seem like much five years from now. We have a convenient financing plan.*

He'd never bought on credit before. His father had taught him better. The old man wasn't up for any best-father awards, but he'd been frugal as hell, managing to pay for both his and Paul's educations, never borrowing a dime.

Then it was the mortgage, the new car. When Zoey came, the private preschool where Heather taught. They got a discount, but still it was a small fortune every year. Then Heather wanted to stay home with Zoey, wanted to try for another baby, and he wanted that, too. *We'll make it* work. We'll cut way back. The bills mounted slowly. The cruise they really couldn't afford, that trip to Disney. As a father, he wanted to give his girl the things the other kids had—those certain jeans, that backpack, the computer.

It just took a couple of months of charging and not paying off the balance. It crept up and up and up.

Until one day, when he sat down to add it all up, he realized that they were buried. It wasn't *that* much. But in comparison to what he made? It might as well have been a million dollars. Day to day, it didn't matter very much. But it was as if there were this weight strapped on his back, invisible to everyone else but making everything he did harder.

But that's not what he wanted to talk to Paul about. It was something else. When he was done, Paul hung his head, folded his hands in front of him.

"What you're saying," said Paul. He paused. "What you're thinking. It's wrong."

"Wrong?" Chad said. "But it's right to deal drugs, make a fortune off of other people's addiction, misery, and death and then have so much cash that you need to bury it in a field outside of town?"

"How do you even know about this?"

"I have a confidential informant on the inside."

"A CI? You trust this person?"

"As much as you can trust a meth head, yeah. He's not lying."

"Why doesn't he steal it himself?"

"Because it's guarded," Chad said. "And he's a fucking coward."

Paul rubbed at the bridge of his nose. "This is just a theoretical conversation, right? Philosophical? Because I know you're not really thinking about doing this."

"Sure," Chad said. He was a little disappointed, because part of him thought Paul might be, *might be* interested in what he had to say. Because he hadn't always been Mister Let's Play by the Rules. It was a low-risk, high-yield proposition. And Chad didn't know a cop who didn't—now and then—choke on how unfair it all seemed. "*Theoretically,* if you were going to do it, how would you go about it?"

Paul dipped his head, drained the last of his beer, signaled to Peg for two more.

fifteen

He threw me to the floor in front of my father's feet. Blood, warm and sticky, sluiced down my neck.

"Daddy?" The word was a wretch, a wail in my throat.

"Zoey."

He started to thrash, the chair he was bound to rocking, his head tossing. It was mind-bending. A horror movie.

"There's no money here—there just *isn't*," he said. I'd never heard him sound like that, voice wobbling with fear. "You've made a terrible mistake. Please. Just let my family go. They don't know who you are and neither do I."

The world warped and pulled into nightmarish unreality. My blood was smeared on the floor, my back screaming. The man, the one who'd pulled me through the window had an iron grip, was on his knees holding my arms behind my back as I thrashed. The knife, I kept thinking. The knife is in his pocket. If I can get to it, I can save us. But my arms were butterfly wings, useless, pinned. The other man stood over my father.

"This can be over," said the other man. He glanced in my direction. He wasn't big. My father was bigger. But the muscles on his arms

210

strained against his shirt, and his neck was thick and his thighs looked like jackhammers. "You just have to tell us where it is and we can go. No hard feelings, right?"

My mother moaned on the floor, shifted, blood pooling. I watched the black-red puddle spread, and I think part of me went to another place. That was the first time I went to the place of the watcher. I had no choice. What small amount of power I had as a person had been stripped from me. A part of me rose up, an impartial observer, and drifted above the scene. I was blissfully separate for a moment.

"Mom."

"Shh," she said, her voice gurgling and strange. She was about two feet from me. "Shh, baby."

"Your wife is going to die," said the standing man. Through the balaclava, I could only see his lips and the dark stubble around them, two flat dark eyes. I started to thrash. "If you tell us where it is, we'll go. You can still save her."

"Dad," I begged, my voice a whisper, no air in my lungs. "Tell them."

"I swear to Christ," he said. He was weeping now. "There's nothing in this house. I would give you anything I owned. You can have our wallets. Take me to an ATM; I will give you everything I have in my accounts. My wife's rings, all her jewelry. Take it."

"That's not what we're talking about, Officer,"

said the man on top of me. "And you. Fucking. Know it. You're beat, okay. You're not going to save your family and get away with that money. Tell us where it is."

My father bowed his head, released a broken sob. "There's—no—money."

In the watcher mind, I saw it all: my mother was dying, the blood slowly spilling from her, motionless now, silent, my father was helpless. What they thought he had, he obviously did not have. The men here, the boy shaking by the door, they were killers, criminals. They were going to kill us all.

"I know where it is," I said.

The standing man lifted his hands. "Finally," he said. "Someone in this family with half a fucking brain."

He strode over to me, leaned down close. His breath stank of cigarettes. "Okay, sweetie, tell the nice men. Where the *fuck* is it?"

"It's in the basement."

"Zoey," said my father. "What are you doing? She's lying. Don't you touch her."

That's when the man on top of me dragged me into the basement, down the steps, pulling me by arms. Air in my lungs again, I screamed and screamed, my limbs knocking against the stairs, the wall, the hard concrete ground, my arms feeling like he might pull them right out of the sockets. Then a cold, hard crack to the jaw.

"Shut up," he growled, his voice taut with anger and frustration. "For fuck's sake, just shut up."

I lay there among a field of stars, my ears ringing. I couldn't move from the pain, from the shock. On my side I curled up, waiting for breath, for strength, for some idea that would save us. The other man dragged my father down next, threw him to the ground, his arms bound. They tied my arms behind my back, pulled at me savagely.

"Okay," said the older man. That voice, gravel and glass, it imprinted itself in my psyche. For the rest of my life I would hear it in my dreams. "Little girl, where is it?"

"It's back there," I said, nodding toward the far corner. "All the way in the back, in a trunk."

"Zoey," said my father. "What are you doing?"

The smaller man went off in the direction I'd indicated. The other man sat astride me. That's when he started touching me, the face, my throat, my breast. I thrashed and bucked, but he must have weighed a thousand pounds. I couldn't get away from him, couldn't move. That feeling of powerlessness, being helpless. Never let them pin you. Never let it be a match of strength alone.

"What do you see?" he called. "What's back there?"

"There's nothing back here." The voice was

213

muffled. He was right. There was nothing back there. I had no idea what they were looking for. I was stalling, buying time.

The man on top of me took out the hunting knife.

"Hey." It was the boy, standing on the stairs now. He was thin and pale, standing masked in the shadows. "Don't hurt her anymore. Please."

"Shut up, kid," said the man on top. "Go upstairs and do your job."

I knew that the blade on that knife was sharp as a razor.

"Where is it?" said the standing man, his voice low and cool, his lips pulled in a grim smile. "Somebody better start talking."

And then the knife was on my skin and I was alone in the world with the pain of my flesh slicing open, my screams seeming to rocket through my father's body causing him to arc on the ground. His voice drowned out all other sounds. That knife, what happened next, most of it is not accessible. The psyche splits, my shrink said, or can in trauma. It does what it must to survive. Again that rising of myself above to watch a man cut and beat a helpless young girl with her father wailing bound and immobilized just feet away, her mother dying upstairs. Until. Until. How long did it go on? It couldn't have been more than an hour. Somewhere in the far distance, a high-pitched wail. A siren.

I didn't hear the shots. The one that killed my father. The one that was supposed to kill me. They didn't need to shoot my mother. She bled to death upstairs.

sixteen

The problem, the real problem was that Raven just felt so floaty all the time. Disconnected from the people around her, even her parents. She'd be standing there—at school, or even sometimes with her friends, and she'd feel herself just lift away. She would start thinking about something else, or the ambient noise around her would become distracting. She'd notice a thing about the other person—like how silky was her hair, or how big were her eyes, or how pretty were her clothes. And then she'd think about that person's parents, and it would get her thinking about her own origins. And then she'd start drifting toward that dark place, that shadowy region. Once she was there, that's when she did or said the kind of things she regretted later.

Raven never felt like that with Troy. He grounded her somehow, kept her in the moment. He had her tightly by the hand and they were striding—*he* was striding because he had long legs and an engine inside that caused him to practically run everywhere and she was half-jogging to keep up with him—down Avenue A toward the club where Andrew Cutter's band Trash and Angels was playing. She was wearing a tight black dress, which she would never be allowed to wear if either of her parents were around. She had taken a pair of thigh-high black boots from Ella's stash of clothes in her father's closet, and this kind of distressed denim cropped jacket. She blew her hair flat, made her eyes smoky in shades of brown. In the mirror, the girl she saw was the polar opposite of her mother—dark to light, soft features to fine. There was something in her mouth—its fullness, its upturned corners. Something in the apples of her cheeks that evoked Claudia. But there was nothing of Ayers. Not a shade or a shadow that she could see.

When she came out into the living room, Troy looked at her funny and didn't look away.

"What?" she asked. She found her bag and crossed the long strap across her body.

"Aren't you—" he started. He took off his glasses and looked away, wiped the lenses on his shirt. The color had come up in his cheeks. *What* was his problem? "Aren't you going to be cold?"

"We'll take a cab."

She *was* cold. The wind had picked up, and she'd opted out of a heavier jacket over her outfit. She didn't want to disrupt the look and have to worry about a coat all night. But traffic was ridiculous, and they finally just got out of the cab that was crawling and costing them a fortune, deciding to walk the last ten blocks. Trash and Angels went on at eleven, and it was already quarter to the hour.

At the door, the line was stupid long, stretching up the street and wrapping around. It was kind of the "it" indie band venue of the moment, Downtown Beirut, named after an old East Village dive bar that had closed long ago. Now, supposedly there was some burgeoning music scene in Beirut and hence the name of the hole in the wall.

Troy stopped at the end of the line. But Raven kept going, and he followed. They were not going to have to wait in line. They were hot and well-dressed, and young—twenty-two-year-olds that looked like sixteen-year-olds. No one was going to know that they were sixteen-year-olds trying to pass for twenty-two. The bulldozer-sized bouncer at the door—complete with shaved, tattooed head—and his slender, leather-clad hostess, lithe with dark skin and bleached white hair, never said a word. She just lifted the rope and shined that light on their fake IDs. They must have been good—like the kind of IDs that would get you in trouble if you got caught carrying them. They must have been the real deal, illegally obtained, and that was a serious crime. The hostess didn't look twice at the cards in her hand, there wasn't that tense moment when you wondered if you were going to get kicked out. She just handed them back to Troy and gave him a hungry smile. Troy flushed again. Raven grabbed his hand and pulled him inside.

"How do you always do that?" he yelled over the din.

"Do what?"

"Just walk in like you own the place." There was that goofy look again.

"I *do* own it," she said. "In my mind."

They both laughed at that, and he dropped an arm around her. At the bar, they just ordered Cokes, neither of them big drinkers. The crowd was pretty edgy—lots of ear gauges and tattoos, black leather. But it was the usual New York City mix—some people looked like they just got off work—loose ties and jackets hung over seats, silk blouses and pencil skirts. Some people were grunge, hair hanging and dirty looking, jeans ripped. Other people looked like they stopped by on their way home from the gym. One guy could have passed for homeless. In New York City, you fit. Even if you didn't fit in anywhere else, you could find a place for yourself there. Not like the place her mother had dragged her. There you were one thing—blonde, pretty, tight-bodied, and rich—or you were a freak, an outsider. Not even a freak. You were nothing.

They found a spot by the stage, sipped their Cokes, and looked around. There was a throb, a deep pulse to the music playing over the speakers. Some of the band members were on stage, milling about, setting up equipment. She watched for him, Andrew Cutter, son of a rapist, her possible half brother. But she didn't see him up there. In his photos he looked like an anime warrior, a mop of black hair, jet eyes, pale skin with an upturned nose and a cupid's bow mouth. He had a mellow, easy voice and was a master on the guitar. There were some riffs from offstage, the drummer beat out a quick rhythm. The music on the speakers started to stutter, and then the rest of Trash and Angels burst onto the stage and immediately launched into one of their hard-rock jams.

He was standing in the rear, near the drummer, not lead vocal on this one. The blond, the one that called himself Charge, was hammering out lyrics about wanting someone and needing her and what was she doing to him. But Andrew—Raven had seen when she was Twitter stalking him that most people called him Drew, sometimes they called him "Angry" she guessed a riff on his @angryyoungman Twitter tag. He was deep, deep into his thing, head bowed over the strings, not looking up at the crowd, not interested in giving or receiving energy. It was the artist's space, the one she could never seem to find, where you only care about the work before you, the rest of the world disappearing.

"Is that him?" Troy yelled, pointing.

She nodded. He looked up then, and she watched Troy's face. Would he see it? How much they looked alike? Sort of. But Troy just shrugged, gave her an easy smile.

"He might look a little like you," he yelled. "A little."

They listened to the rest of the set. Drew never sang, never even moved to lead guitar. Once, she thought he looked at her, but it was brief. He could have just been glancing out at the audience.

"Okay," said Troy, back by the bathrooms. "You've seen him. What now?"

"I'm going to try to get backstage," she said. "Will you wait for me?"

"I'll go with you," he said.

"That's not going to work," she said.

"Why not?"

"Because," she said. "You're a guy."

He nodded, getting it. Alone, with a smile, she had confidence that she could open almost any door. Girls had that kind of magical power, didn't they? Boys not so much. He would just be a tagalong anyway, her conscience, her better judgment. This type of endeavor could not be second guessed. Because it was stupid and impulsive and did not withstand scrutiny of any kind.

Of course, the muscle-bound Latino guy at the door let her right back to where the band was hanging out. And Drew was alone, toward the back of the room, reading. She felt eyes on her, the way men looked sometimes. She tried to make herself small. She wasn't one of those girls. She didn't want weird attention from boys

221

and men; she didn't vamp for it or ask for it. She didn't blossom under it. *You are the chooser,* her mother always said. *You are not chosen. They don't get to pick and have you like a flower. They need to scale mountains and slay dragons. Then, maybe then, you might give them the time of day.* Raven wasn't interested in boys. She liked Troy, that was it.

"Hey," she said. "Are you Drew?"

He looked up from the slim paperback in his hands. *The Stranger*, by Camus.

"That's right," he said. His face stayed still, a little blank. He cocked his head, seemed to take her in, every detail of her.

"Are you—?" he said.

"Butterfly dreams," she said. She tried for a smile, but something about him made her nervous, self-conscious. "I'm Raven."

She saw surprise flash across his face, a kind of angry startle. Then he seemed to shrink up. "What are you doing here? How did you get back here?"

It wasn't exactly the reaction she'd expected. She thought, she didn't know why, that he'd be warmer, nicer. That at least he'd be kind. She realized that everyone around them was laughing and partying, that they were in this dark corner, separate utterly from the group.

"I just wanted to—see you," she said. Her voice sounded soft, stuttery. Her heart was a bird in a

222

cage, flapping. "To see if there was a connection. I don't know if Melvin Cutter is my father."

"Ten minutes!" someone called.

His eyes were so dark, his gaze so level.

"What do you mean, that you don't know?"

"Melvin Cutter—raped my mother." She didn't say the words very often. They sat in her mouth, tasted bitter. "But she had also been with my father—her husband—that night. They never got a test. They didn't want to know, didn't want it to matter."

"But they told you about the rape."

It never seemed odd until he said it.

"They're big on honesty."

He seemed to consider. "A certain kind of honesty, I guess. The truth, just not the whole truth. Like telling you a meteor is headed to Earth, just not telling you how big or whether or not it will destroy the planet."

She hadn't thought of it like that. Her mother had her reasons and all of them were clear to Raven. Claudia and Ayers told Raven exactly what they knew and why they had decided not to know more. She wanted to explain this to him, but instead she just stared down at Ella's boots which were so gorgeous but so painful. Raven's feet were throbbing. She wished she'd let Troy come back with her.

"It's not like that," she said.

"Isn't it?"

223

Did she feel anything? Anything that joined them? Anything that was similar, kindred? No. He was a stranger, not a pleasant one.

"It's ironic, isn't it?" he said. "I've spent my whole life running away, pushing away, hiding from any connection I might have to Melvin Cutter. And here you are, chasing after him."

His tone was musing, not judgmental. "I'm not chasing after *him*," she said. "He's dead."

He blinked, moved back a little as if she'd hurt him. Maybe it did hurt. Maybe all of this hurt him, and that's why he was so angry. She was starting to see her mother's wisdom.

"Five minutes!" That same gravelly voice. Conversations seemed to quiet, people left the room. Drew rose to his feet. He was small, not much taller or bigger than Raven.

"Then what *do* you want?" he asked.

"I want to know where I came from, where I belong," she said. Tears were threatening, tingling at the back of her eyes and tightening her throat.

"Why do you think where you came from has anything to do with where you belong?" His voice was gentle, almost pitying. "I certainly don't believe that. I can't. I have to believe that we create our lives. Do you *get* that?"

She shook her head. She did get it—and she didn't. "I don't know. Maybe."

He shifted as if to move past her, but then he put a hand on her arm.

"Sounds like you have two nice parents that love you," he said. "I'd take that if I were you and leave the rest of it alone. The alternatives are dark."

She felt a heat where his hand rested. "What if you're my half brother?"

He smiled a little. "What if?"

Then he left her standing there. The room had cleared. She was alone except for a couple of girls that lounged on the couches. Outside, she heard the music start up again.

"How old are you, sweetie?" one of the women asked. She was giving Raven a look she'd seen before, a nasty up and down, a sneer over something hollow in the eyes. *Behold the look of jealousy,* her mother told her once. *Not pretty, is it?* But it didn't feel like jealousy, that would mean she had something others wanted. And what could that possibly be? It felt like disdain, like hatred. It drained; it hurt.

Raven didn't answer, just bolted from the room and down the hall, and past the bouncer. *What's wrong, mami? Everything okay?*

Troy was flirting with some girl who looked like she might be in her twenties. He had that face on, that kind of smarmy, smilcy, trying-too-hard look. The woman, a pretty, freckle-faced redhead just looked bored, like she was babysitting. Raven ran past him and heard him call her name. Then she was out on the street, breathing hard,

225

taking in big gulps of the frigid air. Her chest hurt, and then big sobs took her over. People just looked on, indifferent. Then Troy was behind her, wrapping her up and leading her away. She burrowed into him, weeping like a complete loser, absolutely powerless to stop. They leaned against a building until the storm of her emotion passed and she'd left a big wet stain on his New School tee-shirt.

When she finally looked up at him, his was the very face of loving friendship—accepting, concerned, present. He didn't ask her what happened. He knew she'd tell him everything when she found the words. *Why do you think where you came from has anything to do with where you belong?*

"I want to go home," she said. She wiped at her nose with the sleeve of Ella's jacket, shivering.

He nodded, looked to the street for a cab. "To your dad's place?"

"No," she said, shaking her head. "I need my mom."

He looked down at his watch and then back at her.

"Okay," he said. "If we hurry, we can make that last train."

seventeen

When I got back to the hospital, Mike was there, sitting on the floor in the corner like a Buddha, legs folded bcneath him, hands in prayer at his chest, head bowed. He was just a bulky shadow, breathing deep, in measure to Paul's labored breath. White light made a rectangle on the floor. Outside more white rectangles, portals into other lives, other moments, hopefully, most of them better than this one. I sank into the chair, didn't say anything.

On the way in, the nurse asked me if I was Paul's daughter and I had said yes, because it was easier and because in some senses it was true. Is it fair to lose two fathers in one lifetime? I loved my dad but also feared his disapproval, wasn't sure what it felt like to be held in loving arms. He wasn't a hugger, more just a peck-on-the-cheek kind of a guy, a pat on the shoulder, a tight smile. Paul was big on bear hugs, head stroking. He cooked, helped with homework, never angered. He was easy. We were kindred in a way I wasn't with my own dad. At first it felt disloyal to love Paul, but in the end I loved him most. There was a band of sadness around my chest, tightening like a garrote.

"Don't worry about it, kid," said my father

from over by the window. "I loved him better than I did my old man, too."

"Someone was in the apartment," I said to Mike.

He didn't say anything, but the shift in his energy sent a ripple through the room.

"Who?"

"I don't know," I said. "But they trashed it, looking for something."

He blew out a long breath through pursed lips. "I shouldn't have helped you. It was a mistake."

"I'd have asked the questions of someone else," I said. "Answered the questions on my own. I would have wound up in the same place."

Another long breath drawn, held, released. The sound of it filled the room, mingled with Paul's watery breath. It made me think of the ocean, waves crashing.

"Which is the reason why I did," Mike said. "But I regret my decision."

"Does he know? Did you tell him?"

"What? That you have taken it upon yourself to investigate the crime of your parents' murder? That you have drawn some conclusions and taken matters into your own hands? That I helped you? He suspected. After Didion."

He was quiet for a moment. Then, "For the record, I didn't think you would go *there*. I taught you better."

"I don't know what you mean."

228

He shook his head at me. And I could see that he was angry, disappointed. It's not just sad when you part company with your teacher. It's also scary. You're on your own.

We sat in a tense silence for a couple of minutes. Outside the room, a phone rang and rang. Someone let out a laugh. After a few minutes, I started talking. I told Mike about the phone call, the trashed apartment, the key. I told him about what I'd seen online. The house where my parents were killed, now under renovation.

Paul released a low moan, and I wondered how much he was taking in, if anything. Mike popped up lithely; I am always amazed at his speed and agility. Big usually means slow, stiff. Not so with Mike.

He exited the room, and I followed him to the chapel at the end of the hall. It was empty, some weird mix between hospital room and church, all pastel pink and purple with a simple cross hanging high on the far wall. I always liked the idea of religion, a safe place, somewhere you could rest your troubles. I believed in God. My father was a passionate atheist. But my mother believed in a spiritual universe, and she taught me that there was something bigger, something wiser, than I am. I felt it, in a strange, shifting way, like the tumbling crystals of a kaleidoscope. I felt it in the kung fu temple, or when I settled into the watcher mind. There was something there, something benevolent, and light, something other. I believed in God. But I didn't have any faith at all in man, and the church belonged to him.

"What are you going to do?" asked Mike. We sat side by side in the front row gazing up at the gray metal cross.

There in the quiet, with his eyes on me, I knew the answer I hadn't known when I came there.

"I'm going home," I said. "I'm going back there. That's where they'll go if they're still looking for it."

Mike shook his head again; apparently there were no words for his disappointment in me. But he didn't say anything.

"Will you stay with Paul?" I said into the silence. "Stay in touch with me. I won't be long."

He nodded, looking down at hands he'd folded in his lap. Our arms touched; I pushed into him, leaning against his bulk, and he pushed back.

"When Didion—was killed, I think it set something in motion," said Mike. "Disturbed a resting energy. Maybe it's time for closure on this."

"Paul said: *they're coming for it,*" I told Mike. "What did he mean?"

"I don't know," he said. "You said he was out of it, maybe he was delirious. But look. Why don't you just lay low and see how this all shakes out? Focus on Paul, on the school. The girls need you. I need you."

If energy had been disturbed, then I was the one who'd disturbed it. It was my job to bring closure.

"We'll call Boz, maybe ask Seth to spend a couple days staking out the house," said Mike. His brow creased with worry, and he looped his fingers through mine. "We'll tell Boz about the phone call, give him that number, and see what he finds. There's no reason for you to be involved in this, Zoey. Not like this."

I stood. We both knew it was too late for that.

part two
GHOSTS

eighteen

The room came into a kind of slatted, fuzzy focus, and all I could see was Paul, slouched and gray in the corner. I puzzled a moment— where was I? What was Paul doing?—still dwelling in the soft edges of wherever you go when you're unconscious. There were a few blissful minutes of blank disorientation, while I watched him wondering why he looked so bad, what were those sounds, that smell, why did I feel so odd.

Then he looked up, his steely blue eyes meeting mine. He'd aged a million years, looked bent and old, hollowed out by grief. And slowly, slowly, it started to come back.

"Zoey," he said. His voice was just a whisper and it was one word, my name, but everything, all the horror of the universe resided in those syllables.

It's hard to explain what followed in those weeks after my parents' murders. A dark, sucking hole was ripped in the fabric of my universe. Where before I had been loved, secure, thought the world was one thing, after I had been violently instructed that it was another altogether.

Buffeted by the gale-force winds of bone-crushing grief and unspeakable trauma, I was

235

debris from a shipwreck, floating, not even trying to find shore. I began my fifteenth year as one thing, one girl, one kind of person, and ended it as someone else. I survived, but I didn't. I was a zombie. Dead girl walking. No matter what they tell you, some things you don't get over. You just don't. You might still be breathing, walking around. You might still have a cake on your birthday, laugh again, heal some. But you don't "get over it."

It was a long time, too long before I started asking questions. I barely had a language for my new universe for the first year; I was still getting used to its unusual gravitational pull. I could barely lift my feet to walk.

Maybe if Detective Earl Bozmoski hadn't paid us a visit, I wouldn't have ever asked. Maybe I would have accepted the fact that the men who murdered my parents and thought they murdered me got away with it. I couldn't identify them. They had been in no way familiar to me—no one who had worked on our property, who I knew from my mother's life, from my dad's, from school. I had never seen their faces. Their clothes, their shoes were generic—jeans and boots, flannel shirts, black ski masks. I was able to describe builds, the sounds of their voices, the color of their eyes. They wanted something, something they thought my father had. The house was thoroughly searched. They gathered hair and fibers. There was a single boot print outside the door, a size 10 work boot. One set of foreign fingerprints that didn't match anything in the system. Hair fibers were collected from my clothes.

The manhunt that night was exhaustive, the investigation tireless. A cop and his wife had been murdered in their home, their daughter tortured, left for dead. It would not stand, no lead too small, the investigation would not end until someone had been made to pay. It wound on and on, long after other cases would have been shelved. Still. Whoever they were, they got away with it.

Nothing was ever found hidden in our house. Whatever they thought my father had, he didn't have it. Of course he didn't. He wasn't an easy man, but I never doubted how much he loved me and my mom. There is nothing he wouldn't have given up for us. He'd have lain down his life.

"Just one more time, Zoey." Detective Bozmoski, or Boz, as I have come to know him over the years. "As much as it hurts, just tell me one more time."

I looked to Paul, who nodded solemnly. Boz had come into the city where I'd settled in with Paul. I had started school that week, lay in bed every night crying, was plagued by terrible night-mares, was in twice-weekly therapy. I watched a lot of television—cartoons mostly, SpongeBob and *South Park*, even other stuff just for babies like *Little Einsteins* and *Special Agent Oso*. Anything that wasn't real, anything that let me vegetate, not think, not feel.

I told him everything again, from the beginning, starting with Seth. It was he who had called the police. He got to the bridge late that night and followed the path I would have taken home, hoping to catch me. He watched, terrified in the trees, as the men dragged me across the property from the barn to the house, Catcher lifeless on the ground. (Catcher survived that night, lived with me and Paul for another couple of years before we had to put him down for dysplasia. At home he could have gotten around, but in the city, he couldn't manage all those stairs. He was a good boy.) Seth ran, called the police. He probably saved my life that night. For what it's worth. He told me later that he'd always felt like a coward for running. But he was just a kid. If he'd tried to play hero, he would have been dead. Maybe I would be, too.

Boz was a big man with a thinning head of black hair and a perpetual five o'clock shadow. He wasn't part of the Lost Valley Police Department; he was from the state police. The case of a murdered police officer never closes, never goes cold. Detective Earl Bozmoski was a dog with a bone.

We went over it again, every detail. The sound of their voices, the shapes of their mouths, the color of their eyes. What they said to each other. Did they ever use names? He was hoping that as my trauma lifted, as grief lightened, that more details would surface. So far, it hadn't worked that way. Even though that night was on an eternal loop in my thoughts, in my dreams, nothing helpful had emerged from my traumatized recollections.

We sat in Paul's cramped kitchen, the aroma of coffee in the air. Boz pulled a manila folder from his weathered leather case and laid it on the table.

"I've got some pictures here, Zoey," he said. "I wondered if you might recognize any of these men."

His hands were thick and calloused, cuticles ragged, nails short. My mother would have called them a workingman's hands. I liked the sight of them because they reminded me of my father's hands, hands that worked wood, held a gun, held my hand, lifted and fixed.

He spread four photos out in front of me.

My father used the word *mopes* a lot, or *skulls,* meaning low-level thugs, bad men with bad intentions or just the kind moron that fell into trouble because he came from trouble and didn't know any other way around the world. Men who stole, or had the gene for violence, bad tempers, or just something addled in the head. The men in the photos were all one kind or another. Even at that age, I could see it in the deadness of their stares, in the turned-down corners of their mouths, the ragged complexions, sloped shoulders. But they were all strangers. I looked at their eyes, at their mouths. But there wasn't any jolt of recognition.

I shook my head. "I don't know them."

"If you heard some voices maybe?"

"Maybe."

He pulled a recorder out of his bag. "Normally, we'd have to do this at the station. But I didn't want to do that to you right now—when you're just settling in here."

"Is it okay?" Paul asked. I nodded.

"They're all going to say the same thing," said Boz. "A sentence from the transcript of your initial interview: 'You're not going to save your family and get away with that money. Tell us where it is.'"

I must have flinched because he bowed his head and put that big hand over mine. "I'm sorry," he said.

The first voice was too high pitched, almost girlish. I shook my head. The next voice had a heavy New York accent; that wasn't it either. The third voice was deeper. Maybe, but no. The fourth voice sent a bolt of electricity through me, deep, gravelly, cold.

"Zoey?"

"Maybe," I said, feeling my breath come ragged. I couldn't swear to it, but every nerve ending in my body was tingling, my lungs compressing.

"Who is he?" I asked.

"Just a thug, a local screw-up," he said. He fanned out the pictures again. "Look again now."

Two of the men had blond facial hair; I eliminated them. One had too much gray. I stared at the mouth of the man who had dark stubble, at his blank dark eyes. Maybe. Maybe. I was shaking a little, from the inside out.

"I just don't know," I said. "Him maybe. The masks."

"I get it," he said. He raised a palm, gave an understanding nod. "I'm not trying to force you into saying something you're not sure of."

"Okay, kid," said Paul. "Go do your home-work."

I lingered in the hallway just beyond the kitchen door. I heard Paul get up and pour Boz another cup.

"I think we're going to have to face that she's got nothing left to give," said Paul. "She's shattered, Boz."

There was a long pause, a sigh. "Did you know he was in trouble?"

"Who?" said Paul. "Chad? What kind of trouble?"

"He was drowning in debt," said Boz.

A spoon against the edge of a mug. A scraping chair.

"I had a sense that money was tight," said Paul. "How much debt?"

"He was borrowing for private school. There were high credit card balances, multiple cards. He was nearing ninety thousand."

"Christ."

"On a cop's salary," Boz said.

"Okay," said Paul. "So what? So he had debt. Lots of folks have debt."

"A couple weeks before the murders," said Boz. "Some money was stolen. A lot of money, a million."

There was a leaden silence; I slid down the wall to my haunches, vibrating.

"Stolen from where?"

"Word is, from my confidential informant, that three heavily armed masked men shot two guards and absconded with a pile of cash belonging to Whitey Malone."

"The drug dealer you guys never seem to be able to bring in."

"That's right," said Boz. "My CI says that the robbers were trained, organized, and ruthless. They killed the two thugs on guard, collected their rounds and casings. They knew where the money was buried. Came and went quickly. Word is that they were cops, or maybe paramilitary. My guy was hiding, saw the whole thing go down."

"You think the two incidents are connected."

"The men who killed your stepbrother and his wife," said Boz. "They were looking for money."

"And why would they be looking at Chad's?" asked Paul. What was there in his tone? Something I'd never heard.

One of them coughed. "I don't know," said Boz. "Why do you think?"

"How the hell should I know?"

More silence.

"So," said Paul, his voice coming up an octave. "If you think it's connected, make life a living hell for Malone and his thugs. Who else would be looking for that money but them?"

"We've done that," said Boz. "We're doing it. No one knows anything; or no one's talking. Of the locals, these four come closest to Zoey's physical descriptions—size, coloring, whatnot. They're by far the worst guys we have on the streets in the area, armed robbers, drug dealers, rapists, killers—convicted felons every one."

"So it makes sense that they're out walking around."

"Hey, I don't make the laws," said Boz. "Neither do you."

"Did they work for Malone?"

"I didn't find any connections, no."

I heard a chair groan as one of them shifted his weight.

"You've got fibers, the boot print," said Paul.

243

"There's no definitive match on any of it," he said. "This guy, Beckham, has a size ten boot, but so do a lot of guys. We haven't found any guns with a ballistics match in their possession. We brought this guy, Didion, in on gun charges; found a cache of illegal weapons—not the ones stolen from Chad's locker. None of which were used in the commission of the Drake murders. Didion will go back to jail anyway. This other one looks like he's been trying to go straight, has a job at the gas station. Hasn't been in any trouble."

More silence.

"So what are you *saying,* Boz?" said Paul. What was it? Was it menace? Anger? There was something sizzling between them. What?

"Hey, I'm not saying anything," said Boz gently. "I got to look at everything, for my notes, every single angle. You know that. This is a cop killing. All eyes are on me."

There was a hard thump on the kitchen table. I couldn't see what.

"They're going to get away with it, aren't they?" said Paul. His voice didn't even sound like his; it was small now and tight with anger. "The men who did this to Chad and Heather, to Zoey. They're out there."

"I swear to you, Paul, and to Zoey," Boz said, "I'll never rest until we find who did this."

Paul made some kind of strangled noise. It took me a second to realize that he was crying.

● ● ●

Boz was almost an old man now, but he never got the memo. Retirement had agreed with him. He'd grown leaner, had lost the purple gullies under his eyes. We'd stayed in touch over the years, so I knew he'd married late to a much younger woman, drove a white Corvette that he pampered like a baby, took up golf. He still lived in the town where I grew up. I brought my theories to him. He called me sometimes when the odd thought occurred to him.

The lights were burning inside his tidy Victorian when I pulled up in the old truck that Paul kept in a garage uptown.

I walked up the flower-lined path and knocked at the door, heard the television go off inside. In spite of the hour, he didn't seem that surprised to see me when he opened the door.

"Zoey," he said. He wore a tattered old John Jay College sweatshirt. They all went there, Boz, Paul, my dad, even Mike. "Come in."

He held the door open for me, and I walked into the foyer.

There was a mirror there and before I could look away, I caught sight of myself, someone narrow with shoulders hiked high, pale with dark circles under her eyes, hair pulled back tight. Jeans, black hoodie. Not someone who belonged in this carefully decorated home of older people. An interloper, an unwelcome guest. *What's with the getup?* that doorman had asked.

"Mike called you," I guessed.

"Said Paul's in a bad way, that you might be stopping by."

"I want to go over it again."

Even though the people who killed my parents were never caught, Boz has never stopped working the case, even after he retired. He has an office toward the back of the house, where he still pores over cold cases. Lately, he's closed a couple. The new DNA technology and evolving federal and state requirements that mandate DNA samples be taken from anyone arrested have led to new evidence on cases that might have forever remained unsolved.

"Where's Miranda?" I asked. Funny name for a cop's wife.

"She's visiting her sister," he said, motioning that I follow him into the kitchen. He put on the kettle, pulled out a chair for me. I sat at the table, looked around—lots of flowers and ducks, pictures of kids on the refrigerator, a standing mixer, a rack of copper pots. Homey.

"John Didion is dead," he said, leaning against the counter.

"I heard that, too."

"They say it was a hunting knife," he said, putting tea bags in a white porcelain pot. "Through the heart."

"Oh?"

I flashed on it again, that moment where I came in close, one step, one thrust. My strength, his weakness. A pop. A sigh. He let go of life, as if it were a burden he was glad to unload. His eyes went blank; he almost smiled. Or maybe that's what I tell myself. I felt nothing. But there's something that came after, a kind of howl in the back of my brain. I've dreamt about it twice, waking to hope it never happened. But it did.

"All we have are theories, you know," said Boz.

"We have more than that," I said. "I was *there*."

No one was ever arrested for the murder of my parents. The money those men were looking for was never recovered. A few months into the investigation, a cloud of suspicion fell over my father. According to Boz, there was a months-long sideline inquiry being conducted by Internal Affairs into the idea that a group of cops had robbed a local drug dealer, and that the men who killed my father and mother were looking for that money. That investigation, too, died on the vine. There was no evidence tying my father to the robbery.

"There's word that Rhett Beckham is back in town," said Boz. The kettle whistled, and he poured the not-quite-boiling water into the pot. It was slow and careful; he liked the ritual. I could tell.

Rhett Beckham, the tall, thin one. The one who dragged me through the window, who cut me with my father's hunting knife. And then there was Josh Beckham, his brother, the one who tried to say I wasn't in the barn. That's what I think, anyway. Those are my theories, based on my long investigation, the fragments of my memory, the recorded voice, the eyes I saw in mug shots.

According to Seth Murphy, who was also still obsessed with what happened that night, there was another man, a man in the passenger seat of the car, sitting, waiting. We had no idea who that might be.

The car they were in was a big old Caddy, black, run-down. Seth didn't see any tags. It was never found. But Didion had been seen driving something similar a week earlier. All just fragments, pieces that never gelled enough for an arrest, though they were all questioned.

"I heard," I said.

"He was released," said Boz. "He rolled into town a week ago, and now he's living with his brother and mother."

"Someone's moved into the house." The words backed up in my throat. "She's renovating it. She has a blog."

He had his back to me, so I couldn't see his face.

"Mike thinks the energy has been disturbed," I went on. "That it's time for closure."

"That sounds like something he'd say."

He watched the steeping pot, then retrieved mugs from the cupboard.

I told Boz about the break-in, about what Paul said. He brought the mugs to the table and sat across from me.

"Paul was scared," I said. "He said: *they're coming.*"

Boz frowned at that, seemed to go internal for a second. He stood and walked off; I heard him padding down the hall, and I took a sip of my tea. It was hot and sweet. After a moment, he came back clutching a thick file folder covered with scribbling and coffee cup stains.

"So," he said, sitting across from me, putting the folder on the table. He flipped it open. "Three men rob a local drug dealer named Whitey Malone. He's got a pile of cash, around a million buried outside a cabin he owns in the woods. The men, armed, trained, kill two of the thugs guarding the stash, dig it up, and take off, leaving a CI cowering under a bed. They have foreknowledge of the site, move quickly, and take off. We don't know what they were driving. CI says he never got a good look."

I nod. I know all this.

"Two weeks later," he said. "Three men break into your home and proceed to torture your parents—and you—looking for this money. Your father, according to your retelling, has no idea where the money is, or he doesn't give it up."

"He had no idea," I said. This part always makes me angry, that Boz leaves any doubt that my father would allow us all to be killed for money. He wouldn't.

"I'm just saying, Zoey," he said. "It were me?

I wouldn't tell them either. I'd stall as long as I could, hoping for an opportunity, a miracle. They were going to kill you all anyway. He knew that."

"He didn't know anything about it," I said. "I'm *telling* you."

"Okay," he said, lifting his palms. "None of Whitey Malone's men are ever tied to the scene. We have loose, circumstantial evidence that *might,* I repeat *might,* implicate these two men—John Didion and Rhett Beckham—the boot print, Didion seen in an old Caddy, your possible recognition of Didion's voice. But there was never enough to make a case. Didion got sent away on gun charges, got out, went up again, just released last year. Beckham also went away for armed robbery—stabbed some guy in the joint, had some time added. He was just released last month."

He took a sip of tea, looked at me over the rim. We did this. Started at the beginning, ran it all down. Again and again. I guess we'd get tired of it when we found answers to all our questions.

"And Josh Beckham, his brother, no criminal record, has been here all along. Took over his father's business, cares for his elderly mother. The only reason we looked at him was because you said the third man, much younger, seemed afraid and tried to help you hide."

"You talked to him."

"We brought them all in," said Boz. "If it was

them, none of them ever talked. Not then, not in the joint, not bragging at a bar."

"And the money was never found."

"No," said Boz. "According to my CI, the money was never recovered. Whitey Malone died in prison a couple of years ago. That million bucks is like an urban legend now. People look for it, talk about where it might be. Occasionally, cops will find some kids out in the woods behind your old place, digging for it."

"So maybe the guys who took it from Malone got away with it," I said. "They're living in the Caribbean somewhere. Whoever thought my dad took it, they got it wrong."

"That's a possibility," said Boz. "I've considered it."

"But."

"But nothing," said Boz. "It's one of a couple of theories. I don't have the answers, kid. Believe me, I wish I did."

We'd had this conversation so many times. I drained my cup, set it down on the table.

"I don't want to know about Didion, okay?" he said.

"I don't know what you mean."

"But it seems to me like maybe Mike is right. It's set some wheels in motion."

"How so?"

"Now Rhett Beckham is back in town. The house is under renovation, and I heard the new owner hired Josh Beckham as the handyman."

I leaned forward. "Josh Beckham is working at the house?"

Boz nodded, went on: "And you say someone ransacked Paul's apartment, looking for something."

"So what does Paul have to do with this?"

"Maybe nothing," said Boz. "Maybe they were looking for you."

The thought had occurred to me. But who? And why? And why now? Because of Didion? The video footage; had someone recognized me? I got my mail at Paul's, didn't have another address. Maybe someone thought I knew where the money was, had kept the secret all these years.

"I have to tell you." He drained his cup. "I didn't think we'd still be trying to figure this out, more than ten years later."

That's the difference between me and Boz. He's still trying to solve the puzzle, figure out how all the pieces fit together—who took that money, how it connects to what happened to my family, where the money is now. Who was the fourth man there that night, the one Seth saw waiting outside? For him, it's about the unanswered questions. Those things don't matter to me as much. I know who was in my house that night; I know what they did. Even if the evidence isn't there, my body knew Didion.

The Red Hunter only wants one thing.

nineteen

When Heather Drake came home with the groceries, she saw his truck in the drive. She felt it, that mutinous little lift in her heart, that tug on the corners of her mouth. She brought her car to a stop. There was a rattling sound when she turned the ignition off. *What could that be?* she wondered. And how much was it going to cost to fix it? She tried not to do that thing she did, where she thought about how much money was in the account, what she still had to buy, and what was due. There was always too much ahead, and not enough to cover. She tried to make the numbers work and couldn't, and now this weird rattle. But it was always something, wasn't it?

She climbed out into the air cool, growing cold. The trees punched gold against the gloaming. The windows in the house glowed orange. Home. She knew inside that everything was neat and orderly. The laundry was done; there was a stew in the crock-pot. Every surface was clean; every bed made.

He climbed out and walked toward her. She gave a wave and went to pop the trunk so that she could retrieve the groceries. He was by her side, lifting out the heaviest bag, planting a kiss on her cheek.

"Hey, there," Paul said. Just the smell of him.

"Hey," she said, easy. "What are you doing here?"

He frowned. "Chad called," he said. "Said he needed to talk. I figured he meant here."

"He didn't tell me," she said. No surprise there. "Where's Zoey?"

She looked up the drive. "Should be home soon. She had art, Blaire's mom is driving car pool tonight."

Which Heather didn't love. She loved being the carpool mom, the one with the car full of chattering, laughing teenage girls. But she didn't like being the one waiting, watching the drive. She was good at feigning nonchalance, though. Mothers of only children had a bad rap: too overprotective, hovering, nervous. It wasn't because Zoey was her only one; she would have been like that about all of them, if things had gone the way she planned. But it didn't.

"You look—" he started. She thought he was going to say tired, stressed, worried. She was all of those things. "Radiant."

And then she was looking into his eyes. "You're sweet," she heard herself say.

His gaze lingered too long, and she moved ahead of him pushing into the house, balancing the groceries on one hip. The house smelled heavenly, stew cooking.

"I hope we're eating here," he said, putting down the bags.

"I don't think so," she said. "He told me he wouldn't be home for dinner."

"And you didn't ask why?"

She shrugged. "Wife of a cop for nearly twenty years," she said. "I don't ask questions much. If he was going to miss bcef stew night, I figured he had his reasons. His shift is over at eight. He said he was going to grab something at Burgers and Brew."

She didn't say that it was a relief when Chad didn't make it home for dinner, that there were no screaming matches between him and Zoey to referee, no trying to coax out news about the day, wondering why he always looked so worried, so tired. Sometimes when he came home, he brought a kind of pall with him and draped it over the house. It wasn't that she didn't love him. She did.

Paul helped her put away the groceries. He knew the kitchen as well as if he lived there. He always helped with meals when he was there, somehow managing not to get in her way. Chad never came near the kitchen; when he wanted to give her a night off from cooking, they went out or carried in.

"So what's up?" he said. "Why would he ask me to come and not tell you?"

It *was* odd. "I don't know."

A fissure of worry opened in the back of her

255

mind, just a hairline crack, one that would widen when she lay down at the end of the day. Was there something wrong? His health? Something else?

"How have you been?" he asked. He moved in closer, too close. She stepped away, to put the milk in the fridge. He was the only one who ever asked her that. She and Chad were in communication all day—about all the minutiae of their shared existence: Did you call the plumber? Can you pick up some milk? How did Zoey do on her quiz?—calls, texts, email. He never asked her how she was because he knew, better than anyone.

"You know," she said. What could she say? That her life revolved around Zoey and Chad, that lately she'd been thinking she never should have stopped working, that she wasn't unhappy but that she wasn't happy exactly either. "Same old."

There was the slam of the car door outside, then the sound of Zoey's running feet. She must have seen the truck, burst in the door a few seconds later and straight into Paul's big embrace. He lifted her off the ground, gave her a spin. *How's my girl?*

Then it was the Paul and Zoey Show. Belly laughs and high fives and inside jokes. When Heather watched them together, it was as if something heavy was lifted off of her. She felt a big smile spread across her face. With Chad and Zoey, Heather always wondered who was going to draw first blood.

"Hey, Mom." Zoey leaned in for a kiss; Heather gave her one and a pat on the bottom.

"How was your quiz?"

"I did okay, I think."

She didn't worry about Zoey, her straight-A student, driven like her father, maybe because of him, because nothing was ever quite good enough.

"I'm sure you did fine," she said. And he thought she was too easy. *These kids, they're overpraised. Wait until they find themselves out in the real world. No one's handing out participation trophies there.*

She fed them. They sat to dinner like a family, big bowls of stew and fresh bread from the bakery. She had a glass of wine, felt herself go loose the way she did when Paul was around. Everyone was more relaxed when Paul was at the table, even Chad. It was like his stepbrother brought out everything that was good about him. And there was so much; there really was.

After dinner, Zoey had to go do her homework and Paul looked at his phone.

"He wants me to meet him in fifteen minutes," he said. "Burgers and Brew, just like you said."

"Should I be worried?" asked Heather.

He waved a hand at her. "Nah," he said easily.

"Just work stuff probably. Maybe he just wants to talk through a case."

But there was a frown behind his eyes. He reached for her hand, and it lingered there too long. She let it. He seemed about to say something and then didn't. She heard Zoey's voice upstairs, on the phone, chattering happy and high pitched. At the sound of it, he got up and started clearing the dishes.

It was just one night. And it was so long ago, a million years ago it seemed. It was a mistake buried under the debris of years. It could have been so easily forgotten—if he'd ever married, had kids of his own—except that he didn't and it wasn't. She never forgot it. How could she?

"Leave it," she said. "I'll get it."

He ignored her, helped her load the dishwasher, wipe down the table. She walked him out to his truck.

"I'm glad you came by," she said.

He looked back up at the house, and then into the sky. Then he snaked his arm around her waist and pulled her close. She glanced back around her to Zoey's window, which looked out onto the front of the house.

"Don't."

"I never stop thinking about you," he said, his voice thick. Why this night? Was it just because they were never alone without Chad and Zoey?

"Paul," she said. But she wasn't resisting him.

His thigh against hers, the strength of his arm around her back, her hand on his wide shoulder.

When Chad had been away, some fishing trip she hadn't wanted him to take, a weekend of drunken stupidity that would leave him wrecked for a week, Paul had come. She'd seen his car pull up, watched him walk up the drive. She'd come out to stand on the porch. Neither of them said a word as they moved inside, locked the door. She dissolved into him, disappeared. He took her on the staircase, then on the landing in front of the bedroom. Later in the bed she shared with Chad. Again, downstairs in the kitchen. His scent, the feel of his lips, the gentle, powerful way he held her, the way he moaned, deep and desperate, as if he'd never known pleasure—God, it stayed with her. She'd never made love like that with Chad. Never once.

The thing was that Heather and Chad were never *not* going to be together. He was her first everything. They met in high school, were married before they graduated college. He went on to the police academy; she got her master's in education. Paul was older, already gone to the city while they were still in high school. Paul, Chad's stepbrother, best friend. To her, he was someone mysterious, just out of reach, like the coywolf she sometimes saw on their property lately. Eventually he became her friend, too, later their best man. When had it changed?

It was Christmas. She and Chad had been

married a couple of years, they were trying to have a baby. Had been trying for over a year— and it was starting to become *a thing*. They were stressed about it (he didn't really want kids, did he?) and arguing a lot. She was cooking that holiday. Again. For his family and hers, for friends who had been dropping by all day. The house was crowded, overwarm.

Finally, with the walls closing in on her and the sound of the television and everybody talking at once, she went out back and hid behind the shed where Chad snuck his cigarettes (did he think she didn't know?). She just started crying. It was cold; she was shivering in the thin red cardigan, her breath pluming out with each sob. The sky threatened snow, gray-white above her. Even her feet were cold.

"Hey." Paul came up behind her. "What's up?"

She wiped her eyes, embarrassed. "Nothing," she said. "Just. Everything."

He held her. That was it. Chad would be talking, talking, talking, trying to help, to comfort, to explain why she shouldn't be upset. He'd be telling her to relax, to not take so much on, everything didn't have to be perfect. But Paul didn't say anything, just let her cry until it passed, his arms tight around her.

"I'm sorry," she said. "I'm just—"

She couldn't go on, and anyway he held up a hand. "That's what I'm here for."

His face, angular, icy eyes that were wrinkled with kindness. "You okay?"

"Yes," she said, nodding.

"Let's go back into the fray."

On the way back, his arm around her, they bumped into Chad, who had come out looking for her.

"Sneaking out behind the shed with my wife?" he said when he saw them.

"What can I say, brother?" said Paul. "Women just want me. And you've got to give the ladies what they want."

Paul shifted away from her. But Chad wasn't jealous, not in the least. He was so sure of her, of Paul.

"I hear you, man," he said, dropping his arm around Heather. "You okay, babe?"

"Just—*stressed*."

He squeezed her. "Everything's perfect. Just relax."

That was the day when she started thinking about Paul in ways that she shouldn't. And then that night with Chad off fishing—barely a word spoken between them, just the blessed release of all the tension she'd barely acknowledged. Neither of them ever thought it could be more; there was no discussion about what happened next. There was no torrid affair. Just that one moment in time, separate from the rest of the universe, from who they were outside that moment. Chad's wife, his best friend and brother. Those people didn't exist.

Paul left about an hour before the sun came up, kissing her long at the door.

A month later, she was pregnant with Zoey.

"You'll tell me," Heather said to Paul now. "If there's something I need to worry about."

She glanced up at the window to Zoey's room; the light inside glowed orange.

"I'll make sure *he* tells you," said Paul. "If there is. But I'm sure it's nothing."

It was still there, all these years later. He leaned in and kissed her on the cheek, then pulled away quickly and got in his truck.

twenty

Claudia sat and waited, hearing the horn of the train blowing mournfully in the distance.

I want to come home.

The text had come in from Raven at eleven, just as Claudia had finished her final stubborn attempt to get that goddamn wallpaper down.

I'm on the last train.

She hadn't tracked Raven all night. When Raven was with Ayers, Claudia never worried. But there she was, her little blue dot floating on a faint purple line marked Erie Lackawanna.

She dialed Ayers but just got voicemail. She hung up and texted him.

What happened?

She tried Raven, but the call just went to voicemail. Service on the train was always spotty. After about an hour, she got in the car and went to the station.

I want to come home. The phrase filled her with a kind of strange happiness. Claudia knew

263

she didn't mean the ramshackle old house in Nowhere, New Jersey. It was Claudia, her mother, that was Raven's home. As much as her daughter railed and raged, she still needed her mom.

The train pulled in to the station, and Claudia climbed out of the car. A stunning young woman all in black, followed by a tall young man with a mass of blond curls, exited from the last car. It took her a full second to recognize her own daughter and her daughter's lifelong friend Troy.

When Raven saw Claudia, she broke into an awkward run in boots that Claudia had never seen. Troy was carrying Raven's pack and her jacket.

"What happened?" Claudia asked when Raven fell into her arms.

"Hey, Ms. Bishop," said Troy.

"Troy," said Claudia. "Does your mom know where you are?"

He nodded. "She said it was okay if I brought Raven home and stayed with you."

Lydia was a free-range parent. She treated Troy as if he were a twenty-year-old, and always had. Maybe that's why he acted as if he were so much older, wiser than his years—thoughtful, responsible, just sweet. Or maybe Lydia just got lucky.

In the car, Raven spilled it—how she'd lied, what she'd done. Claudia breathed through it; she didn't want to freak out and have the whole thing turn into a screaming match. But her heart was revving; she could feel the blood rushing through her body, heat coming to her cheeks.

"Raven," she said. They were pulling off the road onto the drive to the house. "What possessed you? To seek him out, the son of the man who—raped me?"

She had to pull the car to a stop, her breath coming sharp and fast. She actually felt dizzy. She rested her head on the steering wheel. She felt Troy's hand on her shoulder from the backseat, and Raven moved in close.

"I'm sorry, Mom," she said. "I didn't think of it like that. I was just looking for the place—where I belong."

She looked at her daughter, whose eyes were wide and filled with tears. "It's right here, with me," Claudia said. "Why don't you get that?"

"I do," said Raven. "I get it. He was so—dark inside. So angry. But he said, 'Why do you think where you come from has anything to do with who you are?' It made sense to me."

Claudia bit back the rise of frustration, exasperation.

"I've said that a thousand times," said Claudia.

"Me, too," said Troy from the backseat.

"We raised you," said Claudia. "We love you. You belong with us."

Raven sobbed.

"You lied to me and to your father," said

Claudia. "You snuck out to some club to meet this kid. What if he'd been dangerous like his father? What if he'd *hurt* you?"

"That's why I brought Troy."

She saw Troy's curls and his round glasses in the rearview mirror. He was still the eight-year-old who skinned his knee in the park and cried quietly while she cleaned and bandaged it. The one who used to sleep in his X-Men sleeping bag on her living room couch, Raven on the other couch in her pink monogrammed one. It was so much easier then. They were always right there, a few steps away.

"Give me those fake IDs, please."

She heard Troy shuffling in the backseat, then he handed them over.

"I'm sorry, Ms. Bishop," said Troy. He didn't follow it with any excuses. She slid the IDs into her bag, took a deep breath, and kept driving.

"Wow," said Troy. "It's really dark here. Look at all those stars."

Normally, Raven would take this opportunity to make some quip about the town or the misery of living in the country, but she just stayed silent, looking out the window, her arms wrapped around her middle.

The windows in the house glowed golden. She must have left every light on.

"How close is the next house?" asked Troy.

"About a mile," said Claudia.

"Wow," said Troy.

"No one can hear me screaming," said Raven under her breath.

Claudia couldn't even muster the energy to respond.

"The place is really starting to come together," Troy said.

He'd carried his and Raven's packs in from the car and placed them by the door. The foyer *was* starting to shape up, and the living room to the right. There was a reclaimed oak table in the dining room, with a mix-match of chairs she'd found online and at various shops in town. The restored chandelier, which Ayers had helped her to hang, was lovely and twinkly. The walls had been painted since Troy's last visit.

In the kitchen, it was a different story. Even though Josh had told her to leave the wallpaper until Monday, she just couldn't let it go. She couldn't admit defeat. She'd cleaned up everything that was on the floor and bagged it. But there were still huge pieces hanging from the walls, every gash a different color or another layer of wall paper underneath.

"It's a look," said Troy.

"Yeah," said Raven. "Demolition chic."

They had a good laugh at that, Raven and Troy, as Claudia put on the kettle for tea. They all sat at the table. It had been here, a thick wood piece and two long benches, one on either side. She'd sanded down and refinished the set, created a centerpiece with a piece of driftwood she bought at a garage sale and some bleached starfish shells.

"There are going to be consequences," said Claudia. "You get that, right? I'll talk to your father and we'll come up with something."

"I know," said Raven.

"But I'm glad you came home," said Claudia, reaching for her daughter's hand. "And I get that we need to have a bigger talk about the issue that's at the root of all of this. I thought I was handling things the right way. I did my best, Raven. I'm sorry you felt like you had to do what you did to find yourself."

"I'm sorry, Mom," said Raven.

Claudia thought she might even mean it.

She made a bed for Troy on the couch and tucked Raven in upstairs. She thought about trying Ayers again but figured it could wait until morning. Exhausted, she climbed into bed and fell asleep crying, thinking about Raven chasing after the son of Melvin Cutter. Claudia was definitely going to need a couple of hours with her therapist after this one.

It was after two when she woke, some sound echoing in the air around her. She lay still a moment, listening. She slipped from bed and peered out her door. She could hear Troy snoring downstairs; Raven's room was dark, the door ajar as she had left it. The floor was cold and creaky beneath her feet.

At her window, she saw that the moon had risen high and full over the trees. That's when she saw the shifting of shadows, a form drifting from the trees dark and silent. He moved quickly, then slipped into the hole where the door had been in the barn. She drew her breath in and stepped back, heart hammering. She saw a faint light then, maybe a flashlight beam, brighten the darkness of the barn just a little.

She reached for the phone and called 911.

"There's an intruder on my property," she said when the operator answered. She gave her address. "He's in the barn."

"Stay inside the house," said the operator. "I'm sending someone right now."

"Okay," said Claudia. Her hands were shaking.

"Do you want me to stay on the phone until they get there?" the dispatcher asked.

"Yes," said Claudia. "There are two children sleeping in the house. Teenagers."

"I'll advise patrol," she said. "Can you see the intruder?"

The light inside the barn went dark, and then the form slipped out again. Claudia strained to see his face, but she couldn't. He was too far, and even though the moon was bright, he seemed composed only of shadow. Then he was moving quickly, away from the house, across the clearing behind the barn and into the trees.

"He's moved from the barn into the woods," she said.

"I'll advise patrol," said the operator again. Calm, professional. Claudia was soothed by her voice.

She heard the sirens then, and a few moments later a prowler moved quickly up the drive— lights flashing but silent. As soon as the vehicle stopped, two officers climbed out, one headed into the barn, the other toward the trees.

"They're here," Claudia said, releasing a breath she didn't know she'd been holding.

"Okay," said the operator. "Stay inside until the officers come to the door. Do you want me to stay on the line?"

"No," said Claudia even though she wanted to say yes. "Thank you."

"You're welcome, ma'am." The operator ended the call.

"Mom," said Raven from behind her. "What's happening?"

"There was someone in the barn," said Claudia. She wiped away at tears—anger, fear, exhaustion. Raven moved up close to look out the window. The officers were returning to the house. Claudia hurried down to meet them.

It was Officer Dilbert again, and another even younger looking officer, this one a female. Raven stayed inside the door, while Claudia went out into the cold, slipping on the slippers she kept by the door.

"We didn't see anyone, ma'am," said Officer Dilbert. "But there were boot prints over by the trees."

"We've had a rash of vehicle and empty home break-ins lately," said the young woman, her thick curls pulled back tight. "Some petty thefts. You said just one intruder?"

"That I saw."

"Also, ma'am?" said Officer Dilbert, seeming more like a teenager than ever. "You know with the history of the property and how long it has stood empty, there are rumors that the place is haunted. So local kids sometimes sneak out here on a dare."

Something about the way he said it, she wondered if he had been one of those kids once.

"You know," said Claudia, "folks keep alluding to the history of this house. But I don't know what you mean. What history?"

The two officers exchanged a look. "Sorry, ma'am," said Officer Dilbert. "I thought you knew."

She shook her head, wrapped her robe tight around her. Dread dug a pit in her stomach. She could feel Raven vibrating behind her.

"Maybe ten years ago now, longer, I guess," he said. "A man—a police officer and his wife were

271

murdered here. They had a young daughter; she survived."

"Murdered?" said Claudia. The word shredded her. How could she not have known this? "How? Why?"

"The perpetrators were never caught," said Officer Dilbert. "But they were allegedly looking for some money that had been stolen. They tortured the family in an attempt to recover it, but as far as anyone knows, that money was never found."

"Some folks think it's out here," said Officer Williams. "They come looking sometimes."

"Of course, it's *not,*" said Officer Dilbert. "Someone would have found it long ago if it was."

Claudia couldn't believe what she was hearing. How could she not have known this? Wouldn't her father have said something if his tenants were murdered on the property he owned? But maybe not. The guy barely ever talked; her most vivid memories of him were of him blanked out in front of some game or reading the paper. She thought back. Ten years—Raven had been small. Maybe it happened when Claudia had been at Martha's place in New Mexico, trying to figure out her life, her marriage. Or maybe news of a murder in the tiny burg of Lost Valley, New Jersey, didn't make it to the city.

She turned back to the house. Raven looked

stricken in the doorway, and Troy had come to stand behind her, his mouth hanging open. The house, so full of promise and possibility, suddenly seemed to radiate menace.

"We can request that your house is put on regular patrol, have a squad car loop the drive once or twice a night. When I'm on duty, I'll be sure to come by. I work graveyard—midnight to eight."

Claudia felt herself nodding.

"Now that you're here, fixing the place up, I bet kids'll stop coming after a while. And if someone's casing the place, a regular patrol might act as a deterrent."

Claudia was still nodding, but she felt like the ground beneath her feet was shifting and shaking. She leaned against the porch step banister to support herself.

"I thought you must have known, Mrs. Bishop."

"No," she said.

"My friend Seth Murphy was the one who called the police that night. We went to school with the girl who lived here—Zoey Drake."

"She lived," Claudia said. The words seemed to float from her lips.

"Are you alright, Mrs. Bishop?" asked Officer Williams. Her deep, black eyes were kind, concerned. Just the sight of her young, sweet face made Claudia want to weep. Again. Some more.

"I'm just—really shocked by this," she said. She let herself sit on the top step. Raven came out to sit beside her. How much worse was this night going to get? Her life? How many shitty, wrongheaded decisions could one person make? It was one thing to be a flaky dreamer when you were young, with a million possibilities ahead. As a forty-year-old mother of a teenager, it was downright dangerous and sad.

"Seth Murphy knows all about the case if you're interested," said Officer Dilbert. "You'll find him in town—or just Google him. He's our local PI."

"A private investigator," she said.

"It was a long time ago, Mrs. Bishop," said Officer Williams. "I don't believe in ghosts. Do you?"

No, she didn't believe in ghosts. The living did far more harm than the dead. After her rape, she'd found herself wondering if violence like that left its mark on you. If it opened a hole in your life where other dark things could crawl through. If after something like that you were a magnet for more ugliness. Her shrink had talked her out of that kind of thinking. And she believed, had to, that she created her life, wasn't just a victim. But sometimes, just sometimes, when she was feeling very sorry for herself, she imagined that she'd stepped into quicksand fifteen years ago and all this time, she'd just been very slowly, a millimeter at a time, sinking beneath the surface.

twenty-one

'␣ve had a family emergency. I can ask the night doorman to look in on the cats until I return. I understand if you need to replace me.
They'll be okay. I'll connect with Charlie.
  How long?
Not sure.
Keep me posted.

Why didn't I just quit? Maybe I would. I was surprised to find that I didn't really want to. The truth was that I had grown to like Nate Shelby's place, his energy, his cats. I actually wanted to go back there, sleep in his white bedroom, watch the cats. Maybe he'd fire me and make it easy.

"You need your own place," said my father in the passenger seat of Paul's Suburban. He had a single bullet hole wound in his forehead tonight. I had never seen him like that, but I knew from the files that I read that it was finally how he died. A bullet in the brain. I remembered the sound of it, the cracking report. It's a distinctive sound. Once you've heard gunfire, you never mistake anything else for it.

"You have to move on and build a real life. You can't keep on like this. You're a ghost."

"You should talk," I said.

"Very funny."

I took the key out of my pocket and looked at it.

"What's this key for, Dad?"

But he was gone, and I was parked outside Seth Murphy's office on Main Street. Seth was into his identity as PI, even had a door with an old-timey cloudy glass window. Seth Murphy Investigations. Background checks. Insurance claims. Missing persons and pets. I actually felt a little bad for Seth, as much as I could feel anything for anyone other than Paul. That night—I think it unstitched him a little bit. Even though he'd just grazed the edges of what happened, it got its hooks in.

He couldn't get out of his house that night; his dad had stayed up later than usual. That's why he was late meeting me. An hour late. He'd run the whole way, arrived breathless at the bridge only to find me gone. He could see footprints in the soft earth leading up the bridge, Catcher's, too. He could tell by the pacing nature of our tracks that maybe we'd waited awhile. He figured that he'd just missed me. So he took off running after us through the woods.

What if he hadn't been late? How long would I have stayed out there with him? Would I have been spared the things that happened to me? Would I have returned home to find my parents murdered, never understanding why? Or would my parents be alive? Probably not. They—those men—they were always going to kill everyone in that house. I wonder if they would have found what they were looking for if it weren't for that siren? Maybe my dad did know. Maybe he finally would have relented and they would have gone. Maybemaybemaybewhatififonlyonandonandon, that terrible spaceless run-on into nothing and nowhere.

Seth followed me that night, saw Catcher lying lifeless on the ground. Saw the parked car, the fourth man inside, sitting still in the passenger seat. He watched as I was dragged out of the barn window and across the clearing, screaming, to the house. He said a kind of shock settled, a paralysis. Then he slipped back, backward into the darkness, turned, and with every ounce of strength and speed, he ran for help. It took him just under twelve minutes to reach the Jacob home, two minutes of frantic pounding and screaming to rouse them from sleep, two minutes to dial 911. It took the police six minutes to race to our house and arrive at the scene. Twenty-two minutes. Within that span of time, I was tortured, and both my parents were killed. Still, he probably saved my life.

Seth was kind of a nerd, which was why I had

liked him. I was never into jocks or bad boys. He was sweet, smart, curious—a great lab partner. He had soft hands, a shy smile. I always thought he'd do something more with his life. Maybe he would have—if he hadn't asked to meet me that night.

I got out of the car and walked through the chill night to knock on the door, the glass cold beneath my knuckles, then again. The street was quiet, deserted—all the businesses shuttered for the night or empty. The recession hit this town hard, and it had not recovered. The coffee shop, the bookstore, the hardware store, all closed. Only the liquor and convenience stores still thrived. There was a pawnshop, too. A store that sold uniforms . . . which survived because most people around here were employed by the hospital two towns over, or the bottle factory just a few miles away. There was a lumber storage warehouse, too, down at the end of the street. Off in the distance, there was nothing but trees. There's always a conflict here, between the lumber companies and all the environmentalists trying to preserve the forest.

I say cut it all down. I hate nature. It has so many ugly secrets. It wants you back, wants to swallow your flesh, suck you back from whence you came. I like steel and concrete glass and engines, metal tracks and rebar. Things that man must wrestle into shape. We build whole cities,

278

just to keep nature away, to show it that we're boss—for a little while anyway.

Seth came to the door finally, wearing a Rutgers sweatshirt, three days of stubble, and dark purple circles under his eyes. He wasn't older than I was, but prematurely gray, he could pass for middle-aged.

"Zoey," he said.

Something weird happened then, a kind of hard flash on the moment when I drove the hunting knife into John Didion's heart. You have to be strong, purposeful to drive a knife blade through the powerful intercostal muscles of the chest. That blade was razor sharp, though—it slid right in, and he had no strength to resist me. It was easy. Didion released a soft wheeze, then slumped against me as if we were intimates. His weight, suddenly a ton, pulled us both to our knees. I pressed that knife in deeper. I felt the life leave him, a drain, a passing, something held then released. Then a strange total silence surrounded us, driving away all the noise from outside. I'd hoped for a blast of rage, or a deep surge of joy that vengeance had been delivered. Anything. Anything but the deep nothingness that followed, the yawning hollow inside me. I sat with Didion awhile, watching his blood spill, thinking of the black pool that my mother had lain in. I waited to feel something. Even remorse. Nothing. What does that make me?

"You look horrible," Seth said. He put on a pair of wire-rimmed glasses and inspected me. "Are you sick?"

Maybe. Yeah. Maybe I am. I caught something that night, and it's been wasting me slowly ever since, eating me from within.

"I thought you might come," he said when I didn't say anything.

He stepped aside, and I walked into the foyer, then followed him up a narrow flight of stairs into a large loft space. The kind of space he had—cavernous with exposed pipes and vents, wood floors—would have cost a fortune in the city. He probably paid less than a grand a month. Tall windows looked out over the other surrounding buildings, to a parking lot, to the woods beyond.

I followed him through the room. There were several desks, all the monitors dark. Each workstation had some personal items—photos of people, kids, pets, a mug that read World's Best Dad, a compact, and lipstick.

"Expanding?" I asked.

We walked through a doorway to his living quarters. A galley kitchen, a tossed bed, a plain gray couch, and an enormous television mounted on the wall. The set was tuned in to CNN, with the sound down. President Obama looked characteristically grim, graying, issued a condemnation of ISIS.

"I hired a couple of people part-time," he said. "They have their own gigs, too, pay me a percentage for office space."

"I wouldn't have thought there would be so many mysteries in a small town."

He snorted.

"There are as many mysteries as there are people," he said. "Life is one big unanswered question."

I nodded, my eyes falling on some pictures on his round kitchen table. A woman, youngish, plain with glasses and some acne scarring, mousy hair. There was a professional portrait where she smiled stiffly, one with a friend, one where she sat awkwardly atop a horse.

"Take Mariah Penny for instance," he said, when he saw me sifting through the photos. "Missing forty-eight days."

"I didn't hear about it."

"Twenty-eight years old, CPA, unmarried, lived alone, caregiver for her aging parents. She left the firm where she worked one night and didn't come home. Somewhere between her office and her nice condo, she and her Mercedes C-Class fell into the vortex."

"Drugs?" I offered. "Depression? Caregiving is hard."

"She is a straight arrow," he said. "A good girl. Cheerful, friendly, helpful by all accounts. No debts. No boyfriends. No secrets."

I sat, continued sifting through his notes and photos. "Maybe she just got sick of it all. Took off."

"No withdrawals or credit card usage since she went missing. Phone off the grid."

"Hmm," I said.

"But you didn't come to talk about that."

"No. This is the endgame," I said. "Rhett Beckham is out of jail and back in town."

He rubbed at the stubble on his jaw, sat heavily on a stool over by the counter. "Living with the brother."

"I'm not interested in the brother," I said.

Josh Beckham tried to help me. He was a kid like me that night. It was Didion, Rhett Beckham, and the fourth man that I needed. One down, two to go. Closure.

I reached into my pocket and felt for the key. It was smooth and cold beneath my fingertips.

"What about the fourth man?" I asked. "Any progress?"

Something—quicksilver—flashed across his face. Sadness. Fear.

"What is it?" I asked. He moved from the stool and sat across from me at the table. He folded up the file, Mariah's bespectacled visage disappearing from view.

Seth had long claimed that there was someone waiting in the car that night. He saw the shadow of a figure. I never saw him. Boz wondered if maybe in his state of shock, Seth had been mistaken. But Seth was certain, and I believed him. We'd spent a lot of time talking about him, the fourth man. Who waits in the car? The boss? Maybe Whitey Malone himself, not wanting to get his hands dirty but not trusting his thugs not to run off with the money.

The police questioned Seth vigorously. Had he lured me from the house on purpose? Had someone asked him to do it? Paid him to do it? No, he swore. There was no evidence to the contrary. What did the fourth man look like? He was big. A bulky shadow, wider than the seat he was in. And he smoked. Seth saw the plumes drift up from the open window, the glowing orange tip. But that was it.

Seth and I always stayed in touch. I wouldn't say we were friends, like Boz and I weren't friends. We just shared the same obsession. It bonded us. It has only been the last few months that we've actively been working together, though.

"I want to show you something," he said. "Something I've been working on. Kind of a fluke, really."

He got up and spun around one of the case boards. He flipped on a lamp sitting atop one of the desks and shined it like a spotlight on the clutter that hung there. There were maybe half a dozen photographs pinned, ordered by date, starting about a year earlier, each captioned with a note in Seth's tight, tidy handwriting, addresses, some news articles.

October 3, 2016, Riverside and Ninety-Sixth Street. A slim hooded figure stopped mugging in progress, injuring the perpetrator with a low kick that fractured his shin.

Hanging above these notes, a grainy image showed a man on the ground, gripping his leg, his face a mask of pain, a woman standing stunned, cell phone in hand. In the background, said slim, hooded figure strode away.

There were others.

East Village, November 12, 2016. A little boy pulled from the subway tracks where he'd fallen, apparently pushed by his mother's boyfriend.

The hooded figure is caught mid-leap from the platform, the light from on the oncoming train a moon in the distance.

Harlem, December 1, 2016. A homeless man is saved from a group of marauding teens. Hooded figure delivers a blow to the bridge of the biggest boy's nose with

284

the heel of her hand. Boy tells cops: It was a girl!

Eyes everywhere. Sloppy. On those endless romps I take through the city, every now and then I come across a situation that demands involvement. There were other incidents, too; they just happened not to be caught on film.

"What's all this?" I asked, leaning in closer to pretend to take a closer look.

Seth flipped over our case board, the one we'd been working on, compiling all the events related to my parents' murder, beginning with the drug dealer robbery, our list of suspects, speculations about the fourth man—Whitey himself? Hired man? Dirty cop?—to the whereabouts of each of them. Seth had added a new element, a new story about Didion's death. And that grainy image captured by the camera across the street.

"The vigilante thing—if you want to call it that," said Seth. "It's been kind of a pet project for me. I first noticed it last year—a *Daily News* crime beat reporter did a small piece about that thwarted mugging. Then things starting turning up on Twitter. It's just interesting, you know? Some hooded girl, fighting crime in the city."

I don't feel fear. Not anymore. My heart doesn't race at much. It takes quite a bit to get my adrenaline pumping. Seth, on the other hand, when he turned to face me, was sweating. He dug his hands deep into his pockets.

"It's odd, you know. This girl, she stops bad things from happening. Which is cool. But here"—he tapped at the case board—"if this is her, and I think it is. She killed John Didion in cold blood. Or so it seems."

"So?"

"It's not like her," he said. He sounded worried, disappointed, like a kid who wanted to believe in Santa Claus.

"You know her?" I asked. "What's she like? Who is she really, inside?"

"I thought I did."

I felt the color come up on my cheeks, turned away from his sad gaze. He rubbed a hand over his sizeable belly, then took off his glasses to squeeze at the bridge of his nose.

"Seth," I said. "Have you made any progress on the fourth man?"

There was that look again. He held my eyes for a moment, like he was expecting me to say something. But I didn't.

"Maybe," he said finally. He turned the board around again. "But you're not going to like it."

My dad stood stone-faced in the corner, he nodded at me to look down. When I did, my hands were slick with blood.

I didn't need Seth—or Mike, or anyone—to tell me that I'd crossed a line. It wasn't an accident.

286

Why was everyone so surprised? What did they think I was going to do after I finally caught up with the men who murdered my parents? Bring my case again to the police, beg them to reexamine evidence that wasn't new? Even if they did finally see what Boz, Seth, and I believed to be true, would we seek justice via the courts and prison system? No. No. That's never what I wanted. What is the difference between justice and revenge? Justice is a concept, one agreed upon by a civilized society. Revenge is wild and raw, it's a balancing of the scales of the universe.

My mother wasn't supposed to be there that night. Her high school friend was getting married in Key West. She wanted to go, and she wanted Dad to go with her, their first long weekend away together in years. But he couldn't—or wouldn't—go with her. Because, as I saw it, he could never do any of the things that she wanted or needed him to do, even the little things. All he cared about was the job and disciplining me so that I didn't grow up into a "spoiled, pampered princess." Paul even said he'd stay the weekend so that they could go. But no.

"Go," my dad told her. "Have fun. I can't get away right now."

"You can't get away for a weekend?" I could tell she was upset, even though her demeanor was calm. She did this tapping thing with her foot.

"I have responsibilities, an open case."

"The case of the missing yard tools?" A rare moment of sarcasm.

"Hey, people breaking and entering, stealing private property is not a joke."

"Fine," she said. "I'll go alone, then."

Neither of us thought she would really go. But she bought her ticket. She offered to take me, too. But I made some excuse. My shrink always wondered about this, why I didn't want to go, why I'd prefer to stay home with my father than spend a sunny weekend in Florida. I hated having to choose between them, but there was a big part of me that feared my father's disapproval more than mom's disappointment.

I walked her out to her car that night, my dad stayed sulking in front of the television. She kissed me on the forehead.

"Take care of your dad."

It sounded weirdly final, and I felt a shiver of dread and regret. I should have said yes; I should have gone with her. Another part of the reason I didn't want to go was because of Seth. I wanted to meet him that night at the bridge.

"Don't go," I said. I held on to her.

"I have to."

"It's just a wedding."

She smiled at me, ran a gentle hand down the side of my head. Other than the minor dustups in moments of stress, I don't remember her ever

288

getting truly angry with me my whole life.

"You'll understand when you get older. Sometimes you have to do things—just to do them. Just because if you don't, you're saying who you are. And you don't want to be that person. I don't want to be the person who never goes anywhere or does anything. There's a big world out there." She looked around, her pale eyes sad. "It's not just this little place."

I had no idea what she was talking about, not really.

"He's mad."

"Let him be mad," she said. "Just do your own thing. That's what I'm going to do. For once."

But a few hours later, after we'd eaten in silence the dinner that she'd left for us, she came back. Her flight had been canceled, bad storms in Florida. The next flight wasn't until tomorrow, and even if she took it, she'd miss the wedding. She looked smaller, deflated somehow, as my dad helped her off with her coat.

"I'm sorry, Heather," he said.

He took her into a rare hug, and I watched her sink into him. He meant it. He was sorry—that he didn't go with her, that her flight had been canceled, that she'd miss her friend's wedding. And more—there was so much more to the whole thing. I get that now.

"I know you are," she said.

They stayed that way, kind of holding each other, swaying, for a long time. I left them to whatever grown-up thing they had going on. All I remember thinking was that I was glad I didn't have to spend the next few days alone with my dad.

Boz came back to that again and again. Turns out that Mom's flight wasn't canceled at all. Security cameras caught her entering the lot and taking her long-term parking ticket. A couple of hours later, she exited. She never went into the terminal.

She must have just sat in the car all that time, then, for whatever reason, finally decided to come home. Why? Why didn't she just go?

For a while, suspicion turned to her. Had she met someone there? Had she hatched some plan, then changed her mind? Had it all gone wrong somehow? Crazy. My mom—she was the best person. Kind, thoughtful, faithful, loving. She never even got a parking ticket, freaked out if she found an overdue library book in my room. There just aren't too many people like her in the world.

I wanted to lay eyes on Rhett Beckham. But as I left Seth's, I got a text from Mike.

He's awake and asking for you. Come to the hospital.

And those goddamn cats, Tiger and Milo, they were weighing on my mind. Milo was just a kitten; he needed attention.

I drove by my old house. I couldn't see it from the road, but I could just make out its shape through the trees, the golden lights of the windows. Then I veered off that road and took the one that led to the Beckhams'. Their house was not visible at all. The mailbox at the bottom of the drive was tilted; I noticed a tire track up its side, as if it had been run over and then hastily righted again. It wasn't like Josh Beckham to leave something like that unattended. He must have been unsettled by Rhett's return. I sat a minute, waiting for I don't know what.

Then I gunned the engine and headed back to the city.

twenty-two

When Claudia woke, the bright sun washing in through the gauze of her curtains, she was happy. It was her natural state, a kind of open welcoming of what came next, an inherent optimism.

But slowly, as she stretched, it came back. Raven, the news about the house, the shadowy figure she'd seen. Of course, there were other things, too. The chaos of her kitchen—and the rest of the house, for that matter. And money. Always money. Her accounts were dwindling, credit card balances climbing. She wasn't going to ask Ayers for money; he already paid most of Raven's expenses. She'd left her decent-paying publishing job to take on this project, that optimism of hers in full gear. *You don't achieve extraordinary things without taking extraordinary risks.* That was her mantra; who'd said it? Maybe she'd read it on Pinterest. Shit.

By the time her feet were on the cold wood floor, it had draped itself around her like a cloak. Not despair. No, not that dark, slick-walled abyss—been there, done that, wasn't going back. But more a kind of malaise, a generally blue-to-shades-of-black mood.

Downstairs, Troy was in the kitchen brewing

coffee. He knew his way around the kitchen by now, always felt at home with her and Raven, because he was. She sat and stared at him a minute, the young man in her kitchen. How tall he was, how handsome, how he'd grown. Weren't they just seven, Troy and Raven? Weren't they all just baking cookies together, five minutes ago, their little fingers covered in sprinkles, flour in their hair? There was a weird relationship that sprung up between a mother and her child's close friends. You were part parent, and part friend yourself. She felt like Troy belonged to her in a way. When he was in her home, she was responsible for him. Claudia and Troy had their own private jokes, a shared knowledge and love for Raven. There was an intimacy, and a distance.

"I like it here," he said. "It's so quiet."

"You weren't scared," she said. "After last night."

"Nah," he said. He was the kind of kid who smiled even when he was nervous or sad.

"Thank you for taking care of Raven last night," she said. "You're a good friend."

He did that kind of shrug-nod thing that teenage boys do when they don't know what to say.

"What was he like? Andrew Cutter." She hated herself for asking. "Did he look like her?"

"Honestly," said Troy, stopping with the pot hovering over her cup. "He seemed like a dick. And no, I don't think he looked much like her.

I think Raven looks like you and Mr. Martin."

She looked away from Troy so that he wouldn't see her tear up. He finished pouring. He even knew how she liked her coffee—light with two sugars, though she'd only allow herself one. He set the cup in front of her and sat down.

"Don't they, like, have to disclose something like that?" he said. "About the house, I mean."

"God!" Raven entered the room like a tiny storm, a beautiful bluster. "I had crazy nightmares!"

She breezed by the table, leaving the scent of lilac behind her. Claudia knew that Raven had not had nightmares, that even after everything, the girl had slept like the dead. Claudia had checked on them both every hour, kept looking out the window. Claudia had barely slept a wink.

"Well, I didn't buy the property," she said to Troy. "I inherited it. So no one had to disclose anything. And I didn't really do any research."

"Aunt Martha said that you've always been prone to impulsive action. Is that what she meant?" said Raven with mock innocence. "Hey, let's renovate the murder house!"

Claudia ignored her, sipped her coffee.

"I did some research," said Troy. He glanced down at his enormous smartphone. The thing was practically a tablet. "Like the cop said, a police officer and his wife, renters of the property, were murdered. Their daughter, Zoey, was—"

He paused and looked up at her, worry creasing his brow.

"Go ahead," Claudia said.

"She was tortured, shot, and left for dead," he said. "But she survived."

Raven had grown still, looked down at her nails, leaned on the edge of the sink.

"The theory was that the cop, Chad Drake, was dirty. He'd stolen money from a drug dealer, and the men who came were trying to find it."

"Where did you find this?" Claudia asked, amazed.

"There are a bunch of old articles in area papers," he said.

How could she not have known this? Of course, she'd done no research on the house at all. She'd obtained a survey from the city. But that was it. She planned to, of course, when it was time to start writing the book. But, as far as she knew, it was just an old ramshackle house, whatever history it might have had was long forgotten. If there'd been extensive news coverage of the event when it happened more than a decade ago, she'd missed it, wrapped up, she supposed, in the drama of her own life then.

Troy pushed his glasses up; they'd drifted down his nose. For a second, he was seven years old again.

"The money," he went on. "It was never recovered."

"How do they know that the killers didn't get the money?" Raven asked. "Used it to disappear."

"Because of the girl," said Troy. "She says her father had no idea what they were talking about. They didn't find what they were looking for. Shot her and her father when they heard sirens and ran."

There was the sound of blood rushing in Claudia's ear.

"The mother died right here, in the kitchen," said Troy. He looked around the room. "The father died in the basement."

"Jesus," said Claudia. She dropped her head into her palm. "Jesus."

Nobody said anything for a moment, two. Then,

"So that money?" said Raven. "It could still be here?"

Claudia looked up at her daughter, who had some kind of dark glee thing going on, as if they were watching a movie or acting out a scene. The horror of it was distant, insubstantial to her. But not to Claudia. She felt as though someone had dug a valley through her middle.

"There probably was never any money," said Claudia. "Officer Dilbert said that people have been sneaking out here, looking for years."

"You should totally blog about this," said Raven, coming to sit beside Claudia.

She looked at her daughter. She still had raccoon eyes, her eyeliner from last night smudged into the valleys there.

296

"Don't think I'm going to let this drama distract me from what you did last night," she said. "We have a lot to talk about today. And I have to call your father."

Raven picked at the black nail polish on her fingernails.

"I know," she said. "And we are going to talk about it. But didn't you say that the next time Troy or Dad was here, we were going to ask for help with the basement?"

"You think that's where it might be?" said Troy.

"Where else?" said Raven. "It's the only place we haven't really explored."

"It's not safe down there," said Claudia. "The beams need support."

Raven and Troy got to chattering about it. And Claudia tuned them out. She got up and moved toward the window over the sink. That's when she saw him, Scout. He moved from the woods and loped along the tree line, just a shadow. Raven and Troy didn't even notice him; they were already on their way down to the basement. The whole house thundered with the sound of them on the stairs.

Scout turned to look at her, his fur silver in the morning light. Then he was gone.

Claudia followed the kids. It *was* past time to explore the basement. Raven was right; the only place in the house she hadn't tackled. And with the kids here, it didn't seem so scary after all. The engineer said that he didn't think there was immediate danger of more collapse. But that building a support structure should be a priority. That's what she'd have Josh do first.

"Be careful down there, kids," she said, heading down after them.

A couple of hours later, they were all sneezing from mold and the filth kicked up by moving boxes. There was just the dim light of a few hanging bulbs. And enthusiasm was waning.

"What is all this *junk?*" complained Raven.

Books, boxes of them, old clothes, a man's, a woman's—old bills, tax documents, Social Security statements, magazines, more books. There were tools, old furniture, posters, cheap décor art. All of it belonging to the Drakes. Everything important must have gone to the girl, and all the rest of it was left behind, trash, the detritus left when a life concludes. Claudia's dad was lazy. He probably just had someone box it up and store it in the basement. Or he hadn't even known it was still there. As far as Claudia knew, he'd never set foot on the property after buying it. He was like that, always acting on whims. Leaving someone else to clean up the mess. Now she'd have to do it. Who would she even call to help her get rid of this stuff? Josh. He'd know what to do.

"Maybe it's in one of *these* boxes," said Raven.

They'd opened almost every one; there was just one more stack that they hadn't reached yet. That's what it took to motivate a teenager: the prospect of a million dollars.

"Maybe someone already found it," said Troy. He issued a startling loud sneeze.

"Or it was never here," said Claudia. With the kids down here, sneezing, joking, the lights on, illuminating most of the darkness, the place didn't have the energy of murder or terror. It was just a space, cluttered, dank. Maybe Raven was right. Maybe she *should* blog about it. After all, it was relevant to her journey. And monsters lived in the dark. Once you started shining light, most bad things withered and shrunk away, even memories.

"What would you have done?" she asked her daughter who had sunk down onto her haunches, looking exhausted. "I mean, if you felt some kind of connection to at-angry-young-man."

It was fine to do that. They always leapt between open topics of conversation.

"I don't know," Raven said.

"Maybe I've never said this," said Claudia. "But in my deepest heart, I believe that you are Ayers's child. He *is* your father. That's the biggest reason why we didn't get the test."

Raven bobbed her head thoughtfully. Claudia probably had said it, a million times or more. It was the truth. Or it had become the truth over time.

"I didn't feel anything, though," Raven said. "I didn't feel a connection to Drew. I didn't even like him."

Claudia saw Troy smile a little behind Raven. Claudia felt the energy of a smile, too.

Claudia rested on a large workbench. It was tall, attached to the concrete wall. When her hand settled on an old flashlight, she knocked the item against her palm and was surprised when it turned on, casting a bright beam on the cinderblocks all around them.

Raven heaved a sigh.

"Let's forget it," she said. "There's nothing down here but junk."

Claudia wasn't looking for the money, though. There definitely wasn't a million dollars of stolen drug money in her basement. Her life *did not* work that way.

The kids headed up the stairs, but Claudia stayed a minute in the dim quiet, surrounded by the mess. Raven's and Troy's heavy footfalls upstairs caused a light shower of dust from the ceiling—not a good thing. If the beams were unstable, did that mean that the floor above was, as well? It was the dining room above her, the room that probably got the least foot traffic. Would the next sound she heard in the night be the table crashing through the floor?

All around her was debris, old junk that no one wanted piled high, the piece of beam that had fallen tilting in line with the staircase. It was an exhausting mess, something that seemed utterly beyond her abilities to fix or clean up. She tried not to see it as an allegory for her life. But, of course, it was. That was the whole point of the blog. She took her phone out of her pocket and snapped a few pictures. Then she headed upstairs to write it all out.

twenty-three

When I got to the hospital, the room was dark and Paul was on oxygen still. Mike wasn't there, but a slim nurse stood over Paul's bed, her fingertips resting gently on his wrist. I moved inside and waited for her to finish writing in his chart.

"Are you his daughter?" she asked.

She was young with caramel skin and a pile of curls tied up on the top of her head, deep-brown eyes. The whirring of the machine, the beeping of the heart monitor was a strange, sad song.

"Yes," I said. What was the point in trying to explain when that was as close to the truth as I could get?

"He's stable," she said.

"Better?"

"Stronger," she said. "Yes. He's fighting."

I looked at him, narrow in the sheets, still. The most important battles are fought within.

"He was awake earlier?" I asked.

"For a little while," she said. "Your friend said he would get in touch with you."

"I got here as fast as I could."

She nodded, put a comforting hand on my arm. She looked at me, those eyes connecting with mine. She knew things about life and death that other people didn't know; that knowledge had gathered somehow in the kind, crinkled corners of her gaze. There was a light there, a flat dark, too. I kept myself all wrapped up, held everything inside the shell of myself. But some people give off energy, something warm, positive. She was one of those. Her nametag read: Rose. "He should rest."

"I won't stay long."

I pulled up a chair and sat beside him.

I was buzzing with a million questions. But he seemed far away, his hand limp in mine, the mask over his face. He was on the moon and I was on the earth looking up at him.

"He loved her," said my father from the corner. "You know that."

"Everybody loved her," I said.

"No one more than he did," he said. "I always knew, of course. I didn't blame him."

"What are you saying?"

"I'm saying that we were all people," he said. "Young once like you are now, full of bad ideas, mistakes, errors in judgment."

"Did you rob those men?" I asked. "Did you take that money? When they came, did you know where it was?"

But, of course, he didn't answer me because he wasn't there. John Didion had taken his place; he was bleeding from the wound in his heart. Black blood was a river down his shirt; it dripped

303

slowly into a pool between his feet. His face was blank, eyes looking off into whatever place it was beyond. He didn't accuse or stare at me.

"Who hired you?" I asked him. A smarter person would have asked that question before I drove the knife deep into his heart. The Red Hunter isn't known for her patience. But maybe the truth was I didn't really want to know the answer.

John Didion gave nothing. Just stood there.

I sat with Paul for a while waiting for some flicker from him.

"I have questions, Uncle Paul," I whispered. "And I have some things to tell you. I need you. Please."

But there was nothing, just his labored breathing, not even the faintest squeeze of his fingers, and finally I left.

I was so out of it, so in my own head that I never heard them coming. Some street fighter I turned out to be.

I parked the truck in a lot near Nate Shelby's loft and walked the distance back. I was watching the video screen in my head—Boz, Seth, the pictures on Seth's board, the old house, the Beckhams' place, the things Seth had said— all the pieces turning, jumbled, never coming together. It was right there, wasn't it? I couldn't or didn't want to see how it all gelled.

The first blow came hard from behind, taking me down to my knees. There were two of them, masked, much larger than me. A foot to my back lay me flat on the concrete, chin scraping hard, head knocking. The next blow was a merciless kick to the ribs that left me breathless, a scream lodged somewhere deep in my throat, no air to push it out. All I saw were stars, two masked faces, white eyes, holes for mouths. Silent. Hands on me, arms pulled behind my back. I couldn't even move, stunned, pain exploding white and hot inside. A blow to the stomach, and the hard black point of an elbow coming in fast, connecting to my jaw. And that was it. Black.

Hey! Hey! I heard as I disappeared. *Get away from her. I called the police.*

Next, the cool white of the lobby. A man leaning over me, a crazy pile of hair, familiar kind, worried eyes. Brown. Brown eyes, brown skin. Who was it?

"Little girl?" he said. "Wake up."

The night doorman. Charlie. "I'm going to call the ambulance."

"No," I managed, pushing myself up in time to turn over and puke on the marble floor. It splattered there, ugly and rank.

"Okay," he said, holding up his palms. "Okay. I'll get the mop."

I couldn't believe it. I'd been jumped, never saw it coming. Never got a blow in. I was just like any other girl in the city, vulnerable, a victim. Fuck me. I could taste blood, but all my teeth seemed to be where they belonged; that was good. Ribs bruised, not broken; there wasn't enough pain. My ears were still ringing. It wasn't a real beating. If it had been, I'd be in the back of an ambulance, bleeding on the inside. Those men were big; with the right kind of blows they could have easily killed me. Amateurs.

I patted my jacket. My wallet was still there on the inside pocket. It wasn't a random mugging.

The night doorman came back with a bucket and a mop.

"I'm sorry," I said, trying to stand. "I'll clean it."

"Just sit," he said. "You know how many people have puked in this lobby?"

I looked around at the white leather furniture, the black-veined marble floor, the white carpet, the lacquer cubes that served as coffee tables. "One?"

"That's right," he said with a nod. "You're the first."

I found myself smiling a little, painfully.

"Your face," he said. "You're going to need some ice." I caught my reflection in the glass that looked out onto the courtyard. Even in the dark reflection there I could see the purple swelling. Perfect.

I watched helpless, weak, and wobbly as he

mopped until all evidence was removed. The floor gleamed.

"They dug around in your pockets. Get your wallet?"

I shook my head. I already knew what they were looking for. I'd figured that much out. I reached into my jeans and, sure enough, the key was gone. I felt a hard pulse of anger, more than that: fear.

He held out a hand to me.

"How are the cats?" I said.

He smiled. "I just checked on them an hour ago."

"I might have to leave again," I said.

I dropped my hand in his, used it to pull myself up. The warmth of him, the softness, it surprised me. I never touched anyone like that except for Paul or Mike. All the touching I did—striking, punching, throwing, knee, elbow, fist, worse. I adjusted the girls' bodies, my students. Not much caressing, hand holding.

"Let me know," he said.

How old was he? I couldn't tell. Forty, fifty? Older? His white teeth gleamed; eyes sparkled with something. Mischief? No. A kind of wisdom with a sense of humor about it. "Sure you don't want the police? A doctor?"

I shook my head. He followed me to the elevator, pressed the button. My legs felt weak beneath me; my stomach still roiling. I hadn't even had time to think about who it was. The same people who tossed Paul's apartment? Someone else? Only a couple of people knew about that key, all of them people I trusted completely.

"Never trust anyone," my father said helpfully inside the elevator. Charlie rode up with me. "People are motivated by their own self-interest only. Only."

Charlie opened Nate Shelby's door for me, let me inside. The cats rushed to greet us like dogs, purring, Tiger even reaching up for me. I leaned down to get him, righted myself before I toppled over, held on to his furry softness, buried my face in this fur.

"You should get some rest," said Charlie. "Why don't you? No one's going to bother you here."

He patted his jaw. "And don't forget the ice."

After he left, I could barely stand. I stripped off my bloody clothes and let them lay in a pile on the floor. The last thing I should do was sleep, but the body has limits. I fed the cats, cleaned the litter, took a shower. After, I stood in front of the floor-to-ceiling mirror and regarded myself. Too thin, scarring on my torso, my arms, the mark of my father's blade. Face swollen, light purple on the jawline, the hint of a shiner. I tilted my face up to see the scar that ran along the underside of my jaw. They had all faded, just henna lines on my white skin, raised just slightly, dead of feeling.

It had been so long since I looked at myself,

really looked. I spent a lot of time dodging my reflection, trying to be invisible. I had become invisible to myself. I looked at the paper-white of my skin, the way my collarbone and ribs pushed at my skin, the tight sinewy muscles of my arms and legs, the strain and fatigue on my face. I was a stranger. A ghost, my not-father had called me.

Then I fell into the white bliss of Nate Shelby's bed.

"It's still there in that house," said my father hovering beside me. "It has been all this time."

"Who hid it there?" I asked. "Who?"

twenty-four

Where have you been?" asked Josh.

Mom was still upstairs sleeping; she usually didn't get up until after eight. She'd been asking for Rhett since last night before bed. And Josh had lied, telling her he was working late on the town house job Josh had accepted. One of the contractors had reached out to him, asking if Josh could do all the floorboards and crown molding, installing and painting. It was an assignment Josh could not have accepted if Rhett had not come on; it was too much work for one person. He'd even thought for a second, happily, that maybe it could be a good thing that Rhett had come back. Now he could take on more. Idiot. Though there had been a moment, a pause, when Josh told Bruce that Rhett was back and working with him. But Josh and Bruce had always been good, so the other man just nodded, handed him the materials list and the corporate credit card.

Josh waited an hour for Rhett, using the time to set up the saw, do the measuring, then he just started the cutting. If there had been two of them, one would cut and the other would install. He started after the crew had left for the day at five because it was awkward work walking through the boxy rooms with the long pieces of wood.

It was 10:30 when Josh realized Rhett just wasn't going to show. He was about half where he needed to be if he was going to finish the job on time. He'd have to call Todd, see if he would work a double with him on Sunday (and of course he'd have to pay Todd, cutting into their profit). Josh had to laugh at himself as he locked up the site. He should have known. He did know.

"That's good," his mom said, when Josh told her he'd left Rhett behind working. "Your dad would be so happy."

Except no. Josh didn't think Dad would be happy. Because he knew what Rhett was. He got it toward the end. Rhett was a destroyer. Once upon a time, it had been his dad's hope that Josh and Rhett would take over his thriving business. And that they'd both have families. And that after church each Sunday everyone would gather around that table he'd made for a big dinner. And the grandkids would run around, laughing and playing.

Not that his eldest son—the killer, the felon—would return after ten years away to destroy what little was left of their father's paltry, poor-man's dreams.

"I answer to you now?" Rhett dropped the keys on the table hard. Josh felt himself startle, start to cower inside. He almost backed right down, just plain walked away. But no.

"Yeah," he said instead. "You kind of do. You

311

wanted work. I gave it to you. You didn't show, and now I'm behind on the town houses."

Josh had been to see Lee, his sponsor, about Rhett coming home and the feelings it brought up. Josh hadn't had a drop of booze—or any other substance—in seven years. Last night, he'd had to white-knuckle it past the wine and beer at the grocery store.

You are not the boy you were, Lee had told him. *You are a business owner, a man who takes care of his ailing, elderly mother. You've made a life. You are not his kid brother anymore. He can't bully you and force you to do things you don't want to do.* And with Lee, that sounded right and Josh felt strong. But there was some kind of energy that came off of Rhett, a dark magnetism. It snared him like invisible grappling hooks, and tugged at him.

"Well, well," said Rhett. "Big boss man."

"I wouldn't have taken that job without you," said Josh. "I have a reputation."

Rhett let out a whoop at that.

"Shh," said Josh. "She's still sleeping."

"A *reputation* now," said Rhett.

"The business," said Josh. "I'm fair. I'm honest. I finish what I start on time and on budget."

Rhett lifted his palms. "Okay, okay," he said.

His brother walked over to the refrigerator and pulled out a six-pack he'd stashed in there. No alcohol of any kind in the house, not even cough medicine or mouthwash. That was like AA 101. And beer was Josh's gateway substance. Once he'd had a few of those, there was nothing else he wouldn't do. Rhett held out a beer to Josh, who shook his head.

"That's right," said Rhett. "Clean and sober. Good for you."

Rhett cracked open the beer, and just the sound was enough to start that ache for it. He could taste the tingle on his tongue, feel the cold in the back of his throat—the way all the hard edges smoothed right out after that first sip, the warmth in his center. Josh took and released a breath, looked away.

"Aren't you sick of it all?" asked Rhett. There was some kind of light in his eyes now. Josh recognized it. Damn if it didn't excite him as much as it scared the hell out of him, that look.

"Working for all of them?" said Rhett. "Doing the shit jobs they offer you?"

Something tickled in the back of his mind. Something ugly. "No," he said. "I like what I do, the people that I do it for."

Rhett frowned, shook his head like Josh was the biggest idiot he had ever seen.

"So, if you won the lotto," he said. "You'd still be doing it?"

Josh pushed out a breath. "I'm not going to win the lotto," he said. "And neither are you."

Rhett pulled up a chair and sat across from

Josh, leaned extravagantly across the table. He smiled, bright and wolfish.

"Oh no?"

"No."

"It's there, Josh," said Rhett. "It's been there all this time."

Rhett lay a copper key on the table between them. Josh didn't have to ask him what he was talking about. The guy was obsessed with that fucking money.

Rhett pulled some folded pieces of the paper from his pocket, blue legal-sized sheets. He lay them out over the key, flattening the creases with his big calloused hands. Josh recognized it immediately as the survey for the Bishop property. Claudia had them tacked up on her refrigerator.

"How'd you get those?"

"Missy works in records now," he said. "We stayed in touch. She's still smoking hot, you know."

Missy. Rhett's old high school sweetheart. She was hot the way a cattle prod was hot. She was the only person Josh knew who was as mean and sadistic as Rhett. In high school, she worked in a vet's office. The rumor was that she was the one who volunteered to put the animals down.

"Look closely," said Rhett. "What do you see?"

Josh looked. "Nothing," he said. "Just the house and the barn. I've been through every inch of both."

Rhett tapped on the page, between the two

314

structures. Josh leaned in close to see two faint blue lines.

"What's that?" he asked, digging through his memory for the various survey codes and markings. "Plumbing? Electric?"

Rhett shook his head, that smile practically gleaming. "It's a tunnel, connecting the two buildings."

Josh leaned in to take a closer look.

"I don't know," said Josh. He'd never seen anything in the house or the barn that looked like any kind of door. But to be honest, and maybe Rhett picked up on this, when Josh was looking for that money, a big part of him was trying to prove that it *wasn't* there. Because he didn't want it to be. They'd done a horrible thing; they didn't deserve a big reward. Now that Rhett was back, the enterprise of looking had taken on a different energy.

Rhett fished the key out from under the papers. "That's where it is. Has to be, baby brother. There has to be access from the house, probably in the basement. A million dollars just sitting there, waiting for us."

The basement was a disaster. Truth was—those fallen beams, the mess down there, the heavy mold in the air—maybe. Maybe he hadn't looked as hard as he could have.

Josh nodded toward the key. "Where did you get that?"

"Never mind."

"You've been talking to him," said Josh. "The old man."

"He says he had his doubts until now," he said. "Something happened. Something to do with Didion's murder."

Josh blew out a long breath. "Let me guess."

"He says if we go back for it, we split it with him. Fifty-fifty."

"If he's so sure it's there and he knows where it is," asked Josh, "what does he need us for? Why doesn't he go back for it himself?"

"Hey," said Rhett. "I don't look a gift horse in the mouth, you know."

"We get half," said Josh. "And you and I split that?"

"Well, we have to cut Missy in."

"Wait," said Josh. "She knows about it? About everything?"

"She's cool," said Rhett. "Don't worry."

God, Rhett was so fucking stupid.

"So we do all the work, take all the risk. He gets half, and you and I each get a quarter. Minus whatever you promised Missy. Who now knows what we've done, what we're about to do."

"She always knew," said Rhett, with a wave of his hand. "She's been cool all this time. Anyway, look. If it weren't for him, we wouldn't even *know* about the money. We never would have known about it. Think of him as a contractor;

316

we're doing the work for him that he doesn't want to or have time to do for himself."

Josh wished with all of his heart and soul that they didn't know about the money, that they never had. That Rhett hadn't come into his room that night, that he hadn't gone with his brother. How, how would his life have turned out differently if he'd only had a backbone?

"No one will get hurt this time, if that's what you're worried about," said Rhett, making his voice softer.

"That's what you said last time."

He still dreamed about it. He still heard the girl and the woman screaming, still saw their eyes wide and wet with terror and confusion. The woman, she begged for her daughter. *Please,* she said with her last breath. *Please don't let them hurt her.*

"It wasn't me," said Rhett. "It was Didion."

That was a lie. It was both of them, two wolves in a pack, taking their fill.

That's the thing about addiction, Lee always said. *It's not the substance you're addicted to. It's the person you are, the way you feel, when you're high or stoned or drunk.*

Looking into his brother's face was like looking into the amber face of a cold beer or smelling that first tang on the air when someone lit a joint. It wasn't the taste, the first drag, it was the moment right after when Josh's whole body

317

seemed to release the tension it was holding, when everything that worried or frightened him just receded like players from a stage.

There was something about who he was when Rhett was around. It was like Rhett knew that somewhere inside his little brother, down deep, there was a guy who wasn't that much different than Rhett. There was something dark hidden inside Josh, like a feral animal in a burrow, one that only needed to be lured out.

Rhett took a long swallow of his beer. Corona Extra. Rhett never bothered with the lime.

"We could be drinking this on a beach in Anguilla," said Rhett. "And think about Mom. Think about how comfortable we could make her."

Josh shook his head, had to smile. Rhett knew. He knew how to push every single button.

"And what if it isn't there?" said Josh. "What if that's just plumbing lines or nothing at all?"

"Then it's done," he said, lifting his palms and raising his eyebrows in a show of sincerity. "We move on and start making money the old-fashioned way."

It was a nod to the old man. Their dad loved imitating that old guy on the commercial for an investment firm or whatever it was. *We make our money the old-fashioned way. We eeeaaarrrn it!*

Just remember, Lee had warned. *That guy, the one you are when you're high. He's a fiction.*

He doesn't exist. When you wake up with all of your regrets, he's long gone. It's the real you who has to bear the consequences of his actions. And trying to blame it on him, is like trying to blame your imaginary friend. Everyone knows it's just a lie—even you.

"Look, Rhett," Josh said. "You don't need me. Just do it yourself. Take the money and go."

He felt that surge of strength he always felt after he talked to Lee. Right talk, right speech, words that connected him to that good place inside.

"I do need you, brother," he said. "The big man wants you, too."

"Why?"

"Because we're all in this together from way back," he said. "And because you can just walk in the door. I, on the other hand, will have to break in or sneak in. And no one knows what will happen then. You know what I mean."

That was so true to form. Coax, and if that didn't work, threaten.

"That's a real pretty woman," said Rhett. "And that girl. Oh my god."

Josh felt a hard dump of raw fear, tried to keep it off his face. But Rhett saw it. The predator always saw fear. Jesus, Josh couldn't have any more blood on his hands. He took a deep breath, summoned his strength.

"Then I'll go in alone," Josh said. "I'll bring

you all the money. I don't want it. You take it, go, and don't come back."

Rhett actually looked hurt for a moment, blinking, pushing down the corners of his mouth. And for a moment Josh actually felt bad.

"That's going to break Ma's heart," said Rhett.

"She'll forget," said Josh. "That's what she does. She forgets the things that hurt her."

Rhett seemed to consider. "When are you going back? Today?"

"Monday."

Rhett shook his head. "That's not going to work. He wants the money tonight; he wants to disappear, says things are getting hot for him. He's coming tonight."

"It's got to be Monday."

Rhett's face went dark.

"You find a way in there today," said Rhett. His voice, too, had gone flat and cold. It was almost a relief because now Josh saw the real man behind the Rhett mask, all the masks he shifted around, trying to find the one that would get him what he wanted.

"If you don't," Rhett went on. "Then I'm going to find my way in there tonight. And just hope that no one gets in my way."

twenty-five

Things That Go BUMP in the Night . . .
and other problems with living
in a HAUNTED HOUSE

It has been an interesting couple of days. First, I hired a handyman. And he's going to help with the few (million) things that are beyond my DIY skills.

It will be shocking to some of you that 1) I need help, and 2) I'm willing to admit it. But those of you who have been with me from the very, very beginning remember that this is an important lesson, one that I learned after R was born and the specter of depression loomed. I got help, and it worked. Sometimes you just don't have the right tools in your belt to help yourself. Sometimes you have to call in the professionals.

It was the wallpaper in the kitchen that really did me in. So many (ugly!) layers glued on so thick—I tried the rented steamer, scraping, peeling. But it just came off in these narrow strips, most of it staying fast. I'm sure there's a metaphor here. Help me out!

Or maybe it was really the barn door falling off in the middle of the night, scaring the bejesus out of R and me, leading us to call the cops.

Or maybe it was just that the handyman showed up, eager and ready to help. Or maybe it was some combination of all of those things. Anyway, he's coming on Monday and hopefully that means faster progress toward turning this place from overwhelming project into a happy home.

Given what I learned this weekend, hence the title of this blog, you'll probably be surprised that I even want to stay. I am a little surprised myself.

Last night, I woke up and looked out my window to discover someone sneaking around the property. I called the police (again!). And the same young officer who came out the first night was at my doorstep. He and his lovely young partner (is that sexist to say she was so pretty! And nice!) both grew up here, and they filled me in on the sad, horrible history of this beautiful house.

A family was murdered here. Their young daughter was tortured but survived. The men were never caught. People apparently have been sneaking out here, daring each other to explore the "haunted house." There's a rumor that the killers were looking for money that is supposedly hidden here. And people still come out to search. It was probably someone like that on the property last night. I'll wait while you process the horror of all of this.

Okay. It's bad. I've been sick about it. And I did have about an hour where I thought about packing it in.

But the more I reflected, the more I saw the poetry of the situation, the relevance to me and my journey. Once upon a time, a horrible thing happened to me. A man broke into my home and raped me, leaving me for dead.

I could have abandoned myself. I could have succumbed to the aftermath of trauma, not sought help, sunk into depression and despair, and let those things darken the rest of my life. Instead, I clawed myself back into the light. It wasn't easy. It took time. And the road is winding, with lots of switchbacks and dark patches, even now.

But, likewise, I won't abandon this house. In fact, maybe we found our way to each other for a reason. Maybe we were meant for each other.

Meanwhile, lots of drama with R. The specter of her biology haunts us. Over the years, many of you have encouraged me to face the truth, whatever it is. Especially now that it's what my daughter wants, many of you feel that it's time. I've been stubborn. And I just realized that I'm doing what I said I would never do. I'm allowing a dark corner to stay unlit. I have been choosing the dark place of ignorance. And my reasons are selfish. If it turns out that my daughter is my rapist's child, then—would I have to find a way to love him? Because even in the hatefulness and the horror of his actions, didn't he give me the most important and beautiful gift of my life? How hard it will be to accept that. How deeply we resist forgiving someone who hurt and violated us, how impossible to imagine loving them. But it's not just about me. I have decided that if it's what my daughter really wants, she can have the test. And maybe this is a step forward on my journey, too. Maybe the truth will light the way toward true and total release and forgiveness. Because I will have to help R embrace her biology, and to do that, I will have to embrace it, as well. Jeez. Heavy.

I will move forward and help this house move on, too. We will embrace our past and, in doing so, create a better future. We can make this place a home for us, and be a home for the house, as well. A renovation and rebirth for all of us.

"Mom," said Raven from behind her. "You can't publish that."

Raven had been standing behind her for quite some time, which Claudia barely noticed because it was the usual state of affairs.

She turned to look at her daughter. "Too personal?"

"No," Raven said. "Well, yeah, but what else is new? I mean about the money."

"What about it?"

Raven threw up her hands. "Mom! Think about it! People are going to read that, and even more weirdoes are going to come out here."

The kid had a point.

"But there's no money," said Claudia. "No one knows it's us, or where the property is."

"You really don't know that," said Raven. "What if someone does know? It wouldn't be hard for locals to make the connection."

"Okay," she said. "How about I call that guy Josh, and he helps us look in the basement, move some of the bigger things we can't budge."

"No! Are you crazy?" Raven said. "Then *everyone* in this one-horse town will know about it."

"So what? Everyone *does* know about it. Everyone knew except me."

"Okay, just think about it," said Raven. A lot of times Raven seemed to be summoning her patience, much as Claudia used to do when her daughter was an intractable toddler. "What if, just if, the money is down there?"

She stared at Raven. What if it *was* down there? A million dollars. Troy was standing behind Raven now, leaning on the door frame, holding his eternal smartphone.

"We wouldn't want anyone to know about that, right?" said Raven.

"We'd have to call the police," said Claudia. "Of course."

"Money that belonged to a drug dealer?" asked her daughter, looking incredulous. "Why? So the police could return it to him?"

"The money," said Troy, raising his hand as if he were giving an answer in class. "If it's down there, is evidence in the case of the murdered police officer and his wife. They would probably test it for DNA. It might lead to the solving of a crime. Right?"

Claudia and Raven both stared.

"What?" said Troy, shrugging. "You don't watch *Criminal Minds*?"

"Also," said Raven. "Those men who were

326

looking for it and didn't find it and who are still out there? Maybe they hear about it. And they come back. Maybe they think what we think. That it's still there."

Claudia blew out a breath.

"Okay," she said. "I don't post the blog. I don't call the police. I don't call the handyman. Then what do we do?"

Troy and Raven exchanged a look. "Come back downstairs with us."

"So," said Troy.

They were back in the basement. He was reclining on one of the boxes, his back against the wall, staring at his phone. "It says here that some historic properties in Lost Valley and surrounding areas have tunnels and hidden rooms, and might have been part of the Underground Railroad," said Troy, turning the phone so that Claudia could see.

She squinted at the phone but couldn't really see without her glasses.

"Most of the properties have already been discovered," he went on. "But what year was this house built?"

"The original structure was built in 1855," said Claudia. "But it's been remodeled a number of times since then."

She was embarrassed to admit that was all she knew about it. She remembered her father saying that the house was "unexceptional" but that the land was worth something, which was why he'd bought it. That word had stayed with her; maybe that's why she hadn't done more research.

Claudia felt a little pulse of excitement suddenly. She turned around a couple of times, trying to orient herself. If there *were* a tunnel here, where would it be?

She started walking the perimeter of the large space, skimming the cold, rough surface of the walls with her fingertips.

"What are you doing, Mom?"

She walked the whole way around until she found herself standing beneath the staircase. She hadn't noticed it because of all the debris and junk piled high in front of it. But now she realized for the first time that the empty space beneath the stairs had been drywalled in, with no access to what would have been a lot of area within.

"Help me get some of this stuff out of the way," said Claudia.

The three of them started shoving and lifting boxes, hefting them off to the side. The beam was a bigger problem; it took all three of them to shift it over even a few feet.

The basement itself was not finished, the concrete blocks of the walls exposed. In most unfinished basements, one wouldn't bother to drywall in just the space under the stairs—unless you were trying to create an enclosed storage area. It was just something to get moldy, to be damaged if the basement flooded, which she knew this one sometimes did. In fact, now that she'd moved the boxes, she could see the water damage down near the floor, a black and orange discoloration. No, there wouldn't be any point in the effort or expense—unless.

"Mom," said Raven. "What are you thinking?"

Claudia looked back and forth between the kids, who were both watching her.

"Feel like doing a little demo?" she asked.

"Demo?" said Troy, confused. "Like a demonstration? For your blog?"

"Like *demolition*," said Claudia.

Raven smiled. "Where's the sledgehammer?"

Josh had tried Claudia twice on her cell phone, then on the landline. Then, frustrated, thinking, he went to the workshop to finish up the chair he was repairing for Mrs. Crabb. He'd called Todd, who said he would go over to keep working on the town houses. Josh promised to meet him. Todd was a good guy, did meticulous work, but he was slower than molasses when he worked alone. Working on the chair helped him manage the hard pulse of anxiety. An hour passed, two. She didn't call back.

Rhett appeared in the doorway.

"Tick tock, little brother."

twenty-six

About a month after my parents were killed, Paul and I went back to the house. There were things there that we needed. We pulled up in the old Suburban, and Paul and I just sat there while Catcher whimpered, desperate to get out and run around his yard. When he started to bark, Paul opened the door and the dog bounded toward the house, started scratching on the door.

Catcher was Mom's dog. He loved romping through the woods with me and Dad, but it was Mom he followed from room to room. It was beside her that he slept. He'd been pining, not eating, pacing Paul's apartment with the limp he had now, restless and howling at every siren. Now, it was me from whom he never wanted to be apart.

Paul unlocked the front door and Catcher ran inside, tore through the house. I stood on the porch, hands dug deep in my pockets, and looked at the flat gray sky, the black dead trees, the white field of snow.

"It's been—" Paul started. He took a hard swallow and stared off into the middle distance so long that I didn't think he was going to finish. "Cleaned up."

I knew he had been there a number of times.

I wondered if he'd been the one to clean the place—the kitchen where my mom's blood had pooled, the basement where my dad had been shot.

I nodded but didn't follow him inside right away. He left me to find my own way in, which was the way I needed to do things. Finally, I stepped into the foyer. What got me was how normal everything seemed. It could have been any day. Things were just as they had always been. Mom's house shoes were still by the door, these blue embroidered tasseled things that her world-traveling friend had sent from a distant land I couldn't even name.

Catcher came loping down the stairs, exuberance lost. He padded into the kitchen where he stood whining at his empty bowl. I couldn't even look at him, so clear was his disappointment. He thought she was here.

On the refrigerator hung my math test; I'd earned an A—a big deal for me in math. On the whiteboard were scribbled Mom's notes about milk and the book she needed to get for her book club, the date of my upcoming English test—a test I never took. I didn't know when I was going back to school.

Aborted. Our lives had come to an abrupt and brutal end. I was the only unlucky one still breathing.

I made my way upstairs to my bedroom. It

was full of things—cards, stuffed animals—things that came to the hospital that I didn't remember receiving and which must have been moved home. Paul had retrieved my clothes, some books, my stuffed unicorn Mr. Emma that I'd been sleeping with since I was little. I'd been dragging the poor thing around everywhere since the beginning of time. It was practically a rag, ripped, sewed and sewed again, chewed on by Catcher, limp from lost stuffing.

I drifted from room to room. My mother's purse sat on her dresser, keys beside it, like she was getting ready to head out to the store. The bed was unmade. They'd been woken in the night, never returned to this room. There was a glass of water by my father's bed. Half-empty.

My parents didn't have anything. That's what was weird. My mom had some jewelry from her mother—a pair of small diamond earrings, a strand of pearls. They sat unworn in the black velvet box in a drawer. I took out the box and sat on the bed with it, opened it, and took those pieces out.

"She'd want you to keep those, of course," Paul said, coming into the room. There was a hundred dollars in the box, too.

"Take it," he said. I shoved it in my pocket. It felt like stealing.

"Are you okay?" he said.

My throat was swollen with sadness; my

stomach ached with despair through my center.

"Yeah," I said.

The jewelry, the cash, our photo albums, a framed picture of the three of us at Disney, a red cashmere scarf, the rest of my clothes, other stuff from my room—yearbooks, my laptop, my diaries. The things I wanted from the house filled about four boxes. When we loaded it in the Suburban, it looked like a sad collection of junk.

"That's it?" asked Paul. "You're sure that's everything you want?"

"What else?" I asked.

He shrugged, shook his head, and looked back at the house.

"What happens to the rest of it?" I wanted to know.

"I'll come out next weekend. Some of the guys are going to help me do an estate sale."

I had no idea what that was, but I didn't ask.

"We'll sell what we can," he said. "Those earnings will go into your college fund. Everything we can't sell, we'll donate. Mr. Bishop said we can store whatever else until after probate. He said he won't even try to rent the place for a while."

"What about the money?"

He blinked at me. We hadn't talked at all about that night, though he'd been present for all my police interviews. So he knew everything that happened.

"What about it?"

"Is it here?"

He shook his head. "No."

"He didn't steal it, like they're saying, and hide it here? He wasn't dirty?"

That's the thing, well, one of the things, that had really been eating at me. My dad was a hard-ass, but I always knew he was a good man, someone I could trust, rely upon to be there. He told me the truth about things. He'd never missed a day of work, was never sick. He was upright and strong. If he *wasn't?* If he wasn't, then the very foundation of my world was made of sand.

Paul came in close and put strong, heavy hands on my shoulders, looked at me deep and long.

"Your dad didn't do that, Zoey. Don't believe it for one second. He would never do that to you, to your mom. If he knew where that money was, he'd have given it up in a heartbeat to save you."

"Maybe he thought once he told them, that they'd kill us anyway. Maybe that's why he didn't tell."

"No," said Paul. "Your dad was not a dirty cop. I know he was hard, kid, and that you two had your problems. But I swear to God, he'd have lain down his life for you. He loved you and your mom. Believe that."

His eyes filled with tears and then they spilled over. He bowed his head so I wouldn't have to look, but to be honest I was relieved to see him

334

cry. If it was bad enough for *him* to cry, then it was okay that I did little else.

I wanted, in that moment, to tell him what I hadn't told anyone. That one night, a couple of weeks before the murders, I'd seen my dad leave the house after 1:00 a.m. It wasn't unusual. I hadn't heard the phone, but I didn't always hear his cell. He came back just after 3:00. I watched him heave a bag out of the car, listened as he came in and headed down to the basement. I drifted off again while he was still down there.

I had forgotten all about it—until the night when the men came. That's why I thought to say that it was in the basement. I wanted to tell Paul, but something stopped me. Because what did it mean? That my dad was dirty, that he had stolen the money, that he let my mom and me be tortured rather than give it up? No. It just didn't make sense. Anyway, maybe it never happened. Maybe it was a dream. Everything was so jumbled and confused in my mind, time was so twisted and weird.

We were about to get in the car when Seth came out from the trees. Catcher ran to greet him, nearly knocking him over.

He knelt down to pet the big dog, to hug him.

"Hey," I said, approaching. He rose, looked at me. He looked so tired, so sad. I already knew what he'd done, how he called the police and probably saved my life. But I couldn't bring myself to thank him. He seemed like a stranger. I tried to remember that I had been a girl who had a crush on him, who wondered what it would be like to kiss him. Those two kids seemed like other people. He pulled me into an awkward hug, which I couldn't return.

"I'm sorry," he said. "I'm sorry I was late to meet you. I couldn't get out of the house. If I had . . ."

It was weird to me that he thought he had anything to do with it. It still is, how he allowed the event to define him, drive the rest of his life. Even now, he thought this mystery was his to solve.

"It's not your fault," I said. "You called the police. If not, I don't know."

Above us, some crows circled, calling out. The house looked like a gray shell, something that could crumble and fall. Seth was a ghost. I don't remember how that encountered ended. I think I just got in the car and let Paul drive me away.

Now, I sat in the Suburban—the very same vehicle. I tried to coax it to life in the parking garage, the attendant giving me a skeptical look as the ancient gas guzzler coughed and groaned. Paul had mentioned that there was a problem with the car. I thought he should sell it, but he wouldn't let it go. He hadn't driven it in a year, and I rarely drove it unless I was running errands for him out of the city—usually food errands.

I turned the key again, pumped the gas.

"You'll flood the engine," my dad said unhelpfully. "Give it a minute. It'll start."

I leaned back and sighed. I was a wreck. The blows I took were all aching hot patches of pain. Nothing broken. There's a sharp, breathless, nauseating pain that comes with a break or a fracture. And I didn't have that, which was not surprising since I had taken far worse blows. Either the guys who jumped me were weak, or they were taking it easy because I'm small and a girl. But broken or not, my ribs, my jaw, and my hip (I guess where I first hit the ground) were all a dark purple and aching in a kind of unpleasant misery chorus. Probably someone else would have been out of commission, but I was used to discomfort from years of sparring.

"Pain is just an inconvenience," Mike always said. "Unless it doubles you over or you pass out, just try to ignore it."

He'd been calling since last night, and I'd been sending his calls to voicemail. I didn't want to listen to the voice of reason. The time for lessons was over.

I didn't realize it at the time, but he was right—when I killed Didion, I'd tipped a domino, one that had been poised and waiting for more than a decade. The energy that had been gathering since my parents' murder had shifted from stasis to kinesis. Now was the time to follow the trail to its conclusion, no matter how ugly. You could not reverse the fall of dominos.

How often had I wished that I had died with them that night? There was a part of me that thinks I should have, or that maybe in some real sense I did. Maybe that's why I couldn't muster any real gratitude for Seth. If not for him, I'd be where I belonged.

"She wanted you to live," said my dad. "More than anything, that's what she wanted. She lived her whole life for you. She wouldn't be happy with the choices you've made."

I tried the engine again, there was a loud coughing grind that echoed off the concrete of the parking garage walls.

"Where are you going anyway?" asked my father, frowning.

Somewhere between the information I'd gathered last night, the beating I took on the street where I lost the key Paul had given me, and the dreams that colored my fitful sleep, I decided it was time to go back to the house and search the basement. I needed to go through what, if anything, was still left of my parents. I had no reason to believe that it wasn't all long gone. I hadn't set foot on the property since my last time there with Paul. But I'd read on that blog that the basement was largely untouched and filled with boxes. And I wanted to try to find what my father brought down there that night.

"What did you bring down there?" I asked him. But of course he was gone. He never gave me any new information. He only told me what I already knew or echoed my fears and insecurities.

Finally, finally, with my last attempt, the engine barked to life.

I had no idea how I was going to get into that house. But I had to try.

twenty-seven

The good thing about Rhett was that he was predictable. By the time Josh had finished up the chair, his brother was passed out hard on the couch. Rhett could ingest more alcohol than anyone Josh knew; he'd never show it except to get meaner, darker the more he took in. He never lost control, never got sloppy. But at a certain point, he'd just crash and be out of commission for hours. There would be no rousing him.

Josh stood in the kitchen looking at Rhett, his brother's mouth agape, one leg sprawled wide, his breathing deep. Maybe he'll die, thought Josh. Maybe he'll choke on his own vomit. But no, that was never going to happen. People like Rhett never had the courtesy to die young. They stayed around creating damage as long as they could.

"I thought he was supposed to be helping you," said Jane.

She was rinsing off Mom's breakfast plates and loading them carefully in the dishwasher. Medicare paid for part of Jane's salary; Josh paid part. And part, he thought, was just Jane looking out for Mom because they'd been friends since childhood. Jane's kids were grown and scattered across the country. She liked coming here and helping with meals and such, Josh thought. He was grateful to her, though he wasn't sure he ever said as much. Words didn't come easily to him. They got jammed up inside, never came out right.

"Yeah," said Josh. "I thought so, too."

"Your mama's blind when it comes to that boy," said Jane, casting a disapproving glance at Rhett. From the couch, Rhett let out a long, grunting snore. Josh bit back a flood of hatred for his brother, walked over to help Jane finish up. It wasn't really her job to clean up, but she always did.

Jane's glasses gleamed gold in the light that washed through the window. "He was always bad."

No one knew what they had done, of course. Not really. But there was talk. There was always talk.

"But you're a good boy, Josh," said Jane. "Don't forget that. You're all she has, your momma. She needs you."

Jane used to be the nurse at the high school and everyone was afraid of her. Unless you were really sick, and then she was an angel. Her hair had gone snow-white since then, but her face had hardly aged. To Josh, she looked exactly the same as she always had. Her dark eyes glittered with intelligence and something else, a kind of hard seeing.

"Don't let him drag you into whatever trouble he's got brewing," she said. "You worked hard to get yourself right. You stay in touch with Lee."

Jane's husband, Ray, who was a master carpenter and helped Josh now and again on various jobs, was also in the program. Jane knew well the demon of substance abuse, how it could tear through your life if you let it.

"Can you stay awhile?" he asked. She only worked a half day on the weekends. "I have to go out, and I don't want to leave her alone with him. Not like this."

She looked at her watch, at Rhett, her face turning into a hard scowl. "I can stay till two if you need me."

"I'll pay you time and a half."

She waved him away.

"Just text me if he wakes up?" said Josh.

She nodded. "You heard what I said, right? About not letting him drag you into anything."

"I heard you, Miss Jane," he said. "Thank you."

She left the room, and he stood there a second, thinking. His eyes fell on Rhett's car keys, the sound of his brother's snoring growing louder. Rhett had showed up driving an old blue 1970 Barracuda. The thing spewed black smoke and was rusting along the bottom, but Rhett said he'd picked it up for less than a grand and it hadn't broken down yet. Josh picked up the keys, as well as the single one, the survey, then walked

342

over to where his brother lay. Rhett's cell, an old flip phone, lay beside him on the coffee table. Josh pocketed that, too.

Then he left the house, climbed into his Toyota, and headed toward the Bishop place. What was he going to do? What were his options? He could go to the cops and come clean—about everything. That's what Lee would no doubt tell him to do. *There's power in the narrative. Saying what was, what really happened, so that you can move clean into the future.* Lee was 100 percent about the truth, the whole truth, all the time. Lies took too much energy. They drained you and left you vulnerable.

Josh could call the big man, tell him what he told Rhett, that the money wasn't there. That he needed to leave the house, the people living there alone or Josh was going to tell the police what happened all those years ago. But that was basically like just asking to get killed. No joke. That man, those men, they didn't care who lived or died, especially not Josh or even Rhett. The fact that they'd been left alive after the mess at the Drakes' was basically a miracle. Because they'd proved they could keep their mouths shut, never talked, even when the police brought them both in; that was the only reason either of them was still breathing. The second Josh became a liability, a problem, he was going to find himself buried back in the woods, or in a chipper, or a vat of chemicals somewhere. So far, he'd kept secrets, done what he was asked, kept an eye on the place, an ear out for anyone digging around. He met Dilbert once a week or so at Lucky's. Dilbert—like all cops—was a talker. He had a pet interest in the Drake murders, because Seth Murphy was Dilbert's best friend. So it came up—people got caught digging, kids broke in. In all these years, no one ever found anything. Still, Josh dutifully called the old man every couple of months, just to say he still had an ear out. More than ten years he'd done that.

Or Josh could go to the Bishop house and try to talk his way in, just see if he could get down into the basement, say he wanted to measure or something. If there was a tunnel, the entrance would definitely be in the basement. And if it was there, it would explain where that money was and why in all these years he'd never found it. In the best case, he found what he was looking for and got out somehow.

Or he could just go to Lee's, ask for help. They would talk it through. Josh knew he could trust Lee to keep his mouth shut.

He pulled into the lot of the party store and was parked before he even realized he'd done it. It was the beer he'd watched Rhett drink; it kept popping up in his thoughts—the way it smelled, sounded, that pop and fizz, the swallow. He sat in his car, breathing hard. This was a bad moment; a fork in the road with no good turn. He reached for his phone to call Lee, but then he heard another foreign ringing. Rhett's phone. He didn't recognize the number, but he knew who it was. He answered.

"It's Josh," he said.

There was a pause, an annoyed sniff.

"What are you doing with his phone?" The old man.

"I borrowed his car," Josh lied. "He must have left it in here."

"What's the plan?"

"I'm going over there now," he said.

"Now."

"I know her," said Josh. "I'm helping her renovate. I think I can talk my way in, get it if I can find it, and get out. She doesn't have to know anything. No one gets hurt. She's a nice person, has a daughter."

There was just breathing on the other line. Then,

"I don't give a fuck how you get it," he said. His voice was always flat, no matter what he said, always just above a whisper. "Just get it."

"What if it's not there?" he said. "You know I've been looking all this time."

"It's there," he said. He didn't sound totally convinced.

"What if it isn't?"

345

A sharp inhale like the first drag of a cigarette. "Where's Rhett?"

"I don't know."

"I'll be there by midnight," he said. "You know where to meet."

"Yeah."

The old man hung up, and Josh was alone in the car. A big pickup truck pulled in, and a couple of large, young guys got out—jeans and boots, camo jackets. Josh watched them go in, come out with a six-pack of beer and couple of microwave burritos.

Tick tock.

Rhett was going to wake up. What would he do when he found his phone gone, his keys? He'd be white hot, the kind of anger that made him go blank like an animal. He'd call Missy. Rhett would know right where Josh had gone.

His phone rang then, and it was Lee. Josh picked up the slim cell and almost answered. Instead, he just watched until the call went to voicemail. Josh would bet ten dollars that Jane had called him. *Surround yourself with people who live right and do right,* that was one of Lee's big things. *They'll help you stay on the path.*

The phone buzzed with a text from Lee.

Jane said she thought you might need to talk. Everything okay?

How long did he just sit there, turning over all the scenarios in his mind? The money was there. It wasn't. He got it and ran with it. He got it and turned it in to the police, came clean about the whole thing, took his chances. He got it and brought it to Rhett, hoped he'd just go away for good. Maybe Claudia didn't let him in at all. Maybe he told her what was going on, she helped him out. Maybe he told her and she threw him out, called the cops.

If he came clean to the police and went to jail, what happened to Mom? Who would take care of her?

Another chime from his phone. Lee again.

Just let me know you're doing okay and I'll stop bugging you.

Josh couldn't bring himself to answer. He didn't want to lie. He couldn't tell the truth. He was trapped. That was the feeling he couldn't stand, the thing that got him every time. Every time.

What was amazing was, even after seven years of sobriety, how easy it was. He strode into the party store, bought himself a forty. Took it in its brown paper bag out to the car. There was no tearful struggle, no inner battle. It was just one, just for today, just to give him the swagger to do what needed to be done. In fact, he was doing a

347

good thing. If he could get that money and get rid of Rhett, he'd be sparing himself, his mother, maybe even Claudia Bishop and her daughter a lot of heartache. He could call Lee tomorrow, start over. He just popped the tab and took a sip, then another. The cold, bubbling liquid sluiced down his throat, and his body took it in like a river run dry. And it was just a few minutes before *that guy* showed up, the one Lee always warned about, the one who did bad things and asked the "real" Josh to bear the consequences. Josh had never been so happy to see anyone in his life.

Rhett was waiting by the entrance to the Bishops' drive, the Barracuda idling in the shoulder like a junkyard dog. Rhett climbed out as Josh pulled up.

"What are you up to, little brother? Trying to cut me out?"

Josh regarded him; Rhett was considerably less scary now that *that guy* was here. The Josh who'd been beaten and bullied and tortured by Rhett, the one who still cowered and kowtowed, who backed down was gagged and bound in some back room. Josh felt a kind of easy strength, a calm that he normally didn't feel.

"I'm trying to get this done without more trouble," he said.

"You worry too much," said Rhett. "Where's the key? The survey?"

"I have it," Josh said. "How'd you get the car started?"

Rhett smiled a wolfish un-smile. "I keep another key under the wheel well, just like old Dad taught us. Did you forget?"

Josh glanced over at the Cuda and saw that Missy sat in the passenger seat, watching Josh. She was not *still hot,* as Rhett claimed. She had *never* been hot. She had a hard, vulpine face, mean, dark eyes. She was thin—in a kind of wiry, bony way. She was easy, had made a number of passes at Josh over the years. He wondered if Rhett knew that. She and Rhett were weirdly suited to each other, had a way of looking like a complete set when they were together, and not in a good way. She was a dark whisper in his ear, the last thing he needed.

Josh tossed Rhett his phone.

"I talked to the old man," said Josh. "Told him I'd handle it. He was good with that."

Rhett looked down at the device, back at Josh.

"You can have the money, all of it," said Josh. "Just let me get it."

The air had taken on a hard chill; he'd heard there was a cold front moving in today. There was already that shift from the bright colors of autumn to the dead brown just before winter fell. The leaves fell and whispered all around them. Few cars ever came down this road; there were only a few properties, all of them of large acreage

349

set far back. Two of them were vacation homes. The nearest one to the Bishops' was an old farm, which was empty and had sat on the market for years.

"Okay," said Rhett. "You have one hour and then I'm coming in."

twenty-eight

About an hour later, using tools they found in the basement—two hammers, a crowbar, and a lot of muscle—they'd knocked a big hole in the wall, revealing a gaping space beneath the stairs. They were all coughing and sneezing by the time it was done. Claudia shone a flashlight into the area. Nothing. It was empty.

Claudia was surprised at the weight of disappointment. What had she thought they were going to find under here? If there had been a tunnel, wouldn't some historical society have located it by now? Her father had said that there was nothing special about the house.

Before Claudia could stop her, Raven crawled through the hole they'd made.

"What is *that?*" asked Raven.

Troy and Claudia crowded in together to stare, shining the flashlight into the space. Raven crouched down in the corner.

"Oh my god, Mom," said Raven.

"What is it?"

Raven turned around, her eyes wide.

"It's a door," she said.

She moved aside so that Claudia could shine her flashlight in. She saw it. A small door, more the entrance to a crawl space. This must be it,

351

the entrance to a room or to a tunnel that led to who knew where. Claudia climbed through and squatted down next to Raven. She reached out and yanked on the handle, but it was solidly closed. It did not budge.

Claudia shone the light on it and saw the lock, bright copper glinting in the beam. Something new in a place where everything else was rusted and old.

"Open it, Mom," said Raven, her voice taut with the excitement of discovery.

She sank back and stared at the door, the kids close, looking over either shoulder. How strange, Claudia thought.

"I can't," she said. "It's locked."

twenty-nine

I drove to the house, my mind a roomful of monkeys, thoughts, memories, leaping around, shrieking, and dancing in the rafters.

It wasn't until after that first night, when I saved the street kid from those bullies, that I started asking the real questions about my parents' murder. Before that, I had cast myself as the victim in the story of my life. I saw the events as they had unfolded through the eyes of someone who was fourteen; I saw myself that way, too. Arrested development, my shrink would call it. When a life-altering childhood trauma retards the maturing of the psyche. Or whatever. I couldn't move past that moment of trauma, where I was powerless as men hurt me and took my parents, ripped a gaping hole in my universe. And then in the kung fu temple, but more so on the street that night, I realized I wasn't powerless. Not anymore.

I couldn't talk to Paul. After years of raging, and spearheading his own investigation, and writing letters, and whatever you do when you realize that there's not going to be justice for your family—he just kind of shut down about it. He put away his files and tried to move on. I didn't want to open the wound. That's why I talked to Mike.

He, my dad, Paul, and Boz had all been friends for a long time. Paul, Mike, and my dad since childhood, Boz since John Jay College. Mike took an early pension after fifteen years as a beat cop in the East Village, opened his kung fu school, and did the occasional private investigation work on the side.

I wanted to stop locking people up and start teaching people how to channel their negative energy into something positive. Hence his work with kids at the kung fu temple and the program he ran for at-risk kids in various neighborhood schools around the city.

The morning after I saved the street kid, I had my class to run. I put the girls through their drills. There were just five in that morning session, but they were my favorites. Daisy, who cried when she had to hit someone. Kayla with an attitude a mile wide. Bella, who had real natural talent—speed, agility, and a steely eye of the tiger. Jessa, who worked harder than anyone and had come from not being able to do one pushup to leaving everyone else panting on the floor. And Kym, my mirror—quiet, shy, wrapped up tight. They all lived together in a group home run by a woman named Melba, each removed from their families for various situations of abuse. They were all at the school "on scholarship," as Mike liked to call it. He never turned anyone away, even people who couldn't pay. Which was part of the reason he was always sweating the finances.

We ran through the kicks, blocks, punches, and then we did our forms. Then gentle sparring between the girls or with me. It was an hour and a half of intense physical activity, and afterward they drank about a gallon of water, and we sat around and talked. I was still buzzing from what happened the night before; I could still see that big man crumble, hear his scream. I felt good about it, saving that kid, and I didn't. Maybe my dad was right, maybe there was something more to it. Something dark.

"You know," said Jessa. "I didn't think I was strong when I first came here. But now I do."

"You are strong," I said. "You all are."

"I used to think I was strong," said Kym. "Now I don't."

It was only her third week, and she hadn't said much. I let her be quiet, was soft in my instruction. The other girls, maybe sensing that she was fragile, were careful with her, too. They roughhoused with each other, but not with her yet.

"When I was your age, a little older," I said. "Someone hurt me, too."

I had never talked about it before with anyone except Paul, Mike, and the police. But there it was on the surface, maybe because of what happened the night before.

She looked at me, with big eyes, chewed on

355

her nail. There was a kind of sullen anger there, something I recognized. "Your dad?"

"No," I said. "Strangers."

"Did they go to jail?" asked Daisy, her cheeks flushed.

"No," I said. "They weren't caught. I thought I was weak, too. I felt powerless, a victim."

"Do you still feel that way?" asked Bella. "Because now you're like all *badass*. You're like pow!—and like bam!" She threw some punches to punctuate her words. "Even Mike works hard when he's fighting you."

I tried not to smile. A certain type of girl sees it as mockery.

"I think when you learn to fight, you learn things about yourself," I said. "You come to know your strengths, your weaknesses. You learn to flow with who you are. There's a strength in that. I'm small, but I'm fast. My arms aren't as strong as my legs. I try not to let it ever be a match of strength alone."

The girls were all watching me like I was imparting some deep wisdom. I felt a little guilty; who was I to teach them anything? I had broken a ton of Mike's rules last night.

"What happened to you, Kym," I said, "was not your fault. You are a kid. Your care was entrusted to someone who didn't deserve it. You were a victim in that moment, but that doesn't mean you're a victim for life. You can find your strength, your power. You can create the life that lies ahead of you."

She nodded, but I could tell she didn't hear me yet. If she stayed with us, if I kept saying it, I knew we could make a difference. I'd seen it before—in myself.

After a while, the girls left, and I went to see Mike, who was in the back office, trying as usual to figure out how to keep running a school that most months cost money rather than made money. I could tell because he had his head down in his hand. As it was, none of the teachers got paid; we were all volunteers. We didn't use the heat or the air-conditioning. The rent on the huge space was killing him, but he couldn't find anything cheaper.

"Good class," he said, not looking up at me. "I like what you had to say today. The girls respect you."

I sat in the chair opposite his desk, regarded his office, the towering shelves of books stacked every which way, his countless trophies, awards, photographs at martial arts competitions. There were pictures of Paul, my dad—old ones from when they were all young and handsome, even one of my mom and dad together. Looking at the wall was like time traveling, ghosts captured by light. A milky sunshine washed in though cloudy windows. He swiveled to look at me, the chair suffering beneath his girth.

"What's on your mind?"

"I want to know everything."

"Everything."

"About what happened to my parents," I said. "I know you and Paul ran an investigation. That there are people you strongly suspect. But that you haven't been able to prove anything. I want to know what you know."

Those light hazel eyes in a landscape of dark skin, graying stubble on his jaw. He was the face of New York City, a celebration of mingling cultures, people from all over the world, all different colors, religions, countries meeting in mecca, falling in love, and having babies. It's one of the things I love about New York. Class might still divide us, and maybe nowhere else are the contrasts as stark as in this crazy place. But culturally, we are New Yorkers first.

"Why?" he asked. The question had weight. Not: Why *would* you want to? But what is your motivation? "Why do you want to know? What will you do with this knowledge?"

I wouldn't have been able to answer then. But the idea was already in my head, even if it was just a seed. Something that had burrowed itself into the dark recesses of who I am. It felt *good* to give those frat-boy bullies what they deserved. I *liked* hurting the bigger one and watching him cry out in pain. Even if the boy *was* a thief, it was the dominion of the physically strong over the physically weak that I couldn't abide.

"I want to understand what happened," I said. "And why."

A slow blink, something clicking, registering. Mike saw me. I think he always saw my intention. On some level, I think he always knew what I wanted, even before I did.

"We might never be able to understand," he said. "Even if we find them."

"Please," I said. "Tell me everything. I deserve the truth."

And he did. He told me everything he knew.

Traffic was heavy. I snaked along, praying that the car wasn't going to die on me in the stop-and-start traffic. Seth's words from last night were still ringing in my ears.

"I'm pretty sure that the fourth man was a cop," he said.

"Why?" I asked. "Why do you think that?"

"First of all, he waited outside," said Seth. "Maybe he was afraid your dad would recognize him. Or maybe he just didn't have the stomach for how fucked up it was, didn't want to get his hands dirty."

I nodded, considering.

"They got away with it," said Seth. "I mean, do you know what kind of hell rains down when someone kills a cop? There's no mercy. Those guys move heaven and earth. Unless. Unless there's corruption. A cover-up of some kind. Then people get questioned and released, leads mysteriously go cold, the case starts all thunder and lightning, then slows to a drizzle. Then goes cold."

Seth was, of course, a crazed conspiracy theorist. Which didn't mean he was wrong. The thought had occurred to me, though neither Mike nor Paul ever suggested it. That other cops might have been involved.

"It was definitely cops that ripped off Whitey Malone," said Seth. "It was a surgical strike, swift and trained, zero evidence left behind."

"So cops stole the money," I said. "And other cops came looking for it?"

"Or people hired by cops," he said. "Didion, the Beckham brothers, these were bad guys. They were hired guns, promised a cut. If *we* figured it out, who was probably there that night, why didn't the police?"

"There was no evidence," I said. "They were questioned and released."

"Give me a break," said Seth. "If they wanted Beckham and Didion, they'd have found a way to hold them. Shit, when the cops want someone for a crime, there's no stopping them."

We sat a minute, both of us lost in our own thoughts. I caught him looking at me in that sad, musing way he had.

"Hey, Zoey," he said. "I've been thinking."

"Yeah?"

"Is there any way you can just—I don't know—let this go?" Seth said. "Move on. Live a life."

It wasn't just my dad standing there now. Didion was there, too. Grim and pale, staring, his front soaked with blood, drip, dripping on the floor. If I'd known what I know now, maybe.

I got up. "It's too late," I said.

He stood at the top of the stairs as I jogged down to leave.

"Remember," he said. "You're one of the good guys."

I wasn't so sure. Anyway, it seems like a pretty outdated concept. Overly simplistic, the idea of the good guys versus the bad guys, Mike's position on justice versus revenge. I'm not sure anything is so black and white. Does anyone think he's purely evil? Does anyone ever believe she's purely good? Even terrorists think they're the good guys. Did the men who killed my parents intend to commit a heinous act? How did they justify what happened afterward?

Am I evil because I killed John Didion, because I ran him through in cold blood? He was an old man. One I suspected, convicted, and punished without judge or jury. I *knew*. My body *knew* him. But did I have the right to exact revenge, deliver a form of justice? I don't know the answer. It could go either way. Anyway, it's too late now. Some acts are forever. My point is that I'm not sure that there are any good guys, not in the real world. But that doesn't mean there isn't justice, a kind of code.

I hadn't been back to the house since that day with Paul. I never claimed our things, the detritus of my parents' lives. Mr. Bishop, the owner, died a couple of years later. And the house, Paul told me, sat empty. No one ever lived there after us until recently. I had no reason to think our stuff hadn't gone to the junkyard long ago except that Seth said that the house, the property had sat fallow, no one living there since us. He'd been out to the property a couple of times, wondering, always wondering if there was something that the police missed—on purpose or by accident. And, of course, there was the matter of the missing money.

And then the Bishop woman moved in, Seth and I following her blog, wondering what she'd find. She and the house were right for each other. If ever a place needed a rebirth.

It was afternoon by the time I rolled into Lost Valley. When I'd pulled over for gas, it took me a while to get the Suburban started again. My father and John Didion sat grimly silent in the backseat. Did I feel it? An electricity in the air? Did the sun seem too low in the sky, the sky too dark? I don't know. Maybe.

thirty

Paul was waiting for Heather in the parking lot, just as he said he would be. She never doubted him. He was one of those rare men who always said exactly what he meant, always did exactly as he promised. There was a hard lump in her throat as she pulled in beside him, and her gut was a roil of guilt, sadness, dread. He smiled at her, something sad and sweet.

She'd bought a few things. A sundress, a new bathing suit and cover-up, some pretty lingerie. She'd used cash from her savings account, the one that Chad didn't know about until recently. She owed herself that, this trip. It was only a week ago, a little more, that she'd learned what kind of trouble they were in. She'd known money was tight, of course. But she'd had no idea the mountain of debt that had accrued. She felt like a fool, one of those stupid women who let her husband handle the money. But he had always done, and she trusted him. He worked so hard, all that overtime. He never once told her or even hinted that they were buried, suffocating.

Her credit card had been declined—online, thank goodness, and not in a local shop somewhere. She checked their account and was amazed to see that not only was the card maxed out, but the payment was past due. She went to Chad's desk in the basement, started sifting through the stack of bills, his files. How was it possible? She logged on to their bank accounts, between savings and checking, there was only a couple hundred dollars. Zoey's college fund was empty, closed in fact. He'd taken a loan out against his pension. There was no other way to say it. They were broke. She could see what he'd done, as she followed the paper trail. Ran a card up, then opened another account to transfer the balance for a lower interest rate, then ran them both up again. Then he did it again, and again. He took out a loan against the pension to pay off the cards, then ran the cards up again. There were slips for payroll advances; there was a balance on their overdraft line of credit. Her chest felt tight; her breathing came ragged. How? How could this happen?

If he missed a paycheck, they'd have about two weeks before they were out of money altogether, with no credit to carry them over, if not for her small savings account. Thank God, he hadn't known about it. Or had forgotten about it.

She was alone the afternoon she found out. It was raining, and she felt as if her whole life had crumbled around her. She couldn't have been more crushed if she had discovered him cheating, if he was in love with someone else. Financial infidelity; he'd kept secrets, mismanaged their money, taken out a loan against their future, one he had no way of paying. She felt a hard stab of guilt; she never should have stopped working.

Her small account was all they had. Money she'd inherited as a teenager from her grand-mother. She'd used it mostly for her education. But she kept it, contributing to it from the subbing jobs she took sometimes, things she'd sold on eBay. She'd hoped one day to surprise him—part of the down payment on a house, covering some of Zoey's education costs.

She went to the bank, deposited some money into their checking and paid down some balances, bringing them at least current on everything. She sent him a text:

> Can you come home early?
> What's wrong?
> I need to talk before Zoey gets home.
> Can it wait?
> No.

He'd wept at the kitchen table. She tried to understand, to feel for him. She tried not to hate him, herself. But there was more. Withdrawals, cash advances that she didn't understand, that didn't correspond with their payments due and normal expenses. How could she have been so naïve?

She had the printouts, the last six months of

banking statements, credit cards, pension. It was all easy to get to; she knew all the passwords, so it wasn't like she hadn't had access all this time. She just simply hadn't looked.

She told him about the account she had. He looked at her with red-rimmed eyes.

"How much?"

"A little over ten thousand," she said. "A bit less. I paid down some balances, made us current at least."

He laughed a little, this kind of derisive snort he issued that drove her crazy. "That's a drop in the bucket."

"It's a small buffer at least," she said. "We need to get a debt counselor. I'll go back to work. We can consolidate that debt, and set a budget, work on paying some of this off."

He shook his head, an odd black look on his face. It was the strangest thing, as she sat there with him, the sensation that her husband, a man she'd known since childhood, was someone else. Who was he? A stranger, someone *less* somehow than the man she thought she knew. The kind of love they shared was supposed to be unconditional. Wasn't it? She didn't even want to look at him.

"What else?" she said. It was there, standing in the corner, a black shadow, a wraith. A nebulous, shifting menace.

"This isn't bad enough?" he asked.

"The withdrawals, the cash advances, so much debt. We're not exactly living high on the hog here, Chad."

He shook his head. "You think it's cheap? That school? The rent here. Insurance. Food. Clothes. Vacations. Hell, we spent a hundred dollars on dinner and the movies for the three of us last weekend."

"It doesn't add up," she said. "I know what we spend."

Did he forget that she was smart, educated, good with numbers? She didn't blame him for forgetting if he had. She had forgotten all of that herself. She had let him take the reins of her life and let her world grow small—the house, the school, Zoey, Chad. Her friends had all left Lost Valley. One lived in the city, a magazine executive. Her other close girlfriend was a travel writer, always sending gifts from exotic climes. She never envied them, both of them childless, one unhappily married, the other always with someone new. At least Heather was happy. Well. Happy-ish. As happy as she could be. Or was that just what she told herself?

"What else, Chad?" she asked again. "Where did all that money go?"

She'd gone through his paystubs, too. There were one or two that showed overtime. But mostly not. She wracked her brain for dates he said he was working, events at school he missed.

She checked the corresponding stubs. There were discrepancies. She'd never once doubted, not for a second, that he wasn't where he said he was, doing what he said he was doing. She'd never doubted his love. Other men lied and cheated; friends' marriages collapsed around them. Not Chad. Not their marriage. And here they were. What a sad cliché. Not that she was faultless. Not at all.

"Heather," he said.

"Just tell me," she said. "We'll fix it together."

He reached for her hand. And his touch repelled her. She let her hand rest beneath his for a moment, then drew it away. That dark stranger, the one that resided in his eyes, knew the truth. On some level, he'd lost her. Long before this, they'd been in a slow drift, too busy, too caught up in the day-to-day to even notice.

"I have a way out of this," he said. "Give me a chance to make it right."

One of the things she had always liked about numbers was how predictable they were. Money, too. Money came in. If you didn't spend it, you saved and it grew. If you spent more than you made, you accumulated debt. So, there was the enormous sum that they owed and the paltry (by comparison) amount of his paycheck. Heather would have to go back to work. They'd have to get someone to help them reorganize their debt and get on a tight budget. Chad would need to work overtime when he could. There was no other way to navigate this crisis.

"There's no magic bullet for this, Chad," she said.

Was it gambling? She couldn't think of anything else. He barely drank. She'd never known him to take drugs. She really didn't think he was having an affair.

"What if there *is* a magic bullet," the stranger asked her. The desperate, dark-eyed stranger.

Zoey burst through the front door then. Heather had asked Crystal to take her day on carpool. Zoey planted kisses on each of their cheeks, then breezed through the kitchen, grabbing an apple from the refrigerator.

"Ugh," she said. "I have so much homework. Heading right up."

She thundered up the stairs, oblivious to what was unfolding between her parents.

"What are you doing home, Dad?" she yelled from upstairs. But she wasn't interested enough to wait for an answer. Heather heard her door slam. Homework. Sure. She was going to get right online and play one of those stupid games with her friends.

Chad got to his feet.

"I have to get back," he said, as if he'd just happened home for lunch.

"No," she said, leaning forward. "I need to know everything. What are you talking about? What magic bullet?"

He lifted his palms in surrender. "Nothing," he said. "You're right. I've fucked up and we have to fix it. I assume this means you aren't going to Key West."

He was distant, blank almost. She wanted to reach out and grab the stranger and shake him until her real husband came back. The one, whatever his faults, had always taken care of her and Zoey.

"Well?"

Key West. Mary Jane's wedding. Heather's heart sank. She'd been looking forward to this little getaway so much, even more so when Chad stubbornly refused to come. She wanted the time to herself, without the shadow of his needs and under-the-breath comments, and all of it.

"I'm still going," she said. She held on to it, like a jewel clutched in her fist. The smell of the ocean, the swaying palms. Mary Jane said there would be a string quartet. Heather had begged him to come; part of her had wanted that at first. But he'd said no. Now she knew why.

"Fine," he said. He wasn't even looking at her. She wasn't even there. "What difference does it make at this point, anyway?"

When had she stopped loving him? When had she stopped craving his closeness, admiring things about him? Or maybe she was just angry, deeply angry. She tried to think about how she had felt on their wedding day. Relieved. She'd felt relieved like she had on graduation day, as if she'd accomplished something that her parents had both very much wanted her to do. Her dad had loved Chad, the son he never had. Heather was a good girl. She always did what was expected.

He started to leave and then stopped in the doorway without looking back.

"I'm going to fix this," he said. "You'll see."

"Chad."

But then he was gone. She got up and watched him from the kitchen window. He sat in the truck for a minute, gripping the wheel with both hands, head bowed. Then he drove away. She didn't even wait five minutes before she called Paul.

At the airport, she stepped out of the car and into Paul's arms. The airport was far from home, so she wasn't worried about being seen. She didn't care. She came alive when Paul was there. That night they shared, so long ago, it lived inside her. It sustained her. She clung to him. He put his mouth over hers, and her whole body released the tension, the worry, the deep unhappiness she'd been carrying around. He was coming with her to Key West. She was going to the wedding, and the rest of the time they'd just hide out in the hotel, being together, figuring out the mess they were in. She'd been counting the seconds. But now that they were here . . .

"What's wrong?" he asked.

She didn't even know there was something wrong until he asked. The joy of it, the illicit thrill of what they were planning to do, her suppressed desire for him, her love—was it really about Paul, about her? Or was she just trying to get even with Chad? Doing the thing she knew would hurt him more than anything else, a betrayal to match his. But hadn't she betrayed him, too, long ago? Hadn't she been betraying him all these years?

Heather and Paul stood there awhile, holding each other. She didn't have to say a word.

"It's okay," he said, pulling back from her, smiling. "I'll stay. You go."

They sat in his car and talked—about what had lived between them all these years. About their shared love and loyalty for Chad. How what they wanted could never truly be.

Even after he'd gone, she'd sat a long time thinking. She missed her flight. Then she went home. Because she was a good girl and always, always did what was expected.

thirty-one

L et me see it," said Raven.
    "Just wait," said Troy.

He was lying on his belly in front of the locked door, trying to open it with a bobby pin and a paper clip. Claudia knew, had told them, that there was no way that they were going to pick the lock with those things. But they were convinced. After all, they'd watched a YouTube video. She kind of admired their confidence, their complete faith in themselves and their abilities, a kind of DIY mentality that this generation—Generation Z, was it?—seemed to have. They didn't need to look to authority or professionals for answers. They looked to Google.

Troy pushed out an annoyed breath. They'd been at it an hour, while Claudia looked on, thinking about what came next after the kids gave up. Who could she call? Not someone in this town; Raven had been right about that. Raven and Troy switched places, and then Raven got to work.

"It's just a matter of lifting the pins—that's what he said, right?" she said, sounding like she knew what she was talking about even though they all knew she didn't. "You can kind of feel it."

"I couldn't feel anything," said Troy. He held

the flashlight for her. Claudia used Troy's phone to look for locksmiths out of town.

"Shit," said Raven.

"Language," said Claudia.

"What's wrong?" said Troy.

"The paper clip broke," she said, dropping her head into her arms. "It broke off deep in the lock. It's stuck in there."

Troy issued a sigh. Then, "What about the barn? If you think it's a tunnel, then there would have to be another door. Where else would the tunnel go?"

Claudia shook her head. "If it *is* a tunnel, it could lead to anywhere—out in the woods, even. Maybe it's just a hidden room. Or a crawl space."

"Can we go look?" asked Raven.

"Go ahead," Claudia said.

They were on a treasure hunt, she figured. Let them enjoy it. She used to set up elaborate Easter egg hunts around the apartment and the building, even once at Martha's place in Pecos. Raven would run around excitedly searching for the brightly colored eggs. She'd be so thrilled with any little trinket she found inside, so thrilled with the hunt itself. She had that kind of flushed excitement now.

They weren't going to find anything, but let them look. They pounded up the stairs, and she heard the front door slam behind them. She got down on her belly for a moment and examined

374

the lock. She tried unsuccessfully to catch the broken bit of metal with her fingernails. She lay there a second until she felt a kind of chill move up her back. She got up quickly and hurried up the stairs. She didn't want to be down there alone.

It was truly starting to dawn, now, regardless of the upbeat tone she tried to take in her almost-post about it. A darkness, a terrible sadness had settled into a hard knot in her gut. A family had been murdered here, a young girl tortured and left for dead. They couldn't stay here, could they?

She closed and locked the basement door, crossed the creaking hardwood floor of the hallway and moved into the kitchen. She sat in a chair at the table, and dropped her head into her arms and started to cry. She wept really. Big, gulping sobs. How stupid. What a mess she'd made of all of their lives—hers, poor Ayers's, Raven's. The worst part was that she had been trying to do the opposite. She had always actively sought to overcome adversity, let the light in, move through trauma. But no. Melvin Cutter had marked her that day. Her life since then had been little more than a reaction formation, a fight against the encroaching darkness that he brought with him.

And Raven's, too. Why else would she have sought out Andrew Cutter? Ayers had *told* Claudia about this boy, of course. Claudia kept waiting for Raven to tell her about it. She never imagined that she'd go looking for him. It was Claudia's fault. Who was she to keep Raven's identity from her?

She had to call Ayers, talk all of this through with him. Even now, he was her closest friend, the one she always wanted first when things were good, when things were bad. They spent hours on the phone sometimes, late at night, when Raven was sleeping, just talking and talking. His voice the only honest and sure thing in the world. She needed to tell him about all of it. Where was her phone? Like her reading glasses, she was always putting it down somewhere and then walking all over this huge house looking for them. How many hours did she spend just looking for things she'd lost?

She went upstairs and found her phone and glasses in the room she was using as an office. She was surprised to see a slew of missed calls—two from Ayers and three from Josh Beckham. Ayers, she figured, had returned from his weekend in the Caribbean (how nice for them) with Ella, to somehow learn that Raven had been in the apartment. But what did Josh Beckham want? Why would he call so many times? It was weird. In fact, *he* was weird. There was something off about him. She'd detected it in those first moments, and she ignored it because she was desperate for help with this mess of a house. She'd call him and tell him not to come on Monday. She had a lot of thinking to do.

She was about to call Ayers and tell him everything, eager to hear the measured cadence of his voice. Even when he was mad or worried, he was calm. Through their dating years, the early years of their marriage, he was her counterweight. If she flew off the handle, got flustered, nervous, emotional, he was calm, even, soothing. But it was his calm that eventually undid them. Why in those dark days and years *after* did it seem like distance, like apathy—like weakness? But that was so long ago now. So long.

She picked up the phone to dial when the doorbell rang. Something about the sound of it, and the heavy silence that followed, filled her with dread. Then, it rang again.

Raven kept looking even after Troy gave up. He wasn't that into it. He'd always been this way. He'd be all into whatever game they were playing—hide and seek, or tiger tag, or whatever—and then he'd just suddenly lose interest, say he was tired or hungry. Raven always made him keep playing. Once, he fell asleep hiding under her bed. It took her forever to find him.

He'd been sniffling since the house. Now that they were kicking up dirt and dust and even ancient remnants of hay, the sneezing had commenced. He was sitting on some old empty wooden crates, scrolling through something on his phone (always on that stupid thing, worse than any girl!), sneezing explosively every few minutes.

She kept looking around—behind an empty old locker, rusted and tilting, a riding lawnmower with four flat tires, a stack of leaking paint cans (wasn't that a fire hazard?), a bunch of tarps piled in the corner. Everything was dirty, untouched, obviously sitting neglected and forgotten for years.

"It wouldn't be on the wall," said Troy. "The door? It would be on the floor."

She thought about that. Duh. Obviously.

"Oh, yeah," she said. She shuffled her feet around a minute, kicking up more dirt and some hay. She gave up, too, walked over to her friend to see what was so interesting on his phone. She could see that he was nearly out of charge. He'd mentioned it earlier, that he'd forgotten his charger. Claudia had said he could use hers, but they'd all just forgotten in the excitement. What would he do if his phone died? He'd probably burst into flames.

He then sneezed so loudly that it was more like a shout, causing Raven to jump, startled.

"You do that on purpose," she said, "make your sneezes so loud like that."

"I don't," he said, then he gave her that wide Troy grin. "Those underground railroad sites, by the way? They're pretty rare. Most of them have been found."

"Do you think there could be a tunnel, though?"

He shrugged, looking up at her.

"I suppose it's possible."

She moved in closer to him, so their legs were touching.

"I'm sorry," she said. She'd been wanting to say it since last night.

"For what?" he asked, sitting up and taking off his glasses. He wiped the lenses on the bottom of his tee-shirt.

"For last night," she said. "For dragging you out to that club, then out here. I'm a pain."

He put his glasses back on, and there was that look again. It brought the heat up in her cheeks. Which was weird. Because it was *Troy*.

"I'd do anything for you," he said, his voice low. "Where you are, that's where I want to be. You get that, right?"

She looked away from him, then back.

"You're my best friend," she said. It was almost a whisper.

He took her hand, smiling. "Yeah," he said. "Duh."

He knocked her with his knee. She squeezed his hand hard, then she danced away from him, went back to looking around on the floor. She shoved over a pile of boxes. Nothing. She started stomping her foot, listening.

"I like it here," said Troy.

She shot him a look. "Even after all of this?"

"This place," he said, looking around. "It has a history, a story to tell. Even if it's a sad one, a scary one. It makes this place not like other places."

"Like me," said Raven. "Like Mom. Bad things happened. But we're still standing. There can still be good."

They both heard it when she hit it. Her stomps were these dull thuds connecting with solid earth. And then there was a hollow, echoing sound. She did it again. Troy got up and came over, together they got down on their knees and started clearing away the dirt, the debris, even old hay that had been collecting for years and years. There was a long, wide piece of wood. Someone had cut a space for it in the ground, buried it under earth and hay. If she hadn't been stomping, if they hadn't moved all the boxes around, it would have been totally invisible.

"Help me," said Raven.

They cleared away more dirt and hay, tried to lift the wood out by digging their fingertips in and lifting. No, that wasn't going to work. They needed a crowbar, which, luckily, Raven had carried with her from the basement—just in case.

She dug the edge of it in, beneath the wood, but wasn't strong enough to lift. Troy took over and as the wood came up, she dug her fingers under

380

and lifted, pushing the big flat board up and pushing it over where it landed against the boxes with a thud. That's when they saw the seam in the floor. They both got down on their knees and started brushing the earth away. They saw the latch, locked with a newish padlock.

"Wow," said Raven, breathless. Murder. Missing money. A hidden tunnel. Crazy.

"This one's locked, too," said Troy. "Newish, like the other one. Compared to everything else around here."

"Did you bring the other paper clip and the tension wrench?" she asked, holding out her hand.

"How long ago was it? The murders," he asked, looking at the phone to answer his own question. "Two thousand and seven. More than ten years ago. That's like forever. Why would you steal a million dollars, then lock it up for ten years?"

"They died," said Raven. "That dirty cop stole it, hid it. Those men came looking for it, didn't find it. They killed him before he told them where it was. And no one ever found it. Until now."

"Do you think that's what happened?"

"What else?"

"Maybe whoever took it hid it and then couldn't come back for it for some reason," said Troy. "You know how, like, serial killers suddenly stop killing and the police are all like: maybe he went to jail for something else. Maybe it was like that.

Whoever stole it and hid it went to jail, and when they get out, they're coming for it."

"No one knows about this door we just found, not even my mom."

Troy shook his head. "Someone knows."

Raven felt a little chill come up under the heat of her excitement.

"Can I have the tools?" she said.

"It doesn't work," said Troy.

"Let me try."

She lay flat on her belly and got to work. She wanted to open it herself. She wanted to work on it as long as she could. She didn't want to tell her mom; she didn't want to call a locksmith or the handyman. Because she knew deep down what would happen. He'd come out and with whatever tools he had, he'd easily open the locks. And guess what he'd find. Just an old, musty tunnel leading from the stupid basement to the stupid barn. And there wouldn't be anything down there. It would just be empty. Or, if there was a big bag of money, Claudia would just call the police. End of story. All the mystery, the fantasy, the possibility of things would be gone.

Like Andrew Cutter. Just another loser.

Sneaking out to meet him, scamming her way into the club, flirting her way backstage, she'd been tingling, alive to the electricity of possibility. Who was this cool-seeming guy?

What if he *was* her half brother? Would there be some deep connection, the kind of thing she'd always hoped for from a family member? He was cool, handsome, talented. If he came from Melvin Cutter, and so did Raven, maybe she could still be okay, still Raven, a bright future anyway, no matter the horror of her origin. She wasn't just a mistake, the unwanted result of an act of violence.

But then there he was, the *real* Andrew Cutter, not the imagined guy, subject to all the laws of reality, of cause and effect. He may have been talented, but he was also angry, bitter, and not nice. He had circles under his eyes, and his breath smelled a little. He looked, under all of that, when she stared right in his eyes, sad, broken, confused—just like Raven felt sometimes. And all that sizzling, tingling energy of possibility grew dark and turned to a confetti of ash.

She eased the clip and the wrench in, knowing she wasn't going to open the lock but enjoying the energy of thinking that she might.

Troy leaned over her for a few minutes, then drifted away. Then he lifted his ear to the air, got to his feet, and walked over to the grimy window.

"Who's that?" he said.

"Who?" she said.

"That guy."

Raven reluctantly got up from the lock and went to stand beside him. She saw the hot blond guy from the other day, the handyman. What was he doing here?

"That's the guy who's helping my mom," she said.

They watched him a minute. He rocked back and forth on his feet, looked around.

"You don't think your mom posted that blog, do you?" asked Troy.

"No," said Raven. Although you never could tell what Mom was going to do. She was unpredictable in some ways, did what she wanted. She was flighty. Raven could see her agreeing not to post, then forgetting she wasn't supposed to and pressing the publish button.

"Then what does he want?"

"I don't know," said Raven.

They watched as he waited on the porch. Then the door opened, and he disappeared inside.

thirty-two

There was something different about Josh. What was it? Whatever it was, Claudia didn't like it. She didn't open the screen door right away, blocked the entrance with her body.

"I tried to call," he said. "Sorry to bother you."

"What's up?" she asked.

She felt that tension of which her self-defense teacher taught her to be mindful. That feeling of discomfort, even if you don't know what it means, it means something, he warned. It means stay on guard. Women don't honor their feelings, talk themselves out of it. *But he seems so nice.*

Josh was still doing that boyish rocking thing. But he wasn't looking around, he didn't have that sweet, slightly nervous laugh. He didn't seem shy anymore. Today, he looked right at her, wearing a handsome smile. He seemed older.

"I think," he said, "when I was down in your basement, I might have dropped my best level. I had it in my pocket. Maybe it slipped out when I was moving those boxes."

"Oh," said Claudia. "Really?"

Had he moved boxes when he was down there? They weren't down there for long, and she'd been with him.

"I need it for another job that I promised to

385

finish this evening," he said. "Do you mind if I just run down and check?"

"Well," she said. She didn't want him to come into her house. Why was it so hard for her to say no? "This is not really the best time."

That wall beneath the stairs was all torn up now. How was she going to explain that?

Still, she stepped back and moved to unlatch the screen door. Why was she saying no with her words and yes with her body? She was a pleaser, that was why. She couldn't stand *not* to be nice. According to her trainer, this inability to protect your boundaries was the number one reason most women were vulnerable to predators. Too nice.

His smile widened and he tilted his head a little, then pushed inside. "It won't take a minute, I promise. I wouldn't bother you if it wasn't important."

She had a choice here. She could get firm, get loud. No, she could say. Please go. And I won't be needing you on Monday. But that was harsh, wasn't it? What if he really just needed his level? He'd come and go. She was just jumpy, edgy from everything that had happened. Wasn't that it?

When someone doesn't respect the boundaries you have politely set for yourself, watch out for that person. But she hadn't really set her boundaries, had she?

Then he was in the house, moving toward the

basement door. "I'm sure I dropped it. You know how you hear something, and then it's only later you remember?"

He was lying. She wasn't sure how she knew it. But she knew it. Close up she saw how tense were his shoulders, how frozen his smile. She gave him a tight nod and he moved quickly toward the basement door. She looked around for her phone. She'd left it upstairs. Ugh. As he moved down the stairs, the sound echoing, she went to stand over by the landline. Why was she so nervous? Just the other day, they'd spent hours alone together. He was fine. She was losing it.

"I'll go down," she said.

"No, no trouble," he said, pushing past her. She stood and let him go.

Should she say something about the state of the wall, make a joke? He probably wouldn't think anything of it. You couldn't really see inside the space unless you shone the flashlight. Maybe he wouldn't even notice.

She moved over to the kitchen and looked out the window, toward the barn, but she didn't see the kids. That's when she saw Scout. He was early; she usually didn't see him until later in the day. He sat, gray and regal, his nose up to the air. She'd call Troy's phone and tell them to stay in the barn until the coywolf was gone, until the man in her basement was gone. But when she picked up the phone, the line was dead. She stood there a moment, pressing the talk button a couple of times. It wasn't the first time this had happened, old wires that the phone company was supposed to replace. Usually, it came back up right away. But no. This time it stayed dead.

The guy on YouTube, he was right. He said that you could feel it when the pins lifted. She could visualize from the info on Wikianswers.com. You just kind of patiently worked the edges of the pick in and pushed. If you closed your eyes, you could see the pointed copper surfaces. You used the tension wrench to turn. This lock must have been older or different than the one in the basement, because Raven *could* kind of feel it. She just worked it, worked it, until there was an audible click and the lock snapped open. She stared at it for a moment in disbelief. Then she stood, grabbed the latch and with effort, swung the door wide.

"Holy crap," said Troy, coming to stand beside her. The both gazed down into the black maw in the ground. There were rungs sticking out of the wall, a ladder into the dark.

Raven sat on the edge, dangling her legs down.

"Whoa," said Troy, lifting his palms. "Wait a minute. You are *not* thinking about going *down* there."

"Well, *yeah,*" she said. Was he kidding? After all of this, *not* go down? No way.

"You are *crazy*," he said. He threw his hands up. He always gesticulated wildly when he was passionate about something. "You have no idea what's down there, first of all. Whether the structure is stable. It's dark. What if there are rats? What if it *collapses?*"

Ugh. He was such a baby. She kicked at the top rung with her heel. It was solid. The walls were cinderblock; it wasn't going to collapse. She didn't think. It was *dark*. Like, for real dark. Troy, as usual, was probably right. But what if? What if there was a bag filled with money down there? And all she had to do was go get it.

"Raven."

She spun herself around and started down, looking up into Troy's stricken face.

"Raven Grace Bishop-Martin," he said. He sounded just like her mom. "Don't you dare."

She smiled at him wide, a dare. He shone the beam of the flashlight down on her. She turned and could see the dirt floor below her. It wasn't that far, even if she fell. She carefully tested each rung before committing herself. Then she was down the ladder, the tunnel stretching out ahead of her, total blackness. It was very small; she'd have to crouch or maybe even crawl. Some of her bravery left her, and she looked back up at Troy.

"Are you coming?"

"No way."

"What are you going to do if I go?" she asked. "Tell my mom?"

He looked longingly back in the direction of the house.

"Raven, please don't do this," he said. "Let's just go tell your mom what we found. Let her decide what to do next."

It was tempting. But. "What if it's down here?"

"What if it is?" he said with a shrug.

"Then we're rich," she said. She knew it sounded childish, and he rolled his eyes.

"The money doesn't *belong* to us," he said.

"Finders keepers," said Raven, even though she didn't really mean it.

"It's evidence," he said. "People died."

"Then we're heroes," she said. "We solved a ten-year-old case."

She saw that he liked that better than the idea of stealing money—even though it wasn't really stealing. He was a rescuer at heart. A good guy. Still, he stayed up there, looking down at her.

"Raven," he said. "Just come up."

She really didn't want to go alone, but she would. Maybe it was better if he stayed up there. If the tunnel did collapse, at least he could call for help.

"Toss me the flashlight if you're going to stay up there."

He looked at her, frowning with worry, a moment longer. Then he climbed down the ladder after her.

Claudia waited, listening to him move around in the basement. It had been about six minutes (she was watching the clock), but it felt like a half hour, more. The phone still hadn't come back on; she kept picking it up to check. Raven and Troy were still in the barn. Scout had drifted back into his shadowy world, and the sun was dipping low, shadows growing long, the sky a dusty blue. She had decided to quickly head upstairs for her cell phone when she heard a crash down in the basement. She froze, listening, then moved to the top of the stairs.

She stood in the doorway to the basement. "Josh?"

No answer.

"Everything okay down there?"

Nothing.

She should run upstairs and get the phone. Why hadn't she brought it down with her? She could call the police? And say what? That the handyman she hired was taking too long in the basement finding his level? Maybe she could say that she thought he fell, hurt himself.

"Josh."

She heard movement, a low groan—pain, frustration?

She started down the stairs. She took one creaking step at a time, looking down at her sparkling genie flats that she'd paid too much for on Etsy. Just as she came to the bottom step, he slipped out of the darkness, sweating, looking frazzled.

She backed away from him, up a step. Her trainer wouldn't approve. *Never back away,* he'd say. *Move in. Stand your ground. Only run after you've delivered the incapacitating strike to the eyes, the throat, or the groin.* She knew the drill. Eyes. Throat. Groin. Fingers to the corners of the eyes. Claw of the hand to the jugular. Knee to the groin, hard and fast. Then run. She remembered her training well. Too bad she couldn't seem to put any of it into action. Fear was the factor you couldn't predict or control.

They stood a second, regarding each other.

"What are you really doing down here?" she asked.

He let out a long sigh, leaned back against the wall. "How did you know about it?"

"About what?"

He motioned toward the hole in the drywall; it gaped like a mouth.

A vein started to throb in her neck, a dryness tugging at the back of her throat.

"How did you find this? I've been looking in this house for years. More than *ten years.*"

There was something raw and desperate about his energy now, something that made her body tingle with fear. She didn't say anything, felt her awareness reach out for Raven. *Please stay in the barn,* she silently told her daughter.

"You need to leave," she said, marshalling strength to her voice. "Now."

He shook his head quickly. "That's just it. I can't unless I find what I'm looking for."

What? What did that mean?

"You need to go now before I call the police," she said. She stood aside so that he could walk up the stairs.

He took a step closer to her, palms up.

"Look," he said. "Help me and I'm gone. Otherwise, there are some bad people looking for something that may or not be hidden in this house. If they come here, I won't be able to help you. I won't even be able to help myself. I need to find it and take it to them, and they'll go away."

She shook her head, but she couldn't find words. This wasn't happening.

"They have the survey," he said. "They think there's a tunnel."

He took something from his pocket and held it up. A shiny copper key. For a bending, twisting second she thought she might be dreaming. She remembered when she was in the throes of despair after Raven had been born, and her marriage was falling apart, and the dark fingers of depression tugged at her every morning, she saw a past-life regression therapist who told her that she'd lived a hundred lives as a victim—a slave girl in Mississippi, a prostitute in New Orleans, a housewife with four children, no education, and a mean husband who beat her—and that now, in this life, it was her turn to reclaim her power. She'd survived her circumstances and had the strength to create a bright future. Claudia didn't believe a word of it. She'd never been those things. But she did believe in herself, in her will to survive. *I will never be a victim again,* she'd sworn to herself that day. And now, here she was, standing before a man she'd let into her home who wouldn't leave, who said that worse men were coming.

"Look," she said. She kept her voice low and deep. "I don't know what you're talking about. Get out of my house now."

If that was the key to the locked door, and he found what he was looking for, would he just leave and take her at her word that she'd never tell a soul? If what he was looking for was there, would he leave with a sack of money and trust her to keep his secret? No. He wouldn't. Her whole body was vibrating. She started backing up the stairs.

"There's no tunnel," she said. "Go."

"There is," he said. "That's the door, and I'm going to open it with this key. You stay where you are and don't say a word, then I'll be gone. And there isn't much time."

"There isn't *any* time."

Claudia spun to see another man, just a tall form at the top of the stairs, blocking her only exit from the basement. Panic traveled through her body like an electric shock.

"I said an hour," said Josh.

"I don't have an hour," said the other man. He slowly moved down the stairs. She backed away so that their bodies formed a tense triangle.

"It's really easy," said the other man. He was dark, wolfish, a scar on his face, a roughness to his bearing. Nothing like Josh, and yet there was something in the jaw, around the eyes. "My brother should have kept his mouth shut. But he didn't."

The brother. Wanda Crabb's warning rang in her ears.

The dark man ran a rough hand over the crown of his head. The muscles in his forearms looked like ropes beneath the skin, the thick hair, dark, blurry tattoos.

"So now we have a problem that we wouldn't have had if he let me handle it the way I wanted to." What had Wanda Crabb said his name was? Rhett, that was it. Rhett Beckham.

He moved so fast, it was like a cobra strike. The back of his hand connected hard with Claudia's jaw, knocking her head back against the concrete wall. The world wobbled, a field of stars dancing before her eyes. And then her head was ringing with pain. She lifted her hands to her ear, sinking to the ground.

"What the fuck?" yelled Josh. "What the fuck are you doing?"

But the other man moved away heading straight for the hole in the wall. He used his knee to knock more of the crumbling drywall down, then he crouched low and looked inside. He issued a big laugh, more like a whoop of victory.

Claudia's head rattled, the room spinning. She couldn't think; her breath ragged and deep with panic. *Please, please, let the kids have seen the men come in. Call the police. Run. Just don't come back to the house. Please. Please.* She thought of her phone up in her office, her only lifeline. It might as well have been on the moon. Still, she edged toward the stairs, both of them bent in front of the locked door.

"Give me the key," said Rhett. He wore a wide grin, turned to smack his brother on the shoulder. "I knew it, man. I *fucking knew* it. That dirty cop. It was here all along."

Josh was shaking his head, silent.

Claudia still sat stunned on the floor, tasting blood. All that training and just one blow, she could barely move. She kept inching, finally resting her hand on thc bottom stair.

"Only if we let her go now," said Josh. "Then I'll give you the key."

Rhett released an exasperated breath.

"Can't do that. Not now that you've been running your fucking mouth off," he said, nodding toward Claudia. "Give me that key, little brother, or I'll take it from you."

"No," said Josh. "I'm not going to let you hurt anyone else."

They circled each other, two dogs snarling in a standoff. Josh threw the first punch, missed. He took a hard blow to the gut from his brother, and then they were down on the floor rolling and grunting, delivering punches to head, neck back, rolling. Rhett bested Josh almost immediately, had him pinned, punched him mercilessly in the face.

Claudia got to her feet and ran, thundering up the stairs. The light from the door at the top seemed like it was a mile away, growing farther the closer she got. Fear pulled time long. Then she was almost there, almost to the door. She could get through, slam it closed, lock it from the outside. She'd run to the barn, get the kids, Troy would have his phone, get in the car; she'd left the keys in the ignition, as was her bad habit, but a good thing today. The kids could call the police while she drove them away.

She was almost there, almost there, when she felt the hand, a brutal vise grip on her ankle, yanking her foot and all her weight out from underneath her. She landed hard on her elbows, chin, and knees with a series of thuds and cracks. He pulled her back down the stairs, as she struggled and screamed against him, clawing at the stairs, for the banister. How could he be *so* strong?

She turned to use her legs, kick him in the face, but she missed, her heel connecting only with the air to the side of his head. She came to land beside Josh, who was unconscious on the floor, a line of blood trailing from his mouth, face red and already swelling.

Rhett climbed on top of her as she writhed, kicking. He lay the heaviness of his entire body on hers, holding her wrists with one impossibly strong, huge hand. The other one he clamped hard over her mouth, the hard stones of his fingertips digging into the soft flesh of her face. She heard herself whimpering. He put his mouth to her ear and her nose filled with his scent—sweat, booze, cigarettes. Rank. Vile. Melvin Cutter. How could she be back here again? She'd come so far.

"I have the key to that door now," he said. "If you just lie here and shut up, be a good girl, I'll be gone."

She nodded. He was lying. She knew that. Why didn't he just kill her now? What was he waiting for? She made herself look into his eyes. She saw something there; he wasn't blank like Cutter. There a flicker of something human. He didn't want to kill her.

"I promised my little brother that no one would get hurt," he said, answering the questions she hadn't asked. He glanced over at Josh, whom he'd just beaten into unconsciousness. That apparently did not count as anyone getting hurt, nor did it negate his loyalty.

"He screwed up. But a promise is a promise. I've been watching you. This house. Your pretty girl. I'll come back here or people I know will. You stay quiet. Or better, leave town. You'll never hear from us again. I'm no killer—unless I don't have a choice. *Can* you be quiet?"

She nodded again. He lifted his hand from her mouth. She couldn't believe how helpless, powerless she felt. Her whole body was shaking. Those classes. It was just theater.

"Good girl," he said.

There was something about the phrase, about the way he said it. It was like a match to a gas leak, lighting her up inside. Something pushed up through the fear that had paralyzed her, hot and red. Rage.

"Just stay down," he said. "Five minutes, not even. We never see each other again."

He backed away, watching her. When he turned to the workbench, she pushed herself up. There was a hammer lying on the ground, rusted, dirty. She was going to pick it up and bash his fucking head in. She reached for it, his back to her as he worked the key into the lock. Josh stirred, issuing a low groan, and their eyes met.

"No," he croaked.

Rhett spun on them, saw her hand on the hammer. She was only aware of his fist coming at her like a freight train. She felt her neck snap back with the impact. Then it was dark.

thirty-three

Raven used to dream about tunnels. A long, twisting network of blue tubes that connected all the places in the world. You just stepped through a door in your bedroom, hopped in a cozy pod, and zipped to school, or to Aunt Martha's in New Mexico, or Dylan's Candy Bar—wherever you wanted to be. It only took a few seconds. Step through one door and out another—in your pajamas. No need to get dressed, to go out in the cold or the rain, hail a cab, or wait miserable on a crowded subway platform for a train that may or may not come. This tunnel, the one they were in, was not like the tunnels of her childhood fantasies. It was cold, dark, scary; the rough-hewn walls were damp, only pitch-blackness ahead.

Troy pressed up behind her, shining the flashlight beam onto the ground in front of them. When he held the beam up, it seemed to get sucked up by the darkness, no end to the tunnel in sight. A few feet in front of them was an abyss, emptiness.

"We're heading back toward the house, right?" said Raven. "This tunnel? It must connect the house to the barn." Troy didn't say anything, his

401

breathing shallow. Raven was scared, too, wanted to turn around, the faint light from the opening above shining behind them. They were crouched low, hands nearly touching the ground.

"This is such a bad idea," said Troy. "Let's go back."

"It can't be far, right?" said Raven, pressing ahead. There was a faint dripping sound. Then something else, a distant knock or a crash. She stopped short, and Troy bumped into her, lifted the flashlight.

"What's wrong?" he said.

"Did you hear that?"

"I didn't hear anything. What did you hear?"

"I don't know," she said. "Nothing, I guess."

She kept moving, but this time Troy stayed behind.

"Let's go back," he said, for the twentieth time. "I don't have a signal down here. We can't call for help."

Raven pressed her hands against the walls, reached up to the low ceiling. Everything was damp, but the structure felt solid. It couldn't just crumble around them, right? Even though she *wanted* to go back, too, and she could see why it was a good idea, she just couldn't do it. The tug, the wanting to know, the potential of it—it was too great. In the light, up in the barn, in the house, doing the right thing, it was all known. Dull. Nothing. Just like any other day.

Another thump; Troy lifted the light toward it. Again. Maybe her mom was banging on the door from the other side, trying to get in with a hammer or a crowbar or something. She talked about getting the drill, though she didn't think the bits she had were strong enough to drill through metal.

Raven kept moving, coming to a stop at the curved edge of light cast by Troy. She stepped into the dark. He followed, and the light kept moving ahead of her and she stayed in it, blackness a wall all around them. Then Troy tripped.

Whatever he caught his foot on (probably his other foot, or the too-long frayed bottom of his jeans), he went flying into Raven. The flashlight and the phone sailing up ahead of him. *Crack. Crack.* The light went out. A wash of darkness, the light from the opening above and behind them shone like a beacon in the distance.

"Oh, shit," said Troy. He was heavy, lying on top of her. "My glasses."

"Ugh," she said, rolling out from under him.

"Sorry. You okay?"

"Yeah. Are you?"

"I hurt my knee." She could just make him out. He rubbed it gingerly. She sighed; he was such a baby.

Raven got on all fours, feeling around on the grit of the ground, and found the flashlight first, finally feeling the cold cylinder beneath her fingers. She pressed the button, a couple of times. Nothing. Then it flickered to life. She shone it on him, on the ground behind them. There wasn't anything to trip on. He shrugged as though his clumsiness were a long acknowledged factor in all endeavors. Which it was.

His glasses were a little bent when she found them, but the lenses were intact. He slipped them on. She found the phone next. It was cracked, the screen just a spiderweb of thick white lines. She handed it to him, and he bent his head over it as if it were an injured pet. He cradled it, prodded it with his thumb. It didn't come on when he pressed the center button, once, twice, three times.

"It's dead," he said, bereft.

"Okay, look," she said. "Just stay here."

She took the light and went ahead, moving quickly, crouching low. It couldn't be far, she figured, trying to visualize the distance between the house and the barn. Shouting distance. She looked back at Troy, who was still sitting on the ground, trying to resuscitate his phone.

The tunnel got smaller; she dropped down to her hands and knees and crawled. Her mother would kill her, absolutely lose her mind if she knew what Raven was doing, a thought that scared her and excited her, goaded her forward.

"Raven," called Troy.

"I'm okay," she called back.

It was a few more feet when the beam light fell on something. A blob, an amorphous dark form on the ground. She moved faster, came up close to it. She reached out a hand and felt it, rough beneath her fingers.

It was a bag. A big canvas bag.

thirty-four

See," said Rhett. "You *do* love me, little brother."

"You fucker," said Josh. He spit a mouthful of blood onto the floor.

Rolling painfully onto his side, he moved over to Claudia. Blood ran like a river from her nose and over her mouth. He used his shirt to wipe it away, her eyelids fluttering. A big bulb of regret lodged in his throat. He ached all over from his struggle with Rhett.

"I'm sorry," he whispered. Why didn't he let her hit him? What kind of an idiot was he?

Her pulse was steady, her breathing shallow. Josh took off his jacket and rolled it up, placing it under her head. He should have just let her kill him with that hammer. But it had always been that way with Rhett and Josh. They'd beat the crap out of each other, but God help the outsider that tried to hurt either one of them.

"Why didn't you just let me handle this?" said Rhett.

But it wouldn't have mattered. He knew the night that Rhett walked back through the front door that bad things were going to happen and that Josh would be a part of it. It was just like Lee said. Having certain people in your life was just like keeping a bottle of booze hidden in the house. It was only a matter of time before you twisted off the top and started to drink for whatever reason you'd given yourself. Now that the forty he'd drank in the car had burned off, *that guy* was gone. And Josh was sick, weak from fighting with Rhett, crippled by regret. Seven years sober. All gone.

"Just open the goddamn door and let's get out of here," said Josh.

"Where's that girl?"

"She must be out," said Josh, hoping that he was right. He hadn't seen her when he came in.

Rhett held the key up.

"This is it, brother," he said. He always had a flare for the dramatic. "We've waited for the payout all these years. And now we're here."

"Just open it and let's go," said Josh.

Rhett frowned at him, disappointed in Josh's lack of enthusiasm, apparently having forgotten that they were trying to kill each other just a few minutes earlier, that he'd punched Josh so hard in the face that he'd knocked him unconscious. His whole face throbbed, his right eye swelling shut.

Claudia stirred, issuing a distressed whimper. "Raven," she whispered.

"Shh," said Josh.

He listened as Rhett struggled with the lock. Then there was silence. "There's something

407

jammed in here. Got it." A moment passed, then, "Shit."

"What?" said Josh.

"It's empty," said Rhett. "And the door's too small. I can't get in."

"Empty?" said Josh. "There's nothing there?"

Maybe part of Josh *had* believed it could be there. Otherwise, why did he feel this crushing wave of disappointment? Maybe that's why he'd come here ahead of his brother, even though he told himself he was just trying to keep anyone else from getting hurt. That night, what they did, it stayed with him, poisoned his whole life. It came up in his dreams, hit him every time the table saw hit that high panicked note it sometimes hit. It was why he'd spent so many nights drunk, why he never left for college, why he hid in his old man's shop fixing up tables pretty housewives found at flea markets.

We can't outrun our sins. His old man had been right about that and about so many things.

Maybe on some level, Josh had been hoping for a payday, too.

He moved in next to Rhett and peered into the darkness. The opening was about the size of a microwave oven. He was narrower through the shoulders than his brother, about thirty pounds lighter. He pushed his way in.

The deep black seemed to shift and move. Was there a hint of light? Did he hear something, a shuffling, a voice? If this was a tunnel, then that meant that there was an opening somewhere else. There was a high-pitched note. The rumble of a deeper voice. Holy shit.

"I think there's someone in there," he said, incredulous. Who? The old man? That slut Missy?

"What?" said Rhett. "Are you fucking kidding me?"

With effort Josh got himself through the opening and started to crawl. He heard Rhett thunder up the stairs.

thirty-five

I parked by the bridge and approached the property from behind. The same place I went to meet Seth that night, where I waited with Catcher. I left the Suburban in a little turnaround that was tucked back in the trees. No one would see the truck until they'd passed it, figure it was left by hunters or fishermen looking to pull some trout out of the river.

I was a teenager the last time I stepped on that bridge. Ten years later, I didn't feel like I'd come very far. I was still stuck in that night in so many ways.

They'd hate me, Paul had said, *for how I've failed you.*

He hadn't failed me. He'd taken me in, took care of me with as much love as any parent. He'd helped with homework, found help when things got beyond him. He paid for my education.

"How?" I'd asked him when I first started to understand the size of the expense. I didn't know how much he had saved or what kind of pension he had. But I didn't think it was much, not enough to cover tuition at NYU and still live. "How are you affording this?"

It was a Sunday; I discovered the bill from the

410

university sitting on top of a stack of others. Prior to that, I hadn't even thought about it. In my house, it wasn't *if* I went to college, it was *where*. There was no talk about how it would get paid for. I would strive to get into the best possible school and, somehow, it would get managed. My parents didn't talk about money.

"Your mother had some money saved," he said that day. "When you graduate, whatever is left will go to you. That's what she wanted."

"How much?"

He went into the bedroom and came back with an envelope, a statement that had been opened and stuffed back in the envelope with my name on it. He'd scrawled a user name and password in blue ink.

"She wanted you to go to college," he said. "She worried that if you knew there was money, you wouldn't go to school."

I lifted the statement out and stared at the numbers. The balance, the large withdrawals that coincided with tuition payments, money I had needed for books, room and board, more than $60,000 a year. There was a little more than $300,000 still.

"You'll need another hundred fifty or more to finish school," he said. "But the rest is yours. Don't get your head turned. It's a head start. It's not as much money as it seems."

There was something wrenching my stomach.

411

"I don't understand," I said. "Where did she get this money?"

My parents did *not* have money. They didn't talk about it, but I knew we weren't rich. My mother clipped coupons, searched online for bargains. We got our books from the library, bought what was on sale, not the latest styles. The answer to almost everything I wanted was no or maybe later. And I knew that it hurt her to say no; she wanted me to have everything I wanted, what the other girls had.

"It was an inheritance from her grandmother," he said. "She added to it when she could. You know how she was. Frugal. Then there was the death benefit, pension, life insurance, and the sale of your parents' stuff."

It didn't ring true.

"She told you about it?" I asked.

He nodded, but his face looked gray, his expression strained. It was a look he got when he talked about my parents. Grief, anger, something else I couldn't name.

"I was your legal guardian should anything happen to them," he said. "That was always known. We talked about you, your future, what she—what they—wanted for you."

"But I don't understand," I said. "I thought there was debt. That my dad was in trouble."

He blinked at me. "Who told you that?"

"I heard you and Boz talking, a long time ago,"

I said. "That's why they thought—" I couldn't finish.

That my dad was a dirty cop, that he robbed drug dealers and stole their money, that they came looking, that he let them kill my mother, torture me, kill him rather than say where it was hidden. I still couldn't put my lips around those words in front of him, even though I had been talking to Mike. Even though I had grown strong enough, brave enough to ask questions, to look for answers.

"It's not true," he said. "What they thought. There's no evidence. Your dad—he was a good man. He wasn't good with money. But he was a good man."

"If they were in trouble," I said. "Why didn't she use this money to pay the bills?"

"Because," he said. "It was money she'd saved for you. She didn't want to compromise your future because of their mistakes."

"She told you that?"

He nodded, looked down at a hand he had laid down flat on the table.

"So you knew about the money, but my dad didn't?"

He didn't answer, didn't look at me. Then, "Your mother confided in me sometimes. Your dad wasn't always easy, and your mother and I were friends. But I didn't know about the debt until after they were gone. If I had, I'd have helped them."

I folded up the statement.

"That money is in an education trust," he said. "So, again, it can only be used for those costs until you graduate. Then it belongs to you."

"I'll give it to you," I said. "When I graduate."

"You will not," he said, turning those icy eyes on me. He reached for my hand, and I laced my fingers through his.

"You deserve it," I told him. "How much have you spent on me?"

He bowed his head, and when he looked at me again, his eyes glistened.

"Every second you have been in my life is a blessing, Zoey," he told me. Color came up his neck. "You're the very best of both of them. Every time I look at you, I see her beauty, his goodness, her warmth, his strength. I'm the one who owes you."

We sat like that a minute; I didn't say anything, and I knew he didn't need me to. My love for him was well known, and I've never been good with words. But I knew that my mother didn't have money like that. She'd alluded to an account, a little money tucked away for the future. But that wasn't a little money, not to people like my parents. Where had it come from? Since my name was on the account, it was easy enough to find out that the balance of the account was about $8,000 the month before my mother died. Slowly, about a year later, deposits started to

414

show up—$1,000 here, $5,000 a month later—until just under $400,000 had accrued. Then the withdrawals started for school and nothing new came in.

That was the kind of thing that they'd look for, the police, anyone monitoring a cold case that involved money. Unless no one was looking. Unless the people who were supposed to be looking, as Seth suggested, were intentionally looking the other way.

I stood at the edge of the trees in the shadows. I didn't have a plan, not really. I figured I'd knock on the door and see what happened.

"Is that why you left your car by the side of the road and walked nearly a mile through the woods?" asked my dad. He was following behind me. Didion was nowhere to be seen, thankfully.

It was always better to approach on foot, quietly, when walking into a situation full of unknowns. If I were big and strong, maybe I'd be more direct on my approach. But since I'm small, surprise is one of my few advantages. Not that I was expecting a fight. I just wanted some time in that basement, to go through anything left by my parents. I figured I'd knock on the door, introduce myself, and ask permission. But I'd definitely set something into motion, and I was still aching all over from the bruising I'd taken last night. I couldn't be sure who else was watching the house. That key, the one Mr. Rodriquez had given me, the one I'd been jumped for last night, it opened something. And I had a feeling, whatever it was, was in that house. If they had the key, they weren't going to waste any time.

"What did you hide in the basement that night, Dad?" I asked.

But when I turned around, he was gone, never one to answer the hard questions.

Maybe I felt it when I came through the trees, like Catcher did that night. The door to the barn was gone. The door to the house stood wide open, as well. The blue Toyota that I recognized as belonging to Josh Beckham was parked in the drive. There was a pulse to the air, something not quite right. I waited, a watcher in the woods, listening to the air. There was the wind. The call of some faraway bird. The scrabble of blowing leaves. My own breath.

A dark form appeared in the door to the house, paused there, breathless, then broke into a run across the yard toward the barn. I waited a moment, then followed, fast and quiet.

thirty-six

When the phone rang in the night, Chad Drake was always fully awake before his hand even touched it. It had happened so many times that Heather usually did little more than stir and turn over. For a smallish town, they were a busy department. And adjacent towns had smaller forces, so when something big happened, he usually got a call. He didn't recognize the number on the caller ID.

"Drake."

"Can you meet me?"

"What's up?" he said, surprised. He looked at the clock; it was after 1:00 a.m.

"I need you to come out."

"Okay," he said, sitting up. The floor beneath his feet was cold as he pulled on his jeans, the sweatshirt hanging over the chair. If it was the job, he'd have quickly showered, gotten fully dressed. Instead, he grabbed his sneakers, socks, heading out into the hallway so Heather wouldn't pick up on the fact that there was something different about this call.

"I'm at the rest stop between exit 90 and 93 on Route 80 in Leesburg." Paul sounded level, normal—which in and of itself was odd for a late-night call like this.

417

"What happened?" That rest stop was an hour from the house at least.

"Just come."

"Come to the house."

Chad could hear the sound of cars on asphalt, the distant wail of a horn, a car door slam, voices.

"Just meet me."

He hung up then, and Chad moved quietly downstairs, glancing at Zoey's dark room. He had the urge to look in on her but kept down the stairs. Catcher looked mildly interested in where he might be going, but the dog was used to it, too. If Heather left, he sat and whined at the door. Chad could come and go, no one the worse for wear.

The drive was long. Chad wanted to call Paul from his cell phone. But since his brother was at a rest stop, had clearly called from a phone that was not his own, Chad thought better of it. The highway stretched long and empty, sleep tugging behind his eyes. He used to wake up for a call and be up all night sometimes. It never bothered him until recently. He was getting old.

At first Chad didn't see him. The old black beater—what was it? A rattling old Ford Taurus—seemed one with the shadows. Chad pulled up beside it, aware that Paul had chosen this spot because it couldn't be seen from the road. Chad got out of the car and slid in beside his brother.

"What's up, man?" he said, laying a hand on Paul's arm. "What's going on?"

Paul looked tired, older—there were dark circles under his eyes, deep wrinkles around his mouth filled with shadows.

"It's done," said Paul.

The words worked their way in, and his stomach filled with a toxic blend of dread and excitement.

"What are you talking about?" Chad asked. But he knew.

"It's in the trunk," said Paul. He wasn't smiling. Shouldn't he be smiling?

Chad got out of the car and walked around back to pop the trunk. There was a big blue canvas bag there. He pulled open the metal zipper, and it was loud in the quiet night. Paul came to stand behind him.

"Holy shit."

A huge pile of cash, banded into stacks of ten thousand. The smell of it, that special aroma of ink and paper and a million hands drifted up to his nose.

"What the fuck?" said Chad, looking at Paul. "Where? How?"

"It was just like you said it would be," said Paul. "Those skulls were sleeping when we got there."

"No one got hurt?"

"I didn't say that."

He zipped closed the bag. "You went alone."

Paul shook his head. "I had to cut them in."

"Who did you bring?"

"Better you don't know, right?"

Chad nodded, though he had a pretty good idea. There weren't many guys you could call to help you rip off a drug dealer in the middle of the night. Men who were trained, reliable, had that certain dark ethic you could trust. A code of right and wrong that not everybody shared.

"How much?"

"A hundred grand each."

"So that's four each for you and me," said Chad.

"I don't want any of it," said Paul. He was leaning on the car, looking out at the highway. Up above, the sky was clear and riven with stars, just a few thin clouds drifting in front of the sliver moon.

Relief warmed Chad's shoulders, shifted into his belly. He was *free,* free of that debt, that burden that he carried, thought about, couldn't get out from under. He wouldn't be able to pay it off right away, and this money would have to stay hidden for a good long while. But he'd be able to do it, get them to a better place. She would forgive him; they'd move on.

"Don't be crazy," said Chad. "Take the money. You did all the work."

"I did it for you, for Heather and Zoey," said Paul. "I don't want it. I don't need it. I have no family. I don't even own a house."

Paul got a particular tone when he talked about Heather and Zoey, a softness that never touched his voice otherwise. Chad knew how he felt about Heather. Of course, he did; he wasn't stupid. But Heather belonged to Chad, and he to her; it had always been that way, and all three of them knew it.

"I'll keep it at the house," said Chad. "Half of its yours. It'll be there waiting for you, like a savings account."

Paul nodded but didn't look at Chad.

"Where are you going to hide it?"

Chad looked at the money. "That crawl space we discovered between the house and the barn. I'll pile a bunch of crap in front of the wall under the stairs. Why? You think someone'll come looking."

"No," said Paul. "It was clean. And you had nothing to do with it."

Chad thought a minute. All that money.

"A hundred grand going to be enough to keep your guys quiet? Keep them happy and from sniffing around in a few months asking for more," asked Chad. "They knew what the whole haul was?"

Paul seemed to consider.

"It was your find and my plan," he said finally with a shrug. "They were just the muscle. They're good."

"It was clean?"

"Yes," said Paul again. "It was clean."

"You okay?" asked Chad. He closed the trunk and faced Paul.

"Just tired," he said. "You know you can't spend it right away, right? Pay those bills off slowly, work overtime. Don't call attention to yourself."

"Of course, I know that, big brother," said Chad. It had always been like this. Chad had a problem, Paul fixed it. Paul gave advice, Chad took it. There was no one else he'd ever trusted or counted on in the same way, not even his dad.

"But settle that other debt first," he said. "And remember you promised. No more."

Paul meant the bookie. Chad was into the guy for a couple grand—bad bets on fights, games, horses. Buster had been patient because Chad was a cop, but he was starting to make threats. Chad was most embarrassed about that, how he'd used his overtime money to try to make more to pay off debts and lost that, too. What a mess. But he was done with all that. Done for good.

Chad raised his hands. "I swear to God."

"Take care of them, Chad," said Paul. Something dark had crept over Paul's features, an etched sadness that opened a gully in Chad's center. "Get yourself out of trouble. And take care of Heather and Zoey, or so help me—"

He stopped, shaking his head, let the sentence trail.

Chad stood before his friend, his *brother,* and saw Paul's anger, his disappointment, saw that Paul had brought himself low because of the trouble Chad had gotten himself into. Chad understood that Paul had done it for Heather and for Zoey. He didn't know what to say, bowed his head with shame. After a moment, Paul patted him hard on the shoulder.

"Get the money out of that trunk and go home to your family," he said.

Chad stood a moment, toeing the ground, searching for words to express his gratitude, how sorry he was. But instead he said nothing. He lifted the heavy blue canvas bag, transferred it to his own trunk. Paul was still standing there as he pulled from the rest stop and went home.

thirty-seven

Raven grabbed the canvas handle and started to tug. It was heavy, and she had to use the strength in her legs to move it from where it had obviously been sitting for a decade. Moving it released all the dampness and mold that had gathered beneath it and within its deep folds. Her sinuses tingled and she stifled a sneeze, but more than that, her heart was thumping with effort and excitement. What if? What if? *What if?* She didn't want to open the bag. What if it was filled with paper? Or a dead body? (It would smell, right?) Or something worthless like old clothes, books? As long as it was closed, it could contain anything.

With effort, she got it back to Troy, who pocketed his dead phone and got up to help her and then started sneezing. He folded his nose into the crook of his arm—one, two, three.

"What is it?" he asked with an exaggerated sniffle. He knelt down beside it.

"This is *it*," she said. "It was right inside the door. This must be it."

Both of them stared. "Did you look inside?" he asked.

She shook her head, then reached for the thick metal zipper and pulled.

"Holy shit," said Troy, sinking back onto his heels. "Oh. My. God."

Raven thought of all of those cartoons, where the lid of a treasure chest opened and light radiates out. There was no glow except the flashlight she'd tilted up against the wall and which Troy now shone on the bag. Money. Thick stacks of bills wrapped in white and orange bands.

"No way," said Raven. "No *way.*"

Troy laughed a little, nervous, uncertain. He reached out a hand to touch the money, but then he drew it back.

It felt as if she were dreaming, that it couldn't be quite real. A dream that started with sneaking into the city and meeting Andrew Cutter, one of those long, twisty messes that makes absolutely no sense when you wake up. She reached into the bag and pulled out a stack. It was soft and heavy in her hand. It had so much energy, that energy of possibility—what you could do, what you could buy, who you could be.

"We have to get out of here and call the police," said Troy, breaking rudely into the spin of her imaginings. He gently took the stack from her hand and tossed it back into the back where it lay soft and dark. The envelope slid into the dark of the bag.

"It's blood money," he said. He wore a deep worried frown, such a rare expression. "People died for it. It's tainted."

425

Something came up from deep inside her. At first it felt like anger, because that was her go-to emotion. It was red and hot, burned fierce and bright, lashed out, pushed people away, defended. She was safe behind it; no one could get to her there. But it smoked out fast in front of Troy, fizzled, and died before it burst into flames. Beneath it was the thing she didn't want to feel, that black hole of sadness that sucked in everything even light. It was so much scarier than rage. You could lose yourself in that black place.

The bag of money gaped between them, and her thoughts spun.

The cafeteria on Friday. When Clara sat across from her, Raven had been reading. "Hey," she said. Raven smiled; the kids had been nice so far. She told her mother that she didn't like it. But it was okay.

"So," said Clara. "Does your mom have a blog?"

Raven started to shake her head. Claudia had tried to protect their privacy. But some people back in New York had figured it out anyway. It was only a matter of time before stuff like that got around, especially in a small town like this where no one was doing anything.

"Makeovers and meltdowns dot com," she said. "Cute."

Raven didn't know why Clara didn't like her. But that's when she saw it, that mean glint that some girls got. There was a faux niceness, a smile that tricked, a tone that dripped sweet as honey. But it was a mask. Underneath was something cold, sharp as a razor.

"If I was her, if some animal had raped me? I'd have had an *abortion.*"

The word hurt like a slash to the face. It stung and started to bleed while Clara's friends twittered nervously, though the blonde one looked a little disgusted by her friend, uncomfortable. Raven felt that heat. That white sweater, that faux earnest expression. It wasn't an accident; she did flip the tray and the red viscous (disgusting) sauce sprayed like gore. She got all of them— hair, faces, pretty clothes—and watched as their expressions turned from superior and gloating to horrified and embarrassed. It was a comical shift, one that made Raven laugh out loud. It wasn't until they were being led down the hall by the gym teacher that despair set in. *Why didn't she? Why did Claudia have her?*

Ella's implication that she should find her *real family.* Had she used those words? Maybe not, but that's what she meant, right? Andrew Cutter's rejection; even he didn't want anything to do with her. The people who died in her house. Her mother who tried so hard to make everything right.

Now, with the blood money between them, and the swirling mess of sad-mad churning in her gut, the tears came. She almost never cried.

427

Troy cried more than Raven did. He was a highly sensitive person; a good commercial could make him cry. But now a big sob escaped her, and then Troy was in close, wrapping his arms around her.

"It's okay, Raven," he whispered in her ear. "You're okay."

He knew that she wasn't crying about the money, that it was the whole tangle of everything, that unsolvable puzzle of her life. She never had to say anything to him. Somehow he already knew. *I'm highly sensitive. My mirror neurons are in overdrive, especially with you.*

"You're just Raven," he said. "Smart, funny, wild, the best friend ever. Nothing else matters. Really."

He lifted a hand to push back her hair, to dry her tears. Then, so softly, he kissed her. It was a surprise and it wasn't; it was always just about to happen. There was a salty sweet moment, her heart fluttering like a bird in the cage of her chest. She kissed him back, and he smiled that Troy smile.

"Okay," he said. "Wow."

The light changed, darkening from above. They both looked up to see a stranger peering down from the tunnel opening. An electric bolt of fear shot through Raven.

"Isn't that sweet?" he said. "Young love."

His face was hard, skin rough. His eyes were cold.

"Who are you?" asked Raven, grabbing Troy's wrist. Her voice came out high pitched, afraid. "What are you doing up there? This is private property."

"What do *you* have *down there?*" he said, a wide smile making his face even uglier.

"None of your business," she said, summoning courage. But her voice wobbled and she still sounded like a scared little girl. Troy had a protective arm around her waist. He squeezed a little, which she took to mean he thought she should be quiet.

"I think it *is* my business," said the stranger. "Because you have something that belongs to me, speaking of private property."

That's when she saw the gun, black and menacing in his hand.

"I have no idea what you're talking about," she said. This time she sounded stronger, more sure of herself, even though she wasn't at all. She was shaking all over. Troy was pulling her backward.

It slowly started to dawn who the stranger was, what he wanted. The money. The murders. The men who weren't caught. Oh, God. This wasn't happening.

"It's Raven, right?"

She spun, startled to her core to see another man slipping from the shadows of the other direction, from inside the tunnel where the money had come from. He must have come in the door in the basement.

Where was her mom, then, if that was true? Fear started a boil in her middle. Troy shone the flashlight on him, and Raven saw that it was the handyman Josh.

"We called the police," said Troy. He'd made his voice deep, not the soft pitch that she was used to from him. "When we found the money, we called them. They're on their way, so you should go before they get here."

"Oh, really," said the stranger. He pointed the gun at them and Raven felt chills move down her body. "You weren't going to keep it?"

"Your mom," said Josh. "She's a nice person. We don't want to hurt either one of you."

"Where is she?" said Raven. Her voice was tight, her breath growing ragged with panic. They were trapped, no way up or back.

"She needs help," Josh said, edging closer. Raven drew in a frightened breath. What did that mean? That she needed help. "You need to let us take what's ours and go. And when we're gone, you can call for help for your mother. But you're never going to tell anyone what happened here today."

She found herself nodding, because he was nodding. She wasn't stupid. Josh moved closer, closer, until he was standing right in front of her. He wasn't like the other man, who was climbing down the ladder, gun still in his hand. He was softer, less angry looking. But there was something not nice about his eyes.

"There are people who want this money," he said. "And they're not good people. If you ever say a word, they'll find you. They'll kill you and your family. Is that clear?"

She was still nodding. She didn't have a voice. She was just thinking about how her mom needed help and how she had to give it.

When the other man was on the ground, she could smell him, cigarettes, body odor. He came in close, his eyes glancing over her the way male eyes always did—hungry, assessing as if she was some*thing* they wanted, but not a person. There wasn't enough space down there for all of them. She felt sick—fear, the smell of tobacco, of damp and mold.

"Okay, look. We didn't call the police. Just take it and go," said Troy.

He pushed Raven so that she was behind him, between his body and the wall. "We never saw you. You weren't here, and we didn't see the bag."

The stranger edged toward the bag as if he didn't trust them not to lunge for it, for him, as if they would when he had a gun in his hand. Troy backed them farther away, until Raven was against the cinderblock and he couldn't go any farther.

The man edged closer and looked down into the bag, then he shot a look of glee over to Josh.

"I told you," said the stranger.

Josh just nodded, his face grim. "Let's go."

Raven knew the bag was heavy. But the man lifted it easily.

"You climb up," the stranger said to Josh. "I'll hand you the bag."

Josh hesitated, looked at Raven and Troy. The whole encounter stayed surreal. Raven felt numb, her limbs filled with sand. Beneath the shock, there was a hard pulse of fear, a terrible tension. *Don't leave us down here with him,* she thought.

"You go first," said Josh, as if he heard her. "I'll hand the bag up to you."

The two men stood staring at each other, a stand-off. The way the light fell on them, she could see for the first time that they each had black eyes and bloody noses.

"Have it your way," said the stranger. His lips curled up in a nasty un-smile. Raven knew somehow, she just knew, if Josh left her and Troy down here with the other man, he'd kill them both. Her whole body was tense, lungs tight.

The other man put the bag down and climbed up quickly. He reached down for the bag; Josh handed it up. It disappeared from view.

Josh turned quickly and whispered.

"Go," he said. "Fast. The door on the other side is open and your mom needs a doctor. Don't tell anyone what happened. They *will* kill you; I won't be able to help you."

Before they started to run, the door above them slammed closed, leaving all three of them down there. They heard the click of the lock, then boots running.

"That fucker," Josh said.

The flashlight flickered, browning out then coming back on. Josh turned and ran back into the darkness of the tunnel from where he came. Raven and Troy followed, terror a big knot in her throat. The closer they got, the narrower the tunnel became until they had to get to hands and knees. Raven could see the light up ahead.

"Mom!" Raven yelled. "Mom!"

Troy panted behind her. They got closer and closer to the light; they were almost there. Then the light ahead started to die, and the door, their only way out, closed and locked, as well.

"No." The word came out a hoarse and desperate yell.

Josh banged pointlessly on the door. "Don't do this," he yelled. "Rhett!"

The flashlight chose that moment to die completely, and they were cast into pitch-black. Raven started to scream.

thirty-eight

C laudia dreamed about Ayers.

"Get up, Claud," he was saying. "You can't just lie there. She needs you."

"I can't," she said. God, her head was pounding; her limbs were so heavy. "I'm sorry."

She wasn't apologizing for not being able to get up. But for everything else.

"Don't be sorry, darling," he said. Cool, rational, like always. "Just wake up."

It was actually her fault. The reason she and Ayers didn't make it. She could see that now. At the time she thought it was him. Most people *assumed* that it was him, that he couldn't handle what had happened to her, that he couldn't accept Raven, that maybe on some primal level, he didn't *want* Claudia after she'd been violated. Or maybe, they assumed, she didn't want him, or any man ever again. People made a lot of assumptions about trauma, about rape, about men and women. Old ideas and attitudes clung to the DNA, even if intellectually or culturally we think we've moved on.

But really, when she looked at it in moments of clarity, it was Claudia who was to blame for how it all fell apart. She thought he couldn't understand her pain. Ayers wanted so badly for her to move on, for them to go back to where they were. But nothing in Claudia's body, mind, or spirit could allow that, and there was no way back to the person she was before Melvin Cutter raped her. Ayers wanted her to forget. But every time she climbed the stairs, or the room got too dark, she saw Melvin Cutter lurking in doorways. Ayers wanted her to stop writing, stop posting, stop talking about it, but that was the only thing that made her feel better, that gave her any power.

Claudia grew to hate him for his distance from the rape. She hated him for not being the first man through the door. She hated him for being able to forget—from her perspective—what happened. She even hated him—darkly, secretly—for loving Raven with his whole heart as he clearly did. She was ashamed of that more than anything else; it was baser than she knew herself to be. Because Ayers had promised Claudia that he could love the baby completely, that he would convince himself that there was no way she might not be his. The universe would not punish them in that way. And he did that. And somehow, even though she did exactly the same, she hated him for it. She'd have had more compassion, hated him less, if he'd had to work at it.

Ayers wasn't raging, holding on to anger, filled with a desire for revenge against the man who hurt her. He forgave; he moved forward. She'd been beaten and raped in their home. She'd lost her freedom, her identity, her sense of safety. And Ayers was as evolved as a monk. That's what undid them, she realized much later, how easily he got past it all. She saw it as a kind of betrayal.

She confided in Martha when, after so much therapy, she finally got it.

"It's primal," her sister said. "You want him to beat his chest, turn back time, and protect you. You want him to be in the house with you that night and stop all of it before it happened. But you didn't fall in love with Ayers because he was a tough guy. You married him because he was everything Dad wasn't."

Dad. Distant. Strict disciplinarian. Ruthless businessman. Never showed either of them an ounce of affection. Claudia could never remember him even kissing their mother. He was gone most of the time, a fearful stick figure in their lives. Mom was the soft one, the loving one who was always there—hosting sleepovers, going on field trips. If Mom was unhappy with Dad, she'd never showed it.

Claudia's mother died from ovarian cancer when Claudia was still in college; Claudia never got to ask her the hard questions about marriage, about motherhood, about what compromises she felt she'd made. She got to know her dad a little better then; he was more awkward, maybe with a touch of Asperger's. Distant because he didn't know how to be with people. But then he died from a heart attack two years after Mom.

She and Ayers didn't have huge fights; neither one of them were up to that. It wasn't an angry, nasty split. Claudia took Raven to spend a summer at Martha's retreat in New Mexico. She wrote there, the beauty of the place, the energy of it—it healed her. He called every night after work, begged her to come home. She finally did, but then she moved out a few weeks later into an apartment on the Upper West Side. They shared custody of Raven, who was almost five then—a loved, normal little girl who, like so many kids, had two homes. Ayers, true to form, just let Claudia go. *If that's what you want, Claudia.* Even as she left him, she wondered why he didn't fight for her.

Now, Claudia could see that she drove away a good man who loved her. Melvin Cutter had smashed in the front door of her life and hurt her terribly, left her world in ruin. But she was the one who'd burnt the remains to the ground. In fact, she could smell the smoke.

Smoke.

Slowly, the world came back—tilted, wobbling, in ugly patches. The pain in her head, at the bridge of her nose, the hard, cold ground beneath her.

"Raven," she croaked.

Josh at the door. His brother. Running for the stairs. The hammer in her hand. She tasted blood

437

in her mouth. As she pushed herself up, she saw a deep red swath down her shirt.

There were voices, yelling. Where were they coming from? Her head cleared a little. Oh, God. The men were gone. Where was her daughter?

"Raven?"

"Mom!" Every mother knows the pitch of panic, of pain. She crawled toward the sound.

"Raven!"

Muffled, terrified. "Mom, we're trapped in here. He's coming. He's coming to the house."

But Claudia was alone. The door at the top of the stairs was closed, even though she knew it had been opened. And the door to the crawl space was also shut and locked. She searched around for the key she'd seen, the smell of smoke growing stronger. She pounded—frantically, uselessly—on the tunnel door.

"It's locked," she yelled, her voice cracking with fear. "There's no key."

The drill, that's what she needed. She needed to drill the lock and break it.

"Get back!" A male voice yelled from inside the tunnel with Raven. Was that Josh? Was that freak in the tunnel with Raven? Where was Troy?

"Stay away from her," Claudia screeched.

There was a hard pounding then. She backed away.

Once. Twice. Three times. The door burst open and a pair of work boots stuck out. Josh slid out, panting, red in the face. He pulled Raven out, who leapt into Claudia's arms. Troy climbed out behind them, looking stunned.

"Mom," Raven sobbed. "Mom, are you okay? What happened to you? There's so much blood."

Claudia held on to her daughter, weeping. She couldn't talk, just clung to her girl.

"Mom," Raven said. "It was there. A huge bag of money. He took it. The bad guy."

Claudia could barely hold on to what was happening. It was chaos. She started to cough. What was that smell? What was burning?

Josh was already on his way up the stairs. They watched as he put his hand on the door and pulled it back quickly. He looked back at them, stricken.

"Fire," he said. "He started a fire."

The thinker chatters. She yammers on about this and that, an incessant soundtrack of worries and wants, judgments, observations. She's shallow, distracting, bossy—always telling you what you should do, or could have done, or why things would be better if circumstances were different. The thinker is the enemy of wisdom.

The watcher is the one who knows, the one who sits and waits. The part who connects to the net of universal wisdom. Calm resides in the watcher.

And I was there in the watcher mind. I observed as Rhett Beckham hefted the bag from the tunnel, then slammed the hatch door closed. It was a door I never knew, in all my years in this house, was there. I watched as he fastened the lock and shouldered the bag. I slipped into the shadows of the barn, and he didn't see me or intuit my presence, as he exited—voices down below calling behind him. Ghosts on the wind.

Outside, a woman waited in a primer-painted black car; she got out when she saw him approach and held up the copper key between two red fingernails.

"You closed and locked the door?" he asked. She nodded. "The basement door, too? Latched from the outside?"

"Just like you said," she said. "The woman was unconscious. I just left her."

"Good girl," he said.

"Well?" she asked, looking at him eagerly, rising up on her toes.

"Well," he said. A wide smile cut across his face.

He dropped the bag, and they knelt in front of it. He held it open for her, and she let out a whoop that carried up into the trees.

"Oh my god," she said, face slackening with surprise. "Oh my *god!*"

He stood and helped her to her feet, too. They embraced, and then he started to spin her around and around.

"This time tomorrow," he said, breathless when

440

he put her down. "We'll be in Anguilla."

This time tomorrow, I promised silently, you'll be in the ground.

I watched as he went around to the trunk of the car and retrieved red cans of gasoline, a pile of rags. He stowed the bag in the back of the car, pulled the girl into a long, passionate kiss. They were both dark, clad in denim, both thin in a wiry, tough kind of way. Against the black of the car and the gray of the sky and the ash of the trees shedding their leaves, there was a kind of beauty in the scene, a dark beauty.

"Wait here," he said. "Keep the engine running."

He took the cans inside. I calculated.

Do I need to kill her first? I wondered. Since I didn't know her or who she was or if she deserved to die, I guessed not. Maybe she was just some small-town fool, one who fell for the wrong guy because she didn't know any better. Maybe she was only guilty of poor judgment. I'd only killed one person in cold blood, and I didn't like the way it had changed me. Could I follow Beckham into the house without her seeing me? But her head was bent over her cell phone—like everyone's. Every free moment, no matter what, people reach for those devices. Such a blessing for someone who doesn't want to be seen. Lucky for her, she didn't even look up as I slipped from the barn and took the long way around the far side, and up the tree line to the back door.

I stood there a moment, remembering how I looked inside that night and saw them, how confusing it was, how I didn't understand what I was seeing at first. It was all still there, memories as vivid as photographs in my hand.

The door opened easily, unlocked, waiting for me.

I walked through the laundry room, into the kitchen. I could hear him banging around upstairs, and already I felt the tickle of smoke on my sinuses. I pulled up my hood and walked down the long hallway and came to stand at the foot of the stairs. I felt it rise up, all of it, all my anger and all my pain, the throb of adrenaline and, yes, the thrill of the pending fight.

He stopped halfway down the stairs, frozen, confused, his face sloping into surprise.

"Hi, there," I said, tilting my face up so that he could see me. Slowly, recognition dawned and I couldn't help but smile.

"Remember me?"

thirty-nine

There are two different worlds, two different versions of me. There's the girl I used to be, the one who went to the mall and the movies with her friends, the one whose mother was still reading to her, still tucking her in at night, right up until the night she died. In *that* Zoey's world, it was a big deal to sneak out and meet a boy. That Zoey would be upset if she got anything less than an A on her biology exam.

The night my parents died, I became a different kind of girl, and the world I inhabited afterward was a strange, frightening place full of dark alleys and trap doors, where strangers lurked in the shadows looking to do harm. A part of me died that night; a part of me came alive. This girl is stronger than she was—broken, twisted, but sharper and more dangerous for it.

Rhett Beckham kept coming down the stairs, stopping at the bottom, his dark eyes on me. He'd aged badly, raggedly like Didion. I was taken aback by the deep lines on his face, the gray in his hair. He didn't seem as tall as I remembered; he was thinner.

"You," he said, like Didion. Surprised. As if I only existed in some vague ugly memory he had of his own life. As if I wasn't the person who bore the scars of his misdeeds. I moved in front of the door.

"You knew it was here," he said. He held me in an almost amused gaze. He wasn't afraid of me. He thought I was small, weak, just a girl. Always better to be underestimated. The smell of smoke was strong and growing stronger; it tickled at the back of my throat.

He wasn't wrong. I did know there was something down there in the basement. I didn't know what or where. Just like I knew that there was something wrong with my dad, that he was distant and far away, more than usual. Or that there was something wrong with my parents. Whispered arguments behind closed doors, my dad on the couch in the mornings. But it was white noise in my consciousness; I was aware, but it wasn't affecting me in any real way. I was that other girl, in that other world. There was nothing dark in that place. I was sheltered, protected, and loved.

He moved in fast, tried to knock me aside with the back of his hand. I easily caught his wrist with my left hand and pulled. He was tall, strong, but I immediately determined that he was inflexible, with bad balance. I used the momentum of his swing to lead him off center. I came in close, grabbed his shirt with both hands, and drove my knee up hard into his groin. Then I used my elbow to strike him in the jaw—an ugly crack, a spray of blood and saliva.

He crumbled, curling up in pain too great for noise. Then he lay at my feet, helpless. And I stood looking down.

It was too easy. I wanted a fight, I realized. I wanted Didion and Beckham to be the monsters I imagined them to be. I wanted to fight them and win, emerge victorious from battle with the titans that destroyed my life, that killed my parents, that broke me in two. But in the end, they were just men, weak and dirty, criminals greedy and base. They could only do what they did to me because I was an innocent girl, because my father was surprised and bound, unarmed, because my mother never knew what hit us. There was almost nothing to either one of them.

I dropped to straddle Beckham, turning him on his back, pinning his elbows with my knees. I withdrew my father's hunting knife, the same one I'd driven into Didion's heart.

When life leaves, it's just a breath exhaled and not drawn in again. I had wanted to feel something when Didion died. I wanted to feel something now.

But there was nothing. Just numbness, the emptiness of my actions expanding to fill the world. What would Mike say to me now? That there is no true justice delivered between men and women, the world is too complicated, we are all too tightly connected. You never do something to anyone without doing it to your-

445

self. My rage billowed and plumed inside me.

I brought the knife to Beckham's throat and he watched me, eyes twitching. The amusement and dismissiveness was gone from his gaze. There was fear there now, and I was glad to see that at least, that he knew a fraction of the terror I felt that night. Soon his pain would subside and he'd easily topple me. Then, we'd fight again.

From upstairs, a noise swelled—a kind of blowing wind, a whir. The sound of things being devoured by fire, crackling, snapping, breaking apart. Something else. Voices? Was I hearing voices faint and far away?

"Who were you working for that night?" I asked. It was the question I never asked Didion, my rage getting the better of me. "Who sent you to get that money?"

I used the butt of the knife to bash him hard on the bridge of his nose, but not hard enough to knock him out. He released a deep groan of pain as a river of blood gushed from his nostrils.

"Who?" I yelled.

He moved his head from side to side, insensible. In my imagination, in my child's memory, these men were invincible, and I was defenseless against them, a rag doll. I was almost disappointed that he was so weak.

He tried to buck beneath me, but I brought my elbow down hard on his solar plexus, then leaned in close to lace my fingers through his hair and pull. He let out a desperate wheeze, struggling for breath. I saw another hard flash of fear in his eyes, and I'd be lying if I said I didn't enjoy it. Once, I'd screamed and struggled to get away from him. Now, he was helpless beneath me, in spite of his superior size and strength because I had worked and trained. Because I was the Red Hunter, the embodiment of my own rage.

"Who?" I asked. "Who sent you for that money?"

"Are you sure you want to know?" asked my father, who stood at the bottom of the stairs, looking up at the smoke that was starting to plume. He had a cigarette in his hand, took a deep drag, and turned to me. "Do you want all your childhood illusions dashed?"

"Of course, I want to know," I yelled at him. "I've been looking for answers for ten years."

"No," Dad said, with a slow shake of his head. "You've been looking for revenge. You think it's going to end your suffering. It's not. You get that now, right?"

I turned my attention back to Beckham, who was looking at me with eyes wild. His breath was coming back; he was bucking and struggling beneath me.

I brought the hunting knife to his throat. The blade was so sharp, so carefully honed that just the slightest pressure drew a little bit of blood from the crepey skin of his neck.

I didn't ask him again who he was working for. Maybe my father was right; maybe I didn't really want to know. All I had to do was press and draw the blade across his throat and watch him bleed out. Listen to him gurgle, watch him thrash until life left him. It was the only thing I wanted. Not answers, not justice. Didion stood over by the stairs, ghastly pale and small. I pressed the knife deeper and Beckham began to struggle, lifting my weight with his hips. A thick line of blood trailed down his throat, black and twisting like a snake.

"Then what?" said my father, coming closer. "After that, who are you?"

I hesitated, drew the blade away. Just a millisecond. Who was I now? Who could I ever be with everything behind me, and everything I'd done?

The number one rule of fighting is to never let down your guard. Never leave yourself vulnerable to what may be coming up behind. I saw the flash of hope in Beckham's eyes right before I felt the blow to the side of my head. I toppled, stunned, looking up into the drawn, pocked face of a woman with long dark hair. She stood over me with a shovel, panting.

Then nothing.

forty

wasn't out for long. Either she wasn't that strong, or she chickened out. Because I'll tell you that not many people wake up after a whack to the head with a shovel. That's a killing blow. Still, I grappled to orient myself, my ears ringing, my head throbbing. I held on to my stomach; I could feel bile climbing up my throat.

Those voices were louder, below me. The smoke from upstairs was dark and billowing from the bedroom door at the top of the landing. I heard the rumble of an engine, the squeal of tires, a vehicle racing away.

I heard Seth's voice. "You're one of the good guys."

My parents' murderer, one of the men who tortured me, left my body and my spirit criss-crossed with scars that never healed, was getting away with a bag full of money. I'd had the opportunity to kill him, but I'd hesitated. And now he was gone. If I gave chase, got to the Suburban, and made it to the main road, maybe I could still find them.

But the house was on fire, and there were people trapped in the basement. I could hear their panicked yelling through the floorboards. Probably that blogger and her kid. With shaking effort, I pushed myself up. I was still hurting from being jumped last night—ribs, hip, bridge of my nose. Now there was blood on the floor, on my shirt, some combination of mine and Beckham's. Mike would say I deserved it. I was careless last night, lost in thought. Today, I'd let my anger distract me. I'd hesitated when I'd had the upper hand.

I moved toward the kitchen, but a wall of heat and smoke pushed me back, coughing. The house was groaning, the air growing more toxic by the second. If I'd lain unconscious, I'd have been dead from carbon monoxide poisoning inside a half hour—no doubt what they had in mind when they left.

I raced to the front door, greedily sucking in the outdoor air, still coughing, as I ran to the cellar entrance I knew was on the side of the house. I came to a stop at the two metal doors in the ground locked with an old padlock. I summoned my strength and used the hard sole of my combat boot, drawing strength from my hips to kick at the lock. Once. Twice. Three times. On the fourth kick, the rusted door latch came loose, and I reached down to swing open the doors.

"Here!" I yelled. "Come out this way!"

A moment later, a woman and a young girl, a lanky, squinting boy came into view down below and climbed up quickly. Behind them was Josh Beckham. I watched him as coughing, red-faced, he tumbled out onto the ground. The woman and her daughter fell into each other sobbing. The boy sat beside them, his head in his hands. Josh Beckham just stared, like he was seeing a ghost. I stared back. I never saw his face that night, but I'd seen him many times since then.

"Zoey," he said, finally. He was pale, as if he was seeing a ghost. And maybe he was. Maybe I was a ghost. "Zoey Drake."

All three of the others lifted their eyes to stare; they obviously knew my name. Josh moved closer, but I held up a palm. He was a victim that night, too. Or anyway that's how I saw it. He was in the thrall of older, dangerous men, one of them his brother. I hadn't forgotten that he tried to hide me, to keep his brother from getting to me. Of course, he hadn't done much else to help. He'd kept quiet all these years, never turned them in. But he wasn't much older than I had been.

"Thank you," said the woman.

She extracted herself from her daughter and came over to me. She had the bluest eyes I'd ever seen. "Thank you for saving my daughter. All of us."

She lay a gentle hand on my arm. If she wondered what had brought me here in the first place, she didn't ask. I nodded, words failing me.

"You're hurt," she said, touching a finger to my head. She was bleeding, too, from the nose, a black eye forming. "Let us call the police."

"No," I told her. "Don't do that. Not yet."

"Where is he?" asked Josh from the ground. He got to his feet.

"He left with some woman," I said. "Where is he going? Who is he meeting?"

We stood there, sizing each other up.

"The house," said Claudia with a choking sob, as though she'd just realized it was on fire. "Our house."

A big billowing cloud of black was rising into the sky. Someone would see, call the fire department. When a window exploded from the heat, Claudia grabbed the kids, each by a hand, and dragged them away. In the distance, I heard the first wail of sirens. Once the authorities got here, everything was coming out, all of it.

"Where did he go?" I asked again. I saw some kind of battle play out on Josh's face. In the sad shape of his eyes dwelled fear, regret, a deep despair.

"What are you going to do?" Josh asked.

I didn't answer, just stood waiting, looking at him right in the eyes.

"The only reason I came here today was so that no one else would get hurt," he said. He looked back guiltily at Claudia, who was holding her daughter again.

"That's not the reason I came here," I said.

The world crowded in around us—the burning house, the crying girl, the low gray ceiling of sky, the approaching sirens. He bowed his head and told me where Rhett Beckham was going.

"Wait," said Claudia.

I knew her from the blog, her name, her history, her hopes for this house. I could have told her it wasn't going to work. Some places don't want to be renovated, some things can't be fixed. For this house, for this history, maybe fire was a good thing.

"Wherever you're going," she said. It was weird; I felt a connection to her, as if I'd known her a long time. "Don't. Just stay here, let the police come, let all the secrets come out. Once you're in the light, the healing begins."

The sirens were louder now, the trucks couldn't be more than a few minutes away. It was good advice, true and right. I had a moment. I really did.

But finally, I turned away from her and took off in a run for the Suburban.

forty-one

In the gloaming, I approached the warehouse from behind, pulling up slow through the deserted streets with my lights off. There were other vehicles parked: the black car I saw Beckham toss the bag into, and another, a beat-up old red pickup with New York plates. I snapped a shot of the tag with the camera on my phone. That's when I saw that Mike had called three more times. He'd left a few messages, which I'd listened to on the way up.

"Hey, he's doing better," he said. "He's stable and asking for you. Come to the hospital when you get this."

Then: "What's up? Where are you?"

Then a text: "Zoey, he wants to talk to you. I'm trying to keep him calm. Where are you?"

I wanted to go back. I couldn't, not yet. I wanted to call Mike or Paul, their strong sensible voices always advising temperance, calm. I couldn't do that either. Mike would *know* what I was doing. He'd try to talk me in, and he might be able to. I was weak and tired, hurt. I finally—finally—got what he was saying, what my imaginary dad was saying. When seeking revenge, dig two graves. One for yourself. But it was too late. I was too far gone. I was tumbling, falling into that dark

454

place, and maybe that's where I'd been headed all along. And wasn't there a part of me that wanted to go?

The building was an ominous gray rectangle, dark and vast. There had been talk of this run-down, abandoned area reinvigorating into an arts district. There was a plan, Seth said, for studios and work spaces, hot shops for glass and metal work, clay ovens. Artists being priced out of Manhattan would find a haven here. But the big structures sat fallow, abandoned by the failed businesses that had erected them.

I opened the glove box and pulled out the package of wipes that I knew Paul kept there and tried to get some of the blood off my face. There was a stocking cap in the compartment, too. I pulled it over my head, though the pressure on the gash there caused the world around me to pitch and wobble for a moment. It was never a good idea to go into a fight looking like you recently got your ass kicked. But with the bruising from the night before, there was little chance of hiding it. I was a mess.

Underneath the stocking cap was Paul's old off-duty revolver, a five-shot Smith & Wesson. I knew how to use it; he'd made sure of it. But I didn't like guns. A firearm was a weakling's crutch. Anyone who couldn't go hand-to-hand was a wuss. But since I didn't know what I was walking into, and I wasn't at my best, it didn't hurt to be prepared. I killed the engine and sat, watching, trying to assess the situation. The building was dark. There was only quiet. Could I trust Josh? Would he have called ahead to his brother and told him I was on my way? Were they just waiting for me inside, ready to finish what they started?

I had some theories, some of them percolating for years, some since my visit with Seth. Scenarios that flipped through my mind like an old-time film reel, crackling and sputtering.

First theory: My father took the money. He organized the initial heist with partners. Whitey Malone found out about it, sent Didion and Beckham to get it back. But my dad hid it too well and didn't give it up when they came to call. This theory makes my dad a dirty cop and a coward that let his wife be murdered, his daughter tortured, rather than turn over the money that he stole.

Second: Other men, cops, took the money, and my father was complicit only in hiding it. All the same implications apply to my father—dirty cop, coward. But it would add another layer, other people he had to fear or protect. Maybe he was even forced into this role. It was somewhat more palatable, but not by much.

Third: Someone else stole the money and used our property to hide it. My dad didn't know it was there. So when they came for it, he had no idea how to save us. In it, my dad was just a victim, like Mom and me. Blameless, innocent. This was my preferred theory, though it was probably the least likely one.

But the truth was that I had no idea, even after all these years of poring over evidence with Boz and Mike, who was behind that initial heist and who sent Didion and the Beckham brothers to find the stolen money. Didion and Beckham were thugs, hired men, pirates who took their spoils; there was someone else at the helm. Seth's theory that there were cops involved from beginning to end made sense, but it was hard to stomach. Cops stole the money, sent men to get it from my father, impeded the investigation to the degree that Didion and the Beckham brothers were questioned and released, the case went cold. It couldn't be the truth, could it?

I slipped from the Suburban and moved quickly in the growing dark. There was the silence of the urban wasteland, a particular quiet to buildings that sat empty, something about the way air moves around and through abandoned structures. Life usually finds the deserted places—foliage springs up through cracks in concrete. Birds and small animals nest in windowsills, chimneys and rafters. The faint chirping of an unseen bird was the alarm of my arrival, if anyone was listening. But most people weren't listening, not to things like that.

I found the back door open and slipped inside. Voices carried, echoing. I could hear the tone, measured, but not the words. Through towers of boxes, I crept toward the sound of men talking.

"Why did you do that? I can hear the sirens from here."

"I was destroying all the evidence," he said. Beckham. I recognized the rumble of his voice. "Getting rid of witnesses."

"If you'd done it your brother's way, it could have gone differently. You called a lot of attention." The voice was odd, muffled.

There was a rasping breath, a long, unhealthy cough.

"My *brother* spilled his guts to that woman," said Beckham. "He *told her* why we were there, what we wanted."

Only a tense silence followed.

"And then you bring a stranger here."

"She's cool," said Beckham. "She found the tunnel. Without her, we wouldn't have known about it maybe."

A nervous giggle followed the silence that was growing heavier. The skin on my arms tingled. I couldn't see the other man. His voice was strange, disguised somehow, something over his mouth? I used the shadows to hide, moving closer to the dim light that burned. Even then, I didn't know. A cough, rasping and long. But no—the mind resists. No.

The three of them gathered around a long table, a camping lantern the only light. His back is to me; there's something on his head—a stocking cap, a mask. I can't make it out. Rhett Beckham stood tense and shifting from foot to foot, his hands in his pockets. The woman who hit me with a shovel was behind him, looking back toward the door. She wants to leave. She's scared. She should be.

The stranger's hands are gloved. There's a large plastic tarp on the ground beneath where Beckham and the woman are standing. They don't get it. What's about to happen. I want to stop it. Rhett Beckham is mine. But I was frozen, my body tingling; I don't know why.

"She's taking part of my cut," said Beckham. He smiled, lifted his hands. I had a good view of his face. He was scared, too. Way out of his league. "You don't have to worry about her."

"I'm not."

"Good," Beckham said. He issued a nervous laugh, glanced over at the girl, who was nodding stupidly. "Because I've been quiet all these years. Didn't run my mouth off in the joint like so many of those losers. I promised you one day I'd go back for it. And here I am."

The stranger dumped the contents of the bag on the long table and a pile of cash cascaded across the surface. The girl reached for Beckham's hand in excitement, her eyes bright, but he pushed her away. The gloved man started counting, shifting the stacks into neat piles.

Situation assessment: There were three people, all of them motivated to fight for the payout they've waited years to collect. What were my odds? Poor. I would have to take my moment in the chaos I could sense was about to descend. The thinker panics, goes off half-cocked. Or freezes, paralyzed by indecision. The watcher bides her time, waits for the opportunity.

Then, "Where's the rest of it?"

"That's all there was," said Beckham. His voice cracked and he cleared his throat "We took the bag from the tunnel, some kids had it first. But I brought it straight here."

"What kids?"

"The girl, her friend," said Rhett. "They got to the bag first."

"They got to the bag first." His tone was flat with menace. "How did that shake out?"

"I don't know," Rhett said. He rubbed a hand over his mouth. "I don't how they got to it. Like I said, Josh was spilling it."

"There's only four hundred thousand here," said the stranger.

"That's what there was." I can hear the creep of fear. "I swear."

"You swear." Not a question. I could hear the mockery.

"Yeah," Beckham said. It was only a whisper.

The stranger issued another long cough.

"The night the money was stolen from Whitey Malone, there was a million. Two hundred thousand got paid out that night. Then it sat, locked in that tunnel for ten years. There should be eight hundred thousand here."

Silence. Beckham shook his head and lifted his palms. I thought about the money in my bank account, tried to do the math—the money my mother had saved, my father's death benefit and pension paid to my education trust. An extra three hundred thousand give or take.

It happened so fast.

Two sharp explosive bursts of sound bounced and expanded in the space, causing me to drop into a protective crouch, my ears ringing, head vibrating. When I looked again, Beckham and the girl both stood for a moment, wobbling slightly, their expressions slack. What? What just happened?

Then they crumbled, first him, then her, onto the waiting tarp. She stared at me, unseeing, a neat red circle between her eyes, blood from the hole that must have opened in the back of her head pooling black around her. I felt bad for her, even though she'd hit me in the head with a shovel. Some people were just not smart; they make bad decisions, throw their lot in with the wrong people. It's a problem.

My breathing came shallow. I deepened it. I

pushed myself against the wall. The man at the table, slowly started packing up the money. My whole body was tense, vibrating, ears ringing in the silence.

"I know you're there," he said. "Zoey. Come out."

I stepped into the light, my hand gripping the gun in my pocket. He turned to me, but he was wearing a mask, a monstrous grinning blue face, mouth full of fangs, red-eyed skulls for hair, eyes black holes. The Tibetan mask for the sorcerer's dance. It was a guardian's mask, a protector against evil. I knew it well. No.

He put the rest of the money in the bag, unhurried as if we had all the time in the world. He pulled the zipper. I saw there was a stack left out, sitting at the corner of the table.

That's when another form stepped out of the darkness. He wore a mask as well, the face of a gray wolf with a wide nose and deep-set eyes, yellow bared teeth. He stared at me a moment, and I slowed my breathing, hoping my heart rate would follow. But then he looked away, started dragging Rhett Beckham's body toward the center of the tarp.

I thought about Josh Beckham. Would he mourn his brother? Would there simply be relief? In my limited experience, family relationships are complicated. Love is rarely pure, always laced with something else. Likewise, anger, even

462

hatred was often undercut by love and loyalty.

While I watched, the big man took off his mask and lay it on the table. I knew it was him, but it still felt like a knife through the heart.

Mike. My mentor. My friend. The ground beneath my feet shifted.

"Paul's doing better," he said. "He was asking for you. I tried to call, finally had to make up an excuse that your phone was dead. I told him you'd come after your shift. He wants to talk to you."

I felt a lurch of happiness, relief that Paul was okay for now, but it quickly sank into the pit of dread that my stomach had become.

The other man dragged the woman's body to lie beside Beckham. I was surprised to feel a sob rise up in my throat. The student grows disillusioned with her teacher and so with everything he taught her. I thought of all those hours spent with him, all his words knocking around my head. He taught me so much about fighting, surviving, about myself and the watcher within. How could I reconcile that with the man who stood before me now?

"Tell me," I said.

He released a sigh, long and slow. "You weren't supposed to be there. Neither was your mother. Chad—he was supposed to be alone."

My mind scrambled back there. Mom was supposed to be in Key West that night. I was sneaking out to meet Seth. But who knew that?

"Tell me everything," I said. I searched his face for something I needed—remorse, sadness. But he had his fighting face on, features heavy, blank, eyes lidded, almost sleepy. *Never let your face betray you—your effort, your fear, your anger. Let them look into a clean canvas that they can paint with their own insecurities.* His words.

"Your dad heard about the money from a CI," said Mike. "He told Paul about it, about plans he had to take it. Your father was in trouble—debt, some issues with gambling. He was into it with everyone from the credit card companies to a local loan shark. Paul talked him out of doing the job."

Paul talked him out of it. Of course, he did. He'd never let my dad do something like that.

"So, Paul put together a team, me included, and *we* robbed Whitey Malone," said Mike.

The information landed hard. Words can hurt worse than any blow.

"You and Paul?" I thought of the question my imaginary dad asked me back at the Bishops' house. *Do you want all your childhood illusions shattered?* Had I on some level always suspected?

"You and Paul robbed a drug dealer and took a million dollars?"

"Don't look so heartbroken, Zoey," he said. Impatience curled his lip. "We robbed a drug dealer, not an orphanage."

The other man dragged Rhett Beckham into the middle of the tarp. Then the woman. He left two thick skeins of blood along the blue-white of the tarp. I stared at Beckham. He was mine to kill, but I'd hesitated. Now he was dead, nothing but medical waste, everything he was in this world gone. I wanted to be happy he was dead, that he died ugly and stupid, cowering in front of someone bigger, stronger, tougher. But again, there was only that vast nothingness within me. No joy, no ecstatic sense of vindication, just a dark spiral.

You're one of the good guys.

I wasn't sure that was true. I mean—it obviously wasn't. Maybe there weren't any good guys.

"Paul paid us out," Mike went on. "We were just the hired men, at a hundred each. Which was fine. It was Chad's discovery, and Paul's plan. It was seamless. We were in and out."

I walked over to the man on the tarp, avoiding the slicks of blood. He stood to face me, and I lifted his mask. Seth. The muscles of his face did a little dance of shame.

"I'm sorry," he said.

"I thought *you* were one of the good guys," I said.

"I am," he said, looking down at the bodies at his feet. "We're none of us just one thing, are we, Zoey?"

He shook his head, then bent to fold the tarp over the bodies. Beckham and his girlfriend stared up at me from beneath the folds of the milky white film, surprised, disappointed in how things turned out.

"But Paul didn't take his cut," said Mike, still standing behind the table. "He didn't *want* the money. That's how he was. What he did? He didn't even do it for Chad. That guy—I don't like to speak ill of the dead, of your father. You loved him—but Chad was a user. He used Paul all their lives—not for me to judge. But Paul wanted that money for you and your mom. He wanted *you* to be safe, taken care of. That's why he talked Chad out of doing the job, why he did it himself. If someone got hurt, if someone got caught, Paul wanted it to be him, not Chad. But it wasn't fair that Chad got all of it. It just didn't sit right with me."

"So you hired Didion and Beckham to go get it from him?" I guessed.

Those half-lidded eyes revealed no emotion. He lifted his shoulders.

"We didn't know your mom didn't get on her plane. We didn't know that your boyfriend wouldn't show and that you'd come back so fast. And that bastard," said Mike, shaking his head. I didn't like the way he was talking about my father, even if it was all true. "He wouldn't give up that money. And then everything went to shit.

And Seth—who, by the way, had nothing to do with this back then, just your boyfriend, a stupid kid—called the cops. And that money sat, well hidden by your old man, all these years."

My mind scrambled to put all the pieces together—the fractured versions of my father, of Mike, of Paul. They were in tatters; I couldn't stitch them back together.

"You," I said. "You were the fourth man. The one waiting in the car."

At least he had the decency to hang his head.

"Who was the other guy with you the night you robbed Whitey Malone?" I asked. The world was spinning, but my voice was calm.

"Does it matter?" Mike asked, shaking his head. Then he answered his own questions. "It doesn't. None of it matters now. It's done."

There was a heavy silence, all of us just standing there.

"You and Beckham jumped me last night," I said. "You took the key."

"I'm sorry," he said. "I'm sorry for how all of this intersected with your life. I wish it hadn't. I've tried to make it up to you over the years."

That explained why they didn't kill me last night, why I wasn't hurt worse. They beat me, just not too badly.

"Make it up to me?" I said. "I watched my parents *die*. I was *fourteen years old*."

He lifted his palms.

467

"Because of Didion and Beckham," said Mike. "They were rabid dogs."

"They were dogs that you called," I said.

He dipped his head in a single nod of concession. "And they've both been put down. You got what you wanted, Zoey. Now we can all move on."

Seth used duct tape to bind the tarp around the bodies. He seemed to have some experience with this type of thing, given his calm and the deftness with which he completed the task.

I worked to push through my numbness. Underneath it all, some part of me was screaming in rage and sorrow, but I couldn't get to her. She was buried deep, suffocating. Saving her was saving myself, I knew that. But I was probably too late. Once I drove that knife into Didion's heart, I became one of them. Why hadn't I realized that? I made a decision about what was right and wrong, who deserved to live and die, but the only judge and jury was my own selfish rage.

"He never told you about it?" asked Mike. "All these years. He never told you the truth? You didn't know about the money?"

I shook my head. Paul wasn't a big talker. We spent a lot of time together, but mostly we just talked about me, or ate, or went to the movies. He would never tell me about this dark side of himself, of my father. His only goal in life was to protect me. I knew that on a cellular level. Even if it meant lying to me about them, about his own dark deeds. He'd have figured it was the right thing, to keep all the ugly out of my life. Little did he know I'd been infected long ago.

Mike shouldered the bag and walked toward me.

"Think about the girls; think about what this money can do for them, for the school," he said. "Think about how comfortable we can make Paul. You know he doesn't have much time."

I squared myself toward him, spread my legs, and gripped the gun in my hand.

"I can't let you take that money, Mike," I said. "It's not right."

He smiled, cocked his head. It was an expression he used, the patient teacher indulging his student's youth and naïveté.

"Not right? Come on. This money belonged to a drug dealer, earned off the suffering of others. It sat in the dark for ten years. If it goes back to the police, it will sit in an evidence locker until some other dirty bastard gets his hands on it, one way or another. Let's not get hung up on some paint-by-numbers morality. Your parents *died* for this money. Don't you want it to do some good in this world?"

There was a kind of street logic to this. The school was a force for good in the community, a place where girls learned to be strong, to stand up, where kittens became dragons. But I couldn't teach them unless I could lead by example. I knew that now.

"You don't deserve this payday," I said. "None of us do."

"Who are we to judge who deserves what in this world?" asked Mike.

He looked old suddenly, tired. There were dark circles under his eyes. But his belly was full of chi, and I could see by the twinkle in his strange light eyes that he was ready for a fight.

"I am going to judge tonight," I said.

"Your hands are dirty, too, little girl."

I nodded. "I don't deny it."

"Walk out of here with me, leave the past behind," he said. "Seth will get rid of these bodies. We'll take this money and do good with it. Live to fight another day."

"There are too many hanging threads," I said. "Josh Beckham for one."

"We'll pay him off," he said. "He's weak, has an elderly mother to care for."

Mike would kill Josh Beckham. I knew that; he wouldn't leave it to chance.

"The Bishop woman," I said.

"Threats will keep her quiet."

No. I'd unleashed a chain of events when I killed Didion that led to the opening of a long, dark tunnel that had been locked too long. All our secrets climbed out, and we couldn't stuff them back down there. I felt a creeping lightness, the lifting of a burden I'd carried. Maybe I *had* wanted answers after all, not just revenge. The truth, no matter how dark, shed a new light.

"Drop the bag," I said.

His smile grew wide. It was loving, kind— but there was a shade of something else there—condescension maybe, amusement. We both turned at the hard scrape of plastic over concrete, Seth was dragging the bodies toward the door. How did he fit into this? I couldn't believe, hapless as he had seemed back then, affected as he was, that he'd known that night what his role was. He couldn't have. But then I'd been wrong about so many people, so many things.

"Let's just move on from here, Zoey," said Seth, breathless from pulling the bodies. "We've all made mistakes."

"It's too late for that."

I backed up, blocking their exit from the warehouse.

"We're calling the police. This ends here."

"If you do that, Zoey," said Mike, "you're only hurting yourself. You'll go to jail like the rest of us."

"So be it."

A flash in those eyes, a flicker of anger.

"It'll kill him, you know that. To lose you and me. To understand what I did to your family. He won't come back from it. He'll die alone."

471

The thought put a vise on my heart.

"Who called him that morning?" I asked, thinking of the call he took. "What upset him so much?"

Mike shook his head. "Beckham had some idea that Paul might know where the money was. He may have called, tried to intimidate him. I thought Beckham was crazy. But turned out, he was right. Paul knew where it was all along. Just left it. Well, not all of it, right? I wondered how he was paying for NYU."

I didn't say anything.

"I guess he took his cut after all," said Mike. "He's as dirty as the rest of us."

The thinker panics. The watcher waits. The Red Hunter acts.

I moved in quick, a hook to his jaw flew in so fast that he never even got a hand up to block. He absorbed the blow with a tilt of his head, lifted a finger to the line of blood that trailed from the corner of his mouth.

"Zoey," he said. "I'm not going to fight you."

I took the gun out of my hoodie and his eyes dropped on it. I was aware of Seth to my left. I could hear him breathing

"Where's your gun?" I asked Mike. "The one you used to kill those two."

He held my gaze. It was a look I knew well, the patient teacher, waiting for his student to catch on.

"Don't do this," he said. "I know you're angry. You have a right to be. But let's go home, work through it. We have a long history together, and all of that came after what happened to your parents. Let's take care of Paul and run the school. I can afford to give you a real job there now. No more waitressing."

His face, his voice—so soothing. He knew me. He knew I wanted all of those things.

"The gun," I said.

He was fast, too. He'd dropped the bag and used a lithe sidekick to knock the gun from my hand. It went skittering across the floor and landed at Seth's feet. I dove for it—too late. Seth picked it up and looked at me, worry etched in his brow. He popped the chamber and dumped the bullets into his palm, shoved them into his pocket.

"This is not how any of this was supposed to go," Seth said. He put the gun in his other pocket. I had to recast him. Who was he? Whose side was he on?

"*Did* you know that night?" I asked him. "What you were doing?"

"No," he said, he looked down at this shoes. "Of course not. I was just a kid."

"They knew about Seth—your parents, Paul," said Mike. "They monitored your calls, your email. Your dad was a cop. You think he didn't know you had a boyfriend?"

"He *knew* I was going to sneak out that night?"

473

"He knew," said Mike. "Your dad was going to wait and follow, scare the bejesus out of the kid. He mentioned it to Paul, who told me. Just in passing, just conversation. I knew Heather was going to be away, as well."

"But she *wasn't* away," I said. "Why didn't you stop it? You were the fourth man. The one waiting out in the car. When you knew she was there, when you saw me come back—you didn't stop it."

"It was too late by then," he said. The weight of regret in his voice only made me hate him more.

"Too late because if you left us alive it would have come back to you. You would have been caught," I said. "They were always going to kill him. No matter what."

"No," said Mike. "No. If he'd given up that money, they'd have taken it and left. That was the plan. But he didn't. He *wouldn't*."

I wanted to believe that, that Mike never planned on hurting my father. I know he wouldn't have planned to hurt my mom and me. He just wanted the money that none of them deserved. He hired Didion and Beckham to get it. If my dad gave it up, that would have been the end of it. He could hardly report the robbery. He'd have to let it go. Or tell Paul. Or go after it himself.

"Paul would kill you if he knew what you did," I said.

Mike shook his head as if I were annoyingly

stubborn. "You're not going to let this go, are you?"

There was a red pulse moving through my body, a dangerous amount of anger like a tide washed through me.

I flew at him, an elbow to the jaw hit hard, eliciting a grunt. My upper cut headed for his thick chin, which he deflected. My knee to his groin—which he easily sidestepped. My movements were clumsy with rage, too much power, not enough accuracy.

"Don't," he said, barely out of breath.

I came at him again. But a palm strike to my solar plexus sent me flying back, landing hard beside the wrapped up bodies. Winded, I lay there, looking at Rhett Beckham's dead face through sheets of plastic. Pain throbbed from my center; adrenaline, cortisol raged as I struggled to regain my breath. He was stronger than I was, a better fighter. Always had been, always would be. He came to stand over me.

"Are we done?" He looked to Seth. "Get these bodies out of here."

Seth looked uncertainly at me but did as he was told.

"When did you start working for him?" I managed, staring at Seth.

"He's been keeping an eye on the place for me for years," said Mike. "To see who came after the money, he thought so we could find out who killed your parents."

"You knew," I said. "At some point, you figured out who was behind it."

"I suspected," said Seth. "I wasn't sure until recently."

"I thought you were one of the good guys," I said. He looked away from me, grabbed the tarp, and started dragging until he disappeared into the dark of the warehouse.

"Don't be too hard on him," Mike said. "He struggled with it. But he was broke, about to lose the firm. Money. There's no seductress more alluring, no corruptor more total."

I scissor kicked, taking Mike's feet out from under him. He fell hard, surprised, but he pencil rolled quickly away from me, leapt to his feet. I was up, too, and it was on. We danced around the warehouse space in the dim light. I am small, so I must be fast, come in tight. He is large, at least three times stronger. My first order of business is to tire him out. You can't fight for long; your body can't handle all those brain chemicals, the effort it takes to punch, kick, deflect, evade. A cheetah can run sixty miles an hour, but only for thirty seconds.

He threw three powerful strikes: A roundhouse kick. I ducked; it flew over my head and sent him spinning off balance. A hook intended for my head. I backed away and felt it graze the tip of my nose. A claw headed for my throat, which I deflected and stepped around, bringing my elbow hard into his kidney.

He kicked his leg out and tripped me as I came around. I landed hard on all fours, but hopped up quickly to my feet and turned in time to take a blow to the side of the head that sent me staggering back. Then he's a freight train, coming at me with blow after blow, some of which I evaded but most of which I took—a crushing strike to the ribs, a hard kick to the shin, punch to the jaw. Then I'm down, the ground rising up, the world in an ugly spin. His face, blank and hard hovered, a face I loved, a man I trusted. All the fight left me. I was beaten. I was beaten long before it ever began.

My father stood on the edge of the light. Didion lay on the floor bleeding. My father was stoic, but a single tear drifted down his face.

"If I told them where it was," Dad said. "They'd have killed us all. I was buying time, I swear it."

I knew it was true. My father may have been a dirty cop, a gambling addict drowning in debt, but he loved us, and I always knew that. He wouldn't have let us all die for money. He was stalling, trying to keep us alive until help came.

"I thought maybe, maybe you'd come back," my dad said. "That you'd know something was wrong before you came through the door. I thought you'd run for help."

"I tried," I said.

"I know you did," said Mike, thinking I was talking to him.

"I know you did," said my dad. "I'm sorry, Zoey. I made so many mistakes—with you, with your mom, with my life. I fucked up. But the only thing that matters is that you got out of there. That's all she would have cared about, your mom. We would both happily die if it meant that you lived and went on to live a happy life."

But I didn't do that. Trauma was a wrecking ball that moved through my world. The pieces never fit back together quite right. I was a zombie, or had been, the walking dead.

"I'm sorry," my dad said again. "I love you. Forgive me."

Then he turned and walked into the dark. Didion was gone, too.

"Dad," I called. "Daddy, don't leave me."

But he was gone, and I knew he wasn't coming back. It was just me and Mike, who shook his head with pity.

"I didn't want it to be like this," said Mike. "But you can't say I didn't warn you."

The gun glinted silver in his hand.

When you seek revenge, dig two graves. One of them for yourself.

forty-two

C laudia watched, disbelieving, as great plumes of white showered her house, dousing the flames that shot up through the roof. Troy under one arm, Raven under the other, they watched from the bed of the pickup. Raven softly wept. Troy just looked stunned. And Claudia—well.

You never understood the power of things. You saw a lot on television—raging forest fires, tsunamis, hurricanes. You knew that people got raped, beaten—killed, murdered, life wrested from them in all kinds of horrible ways. But there was a kind of safe distance—the sense that it was happening elsewhere to others. Until you had a violent man's hands on you, until your body was violated. Until you felt the massive, frightening heat of fire, knew its roar, how it sucked the air from a place and replaced it with poison. How just its nearness could overcome you. How you couldn't fight. That was the hardest thing to learn, that sometimes, some things—you just can't fight them.

"They got away," said Raven. "With all that money."

"Shh," said Claudia. "The important thing is that we're all alive and okay. Nothing else matters."

"It doesn't matter that the house burned down?" said Raven, reaching for sarcasm through her tears.

"No," said Claudia. "Not really."

She even believed it.

Josh Beckham sat in the back of a squad car. They'd all been questioned. Claudia, Raven, and Troy each gave their version of what happened. Claudia told Officer Dilbert about Zoey Drake running off on her own to stop Rhett Beckham, that Josh knew where she'd gone. And he promised to find her, to help her.

Josh Beckham had asked for a lawyer, said he had information about the case ten years ago, was ready to come clean. She felt bad for him—in a way. You can't carry a secret like that around without it doing some damage, even though he was probably just a kid at the time—maybe too stupid to know what was happening until it was too late. He didn't seem like a bad man, but really—what did she know? She was literally the worst judge of character imaginable.

Claudia saw the headlights of an approaching car and recognized the sleek lines of Ayers's Mercedes as it came to a stop and he burst out of the front door.

"Daddy!" Raven shrieked, pulled away, and shimmied herself out of the truck, ran for her father. He grabbed her and held on tight, but he was looking at Claudia.

"What happened?" he said. "What on earth happened here?"

What *had* happened?

One minute she was young and beautiful and happily married, trying to have a baby with her handsome, sweet husband. The next minute, she was sitting in the back of a pickup truck, watching the house she'd been trying to renovate go up in flames. How had she gotten here? How many accidents and mistakes and choices had she made? How many of them had been wrong or right, good or bad? Maybe that's all life was, this impossibly complicated helix of choice and accident, things you could control and couldn't. And when the day was done, the only measure of success was how happy you were, how much you loved and were loved.

"Is he her father?" asked Troy. The kid seemed stunned. They'd wrapped him in a blanket, and she swore he looked just like he did when he was seven years old, curled up in his X-Men sleeping bag. Claudia remembered that it was the whole reason poor Troy was here, because he was trying to help his friend uncover the mystery of her identity. Poor kid.

Claudia looked at the sweet boy who loved her daughter. It was so obvious. She touched the still soft skin of his cheek, felt with surprise the stubble on his jaw.

"Of course, he is," she said. "Look at them."

481

Ayers and Raven walked over toward the truck, their steps wobbling as Raven clung to Ayers and he held her with a strong arm. She could hear Raven talking—tunnel, bag of money, these men came, locked us in. We were trapped. She was rambling, not making sense. Ayers looked confused, worried. Claudia shifted herself out of the truck, came to stand before Ayers.

"Let me tell him," said Claudia. Raven looked between them and nodded. She went to Troy, and the two of them walked off.

"Don't go far," Claudia called. "Stay away from the fire. And the woods."

Raven nodded, for once without snark or comment.

"What in God's name happened?" whispered Ayers. "Claudia."

He put a gentle hand to the bandage on her nose, to her jaw.

She sat, and he sat beside her. And she told him everything.

forty-three

Still lying on the ground, I stared at the gun he had pointed at me. I had to admit, it was disappointing.

"You're going to shoot me?" I said. "What a cop-out."

I literally didn't have the strength to lift myself up. I always figured it would end like this, with me on the ground, bested by some thug with a gun. Maybe Beckham or Didion, maybe some thug on the street. I didn't expect it to be a man I trusted and loved. But that's the statistic, right? A leading cause of death in young women is homicide. Most of which were perpetrated by men they knew.

"You're a good fighter, Zoey," he said. He was breathless and, I could tell, hurt. I'd gotten some good strikes in. "I taught you well—a little too well. And you have youth on your side."

He chuckled, as if we were just on the dojo floor discussing a sparring session.

"So how do you want this to go?" he said.

"How do *you* want it to go?" Another voice.

He came out of the darkness, resting heavily on his cane. He had a portable oxygen concentrator in a sling around his chest, the nasal cannula in his nostrils. It emitted a strange rhythmic squeak like a hamster slowly turning a wheel. In his free hand, he held his revolver.

Paul.

He did not look well, pale and sweating. Seeing him gave me the strength I needed to get up. I limped over to him, wrapped him up, and he held on tight. He felt so thin.

"Zocy," he said. He kissed my head.

"Christ on the cross," said Mike. "How did you get here, man?"

"In all these years," said Paul. "I never once suspected you. You know that?"

"So when did you figure it out?"

"I heard you on the phone," said Paul. "You thought I was sleeping. I heard you talking, and it all clicked in. Stupid. I was blinded by friendship. I never dreamed you'd hurt them."

"How'd you get here?" Mike asked. "From the hospital."

"Car service," he said. "I came to get my girl."

Mike bowed his head. When he looked up, I expected to see regret. "Where is the rest of the money?" he asked instead, his face blank.

"You got your pay," said Paul. "That was always the deal. A hundred grand for an hour's work. Why did you want more?"

"We always want more." He laughed a little.

"Not all of us," Paul said. "I told you that money was for Zoey and Heather."

"The woman you loved and her daughter."

"That's right."

Mike nodded in my direction. There was a coldness to him I'd never seen. I'd seen him angry, worried, sad. But I'd never seen what I saw in him tonight. You need it to win, to really win. You have to be willing to kill—or die.

"Does she know?"

"Don't do this, Mike," said Paul.

"Does Zoey know you had an affair with her mother? Does she know that it was you Heather was going to run off with that night? But that, in the end, guilt got the best of her and she went home."

"I loved your mother," Paul said. "It's true. But I loved your father, too, and so did she. We made mistakes, but we did what we thought was right in the end."

I knew, didn't I? On some deep level, I knew that they loved each other, that there was a lightness and an ease to her when Paul was around that wasn't there any other time. He made her feel safe; he looked at her with a smile in his eyes. My dad—I don't think he was much of a husband. I couldn't be angry with Paul and my mother for loving each other, for any of it. I couldn't be mad at my father for the mistakes he made.

In fact, the rage I'd been carrying, that bloody passion for revenge, it had left me cored out. I was drained. All that sizzling energy of righteousness,

485

the zeal for justice, it was armor, a veneer I wore to protect the sucking emptiness in me.

"Put the gun down, Mike," said Paul.

"Where's the rest of it?"

"That was my cut," Paul said. "Four hundred. You've got more than your share now. Just take it and go."

I heard it, but I wasn't sure they did. It was high and far, like a mosquito you couldn't shoo, sirens in the distance.

"Where's Seth?" asked Mike.

"He's indisposed," said Paul.

I watched Mike's face, his shoulders, just like he'd trained me to do. The eyes narrow to a tight focus, the nostrils flare to pull in more oxygen. The world slowed down.

First, he lifted his eyes. The sirens had grown louder and he knew time was up.

"You called the police," said Mike, looking at Paul. "You screwed us all."

"No," said Paul with a tight shake of his head.

Mike's shoulders tensed and he drew in a breath, looked between us. His chest rose as he lifted his arm, muscles flexing. It was just one step for me to put myself in front of Paul and I did that, just as Mike squeezed the trigger and the world exploded in a red flood of pain.

I was at the edge of the wood again, Catcher at my side. The night was cold and the moon a silver face in the sky looking down at me. I looked at the house, sitting still and peaceful at the edge of the field. My heart thudded with disappointment. Seth stood me up. And I waited like a fool, for an hour. Now the light in the kitchen was on, and I was going to be in so much trouble. *So* much trouble.

Catcher released a little growl, a little half bark, more like a huff and then I heard what he heard, footsteps behind me. My name in a whisper on the wind.

Zoey. Zoey wait up!

I turned and there was Seth, breathless, flushed moving through the trees. My heart did a little rhumba. He was bigger than the other boys, with dark, heavily lashed eyes and full lips.

"My dad," he said, panting. "He wouldn't go to sleep. It's like he knew I was waiting to sneak out. I'm sorry."

He dropped to his knees and rubbed Catcher behind the ears and was rewarded with a big slobbery lab kiss.

"Hey, Catcher," he said. "Hey, boy."

"I waited," I said, not ready to let go of being mad at him.

"I know," he said, looking up. His smile was sweet. "I'm glad you waited."

He stood. Catcher whined a little, looking back at the house.

"I have to go," I said. I nodded toward the house. "They're up. And I'm dead."

He laced his fingers through mine. "So if you're already in trouble, what's a few more minutes?"

"They're probably worried," I said, moving away. He tugged me back and then his arms were around me.

"Don't go," he said. "Don't leave me, Zoey. Stay with me, baby."

I'm not in the woods with Seth. I am not fourteen. I am looking into Paul's face, which is wet with tears. He's holding me on his lap, rocking me back and forth. His gun lays on the ground. My shirt is black with blood, but I don't feel anything. Mike is lying beside me, eyes sightless, staring into nowhere. Beside him is the sack of money, useless to him now.

Then I'm with Seth again, unlacing my fingers from his.

"It's too late," I tell him. "I have to go."

"No," he says. "It's not. Come walk with me. Just for a little while."

I look back at the house. I'm dead anyway. Might as well have a little fun first.

SIX MONTHS LATER

forty-four

t's a brutal ninety-three-degree summer afternoon in Manhattan. The kung fu temple doesn't have air-conditioning and the girls are drenched, red-faced, and breathing heavy. I stand in the corner, watching—encouraging, admonishing, cajoling. It's good for them to suffer and to push through anyway. And there are no worried moms sitting in the sidelines for this class, so I push even harder.

"You're almost there," I tell them. "Cool down in five."

Really it's more like fifteen, but who's counting? Hope is a good thing.

The new girl is in the corner sipping on ice chips.

You're not really studying kung fu if you haven't thrown up at least once, I told her in the bathroom.

Great, she said.

When she comes back of her own accord and joins the girls for the final striking drill, I smile. She'll make it.

Then we're done, and the girls collapse, laughing. They take turns at the water fountain, senior students letting the less experienced drink first.

"Don't gulp," I warn. "You'll be sick."

I'm still limping badly, tire easily, should really be using a crutch. But here I try to walk without it. When the elevator pings, I look up to see the guardian from the group home where the girls live. Melba is a tall black woman, fit and elegant in white linen pants and tank top.

"It's an oven in here," she says, bowing at the entrance and slipping off her flip-flops. She's a student here, too.

I flip on the ceiling fans that literally do nothing except move the hot air around. The tall windows are open wide, just letting in the sounds of the city. There is no breeze.

"How'd they do today?" she asks

"Marisol got a little overexerted," I say. "But she's okay. They all did great. They're getting stronger."

She nods. "It's a good thing," she says. "What about you?"

"I'm getting stronger, too."

She regards me with kind eyes, someone used to seeing beneath the surface. I am still getting used to talking to people, allowing myself to be seen. "You seem—well."

"I'm—um—getting there."

"That's a lot," she said. "Considering."

When the girls leave, the space is quiet except for the continuous music of the city streets—horns, and tires on asphalt, air brakes, and manholes clanking, construction and voices, the hiss of buses. I sit a moment in the center of the room, and draw in and release several deep breaths.

Inhale: I dwell in the present moment. Exhale: It is a wonderful moment.

I almost mean it.

In the back, Paul is doing the books. He is thin, drawn through the face, but stronger than he has been in years. A new cocktail of meds, stem cell therapy, and a new technology called an Aerobika Oscillating Positive Expiratory Pressure Therapy System has him stable and moving about more. There's no cure for what he has, but he has more time than we thought. And none of us can ask for more.

"How are we doing?" I ask.

I sit in the chair across from my desk, which used to be Mike's. I haven't changed much in this space, though I did take down his display of Tibetan masks. I still see the one he wore that night in my dreams. Another nightmare among many that visit me when I am unquiet.

But I loved Mike, and that hasn't changed much either. I hate what he did, what he would have done. But there was also a man who pulled me back from the edge and taught me everything I knew. He held me, bandaged me, massaged me, iced me, and taught me how to grab the harness of my power and never let anyone take it back, not even him. That was the real Mike, too. And I can keep that Mike, I decided. And I'll let the other man—the dirty cop, the man who hired the Beckham brothers and Didion to take the money back from my father, the one who didn't stop it when he could, who was responsible for all the horror in my life—whether he intended that or not—go.

Paul put a bullet through his heart in the warehouse. Mike is gone. That Mike is not going to be a part of my life moving forward—not in anger, or hatred, or thoughts of revenge. I've finally learned the lesson he tried to teach me. I wish it hadn't cost so much to understand.

"You're in the black, kid," Paul says, looking away from the screen.

He issues a cough, and I brace to race for the inhaler, but he gives a quick wave to indicate he's okay. "Last two months, you're turning a profit."

Mike left the school to me in his will, along with all its mountainous debt. When I recovered from my multiple injuries, including a bullet wound in the abdomen, I infused the place with the cash left in my account, hired some teachers and a marketing firm. We have an after-school pick-up, some teen volunteers who get free instruction, a kiddie class on Saturday mornings, and the free Saturday afternoon for the girls from Melba's group home.

That money. It will do some good.

We hear the elevator ping and I go outside to see Boz shuffling in, sweating like he's run a mile.

"Christ," he said. "Is there any place worse on earth than this city in the summer? I don't know how you do it. And—hello? Air-conditioning."

I get him a water in a paper cone from the fountain and take him into the back, where it's cooler. We have an ancient air-conditioning unit that barely works in the window. He sits down hard across from Paul.

"I thought you might like an update," he says. "I heard from my buddy at the precinct."

Paul and I exchanged a look. It was tricky. There were things that I knew now, that Paul had always known, that Boz didn't know. Boz didn't know that Paul had organized the original heist. I had not been linked to Didion's murder.

"Josh Beckham has been released with time served," said Boz. "You probably heard that. Because he was a juvenile at the time of the initial incident and he was acting under duress from his brother. Your testimony that he tried to help you escape, and the testimony from Claudia Bishop that he came to the house to try to keep his brother from coming for the money helped him. Now he's free to take care of his elderly mother."

I am happy about that, as happy as I can be.

"We know that it was Rhett Beckham and John Didion who were guilty of murdering Chad and

495

Heather, and the crimes against you, Zoey. And that it was Mike who hired them that night."

Boz stops to look between us.

"So I guess what everyone's thinking is that your father organized or helped carry out that heist and hid the money. Mike, we're supposing, felt that he didn't get a fair shake and that's why he sent Didion and Beckham to Chad's place."

Paul nods, looking solemn, rests his head in his palm. And my body is tense suddenly. Boz didn't come out here to tell us things we already knew.

"But—you know," he says, looking back and forth between us. "With everyone dead—Mike, Didion, Beckham—there are things we just may never know."

Poor Boz. This thing had been haunting him for years.

Paul found me that night because he'd installed the Find My Friends app on my phone. He'd installed the app on my phone when he started to suspect that I had killed Didion. When he figured out where I was that night, he'd ducked out of the hospital and took a car service, following my blue blip on the screen of his phone.

"With Seth gone, and that phantom bag of money, too," said Boz, shaking his head. "He's the only person who Mike may have talked to. And the money, the bag it was in. Maybe there might have been some DNA evidence even after all these years."

"They still can't find him," said Paul. "That's amazing."

"All that cash, untraceable bills," Boz said. "He could be anywhere."

Seth. He was the piece that didn't fit into the puzzle. I couldn't believe he'd go to work for Mike. Also, that money. I'd seen it there next to Mike when we were both lying on the ground. Could Seth have taken it and Paul not seen him? Paul claims that it was there one minute, but that he was so consumed, thinking that I was dying in his arms, that he never noticed that it was gone. The idea that Seth would take it and run off. It did not fit. But what else?

"There were other people involved," says Boz. "Must have been. We know that. I'm sorry. We just may never know who."

We all sit for a moment, listing to the *whoop-whoop* of a police siren passing down below.

"Do you think you can live with that?" asks Boz.

A long moment passes among the three of us.

"I think we have to," says Paul.

It's then that my eyes fall on a picture I've been looking at all my life. It was hanging over Mike's head as he sat at his desk as long as I'd been coming here. Paul, my father, Boz, and Mike all in the stern of a boat. Florida, I think it was. They're holding a marlin, a big one, grinning ear to ear. My dad has a beer lifted at the camera, the water a glittering green all around them. That's when I get it. The third man in the heist. Boz.

We have all made mistakes, done wrong. Boz, Mike, and Paul, police officers charged with the duty to protect and serve, organized the robbery of a drug dealer. Maybe Paul did it to help my father. Maybe he did it for some other reason. Boz and Mike were likcly just greedy. Like most cops, they had an idea of who was good and who was bad in this world. And robbing a drug dealer to help another officer in trouble maybe didn't seem like such a bad thing.

Paul had an affair with my mother, his best friend's wife.

Even Mike didn't know how bad things would get when he hired Didion and Beckham to get what he thought belonged to him.

I murdered a man in cold blood. I have taken to the streets, fancying myself a hero, a crime stopper, and there are more than a few people walking around this city with wounds that I have inflicted in the name of justice. But some people would just call me a vigilante, a thug no better than any other. Street justice is not justice, they might say.

Who's right?

Paul turns, and his eyes fall on the picture I was looking at. When he turns back to me, he has his cop's face on, blank, waiting, giving nothing.

"Can you live with it, Zoey?" asks Paul.

Boz and I lock eyes. "What choice do I have?" I ask.

After a moment, he gets up and moves toward the door. He turns and looks back at us.

"Hey, you heard about that girl they're looking for? The vigilante. The one that they think killed Didion?"

"Helluva thing," says Paul, putting his reading glasses on again. He turns back to the screen.

"They say she's disappeared," says Boz. "She hasn't been around in a few months."

I look at him and smile a little. *I hear you, Boz. I get it. We all have to agree to live with, to let it go, or none of us can.*

"I hope they never find her."

"Me, too."

Later, I am alone in the school doing the glamorous work of washing towels and wiping down surfaces. The dojo is a sacred place and must be kept clean. The altar especially. For ours, I have chosen the laughing Buddha surrounded by children to remind me that this place is for turning kittens into dragons. As I wipe his shiny head, my phone starts to ring.

I look down and see that it's Melba. When I pick up, she's crying on the other end.

"Melba," I say, alarmed. "What is it?"

"Do you know about this?" she asks. "Did you have something to do with it?"

My stomach hollows out. One of the girls? Something horrible that one of them did or was done to them.

"What is it?" I say, my throat tight. "Tell me."

"I just heard from my attorney," she says. Then she lets out a laugh. "The group home has received a donation of three hundred thousand dollars."

Relief is a flood. I sink to my knees.

"Do you know what I can do for my girls with this money?" Melba asks, her voice joyous, a person who knows that the only true happiness in this life is doing for others. "Do you know how much it will help us?"

"That's—so wonderful," I say, even as my mind struggles for meaning, for understanding. "Do you know who sent it?"

"My lawyer said there was just a box of cash and a note on plain cardstock," says Melba. "It just said: From one of the good guys."

The world is a tilt-a-whirl, and I just barely hold on.

forty-five

Who brings her parents to a concert? *No one* except dorky only children (*single children* was the correct term because *only* implied paucity, according to her mother). Pathetic, single children whose parents were sadly laboring under the delusion that they were still half cool. Which they so were not.

Okay, even Raven had to admit that her parents looked pretty good—Claudia in a simple sheath dress with platform peep-toe red shoes, and Ayers in triple black with a nice Armani belt with a brushed nickel buckle. And they were happy. And Raven was—weirdly—happy. What had started as an extended sleepover, where Raven and Claudia were just staying with Ayers until Claudia got back on her feet, had turned into a formal announcement to Raven that they were getting back together and going to be a family again.

And it was good, and weird. Because her parents, in her memory, had never been together, always separated. And some of the games she'd gotten used to playing no longer worked. But she could live with it.

"So," Piper gushed. "Is it official? Is Troy, like, your *boyfriend?*"

"Um, yeah," said Troy, coming up behind them. "It's official."

"Yeah," said Raven, leaning into him "It is."

Claudia and Ayers promised to give them a "wide berth," whatever that meant, but there was no way they were going to see Above & Beyond at the Beacon Theatre without chaperones. Raven's parents had paid for the tickets, too, seating themselves a few rows behind Raven, Troy, Piper, and her maybe-boyfriend Todd, who Raven didn't really like.

Claudia and Ayers were at the bar, pretending they didn't know her, and Raven excused herself to go the bathroom, waiting on the predictably endless line that was *always*.

"Hey, Raven."

She jumped a little. It had been a few months, but she was still jumpy, having bad dreams about being locked in a tunnel, about fires devouring their apartment building. She dreamt about that bag of money, which had disappeared *again,* and the hideous face of Rhett Beckham. She didn't like her parents to go out at night, and so they didn't. This was the first night out for all of them in a long time.

She didn't recognize right away the guy standing in front of her, and then it slowly dawned. She felt a little flutter of nerves. That dark hair, those intense eyes. Andrew Cutter.

"I saw on Twitter that you had your test."

She remembered that night, how mean he'd been to her. She talked to her mom about it, and Claudia had asked Raven to think about what Andrew's experience might be. How angry he must be, how damaged. Raven thought about it, but she still hated him a little. He had dark circles under his eyes, looking a little more ragged out than she remembered him.

"I thought you unfollowed me," she said.

"Twitter feeds are public."

"Okay," she said, not knowing what else to say. She wouldn't have imagined he'd given her a second thought.

She looked out into the crowd for Troy. She could see the golden crown of his head above some of the others. "So, yeah I got my test."

"We're officially *not* related," he said.

"Right," she said. "Lucky you."

He smiled a little, but it wasn't a nice smile. "No," he said. "Lucky you."

Then he walked off, disappearing into the throng. She stood there shaking for a moment. Then, no. She wasn't going to freak out and leave. She was going to find her friends, her *boyfriend,* and have a good time.

She was still unsettled a little when her mom came up behind her.

"Who was that?" Claudia asked.

Her mom had white glitter shadow on her eyes—which might be a little young for her. But she just looked happy, lighter, freer than she had in as long as Raven could remember.

"No one," said Raven, in what she personally thought was a stunning act of maturity. She deserved some kind of a reward for how grown-up she was being right now.

"You gave him the death stare," said Claudia. There was a little wrinkle in her brow, as though she detected something was not right. Mom radar, always on.

"I don't talk to strange boys, right?" said Raven. "Isn't that what you taught me?"

"Yes, it is," said Claudia, kissing her on the head. "Good girl."

She might tell them later, but not now, not tonight. Tonight, they were going to be happy, have fun. The shadow of Melvin Cutter was gone from their lives for good. She biologically belonged to Ayers and was surprised to find that it didn't matter all that much. Because it was the life they shared that mattered, the hours they'd spent in the park, the million Band-Aids he'd put on her knees, how he carried her bloody tooth in his pocket all day while they were at Great Adventure and still remembered to put it in the little pillow so the Tooth Fairy would come. Those were the things that made Ayers her dad, not the blood running through her veins. She didn't love him any more totally. But she would never have known that without knowing. A pall had lifted from her mind, from their life, and they were free to move into the future.

"I think we're going to have a wedding," said Claudia in the bathroom. Her mother had no issues whatsoever raising her voice so that Raven and everyone else could hear over their peeing. "*Another* wedding."

"Okay," said Raven pushing her way out of the stall and over to the sink. The thought of a wedding excited her, and also freaked her out a little. How many teenagers had to go to their parents' weddings? It was—*odd*. Why couldn't they just be normal? Her mother squished in next to her.

"So, I was thinking," said her mom. "Will you be my maid of honor?"

Raven rolled her eyes. "Mom, that's weird. I'm your *daughter*."

"So what?"

"Mom."

"So that's a no?" Claudia pouted. She reapplied her lipstick, a deep berry plum. "I suppose Martha would do it. Again."

"Mom!"

Claudia looked at Raven in the mirror, and Raven smiled. Claudia pulled her into a tight hug.

Raven laughed. "Of course, I'll be your maid of honor."

Claudia, embarrassingly, teared up a little. "I love you—so much."

And all the other ladies in the bathroom broke into applause. It was New York, after all.

They danced that night, and cheered, and jumped around. Her mother was still working on the house, now repairing after the fire, but they weren't going to live there. And Claudia was doing what maybe she was always meant to do: she was writing a book. Raven felt like every ugly thing was behind them. And even if it wasn't true—it was true tonight.

forty-six

My head is still spinning as I return to Nate Shelby's apartment. Tiger and Milo meet me at the door, wrapping around me, mewing. Milo reaches up and I lift him, nuzzle against his snow-white fur. I go into the kitchen and fill their food bowls, refresh their water. Then I head up to the roof. It's slow going, but I make it.

I don't sit on the ledge like I used to. I sit in the center, on the tar paper that is still warm from the day's heat, even though the sun is setting, a big red ball in the sky dipping below the city buildings. It is quiet, as quiet as this place will ever be. I can't hear the wind, though it is blowing, just the traffic noise carrying up. Even when it grows dark, I won't see many stars, the city is too bright. The city is alive, with a beating heart. I feel its pulse inside my own.

I try to make sense of the things that have happened today. What I know. What I suspect. What I may never know for sure. I draw in and release long, slow breaths, let my thoughts swirl and pass through me. The Buddha says, "There is no external refuge."

Meaning, you cannot look into the outer world to feel safe, to feel at peace. You cannot look without for understanding, or for justice. You must look within.

I think about the money. A million dollars stolen from Whitey Malone. One hundred went to Mike and a hundred to Boz ten years ago. Paul took four hundred thousand after my parents were gone, and sealed up the other four hundred thousand in that space beneath the stairs. Slowly, over ten years he deposited it in my college account. It paid for my education without my knowledge; what's left of it is being used at the school. Three hundred thousand was just given to Melba's group home. That's one hundred thousand still missing. Seth? Maybe he's on a beach somewhere. Maybe the money's doing some other good work. Or maybe Seth is at the bottom of a river somewhere, and someone else, maybe Boz, has a fatter bank account.

Can I live with it? Do I still have work to do? I don't know.

The thinker panics. The watcher bides her time. The Red Hunter acts.

Is she dead, I wonder? Did The Red Hunter die in the warehouse that night? Was her only power rage? Now that my rage has cooled, now that a kind of justice has been served, will she find her way back to wandering the city streets? I don't know.

Back downstairs, he's waiting in the kitchen. Nate. I'm not the cat sitter anymore.

"There's someone here to see you," Paul said one day while I was recovering in the hospital. But Paul had come in through the door alone, with only his oxygen tank in tow.

"Your invisible friend."

"No," said Paul. "Yours. I found him in the hallway. Nate Shelby. He's says you're his cat sitter?"

"Nate Shelby?" I said. I am not vain by nature, but I had to wonder what I looked like after my recent adventures, convalescence, and depressed state.

"Bring him in?" asked Paul.

"Um," I said, shifting up. "Okay."

Nate came in carrying a bouquet of calla lilies which, I thought, seemed a bit funereal and much like those that adorned his lobby. But sweet.

In my mind, I'd created him tall and swash-buckling, long dark curls and leather pants. I imagined him in studios, angrily splashing paint on his huge canvases, or drifting though swank galleries with a beautiful woman on his arm. But in reality, he looked somewhat bookish—with short, shorn dark hair and glasses. His jeans were paint splattered. He *was* tall, lean in the waist and broad through the shoulders.

"How—?" I started. He had a kind, arresting

509

smile. "What are you doing here? How did you know?"

"Well, you're all over the news, for one," he said. "And our doorman friend, Charlie, called to say that you might not be up to looking in on the cats. I had to come home anyway, so I thought I'd drop by while I was in town."

"I had my uncle call him," I said. "To say there had been an accident. Are they okay? Milo and Tiger?"

"I think they miss you," he said. "But yeah, they're okay. The more important question is how are *you?*"

"Um," I said. I like the way his energy fit into the room. It was quiet. He sat in the chair by my bed. His eyes, they never left me. I could feel him taking in all the details, easily, without judgment. He was a watcher. An artist who wanted to see it all—all the lines and shadows, all the lights and darks. I found I didn't have the urge to hide from him. "I'm here."

"That's something," he said. "That's a lot."

"I suppose it is."

He smiled and for the first time in about a million years, I felt a smile turn up the corners of my mouth.

Paul seemed to think that it was his cue to leave. He slipped from the room.

"Your uncle," he said. "I would have said he was your father. Something about the eyes."

"No," I said. "My father died a long time ago. But he's like a father to me."

I was my father's daughter. I knew that and Paul confirmed it. Our bond, whatever Paul and I shared, was more than biology. We were family in every important way but that.

"There you are," Nate says now as I enter the kitchen. "Where did you go?"

"Up on the roof," I say.

"You climbed the stairs." He frowns.

"It's good for me."

"Hmm," he says, which I'm just starting to learn is the sound he makes when he disagrees but knows it's not his place to say. I wonder if that will annoy me sometime down the road. I doubt it. He's careful, gentle, everything a boyfriend should be.

I've never had a boyfriend before, if that's what you call the person who offers you a hand back from the brink. Who then shows you what it's like to walk through the park (not searching for crimes in progress), and linger in cafés over brunch until the afternoon (not counting exits), or stay up all night talking (not obsessing about revenge)—or not talking, which is better. But it's nice.

We're still getting to know each other, of course. There are things about me he doesn't know.

For instance, I won't tell him about what

happened today. There are too many shades of gray to ask anyone to go along. In some real way, a lot of people, including me, got away with things we shouldn't have. But justice has a way of creeping up on you. (And, I'll be watching my back.) He only knows what everyone knows about the heist, and my parents' murders, about the huge sum of money that was stolen and never recovered and, for now, he doesn't need to know more. Because Nate Shelby says he's in love with Zoey Drake, the cat sitter, the martial artist, the teacher who helps girls get in touch with their power and strength.

Around his apartment are sketches of me—pencil, charcoal, pastel. I'm not sure I know the girl in those pictures—fragile-looking, with a shock of spiky strawberry-blonde hair, delicate features and sad, sad eyes. She's not the watcher, the thinker, or the Red Hunter; she's all of those things, and something more.

Maybe now, for the first time, I'll give myself permission to get to know her.

acknowledgments

Though a novel is written in solitude, publishing takes a village. I am blessed with a stellar team of supporters, colleagues, and friends.

I owe a big thank-you to my editor, Tara Parsons, for her insight, enthusiasm, good humor, and talent. The relationship between writer and editor is an intimate one as we work together to make a manuscript the best it can be. Her thoughtfulness, wisdom, and careful reading were invaluable in making this book better than I could have made it alone. And we had fun doing it!

Thanks to my agent, Amy Berkower, at Writers House for her support and hard work on my behalf. Every author needs a captain, someone to help navigate the big waters of publishing. Her intelligence, experience, and friendship are a beacon. Thanks to Alice Martin and Genevieve Gagne-Hawes for their kind words, careful reading, and support.

The folks at Simon & Schuster Touchstone and Pocket are an absolutely stellar group. Each and every person brings their own special gifts and talents to the table. My heartfelt thanks to: Carolyn Reidy, Susan Moldow, Michael Selleck, Liz Perl,

Louise Burke, Jennifer Long, Liz Psaltis, David Falk, Brian Belfiglio, Jessica Roth, Cherlynne Li, Wendy Sheanin, Paula Amendolara, Teresa Brumm, Colin Shields, Christina Festa, Charlotte Gill, Gary Urda, Gregory Hruska, Michelle Fadlalla, Meredith Vilarello, Lauren Flavin, Paul O'Halloran, Irene Lipsky, Etinosa Agbonlahor, and Isabella Betita. And I can never heap enough praise on the top-notch sales team, out there on the front lines in our ever more competitive business, getting books in every format into as many hands as possible. It's everything; thank you.

I have an amazing network of family and friends who cheer me through the good days and carry me through the challenging ones. I am so grateful for my parents, Joseph and Virginia Miscione, and my brother Joe who have supported me in every way—all my life. Thanks to Heather Mikesell for being one of my first and most important readers. Thanks to Tara Popick and Marion Chartoff for their unfailing friendship—though too much time passes between visits! They've been with me every step of the way.

My husband, Jeffrey, and our daughter, Ocean, are the center of my universe. A day doesn't go by that I don't thank my lucky stars for the cutest, funniest, sweetest, most loving family a girl could have. The life of the writer is full of beautiful gifts and challenges, dizzying highs and crushing lows. My family helps me to keep my focus on what's important, what's real; they keep me centered. Our labradoodle, Jak Jak, offers daily cuddles, kisses, and comic relief. I'm so grateful and so in love.

Special thanks to my readers who have followed me through all the dark, twisty passages I have wandered. A writer is nothing without her readers and certainly I have some of the kindest, most supportive, most involved and vocal out there. Thanks for turning out, for writing, for promoting, for connecting on social media. And, most of all, thanks for reading.

about the author

Lisa Unger is an award-winning *New York Times* and internationally bestselling author. More than two million copies of her novels have been sold, and her novels have been translated into twenty-six languages. She lives in Florida. Visit LisaUnger.com.

| Books are produced in the United States using U.S.-based materials | Books are printed using a revolutionary new process called THINKtech™ that lowers energy usage by 70% and increases overall quality | Books are durable and flexible because of smythe-sewing | Paper is sourced using environmentally responsible foresting methods and the paper is acid-free |

Center Point Large Print
600 Brooks Road / PO Box 1
Thorndike, ME 04986-0001 USA

(207) 568-3717

US & Canada:
1 800 929-9108
www.centerpointlargeprint.com